HILL PEOPLE

HILL PEOPLE

A Novel

James Riley

For Miko, Jade, and Grace

Introduction

At half past three in the morning, on the twenty-seventh of June, eight hundred and eighty-two residents of Cheronkin County, California, vanished, never to be seen again. They left behind children dreaming of beanstalks in their beds, dessert dishes stacked on the kitchen counters, bathtubs filled with steaming water, and dogs baying in a chorus long into the night.

The only available evidence in the mass disappearance were pieces of clothing and other personal fare, including watches, sunglasses, wallets, car keys, and jewelry found in the streets and on the sidewalks throughout town. The trail of these belongings led to the hills north and west of Cheronkin, to a patch of land mysteriously blackened as if by fire, and covered in a fine layer of glass; it has been assumed those who "vanished" died there.

Theories abound. Investigations and interviews uncovered a fine web of detail without ever catching sight of the spider. As one whose life was forever changed that night, I have sought to understand the events of the days and months prior to this event. If it is only by the act of remembering that one is able to forget, then that is why I choose to tell this story now. I want to put it all down; I want to stop carrying it all around with me.

Regardless of any other fact or fancy regarding these lost souls' last days, this can be verified as true: that patch of land to the west of Cheronkin County is now a verdant garden tucked inside a thriving forest, once more home to woodland creatures. It is a place abundant with the colors of life, representing a diverse array of rare flora and fauna. The locals know better than to go there. It can be found at the heart of the abandoned, overgrown woodland suburb that once was our home. This is all we can really know to be true.

—*M. P.*

Prologue

An excerpt from Dick Arthur's *Surreality Reigns*
(© 1962 Coal Box Classics, Out of Print)

The new neighbors intrigued me immensely. I knew they were happy people by their meadowlark voices, having spent many a lonely hour in my youth entertaining myself in the back yard by listening to those lovebirds as they sang to each other and laughed and chattered the summer days away.

He doted and hung on her every word, his voice so filled with devotion it would seem to float higher into the air the closer she drew to him. She was more reserved, and I wondered if she truly heard the gratitude with which her expressions to him were received.

The Cheronkin County of my youth was pre-rural, populated in the main by those who were between obligations—jobs, marriages, families, probation appearances—folks who couldn't afford to live anywhere else, and who wouldn't know how to comport themselves if they could afford to escape to the middle class. My view of it was that these were people who had taken a shot at living in the city, and when it didn't work out for them, for whatever reasons, they ended up in a backwoods place like Cheronkin. They were people who appreciated their privacy, who kept their gates closed, their windows shuttered year in and out, didn't mind their neighbors' ways, and expected the same courtesy in return.

Before the new neighbors arrived, the house next door had been locked tight and sitting empty for all of my remembered days. Many times over many years my refuge was that untended yard, my staging ground for imaginary battles and football games. Rows of dead rose bushes served as rolls of barbed wire, and the browned cypresses filled in for goalposts. By every summers' end even the weeds were dead from the combination of heat and neglect, leaving the yard filled with foxtails and burrs and dandelions, and after my first good sticking, I would not play there again until the next spring.

These new arrivals to the neighborhood were apparently related to the woman who had lived and died in that house long before I was born. At least, that's what my

3

mother said. My mother was a petty and intolerant woman, as square as the frames of her glasses when it came to judging people. Short months after the neighbors had moved in, and without having met them or spoken to them, she began to question the exactitude of the new owners' relationship to the previous owners. The resentment she exhibited was a result of their failing to confirm or deny what at best was gossip and at worst pure invention about their origins and their reasons for moving to Cheronkin. That mother had invented much of the gossip and spread it around did not enter into the debate.

"Newcomers should come around. Explain these things to the people they're going to be living among," mother would say. "Otherwise, people will be glad to assume the worst."

The husband wasn't seen around the house a lot. Most every neighbor I spoke with was unaware there was a man living in the house at all; they had only seen her. It seemed he rarely ventured outside the front door, apparently because he was so hard at work fixing the place up.

It was her voice alone that I heard one night toward the end of my last summer in Cheronkin, a full six weeks after their arrival. I was bouncing a tennis ball against the exterior of our house, caught up in an imagined game of baseball. My parents were getting loaded inside in preparation for a visit to the local drinking hole, the Hat, where they would drink more and listen to jazz and perhaps find someone else to bring home with them for the night.

The voice of the woman next door carried on the wind as she sang to herself under the full moon, her music barely louder than the chorus of frogs and owls. I breathed in the sound as crickets sang and butterflies skittered through the wildflowers that were opened wide in longing, as if it were the sun itself upon them and not just its reflection.

By the time my parents were off in their car, I was already searching for a viewing place, a section in the fence with a hole in it, or two planks placed farther apart from one another. There was a loose plank in back, a convenient throughway between our yards, but that was in the far corner of the yard. The fact I could hear her so clearly meant she was not far from the fence, and though I did not want to get caught, I wanted to be able to actually see something for once.

4

I settled for a knothole closer to her than I wanted to be because it was an area shielded on our side of the fence by overhanging branches. I was too easy to see, should the parents return unexpectedly, from the street out in front of the house anywhere else along that fence, and in the bright moonlight.

This was the first time I had seen her. In the light of the day, I would have been upbraided for lingering so close to the fence, and so I had not yet otherwise found the chance to do any spying.

The view brought a blush of heat to my face.

There she was, dressed in the sheerest of robes, and nothing more. My view was of her backside as she stood in front of the dead maple tree. She was doing something to the trunk with her hands. She wasn't overweight, but she did look soft and maternal, and round around the edges in places. The pale shine of her skin in the moonlight made her look as though she were glowing. Her hair was teased out and frizzy, and either silver or gray. One wink of her doughy, white bottom peeking out from underneath that sheer veil had an immediate and noticeable effect upon me.

When she turned and moved to the first row of rosebushes, there was nothing self-conscious about her movements. And why should there have been? She held a small brush and a bucket. Her pale breasts, which were fair-sized, sagged a little, though that didn't alter the pleasure I felt at finally seeing a pair of them.

She mouthed words to herself as she hummed and dipped the brush in the bucket and painted the stalks and stems. Paying closer attention, I could see she had already done this with much of the yard: The trunks of the dead fruit trees, the soil in the flowerbed by the walkway to the house, and the fronds of withered palms all glistened with the stuff. A glob hung in the dying cypress closest to my spy hole; the liquid looked gray and frothy. It dribbled from the branches in long, gooey strings.

At some point, I stuck a pine twig through the knothole, but could not reach the cypress, although, eventually, I was able to swipe a spot of the stuff from a browned leaf on a dying jasmine vine nearby. I looked at it and smelled it, and thought it might be cleanser. When I touched it, it was sticky and repulsive. I quickly wiped my

5

finger off on my pants. Then I sat and listened and watched for a while longer, my face flushed and my blood boiling at the forbidden feel of my view.

Oddly enough, in this excited state, I must have fallen asleep. I attribute it to her quiet and unintelligible lullaby. I closed my eyes only to blink, and slid off through fleeting and ghostly imaginings of the home she might keep were I her child, asleep in my crib in my patchwork quilt of a bedroom.

There was a wicked gleam in the far corner of her eye when in this dream she leaned over the crib where I slept, an intoxicated, maniacal smile on her lips. Her breasts swung above me, her engorged and reddened nipples presenting an open invitation. She picked me up and coddled me, pushing my face into soft, padded skin that smelled of rose and jasmine and orange blossom. A pleasurable warmth rushed through my loins that momentarily had me thinking I'd wet myself. She mussed my hair and whispered words in my ear that triggered an equally startling explosion of images across my mind's eye.

It was as if we were having a conversation, though no words were spoken. I understood that there was something inside her that was much older than she seemed to be, that a voice echoed through her which was a thousand years old. And that there were others like her to be found in the world.

She shushed me as she rocked me back to sleep. Her voice continued to fill my ears with stories of wonder and dread, secrets great and terrible, words never before spoken aloud, all of it history, she told me, preserved and passed along through generations on the buried bones of the dead.

I did speak to her before I fell completely asleep.

I asked her where her husband was.

She paused and she frowned. And then her face was momentarily overcome with great sadness.

Blearily, I said, "I've heard his voice in the garden."

"It must have been his ghost you heard. I didn't know he'd followed me here, although still I often find myself talking to him as if he were here. As if I were the person I used to be. He was a lovely man. Perhaps that is why. He died before I came here."

"Are you sure?"

"Yes, child. I killed him with my own hands."

6

I awoke an undetermined time later with a start, in time to see a light flashing over the bushes that shielded me. Momentarily disoriented, hard-learned instinct had me on my way and running for my bedroom before my brain had entirely grasped that the lights were the headlights of my parents' car careening up the long driveway.

I rushed into my bedroom where I stripped out of my clothes and stuffed them into the closet. I took care to put my pants, which were stained with goo and semen and covered with pine needles, at the bottom of the pile. I was in my pajamas and under the sheets well before Frank and Faye staggered through the door with what sounded like more than one of their male friends.

They never looked in to see that I was there. They all just went and locked themselves in the rec den at the back of the house. For my part, having escaped detection, I had already forgotten all but the most vivid impressions of my dream, and was far more interested in further investigating the sensations that had wracked my body that evening. (I have been similarly occupied ever since.)

I was home free, and smug about it in the morning, overly pleased with myself for having done so well at avoiding trouble at home, and wondering when if ever I might be able to repeat the experience.

My self-satisfaction lasted exactly until I opened my closet door and found inside a small pine tree, three feet tall and bushy, growing out of the pile of clothes I'd left there the previous night. Strands of jasmine were woven throughout the branches, filling my closet with the flowers' powerful perfume. The pants I had been wearing only hours earlier were pinned to the carpet by roots which had grown through the fabric and into the wood floor, where they appeared to have done a great amount of damage.

I immediately packed my duffel bag and was soon ready to be on my way.

I walked out through the front door. No one had yet emerged from the back of the house. I did not take time to peer closely into my neighbor's yard again before I went, but I did note that the green tops of several trees could be seen peering over the top of the fence, where yesterday there had been only a dead tangle of branches. Flowering vines were now

7

well grown in and wrapped around individual fence planks. Had I been able to take the time to peek inside, I'm sure I would have found a dense curtain of brush and branches obscuring my view of a garden ripe with bloom.

In retrospect, I half wish I had remained at home, at least until the damage to my room had been discovered and the punishment meted out. The pain my father would have visited upon me would surely have cemented my memory of him more firmly, and left it unshaken after so many years. As it is, I can hardly remember his face.

I have long wondered how much time passed before my parents realized I was gone and went looking for me. I have since frequently and fervently hoped they didn't open the closet door and notice the tree until its roots had had the chance to sink deeper, to split the foundation, and the branches had grown long enough to break through the roof and bring the whole house down on them.

Chapter 1

Cheronkin County, California,
February

As soon as the dog saw that Michael was headed in its direction, it thumped its tail against the ground. It didn't lift or move its head, but he felt its eyes tracking him as soon as he stepped into its view. It was a handsome dog, sure enough; a well-groomed Golden Retriever, with its legs bent in ways they shouldn't be, lying in a pool of blood on a landscape speckled with roadside debris. It had been tossed aside and left to die in a place someone had assumed no one would notice.

Poor pup. He was ready to befriend whatever human came along, whether it was someone looking to help him or put him out of his misery.

Mary backed the car to a position parallel to Michael as he crouched down beside it. She rolled down the passenger window. Her voice projected mock concern across the night. "Careful. Ooooh. He might have rabies."

"Not helpful."

The tail slapped the ground more enthusiastically at the sound of their conversation.

Mary's tone softened into sympathetic noises. "He likes your voice. He's wagging his tail harder."

The dog sighed when Michael rested his hand on the back of its neck. "Go home and call the Pet Vet."

"It'll take them an hour to get out here."

"We can't leave him now that we've stopped."

"Which is why I didn't want to stop, Michael. Do you really want to be alone out here?"

"There's no room for him in the car with the pimples strapped in their chairs in the back."

While Michael waited for her reply, a familiar-looking piece of paper caught in a tumbleweed beside him caught his eye. Aged by sun and rain, its faded type read:
COME ONE COME ALL COME JOIN THE HARVEST BALL!

This was something his mom used to be involved in. She'd probably printed this up and handed it to someone outside a store or stuck it under someone's windshield wiper— years and years ago.

Mary tossed two sticks out the car window. Each one flared incandescent pink when it hit the pavement. "Glow sticks. I got them at the truck show. In case the Hill People come to take you." She snickered.

"Thanks."

"I had fun today. I'm glad you're home."

"Me, too."

"Stay back from the road, okay? People drive crazy out here."

She looked in the back seat at their nephew and niece, Max and Lorraine, who were apparently still asleep. Then she closed the window and pulled out slowly, offering Michael a last chance to change his mind.

Most locals avoided the roads winding through the mountains west of Cheronkin County. Landscape which by day offered fields thick with chaparral and wild grass underneath groves of oak and eucalyptus were nearly impenetrable in the darkness of the night. Beyond the range of the headlights, the next bend in the road was hard to see, and it might be a hairpin turn. It was easy to miss a turn-off. Sometimes cattle blocked the road. Often the fog was heavy.

Mary preferred the network of back roads to the town's main artery, Marble Canyon Road, because there was rarely anyone to get in her way. And she knew the roads well because she loved to drive them—something their mother was undoubtedly thinking about when she splurged on a security/safety system for Mary's car that included something like twenty airbags. Mary was able to speed along for the most part without impediment, nestled in her own little Zen zone, chatting idly away, same as she did, Michael imagined, whether or not there was anyone in the car to listen to her.

Mary had long since mastered the art of making everything seem equally important, whether she was discussing their mother's latest dabblings in holistic medicine, or her disgusted reaction to the size of the toe jam she once pried out from under the nail of an ex-boyfriend's big toe. She was never like that as a kid; the family assumed it was one of the skill sets they had over-cultivated at Cosmetology School.

She was driving so fast that night, and chattering away so fast, it was a wonder Michael spotted the dog at all.

". . . His name is Dr. Wen, I think," Mary was saying just before they passed it by. "He's like Chinese and Indian, something like that, a therapist in that new round brown building on the other side of the freeway? Indian as in dot, not feather. It's supposed to have an incredible Zen meditation garden. Short of it is that I have to go with Mom in the morning. She wants me to keep an eye on the session."

"What is she thinking she's going to find out?"

"I guess she's been having anxiety attacks, and I guess they've been happening at times when it doesn't, like, fit the mood. For example: She's not anxious driving with me to the flea market up north in a hail storm, but she's reeling with panic when she's putting seed in the bird feeder on a beautiful, sunny morning. She can't connect the panic to anything rational, and she's thinking—probably because someone on her phone tree saw it on television and told her about it—that hypnosis might not only get to the cause of her anxiety but also train her to not let herself be overwhelmed by it when it comes on."

"What do you need to keep an eye on?"

"I think I've told too much. So. Carina and I were supposed to go to the Tuesday Sale at the mall tomorrow—"

"And I hate the whole don't-tell-Dad part of it."

"That's easy to address, Michael. Just forget about it. Empty your mind. I wasn't supposed to tell you. Dad thinks she's seeing a therapist, which she is, and he's glad about it because she's driving him nuts. And when you're around Dad, your position is that I never said a thing. Or I will deny it and say that you're lying. You can go on pretending everything is fine with her just like you have been."

"And you just go on validating her craziness," Michael said.

"We all have our crutches."

"Is that your crutch or hers?"

That was when he saw the blur of fur by the roadside.

Michael watched Mary zip her car around the corner. The sound of the engine gunning was quickly replaced by the sound of the dog panting beside him and the background white noise of the crickets

"So it'll just be us for a little bit."

It was hard for Michael to look at the dog again after his initial inspection. The sight of his legs so unnaturally bent made him want to avert his eyes from anything but the animal's face, and its sweet face filled him with sadness. Michael was afraid that if he touched it, he might mess something up worse. There was a long trail of dark spatters curving from the puddle under the dog to the place by the side of the road where it must have landed after being hit. Or when it fell out of whatever truck bed it was riding in. Or whatever happened to it.

There was no blood on the side facing up. This meant he was lying on the worst of it.

Michael wiggled the flyer out of the tumbleweed, stared at it a minute, folded it, and put it in his pocket. He stood again to pace around some more, and something rustled around behind some nearby bushes in response to his movement. Just as quickly it stopped. Some animal. He hoped.

It was a moment before the sound of the crickets returned.

Michael's Aunt Rachel had had an affair with Michael's Uncle Stan. That's what finally brought Michael home to Cheronkin. It was a huge scandal for the Phillips family, and it had ended all communication between his father and his half-brothers. That and the fact that there were already a lot of divorces in the family tree already; it all worked to Michael's disadvantage. When all that happened, and high-school-sweetheart Danielle saw it as an opening to start talking about exploring her sexuality outside their relationship—they were two years out of college and living together in the city at the time—Michael felt it was time to move on.

And that brought him home. Because there wasn't anywhere else to go? Not entirely true.

But it did feel like it was what he was supposed to do. Something here was calling him back.

12

It was different to be in the rural setting again. Not that he hadn't been back to visit regularly; it was simply a different sensation returning to Cheronkin as a place to stay when he thought he would never come back to stay for good. How many years did he spend just wanting to escape these hills? He remembered, when he left town after high school, he'd felt like the kid in that Dick Arthur story---like there wasn't a place for him in Cheronkin anymore.

Michael sat down next to the dog, and patted him lightly.

And was almost immediately startled by a voice calling out of the night.

"Hello?"

The dog was equally surprised, first flinching, then whimpering, then, as Michael searched for the owner of that voice, growling.

"Hold on there a minute, big guy." Despite the fact he seemed half-dead, he had an intimidating growl, and Michael was glad for the effect. "Let's see who it is first."

"Is everything all right over there?" A woman was standing at the edge of the area of light cast by the glow sticks. She took a purposeful step in his direction. She asked again, "Is everything all right?"

"Not really. This dog is pretty bad off. My sister went to call the pet hospital."

Michael recognized the voice, although he didn't know from where. And then, as incongruous as it seemed out there in the desert brush, he watched her silhouette as she drew closer and connected the voice to the name to the place where he'd heard it, and his heart jumped again.

"So, you *found* the dog here . . ."

He listened with his eyes closed. It was her. "No, don't say it like that." He opened his eyes. "We didn't hit him. I saw him while we were driving by. I just stopped to help. If I could." It sounded like a lie, even to him. "Where did you come from, anyway?"

She pointed behind her, to an area outside the radii of the flares. It looked like a bicycle.

"I didn't notice it there at all."

"Your eyes aren't too good," she said.

"I compensate with my hearing." Was she making fun of him? "Is your name Talia?"

13

She stiffened a little. Did she smile, too? She wasn't close enough yet that he could see her face clearly, but he'd surprised her, at least a little.

She didn't let it show for long. It pleased her to be recognized.

"Murray's Hat, in Cheronkin, about seven years ago. Your first show went over so well that you came back and did two other shows. And then you were just, like, gone. Vanished. I thought there'd be a record by now."

And then she was finally close enough that Michael could see her face.

"There hasn't been a record, has there?"

She waited for him to continue.

"At that last show, you said that you grew up here, but I don't remember seeing you around when I was a kid. And I'm sure I would have remembered. You know. You."

He couldn't help staring; his mind was swimming. The dog might as well have been in another dimension. It was much more than a fan's adulation, though that was undeniably a part of his chemistry at the moment. It was almost overwhelming. There was this incredible sense of synchronicity, the two of them out there at this seemingly arbitrary moment in time; there was a connection he felt, an instant, unspoken exchange, and a sense of something that was almost like recognition. Michael felt something; however, there was no affirmation in her expression that she felt the same. When he looked away, embarrassed for staring, the feeling stayed with him. Recognition. A voice inside him said *I know you!* It said *I recognize you from somewhere before;* it said *Where have you been all this time?* The intensity of the feeling caused a feeling like hurt in his stomach.

It was like nothing he had ever felt before.

Michael was glad it was dark. What showed on his face could only have been flustered embarrassment.

The dog growled at her.

She sneered at it in response. And then she barked at him. And the weight of the spell was broken.

Surprised, Michael laughed.

"Dogs are always growling at me," she said.

"Says something about a person."

"What does it say?" she asked sharply.

He didn't answer. Nowhere good to go with that . . .

14

She crouched down across the dog from him. "You're the one who hit him?"

"No."

"Are you sure?"

"I wish you'd stop saying that. Think about it. You look as suspicious as I do. More so. It's just as strange for you to be here as it is for me to be here. Even more strange. This is a crazy place to be out riding your bike in the middle of the night unless you're just returning to the scene of a crime. "

"Fine." She studied his face silently. While she inspected him, he noticed that she had a really big forehead. That gave him an imperfection to focus upon. Covered it up a little with her hair. Not a beautiful girl, but definitely attractive. There was a hint of masculinity to her face that lent to her exotic look.

Michael wanted her to talk to him. "What kind of person leaves a suffering dog at the side of the road? And why not drive a little slower, by the way?"

"That wasn't you passing me by doing ninety just a little ways back?"

He grimaced.

"Did you even see me, eagle-eye?"

Obviously he hadn't. He stammered. "That was my sister driving. Maybe she did, for all I know."

"For all you know."

He shrugged at her. "You know what? I'm here to keep him company. He shouldn't be alone when he dies."

"When he dies, he'll still be alone."

It was almost as if she wanted an argument.

Michael changed the subject. "Maybe it's time for you to sing at the Hat again. It's reopening, you know."

"Really?"

"Yeah. And after you do that, then you should stop wasting your time in places like the Hat. You're better than that."

"I find a lot of the advice people give they would do better following themselves." She crouched down on the other side of the dog and watched me, her eyes glittering with interest. "You know my name. Who are you?"

"My name is Michael."

That seemed to confuse her. She was expecting something else? She stood again, staring at the dog. "Were

15

you going to tell me my future? What I should be doing? Starting with the singing? I'm really not sure if this is where I am supposed to be."

Was she being sincere? Or was she still mocking him? "I know how you feel," he said.

The dog whimpered pathetically. Its tail slapped the ground.

Talia sucked in her breath, startled by the movement, and her gasp made Michael jump. "I've been asking for a sign, myself." She reached out to touch the dog. "I could never resist an orphan."

It growled again, and bared its teeth at her hand.

She pulled away.

Michael snickered, the same sound Mary had made at him earlier. When he patted its head, the dog sighed. And then it started to choke. A shrill squeal of air got stuck in its throat before it broke out with short, ragged breaths. Its heartbeat raced under his fingertips. Each gasp that followed was a struggle. Every breath came harder than the one before. Michael could feel the fluid in his lungs through his fingertips. Its eyes glazed over.

The night at that moment was silent, waiting. No rustling of branches in the night, no singing of crickets; only the sound of the dog's labored gasping and wheezing. It was too much. Michael stood up again to look toward town. The ambulance obviously wasn't going to make it.

There was a blur of movement in the underbrush nearby. It was not far from where they were situated. Something like a coyote skulking around, waiting for its dinner to die.

"Take it easy, big guy. We're here."

The dog sighed one last time. A long, deep, heavy sigh, the one he had just been struggling to catch. His eyes closed, and his head rolled to the side. The panting stopped. The body was still. There was a final gurgle, and foamy saliva ran out of its mouth.

And then it wasn't breathing anymore.

It wasn't breathing. It still wasn't breathing.

They both stared at it.

"I've never seen anything die before," he said.

Michael leaned down, touched it, thinking it was so very strange. Its fur, its body, felt different under his fingertips than it had moments before. Not just dead. Lifeless. Empty.

Talia and Michael waited a few minutes in total silence.

Finally, he couldn't stand looking at it any more. He shrugged, and stood up.

Talia wasn't ready yet to move or speak, so he waited several more minutes without a word. The whole time, Michael was thinking about what he could say, something that would break that silence and end the moment. That stillness was finally broken when the dog's body twitched violently, and it gasped a wet gasp again—some sort of horrible post-death-rattle reflex was what Michael thought it was—and then, impossibly, it jumped up onto its feet.

Talia shrieked and Michael nearly fell over trying to back away from it.

More, and worse, all their startled, frantic activity startled the somethings or someone elses that were watching from somewhere out there in the darkened brush. And there were definitely more than one of whatever it was. The dog jumped and scared them, and then Talia and Michael reacted, and they scared whatever it was that left the bushes around them shaking as it or they scurried away into the night. Whatever it was—Michael told himself that it was coyotes, though he knew it wasn't—their feet made almost no sound as they rushed away, but they shook a lot of plants as they went. For a moment he just stood there, trying to discern any other evidence of their retreat over the sound of his heart thumping in his ears.

Hill People.

What flashed through Michael's mind was the explanation his father had provided when Michael was ten years old and about to spend his first overnight campout in the hills with his Early American Pathfinder club: "There is no such thing. The Hill People are a myth. Like everywhere else, there are homeless people, and that's all they are. That's all you're ever going to find in the hills, and none of them are ever there for long because the Park Service escorts those people out of town whenever someone reports them. There is no such thing. It's just the kind of story people like to tell to scare each other."

17

Michael's feeling now was that when whoever or whatever it was had left, they hadn't moved off too far.

Talia was watching the dog. Both of them looked stunned.

He heard his own shaken, feeble voice saying to the dog, ". . . You got a cut . . ."

It teetered on its hobbled legs, and Michael thought it would fall over again; somehow, it balanced itself. Once it had its equilibrium, it lifted its crooked back leg, and with a stretch and a pop, the leg was back in alignment.

Michael's mouth dropped.

A minute later, it similarly adjusted its front paw. Then the dog gave itself a great shake. Dark pieces of blood-soaked dirt and clumps of hair fell from the side it had been lying on.

"What did you do?" Talia asked breathlessly.

"I didn't do anything. What did you do?"

She stared at him with open disbelief.

And a minute later, the dog ambled off into the brush.

"It was dying. Look at the blood! It was dead!"

"There is our sign," she said.

"Our sign of what?"

There was that look again, almost as if Michael were the true curiosity on the scene. "I guess I'm done with you," she said. She readied herself to leave. As she walked back to the road, Michael heard her say, "You picked a bad place to hide out from the world."

The sound of a siren rose in the distance as she rode off.

Michael thought about the night that followed his father's explanation for the Hill People. He'd woken up in his sleeping bag, lying on the ground in a clearing under the open night sky with the other Pathfinders spread about around him, and realized that he needed to pee. Lying perfectly still, he'd listened to hear if anyone or anything might be nearby, human or animal, which could hurt him or grab him and run off with him before anyone else had time to respond to his cries for help. And in the seconds before he was finally going to move, a man stepped out of the bushes that were closest to where he was lying, moved right past Michael's sleeping bag, threaded his way through the other sleeping bags without stirring anyone else in the camp, and

18

then walked off into the bushes on the other side of the clearing.

At that moment, Michael could see the truth in his father's words, that this was just a dirty, ungroomed person dressed in ratty clothes, and that there was a good chance he was living out here in the hills. Classic definition of a Hill Person, except that he wasn't mumbling to himself as he went by. Yet he clearly had no interest in their group—whereas the Hill People in stories were always interested in acquiring odd human paraphernalia, like the zippers off sleeping bags. At the same time, the sight of that shoe coming down out of nowhere had nearly made Michael wet himself, and left him disconcerted that random people might walk through what was clearly a campsite in the middle of the night. He'd held his breath and not moved a muscle until long after the man had disappeared from view, and even then he'd waited a while. And when he'd peed and returned to his bag, the thought that there might be more people like that man lurking about left Michael disturbed and unable to fall back to sleep for the rest of the night.

The ambulance driver was a guy Michael knew from high school. Because Michael's shirt was covered with bloodstains and there was no body to show for it, just a puddle of blood and clumps of bloody dog hair a short distance off the road, the driver was clearly uncomfortable with Michael and his story. Once they were on the road back to town, he made several comments about Michael making him an accomplice to murder, and when they were about halfway home, he asked Michael to move to the back of the ambulance.

Michael only realized riding home that Talia had ridden off in the other direction, heading back into the hills rather than into town. He couldn't imagine where she could be headed to or where she had come from, as there were no houses he knew of in the back hills. He would puzzle over the night's events later. Right then, Michael was glad to be back home for a while. His old home that was now his new home again. It had to be a good omen when a dead dog came back to life and a guy met one of the girls of his dreams.

Besides, he asked himself, if something really bad was going to happen, wasn't home where he would want to be?

19

2

The Next Afternoon

The ten o'clock patient was a referral. She'd brought her daughter along, which was not exceptional. So many patients experienced anxiety before their first visit that Dr. Wen had made it a policy to call in the days before to reassure them by answering any of their questions, as if he were to be operating on them, and they often asked to bring a companion along, as if as a witness to protect against something they greatly feared.

Look at my chest, Dr Wen wanted to say to some of them. He wanted to lift his shirt and show them the scars of heart surgery. Now that was something to fear.

He said this to his students, but never to his patients.

The daughter entered the examination lounge with a cell phone to her ear. She continued to chat after acknowledging him with a smile, and then ended her conversation with a comment about energy vortexes interfering with the reception.

"I have a cell phone, but it only works north of the freeway, and most of my nonworking life is lived south of the freeway, so getting a call or two in on my days off is always a thrill." Her expression was completely unapologetic.

For her benefit, he briefly outlined his examining room policies. First among them, no cell phones.

The mother took some comfort in her daughter's distractions, though the quiver in her eyes and in her handshake revealed the depth of her internal discomfort instantly. She was so tired that she was now ready to subject herself to "borderline nonsense," as he believed she had expressed it to him over the phone.

The daughter, he thought, was very attractive, flawless and golden in a way only a blonde could be. Fit body, athletic legs, real breasts, late twenties, confident, with too much but perfectly applied makeup, dressed in a gold and blood-red mandarin-style outfit that resembled pajamas. The doctor guessed either she had either expected to witness some

Asian mysticism or she had had a sushi-themed date for lunch.

What was troubling her mother? Was it more than discontent with her present life? Boredom or disinterest or depression? There was a great weight of anxiety, and much sense of anticipation. Her words to him on the phone— "Something is coming, something necessary, some big change is coming. But instead of excitement, I feel dread"—were not entirely unfamiliar sentiments among the patients he saw, some of whom he would have described as experiencing personality disorders leaning toward paranoia and schizophrenia. It did occur to him, too, that she could be experiencing the Change of Life herself.—"I don't know what it is, or when it is going to happen. But I know the whole world will be a different place afterward."

Her name was Melinda Phillips. Her daughter was named Mary.

Wen frequently had to explain to his patients that there was nothing magical or mysterious about what he did; at the same time, he owed the success of his practice to the fact that many in some small way believed there was. He utilized many alternative forms of treatment in his practice; in this country, where there were so few alternatives in medical care, that had helped this overweight, Thai-born war veteran with a mere chiropractic license and a background in village medicine to develop a thriving and exclusive practice in alternative medicine. He was most often called upon by colleagues in more traditional practice for what they have termed hypnotherapy—an official-sounding title for the discipline that he believed was intended to lend legitimacy to the perception of what it was he did. Hypnosis drew upon both his traditional therapeutic training in the States and his childhood apprenticeship at the side of his father.

He started all his therapy sessions with a short relaxation breathing movement, and a short narrative that he recited; there were lights built into an ingenious wall screen that flashed in a random pattern that he believed resembled spinning DNA strands, but which caused him to fall asleep if he stared at it too long. He posed two questions in the quiet that followed, and he asked them to withhold their answers, to consider them silently. The first thing he

21

asked was for them to recall the happiest day of their lives. And then, after a moment, he asked them to recall the saddest moment in their lives. This helped to open them up to sharing with him.

In the end, these tools were all distractions. As with the trade practiced by any skilled illusionist, it was all in the movement of his hands—he was communicating silently from the moment he rested one of his hands on his patients' shoulders: firmly pushing them back to hold them against the seat, as if they were children to be secured, a certain movement of the fingers, a flash of a ring, a repetitive pattern that caught and spoke to the eye and lulled and calmed the mind.

Because he had learned this from his father when he was still very young, he considered it a skill as easily learned as knotting a hook on a fishing line.

Everything was growing, Mary thought.

By the time Dr. Wen had asked her to "Please, young miss, keep the phone off and sit silently," Mary had already seen it coming, ended the conversation, and moved along mentally, having realized after shifting uncomfortably in her chair a few times that she was going to have to begin her hair removal regimen again. She would swear she remembered enduring a wax and a facial with much plucking the week before last.

Now her legs were all prickly.

There was also the tomato plant in her kitchen, which months before had withered and died of thirst despite its proximity to the kitchen faucet. The idea of throwing it away had not yet impressed itself on Mary's mind. She just sort of looked at it occasionally and thought about how badly it reflected on her as a nurturer, and in a strange way had appreciated it for playing that role.

Then this morning she'd noticed a stalk of green in the planter.

Mary looked at her toenails and nearly gasped at how out of control they were. She tucked her feet under the chair. She had chosen these specific sandals and looked in the mirror before she left her apartment; she hadn't bothered to linger on her toes or how they looked up close. Now she was sure they would look like the kind of nails you found on the end of a paw. Further investigation of the matter would only cause further obsession.

Her mother's voice somewhere in the back of her mind reminded her that *the good men don't date hairy girls* as she reached for her cell phone, fully intending to call Geoff at the salon to ask him to try to fit her in between appointments tomorrow. This was her mother's fault, too, with all her talk on the way over about the groundcover spreading through her plumbing.

Doctor Wen, who was indefensibly overweight, had indicated her mother should sit down. He firmly pushed her shoulder back against the lounge-like chair's leather backing and held her there a moment, as if expecting her to resist. And then he was off and talking about spirals and connective strands and binding energies, with lots of hand-waving going on as he spoke.

Mary didn't quite follow all of it, and wondered if whatever her mom was watching on the screen made it clearer. And she wondered when the session would begin. She'd never witnessed a hypnotism before.

Mary looked down at the phone in her hand and wondered if Carina might be able to meet her for sushi for a late lunch. She could send a message without making a sound. At least her outfit wouldn't be wasted. She reached for the phone again, but stopped herself, and forced herself to focus on the session.

"Melinda, are you comfortable?"

Her mother, sort of dreamy, answered, "Yes."

Most disturbing to Mary was that her mother's eyes were half-open. There was a muscle twitching beneath her right eye, ever so slightly, but uncontrollably: Did that mean she was dreaming? And, as unusual as it was to see her mother in such a seemingly relaxed state, Mary was skeptical. However, were her mother not hypnotized, would she be able to sit still much longer? Not likely. They would all have to wait and see.

Even in her quiet moments, her mother tended to look as if she were mentally sprinting through an inventory of current and future concerns. Always trying to identify the next target of her attention.

Dr Wen said, "Can you tell me your name?"

Her mother responded, "Blrrg."
Mary snickered, though she tried not to.
And there it was. Supermom was dead.

Melinda was confused when she found herself in a different place. She was no longer in the doctor's office. For a fleeting moment, she experienced a loss of equilibrium, a feeling of dislocation accompanied by a calm that eased both dread and anticipation.

The doctor's office started to feel like a dream she'd had. And this new place she was in, it wasn't a new place at all. This had once been her home. She'd never wanted to come back to this place—where she was first raised—but she had always tried to remember it, as if there were a more powerful lesson to be drawn from it which she might have overlooked. As if there had to be a deeper reason for the fact that it existed at all. Why was this where life had started for her? Why would the universe do that to a child? She had never wanted to see her mother again—and seeing her was all she wanted, too. To give her a chance to make it up to her? To see if she could understand her mother as a real person? She didn't know.

Her mind on its own had done her the favor of never forcing her to relive her childhood, even in her dreams, much as she always wished in her heart she could see her mother's face again.

A voice said, "Some believe the only way to truly forget something is to relive it."

That she could not attach the voice to a body didn't startle her. Its presence didn't alarm her.

"By remembering, one can also forget," it said. "Remembering is the first step."

Calm suffused her.

She stood in an apartment living room. Three doors—one to the bathroom, one to the bedroom, and a third, the front door— were closed. It was clean on the surface—no trash on the floor or countertops, the carpets were cleared of clutter—but it was filthy underneath. Ground-in dirt and mildew in the carpet, smoke stains and fingerprints and food on stark walls, watermarks and smears and dust on the windows.

And that carpet! She'd forgotten the carpet. Old, worn, green, floral-printed, and distressing. It brought back to her that this was the loneliest place a child could ever be.

All the cabinet doors had been removed, and all the shelves inside were empty. It had the look of a room in the midst of renovation. The electric sockets were duct-taped. Sharp corners—the table, the counter—were padded with cloth. There was nothing to fall off or break into or hurt herself on; there were also nothing but dirty, balled-up socks to play with.

This was where her mother left her all the time. When she was gone for the day or the night. When Melinda would worry and cry and then still her mother wouldn't come home. And this was where she was sure Melinda couldn't hurt herself when her mother blacked out on the couch from drinking. And when she had overnight guests.

Melinda wanted to leave before her mother returned home.

"Breathe, Melinda," the voice said protectively. "Close your eyes and focus on your intent. Do you see the light that surrounds you like a skin, from head to toe? Keep that light in your mind. It is like armor. Nothing you see here can hurt you through that light."

Melinda saw no light. Why should she trust that voice? Why did she want to?

"You don't belong here."

"Yes, you're right, Melinda. I don't belong here. But I'm here now to help you, to make this easier."

Haltingly, her mother regained her tongue. Her words came slowly as she described the apartment she had lived in with her mother as a child. She was eerily calm and candid; Mary thought this must be something like the state of equilibrium her mother was always talking about, the one her general practitioner had been trying to achieve in the escalating mix of antidepressants and tranquilizers he was prescribing.

Then again, Mary thought, if this were the only alternative, she might prefer the drugs.

At one point, Melinda said in a very sincere and vulnerable voice, "I want to leave here before she gets home," and Mary felt both sympathy and outrage at the dread, the fear in her mother's otherwise mellowed tone.

Dr. Wen said, "Breathe, Melinda. Close your eyes and focus on your intent. Do you see the light that surrounds you like a skin? It is like armor. Nothing you see here can hurt you through that light."

"You don't belong here," she said. She sounded wary, distrustful.

"Yes, you're right, Melinda. I don't belong here. But I'm here now to help you, to make this easier. Melinda, I want you to tell me something about your mother, if that is possible."

She said, "Screaming. She's screaming. The air smells like vomit and . . . crap. Screaming, screaming, screaming," she paused, as if listening. "My father is telling her to shut up."

Her voice trailed off.

"Hm. Can you describe anything about the circumstances?"

"It's my birth. My whole being is filled with her screams. Nothing else comforts her."

"Hm."

Over the years, many patients had come to Dr. Wen in emotional disarray and confusion. In his efforts to help, he had come to understand the importance of striving to hear the voice within.

He modeled his practice on so-called homeopathic practices that he had encountered in Europe after his studies, where the focus was on strengthening the body to resist infection through diet, vitamins, and posture adjustment. It was at that point he recognized the potential of applying in his own practice some of the alternative medicine and remedies used by his father and passed on to him. In America, his practice was categorized as alternative; as such, it attracted more curiosity-seekers than the standard medical clinic. And some of those could be very eccentric.

It was not extremely unusual for a patient to experience a rebirthing. Dr. Wen had witnessed several in recent years; however, the speed and ease with which Melinda confronted and released the experience were remarkable and very unusual.

He had kept all of his patient notes for a possible book one day.

And Melinda, Dr. Wen sensed, was going to make an interesting case study.

Melinda felt as if she were falling, or being pulled, backward. There was a flash of light. And then she was in another place—a small, impoverished-looking room. She was turning away from it even as she saw what it was, because it was not something she wanted to see any more of, in this life or any other. A family of children's bodies littered about, dehydrated, malnourished, too weak to stand. Stinking of vomit and bile.

Had she been one of them in another life? Was that why she was seeing this?

One of them, the oldest girl, looked directly at Melinda, as if she could see her, although Melinda felt like she was a ghost, invisible, hanging over a scene that had long been swallowed by the past. Melinda instantly believed that she recognized something of herself in this girl. This was who she had once been, Melinda thought, even as she continued turning away.

Her lifetimes spread out before her, a panoply of ghostly silhouettes, each beckoning, inviting her to relive the memories they held. She had immediately taken this first view of a former lifetime as a cautionary warning—suddenly her daydreams of being wealthy or royal-born or otherwise notable in a previous life seemed far less relevant than the worldwide historical record on living conditions for women and children. With rare exceptions, wherever and whenever she had lived in previous centuries, if she'd been born female, there was a great likelihood her life had not ended well.

Yet this was where she was headed, she thought, back through her lifetimes. This is where that voice had wanted her to go.

She heard a voice speaking, a new voice, softer in tone than the first, but the sound was nearly unintelligible. It seemed to be a woman's voice. For a moment, she longed for that first voice, the man's voice, which had been so comforting and sure and clear; but still, she found herself drawn in the direction of the newer sound. Melinda thought it might be her own voice echoing back, but the more closely she tried to focus on the sound, the farther it drifted off. Or was it she who was drifting off after it?

. . .

Where was she now?

She was charging through a magnificent garden on a hilltop. The sun was blazing overhead. She paused for a moment at the garden wall, looking down the graveled slope to the thicket of dense brush at its base. The forest stretched uninterrupted beyond that thicket, to the horizon. Another woman led the way, hunting knife in hand. Her hair was a red burst of fire racing down the hillside.

A chattering flush of birds took to the air from inside the dense greenery. Something surged behind that bramble of thorned

27

leaves and branches. What Melinda recognized was its surprise at being discovered, the reckless scramble of its flight.

If not for the dominating scent of pine, would she also be able to smell its fear?

Alone, Melinda would have stopped there; it would be enough if they had driven it off.

Her companion, though, was an irresistible force; after she charged to the thicket, she thrashed her left hand back and forth, the foliage melting under her blade as she carved her way forward.

If Melinda could have seen her own reflection at that moment, what face would she have found staring back at her? What would her name have been? Her hair that she could see was a familiar hue, but a different length, and thinner. This body felt younger and stronger than she could ever remember feeling.

Exhilaration filled her as she followed behind her companion.

When had she forgotten that she could feel so strong?

After the reenactment of the birthing, the session got stranger, if that were possible. Mary almost didn't want to hear anymore of her mother talking in her hypnotized voice, which could be hard to understand because it was quiet and sort of childlike and dreamy, or the way Melinda seemed at times to struggle to say a sentence, slowing pulling it out word by word.

Regardless, her mother segued into a whole other, totally unidentifiable scenario. One minute she was curling herself up into the fetal position, and the next she was struggling with what sounded like a string of names in another language. Wen followed it better than Mary; she couldn't understand exactly what was being said between the two.

Wen asked her grimly, "These were your brothers and sisters?"

Her mother nodded in response. "We were poisoned by the water," she said matter-of-factly

Her mother's voice trailed off occasionally as they continued, not like she couldn't remember something right but more like she was distracted. Mary thought she was talking about something terrible that had happened to some kids, but had no idea what it might be about.

That part of the session just didn't click with Mary until Dr. Wen took out his notebook and started to probe for detail—a family name, geographical markers, materials used in their home, clothing fabric, style of footwear.

And, slowly, Mary realized that her mother was supposedly talking about another life she had lived before this one.

Mary studied her mother more closely.

She wondered if any of it were true. Or was this all something she read up on somewhere? And was there something different about her now, now that she was remembering a life as someone else?

Mary's mind wandered to her brother. He would be having a riot with this going on in front of him. She wondered if hearing about this was going to get him too agitated. He was so like dad that way, resistant toward anything that went out of the mainstream.

What was Michael doing back in Cheronkin, anyway? How long was he going to stay? She knew his breakup with Danielle had been hard on him, even if he was the one who made the final call to walk. But wasn't it strange that he'd left everything else in his life, too, and that it didn't seem like he'd had a second thought about it?

He hadn't mentioned any of it during their afternoon together yesterday.

He would be scared to hear it, but when Michael did get around to asking for dating assistance, Mary had a hundred prospects for him; she just had to give him time to settle in.

Mary was still a bit envious of the lightness in Michael's voice over the telephone the previous night, when he'd described his unlikely encounter over the corpse of a dog with this longtime object of infatuation. A singer he saw at the club years ago. For him, for the night, for the week, for a while into the future, he would be able to summon the memory of meeting her and all of his troubles would shortly fade into the background and he would believe that life might have a reason to it. At least for a while.

If only someone felt that way about her.

Mary looked at her watch. This session was approaching its anticipated end, and she thought Wen was a bit off still from any sort of finishing point. She was sure he noticed her movement and understood the message. After a moment, he cleared his throat, stood, and adjusted the screen in front of her mother, so that Mary was actually able to see the colored shapes floating across the black background in winding spirals. She stared, intrigued.

Wen did something with his fingers. First, she thought, there might have been something in the air, a fly his hand was chasing. Then she thought—or was it her imagination?—that he might be holding something in his hand? But she couldn't quite see what it was.

Her eyes felt heavy.

It might have just been his fingers, that was all. Fluttering there, fluttering like the wings of a butterfly buffeted by the wind . . .

Once the daughter was asleep, Wen decided to make a more focused effort.

"Melinda, I am curious about the period of time between the moment of passing in one life and the moment of birth into another. Where do you exist during this time? Where do you go?"

"Someone is there, always waiting for me. A friend."

"Always? If we were to continue down this path, how many lives have you experienced?"

"Many hundreds of lives."

"Melinda, is your friend present now?"

"Yes. I'm never alone."

"May we have a conversation?"

"Of course," she said.

Her lips continued to move, but Wen could longer hear her words. Instead, he heard the sound of rain. His arm had gone numb. The sound was almost like a bad memory. Rain on the river. The sound was most disconcerting. Rain on the river has so many different meanings . . .

Although it was a forest, there was the feel of walking through an ancient and endless temple, accompanied by the hush that falls in places where men dare not walk. Tree trunks like columns stretched to the sky to hold the green canopy that sheltered all worshippers.

Melinda wondered: Why has it been so long since I walked here?

Momentarily overcome by the majesty of her environment, she didn't notice at first that her hunting companion was gone. There was a certain charge to the air in one direction, a sense that the silence of this place had recently been unsettled; it wasn't after more than a few steps that she heard a voice, small, yet carrying clearly—familiar, but from where? Which one of her lives?

"I have encountered many so-called past-life experiences in my practice," that voice said, carrying on the wind through the trees. "I have not found many of these accounts to be credible; most often, there is countervailing information related to the patient's psychology which causes doubt on my part."

She followed the sound of the voice, surprised that its tone was not what she had expected. There was no fear, nor panic. It wasn't even out of breath. How could this have been the person they were pursuing?

She saw through the trees to her side a man, a roundish Asian man with a round head seated in a meditation pose, naked, eyes staring ahead as words spilled from his lips.

Her companion appeared in the trees on the other side of the man. She moved through the trees toward him like a lit fuse.

The man said, "I have to consider how to get at the heart of the matter. If indeed this is a legitimate testimony, what part of a person is it that moves from life to life to life with each rebirthing? Is it the soul, and does that mean that throughout these lives where all physical, external characteristics have changed, that the soul is eternal and unalterable?" His tone was strangely hypnotic. Comforting and sure. It seemed so familiar.

He did not react when the redhead reached him. He did not even seem to see her. Not when her blade flashed again, not when his head tumbled from his posed form with such force that it bounced and turned and rolled after it hit the ground. His lips continued moving all the while. "Or is that soul a consciousness that learns and grows and changes through these lifetimes? If so, what purpose do the barriers of memory serve in the process of developing such a consciousness? Why would we not be allowed to remember?"

No more questions, Melinda thought. The redhead nodded her head, as if in silent agreement.

Mary woke from her trance. It took a moment to understand she was sitting in Dr. Wen's office.

What the hell was that? Did she fall asleep? It didn't feel like falling asleep.

She tried to assess the moment in the room, to figure out if and how long she had been out. The Doctor was still standing with his back to her. Her mother was staring blankly ahead. She considered, for a moment, her last memory: the machine with the flashing lights.

Had he hypnotized her, too?

Wen was speaking. He was finishing a question, ". . . external characteristics have changed, that the soul is eternal and unalterable?"

And then nothing. For a minute, she waited, listening. Not a word more was said, adding to the challenge of getting her bearings.

Was he waiting for Mom to say something, or vice-versa?

The room was too quiet.

Something was not right here.

"Doctor Wen?"

He turned his head just a bit, starting at the sound of her voice. He made a short, choking noise, and grabbed his throat with his right hand. His left hand hung at his side.

And then he leaned forward and fell over, a great grunt of air pushing out of him as his stomach compressed against the floor and a smack! as his face hit the floor.

Mary had no idea what it was that finally woke her mother. With a gasp and a start, Melinda just suddenly opened her eyes and sat up.

The room was empty by then; Mary had been waiting so long in that disquieting silence for a trauma therapist to show up that *she* had started to feel genuinely traumatized. She worried that the hospital staff had forgotten her the minute they'd seen Wen on the floor. She also began to worry that Dr. Todd, one of the doctors who came to assist Dr. Wen, and who now had her phone number, might not call her.

Mary already knew which dress she wanted to wear on their first date.

"Oh, thank God, Mom."

"What happened?" Melinda yawned and stretched her arms over her head. "My goodness, what a strange feeling—I don't think I remember feeling this rested in a long time. Where did the doctor go? Have I been out long? Did I have anything interesting to say?"

Her mother looked her in the eyes, saw something worrisome there, and asked again, "What happened?"

3
One Week Passes

4:00 PM

The sky above the bay was thick with birds. Arriving from every direction, they joined the thousands already circling above the water, forming what looked like the bottom spout of a tornado. If there was any menace to them, it was in their numbers—they nearly blotted out what was left of the day's sun—and in their unified purpose—spinning in a churning funnel in the air above the bay. Were they feeding? Were they mating? Or was it a call more primal they were answering?

Michael looked at his watch as he waited in his car in a dirt lot just off the coast highway, watching the spinning, turning swarm. The dying light made their wings all look black.

At one point, he caught a glimpse through the winged mass of a boat moving slowly out to sea. Was it some kind of fishing boat they were circling, hungry for its catch?

Michael wondered whether the mystery guy his aunt had asked him to pick up was ever going to show. How was he getting here? Michael didn't even know where to wait for him. A speeding car passed through the nearby intersection of the highway with Marble Canyon Road. On the corner was a boarded-up gas station which had been boarded up all of Michael's life, with the main difference now being that it was surrounded by a chain-link fence. There was a cardboard sign nailed to a telephone pole across the street from the gas station, on the coast side of the road. He had seen it before, though it had since been updated after the last accident in the canyon. Someone had written in dark red paint:

MARBLE CANYON   ~~12~~ 14
HUMANS   0

Later that evening, Aunt Laura was hosting a beach party for the employees of her restaurant, of which he now

34

was one, on a strip of beach at Cheronkin's northern county line. He'd thought about going, much as a beach bonfire wasn't his sort of thing, but the timing was all wrong, too. It was happening not five miles from where he was now, but nothing was going to be happening until hours later, so he was going to have to drive all the way home, drop off the guy he was picking up, then come back again. His other option would be to hang out until dusk with the guy, if the guy was game; the problem being it was someone Michael hadn't even met who he might not like at all or who might not want to go to a bonfire.

He'd already been thinking of calling Mary to ask her to meet the two of them—but was sure she'd turn him down. Both Mary and his mother had been incommunicado since the "therapy" session, where Michael guessed something heavy must have gone down. He was confident one of them would spill the story and was hoping it would be later rather than sooner. So he hadn't bothered asking Mary about the party. Besides, although she went to Fandango from time to time, she'd never been into the club the way Michael was.

Still, he thought her conversational skills would help with whoever this person turned out to be. If Michael was basically going to play the part of local groupie trying to make inroads with the staff—the only reason he would go to the party—wasn't it going to be more difficult to do that if he were hosting a guest?

And what would they talk about until the party started? Michael's new haircut?

Michael saw someone making his way up from the harbor a short time later. He had expected the visitor to arrive via the highway, either by bus or by car. Why hadn't Aunt Laura told him to drive down to the pier to pick him up there?

He held out his hand as he approached Michael. "You're my ride?"

"Michael. Sorry you had to walk. I was expecting you by land, not by sea."

"Jack."

They shook hands.

There was a noise that sounded like a string of firecrackers going off on the other side of the mountains, in Cheronkin's direction.

Jack looked questioningly at Michael, who shrugged his shoulders. "I have no idea what that was," Michael said.

Jack had the look of a person who'd been out to sea for months. His face was all peeling skin, sunburn and, like his hair, whitened by crystallized salt. His eyes were glazed and glassy; likely he was stoned, and he smelled strongly of cigarettes. He was unshaven and unwashed, his clothes dirty and smeared with unidentifiable substances, and he smelled like fish and garbage. None of that dampened his demeanor.

"You came in on a trawler?"

"I hitched a ride with those guys for the last leg north. I took a roundabout route here." He laughed in a good-natured way.

"That's where my aunt met you?"

"Yes. Okay, so you're the nephew." He looked out at the boat, a speck in the distance. "Took some time, but they were going my way." Jack sniffed at himself, and grimaced. "We better get going before those birds catch a whiff of me and realize I've come ashore. I did leave my socks on board to throw them off." He chuckled again, showing Michael that he was indeed not wearing any socks.

Michael wished he'd brought a towel to cover the car seat.

Jack looked Michael over after they were both seated in the car. Michael was pulling on his seatbelt and eyeing Jack in a way that said he expected him to do the same.

"It's not a party town I'm arriving in, then? You look like a guy who minds his hours." Jack snapped on his seatbelt.

Michael didn't know how to respond.

"Well, good. I could use the rest. And we're not that far from the city, right? You can at least point me in the right direction if I want to find some fun? Is there someone you know who can direct me to the hot spots?"

Michael started the car. It sounded like the guy might be making fun of him.

"Another day," Jack said, "another dollar."

6:00 PM

"Do you think I left them up in the car?" It was the third time Jack had asked. For a third time he rummaged through his knapsack looking for the cigarettes he'd supposedly had.

"We could go look." He didn't seem like he was a bad guy, but Michael wasn't giving Jack his car keys to go look on his own.

"Yeah, but what if they aren't there?"

The sun was just beginning to set.

"Is that all the stuff you brought? One backpack?"

"It's pretty much all I had left."

One of the bartenders—he thought her name was Janet—and a group of waitresses were setting up when they got to the beach. They had wine coolers, blankets, firewood, a basket of sandwiches and bowls of fruit, all the comforts, but they insisted Michael and Jack wait for some of the others to arrive before they ate anything; which meant there was little distraction while Michael and Jack sat nearly silently in the sand facing the shore.

Michael had been working at Fandango for only a week now, and he'd been feeling there was some attitude toward him from some of the staff. Likely because he'd gotten his job because his aunt owned the club, and also simply because his aunt now owned the club. A lot of people were having a hard time with the idea of a new manager, a new name, a new ambiance, a new everything.

Some of them just might never accept that the Hat was gone. They would continue working at the new establishment, wanting it to fail, and then what? Somehow, magically, it would revert to what it was?

And because Michael was a longtime Hat aficionado, he was actually sympathetic to their feelings, so he'd just decided to take the flak quietly.

Jack pushed the backpack away, an irritated look on his face. No cigarettes.

7:00 PM

A younger guy Michael recognized as one of the busboys and an older woman who worked behind the bar on the weekend crossed the sand, chattering and smoking cigarettes. They set up chairs and towels nearby. The guy, whose name he couldn't remember, waved at Michael and Michael waved back.

"We got on the road just in time," the woman said to Michael. Who was she? Another name he didn't have down. "There's a fire out in the hills. Someone said a gas main exploded and set a couple of houses and a church nearby on fire . . . it was all on the east side of town," she said quickly when she saw the worried look on his face. "But the roads were just clogging up something all around."

If there was any smoke in the sky in the direction of Cheronkin, it was too dark to see. Michael hoped they would be able to take the canyon drive home. Otherwise, it was going to be a two-hour haul getting back.

"Where did you live before you came to Cheronkin?"

"Texas," Jack said. "I was in Texas."

"For a while?"

"A couple months. Yeah."

"Doing what?"

"About the same as I've ever done, Mike. Trying to stay alive. Trying to stay ahead. Different things. I was working with a band at the time, but it was just a part-time thing. I did some artwork. Just kicking around."

"What did you play?"

"Drums."

"Why did you leave?"

"Something on your mind, Mike?"

"Nothing," Michael said. "Just making conversation."

"Well," Jack said, "I'll tell you the story, but I'm not going to make a big deal about sharing it with everyone I meet here. So you can be my liaison for whoever wants to know who you think should be in on it.

"The roof caved in at a club I worked in, in Austin. I was in a house band." Jack scratched the back of his head. "I guess part of it landed on me. I don't remember any of it, but I heard the story enough afterward that I know what happened. Thirty-seven people died, and, strangely enough, the township I awoke to expressed its grief with days, weeks of celebration, drinking, popping pills, partying, and music all over the place, like Mardi Gras sprung up. The whole place was under a crazy spell of grief. I remember part of the party, There was a fundraiser for the victims and their families, and I contributed some sculpture work—which is something I do on the side—and your aunt saw the pieces and hired me to design some of the same for her club."

38

"I remember reading about the accident," Michael said.

"Major property damage. Oh, yeah. My notable achievement apparently was surviving the experience."

"That's crazy."

"I had my ID on me, so I knew my name, but that didn't help me get very far beyond figuring out where I lived. I remember, as far as I can tell, all the things I learned to do—reading, writing, I can still drum and do the artwork—but I couldn't tell you a thing about where I came from before Texas." Jack smiled. "'People died. Hearts were broken, too many drugs were taken . . . all the survivors just about went out of our minds in Texas. 'Wasn't that just the way it was there?' Before I left Texas, I ran into a guy who was apparently in that same band. Those were basically the words he used when he was recalling the experience. I can't remember any of it. That and a lot of other things are gone. In my mind, everything before the accident is still a blank space."

7:10 PM

Another busboy came running across the sand with a bundle of tiki torches in his arms. He went straight to the group of waitresses first thing, and after ruffling his hair a little, they directed him to the area where they thought the torches should be set. He was also in training for a prep cook position.

"There's Aaron," Michael said. They had moved on to playing backgammon by now, with a game set Jack had finagled from the waitresses. Jack was winning, three games to Michael's one.

Aaron noticed them after he had jammed the third tiki torch into the sand. And when he recognized Michael, he ran over, and fell to his knees in front of them.

Jack immediately asked Aaron if he had a cigarette.

"Uh . . . Aaron, Jack," Michael said.

Somehow, Aaron already knew this. "The art guy, right? No," Aaron said, "I never smoke. I don't have dreams at night when I partake of tobacco." He said this as if he were revealing a solemn secret. "But I did get my hands on some dopage."

"So what are we doing here?" Jack leaned forward in his chair, clapped his hands twice, smacked his lips and

39

finally brought his hands to rest on his knees. "Start spreading the happiness around."

Michael thought this forward, but Aaron seemed not to mind.

Aaron pulled a plastic baggie from one of his pockets. "Ten bucks and I'll roll you a big fatty," he said.

"Ten bucks?"

"Gotta pay for gas."

Jack snorted. "Five bucks for half a fat one. I don't have a lot of cash on me. I just got here."

"Cool, man. Deal."

Michael heard a horn beeping up in the parking lot. Five or six cars were slowing on the highway to make the turn-off. The party was starting.

When Aaron and Jack completed their transaction, Aaron ripped the joint in half and then walked off, lighting his portion.

Jack looked sort of decrepit crouched over trying to light the stubby half-joint in the wind.

Someone tapped on Michael's shoulder. The cutest of the three waitresses who had been overseeing the setup. Her name was Kirstin. Slim, kind of boyish figure, knockout eyes and smile. Michael said hi.

She handed him a wine cooler, and smiled warmly. "I thought you might like a drink." She rested a hand on his arm briefly. Long enough for him to stare at it. And then she walked off.

"It must be your new haircut," Jack said.

To Michael, the best thing about the short exchange was that Jack had witnessed it. Derelict as he appeared at the moment, it was obvious Jack wasn't a bad-looking guy. And then, thinking of him as some accomplished artist only magnified his presence.

A little something to buttress the ego against the guy sitting next to him.

The potential downside of the visit he considered as he inspected the drink.

There was no telling what might be in there. Could be beer, wine, or spit.

7:30 PM

Jack said, "I'm ready to go dig in the car for those cigarettes."

Soon they were walking back across the sand, smoking the joint with all the new arrivals walking past them. Most of the smiling faces casting mischievous glances at their exhalations were recognizable from the club in both its incarnations, the current Fandango and the former Murray's Hat. Though Michael didn't know that many names, it reassured him to think that he did now fit in with the history of the place. He was glad that he decided to attend.

Jack searched the car when they got to the parking lot. No cigarettes. He cursed under his breath.

A red Porsche made the left turn off the coast highway into the lot. Whoever was driving sat on the horn.

Jack got out of the car, closed the door. And by the time he and Michael had walked to the other side of the car, the Porsche was stopped in front of them.

"Is this where the party is?"

Andrina Sorenson. Once married to a friend of Michael's dad—part of his middle-age crazy, his dad would say. Michael had met her before at a party or two, and the wedding. Not that there was any acknowledgement from her. She was all about Jack.

Her left arm was hanging out of the car. She had long, plastic nails.

Jack leaned in and said something that set Andrina laughing while Michael stepped out behind the Porsche, admiring it. Andrina ran her nails along the dashboard, and up to the top of her windshield as Jack looked over at the girl in the passenger seat, a bored-looking blonde with high cheekbones and what looked like a severely tight bun of hair on her head.

Andrina asked if Jack liked her new friend. Clearly referring to her car.

"I've seen better," Jack teased, clearly referring to the girl, who curled her lip in response.

Andrina laughed again, and told her friend to settle down. "It's all play. Well, aren't you the card?" Andrina asked. "Seriously, what do you think of my new car?"

Continuing his inspection of the car, Michael reached the passenger side, and found himself looking at the blonde, who had intentionally turned her head away from the conversation.

She didn't look so bad to Michael.

Andrina asked Jack if there was any kind of party going yet.

"No, not yet," he said. "Mostly just a bunch of beach grubs. Listen, do you have a cigarette?"

Michael said hello to the blonde, thinking she might be feeling snubbed.

She said hi.

Michael leaned into the car tentatively, as if to look at the interior. And, thinking he was being witty, he repeated the car's campaign motto, as he remembered it from his youth. "Porsche." Michael said. "There is no substitute."

The blonde rolled the window up, forcing him back a step.

Inside the car, she shuddered, and turned her eyes to the horizon beyond the dashboard.

As he walked away, Michael yelled out to Jack that he would meet him on the beach later.

8:05 PM

"Women, the source of all our tribulations," someone said as Michael dished himself a plate at the buffet. "Can't live with them."

Michael was hungry. His mouth was dry.

Down the table was a tall, skinny guy decked out in ragged jeans, a black dinner jacket, a cape and a straw hat. A briefcase was lying open between them at the end of the banquet setup, balanced on the rim of the punchbowl. Inside were cigarettes, lighters, penlights, and two jars filled with joints.

"How much for a joint?"

"Ten dollars."

"Five for half of one," Michael said, feeling better versed in the way these things were handled. "I don't smoke very much."

The guy didn't argue. Michael pulled a bill out of his wallet, and dropped it in the briefcase. The guy leaned in, pulled out a jar, and unscrewed the lid. The only part of his face not lost in the shadow of the hat's rim was his chin. Michael had seen him at the club before, he was sure.

He snapped the joint in half, passed the bigger side to Michael. His hand came up again a moment later with a lit match in it. "Full service," he said.

42

"No kidding."

"It's good for business."

Michael coughed a whole bunch after his first drag.

The guy closed his briefcase. "Happier trails," he said as he walked off.

8:35 PM

Halfway through his beer Michael felt sick to his stomach, and a little too lightheaded. A little too stoned, maybe, he thought. Jack wasn't anywhere to be seen. There were about sixty people moving around the area lit by the tiki torches, dancing, eating, laughing, playing instruments, or else just working their way through the crowd around the bonfire. Farther from the fire, on the broken line of blankets on either side of Michael, there were small clusters of people in groups of two or three, or like him, sitting alone, just kicking back.

The guy with the briefcase moved from blanket to blanket to towel, working his way around the fire. At each stop his silhouette would bend slightly as he pushed back his straw hat. The briefcase would swing open. At almost every towel, the guy unscrewed the lid of the joint jar. After each transaction he stuffed the cash into his jacket pocket.

He approached Michael after selling a joint and a pack of cigarettes to a guy on a towel about five feet away from him. When he pushed his hat back, Michael was mesmerized by the strands of straw that formed the dark and pointed bramble around the rim of the hat.

The guy planted his feet like a salesman, and bent down from the waist.

"Smokes?" The briefcase flew open.

The guy next to him lit up his joint, and the smoke wafted past him. Michael grabbed his stomach. "No thanks," he said. "You did me at the banquet table." And when the guy didn't seem to understand, Michael started to explain that he bought something from him earlier.

But then it stopped him. *His face.*

The face that went with the chin and the voice, it was somewhere in the back of his head. The voice with the face he was seeing in his head was saying something like "Dots we got lots of dots."

"Oh," Michael said, stunned.

Lots of dots lots of dots.

43

Years ago on the sidewalk outside the club, there had been a chattering, nervous-looking transient waving around a sheet of white paper covered with tiny, multicolor dots. Someone later had said it was acid, which Michael was not at all into and had never actually tried.

"Dots," was what he had said to Michael, "I've got lots of dots."

A guy has to ask himself how many dots a guy like that could hide in half a joint.

Michael leaned forward and threw up.

While he was still retching he heard the briefcase clicking closed.

9:17 PM

Michael tried to be very, very still. He wanted very much not to freak out, so much so that he was hoping he would just sort of pass out and it would be over when he woke up. He didn't want to make any kind of scene, attract any kind of attention. He just wanted it to go away.

His head was spinning and a nauseating ache settled in his stomach.

He thought he would just close his eyes, still his thoughts, and go to sleep.

He didn't know how long he was lying like that. It could have been a long time. It could have been a short time before he sat up and the throbbing in his head had vanished. The nausea in his belly had lifted. He giggled a little about what an idiot he was. This was dumb.

And then he wondered if he should maybe have warned people what the guy was doing.

"Hey," he called out to the guy next to him, who had finished his joint and was now smoking a cigarette. "Hey!"

The guy next to him nearly fell over and off his towel at the sound of Michael's voice. He was wearing a blue shirt with big white dots all over it, and striped shorts.

What was he going to say? Michael looked at him, then averted his eyes. It hurt a little to look at him. Who should apologize? "It's okay. I won't yell anymore," Michael said, but didn't know if the guy could hear him.

It was really too late for warnings, anyway. People were tripping out all over the place already.

44

Looking around he could see some partygoers spinning in circles or wobbling around, laughing wildly and shouting, others lying in the sand and flailing their arms or else just sitting completely still—simply engrossed in some object in the sand like a piece of glass or a cigarette butt.

Michael quickly became absorbed in watching the shadows that were cast across the sand by the light of the bonfire, which had seemingly outgrown the fire pit that contained it. It was now burning brilliantly white, casting sparks into the night sky.

On another blanket nearby, a girl let out this crazy, shrill, cackling laugh. It looked to him like she had seaweed for hair. She had hoop earrings, and there were kelp pods hanging in chains down the sides of her head, cascading over her shoulders. He could make out every feature on her pretty little mermaid face as she laughed and pointed out at the water.

She looked very fucked up.

Everybody got those dots.

The stars were out, puffy little white points of light moving, spinning here and back, in cadence with the rhythm of the music and the dancing of feet and the rush of the waves.

The shrill girl kept laughing. People kept on dancing. One guy started weaving in and out of the tiki torches as he went. A girl behind him started to do the same.

Striped shorts next to him leaned over, and said, "If I start having a bad trip, please ignore me."

"I got lots of dots," Michael said, nodding and giggling. "It's just silly. And dumb."

Michael didn't know if the guy heard him. They both had a good laugh.

There was a waitress sitting closer to the bonfire than anyone else, just apart from the gathered crowd. He'd seen her once at the club. She'd just gone back to school and was only working weekend shifts for the fall. She was so close to the fire that her hair was smoldering. Her clothes might have been melting off her perky little body. She didn't mind. She looked like she was lost in her own world, and seemed to be enjoying the heat.

A guy who looked like a surfer walked over to her. She turned a little to talk to him. He stood beside her and put

45

his hand in her hair and looked mildly amused as he surveyed both her condition and the condition of the partygoers around him. She reached into his shorts, and though he seemed surprised, he didn't stop her. He rested a hand on one of her breasts and stepped in toward her.

Michael was shocked, and looked away in embarrassment, only to realize there wasn't anywhere he could turn his attention where there wasn't someone's white butt winking at him, like a silent signal to disrobe had been telegraphed across the sand. Suddenly, throughout the crowd, a good portion of the people dancing, having chicken fights, and throwing food, were now naked.

No way.

Michael was hypnotized as people coupled up and the light glowed golden on their baked, naked skins. Touching and tongues, hips and shoulders and feet, patches of dark hair—which were one of the things that made naked people look so weird, he thought, those odd little patches of hair just below midsection of the human body, some with fleshy bits hanging out.

There were singles and couples and threesomes and just all these people getting down right there in the sand in front of him.

Then he heard someone call his name.

Michael.

A girl.

Was there someone there for him?

He worked himself free of the groove he had formed in the sand. The show wasn't even giving him a hard-on anyway. He must have gotten something different than everybody else did.

Michael looked around.

There were two girls climbing the staircase to the parking lot. Had one of them called out his name? One of them was harder to make out than the other, because she was dressed in black. Was that Talia? Or was he hallucinating that too? Just wishful thinking?

It was hard to be sure there were two people really there. One he could see plainly, because her red hair was so bright. It was like a fire.

By the time he'd crossed the sand and reached the bottom of the stairs, they were already out of sight.

He kept moving. He thought he could catch them. He tripped halfway up the stairs. He caught himself with his knee and his right hand and impressed himself by managing not to crack his face on the corner of a step. . . . just get up get up, he thought, before anyone sees . . . didn't want to be a topic of conversation at work on Monday . . .

But getting up wasn't easy. Something had wrapped around his shin when he fell; it threw off his balance when he tried to stand. There was a vine of ivy curled around his leg just below the knee. As he stared at it, wondering where it could have come from, he became aware of an odd prickling sensation under his palms.

Thinking he might have set his hands on some bugs, he flinched, and moved them. There were no bugs. There were instead sprigs of green pushing out of the rock underneath.

And it wasn't just under his hands.

It was under all of him, plants sprouting up and down the steps, leaves unfurling, and flower buds fattening before his eyes. He tried to yank the vine off his leg, but pulled his hand back in disgust at the feel of it sliding and pulsing in his grip.

The top of the staircase was already gone from his view, covered with blossoming sunflowers and reedy shoots that ended in sprays of small flowers.

Another vine circled his hand, and pulled his arm out from under him. His face landed in a bouquet of flowers, kicking up a puff of pollen. He pulled that hand free, and pushed himself up a step closer to the top before his foot smashed and slid on something crisp and wet, and he fell again. More vines wrapped around his arms and his neck, and he flailed helplessly, buried in wet, green leaves. Flower petals tickled his eyes, blades of grass poked up into his nose. The plants were all taller than he, and taller than he could see over while he was on his knees. The vines that held him were growing inside his clothes, the slithering leaves rubbing cold against his skin. The less he moved the less he could move, the more the plants gagged and tied him. The smell and taste of pollen nearly overwhelmed him. And the crawling tangle of vines tightened around him, squeezing slowly under his armpits, twisting tighter around his neck.

Michael tried to catch his breath and ended up choking and coughing on thick, chewy leaves. When he spat those out, he thought to scream for help, and ended up with another mouthful that set him off choking again. He feared he might not be able to catch his breath again.

Panicked, he pulled his hand free again, but his whole body was pinned and there was nowhere for it to go. Another vine lashed around the wrist and pulled it down. Gagging, he fought in vain to pull it free again. The moon seemed to swell in size.

He hoped this wouldn't be a long way to die.

Something tugged on his arm, and then again, and then he was moving up the last remaining steps. A gnarled and hairy hand with fingernails that looked like dirty animal claws had grabbed hold of his arm, and was pulling him away from the plants, while another matching hand, nails gleaming, slashed at any vegetation that moved in Michael's direction.

Michael was lifted over the last two steps as if he weighed nothing. He rested on his hands and his knees once on the asphalt, regaining his breath and a portion of his composure.

While the horizon teetered, a voice growled, "Quiet down."

A car skidded at the far end of the parking lot. Michael looked up in time to see Andrina's Porsche squealing away on the coast highway.

"Stop yelling," the voice said again, firmly.

The voice sounded more familiar this time; Michael thought about it and realized that he was indeed making a lot of noise, and instantly he was quiet.

The voice continued to talk calmly while Michael crouched, breathing hoarsely, feeling the cuts and scratches that covered his legs, feeling the stings and scratches that thorns and thistles had left across his palms.

His rescuer lit a cigarette. Michael was almost afraid to look, because of the hands. And the claws. He was half-expecting the devil himself. That would someday be his anti-drug testimonial: "I just wanted to be part of the crowd. Then I saw the devil."

He giggled.

But it wasn't the devil. Or, if it was, the devil had amnesia. It was Jack.

IN THE NEWS

ain'titwickednews.com, Web log, March 15
Thirty-three people were admitted to hospitals in Buenaventura and Cheronkin after buying and smoking cigarettes laced with an as-yet-unidentified hallucinogenic from an unidentified man at a beach party. Officials were alerted when three teenagers returning from the party arrived concurrently at two local hospitals complaining of nausea, headaches, and hallucinations. An artist's sketch of the suspect, who is still at large, will be released by police "as soon as we can get two of the kids to agree on a single, coherent description," one official said. "A lot of them liked his hat."

ain'titwickednews.com, Web log, March 23
It was reported in this column that the 10-day-old search for two missing children, Keith Pollack, 4, and Jennifer Sayles, 5, had ended with the startling discovery of a stone altar marked with unusual symbols and other suspected indicators of satanic worship. This week, after police determined that the crushed bones found on and around the altar belonged to dogs, cats, turtles, hamsters, and other household pets, and were not the children, as was initially feared, the massive search effort has been reorganized, with hundreds of volunteers from adjacent communities lending support. This time around, efforts have been hampered by late evening and early morning fog. The two children became separated from their parents during a family reunion taking place in the hills west of our recent favorite little rich burb, Cheronkin County.

West Coast Regional Reporter, April 2
Southern Counties Mercy Grace Hospital announced that for the fourth straight week no one has died in their trauma ward, a new record in the hospital's 60-year history. "While many of our patients remain in serious condition, we have seen improvement nearly across the board in terms of critical care patients and patients undergoing long-term hospitalization. There's not a few of us who feel like we have been witnessing a miracle."

4

Family Dinner
April 4

Mulligan Water-conditioning Company
1085 Marrino Blvd.
Cheronkin County, California

Dear Sirs,

After being informed one last time that there is nothing wrong with my water-purifying unit, I have taken matters into my own hands. I fixed it myself and I fixed it good.

What's left of it should be arriving at your offices after the holiday.

The fact is, I don't know what is going on here. But I have a feeling you do. I've seen the look in your "service" technicians' eyes. I am not naive. And I simply refuse to spend the rest of my life pulling weeds out of my kitchen sink, whatever part they may play in your purifying process.

I can't tell you the hell I've gone through because of this. My husband thinks I'm insane. Mulligan Man, my ass. We'll be eating our holiday dinner off paper plates this year because of you.

This house is going back to bottled water.

Sincerely,
Melinda Phillips

Mary was certain that something wasn't right in the world as she set the parking brake and opened the car door to step outside. The neighborhood looked perfectly manicured, in a way it never had before, with every tree, bush, and shrub up and down the sidewalk pruned to a bare minimum of foliage. Houses on the block that Mary had literally never seen were exposed to the view from the street. None of the trees on the connecting streets or on the next block over were similarly landscaped; this street looked like a new development slapped into a recently clear-cut section of Cheronkin.

She would bet that the whole block was up in arms.

50

The properties here were two-acre lots, the houses elegant, on streets lined with willows, eucalyptus, and pepper trees, and bougainvillea, ivy, and jasmine camouflaged every light post and telephone poll. No one driving down the street would have known it was a well-to-do part of Cheronkin they were observing. It always felt like you were out in the brambles. The older part of town had for a long time been inhabited, for the most part, by one-time hippies who one way or another had come into a load of money, and their heirs, as well as the descendents of the families who'd been in Cheronkin from the early days of the town's history. As a community they had fought fiercely to prevent the development taking place in the northern part of the county from spreading their way, insistent on maintaining the area's natural high desert look.

Now this street looked like the suburbs.

It looked like hell.

But what was bothering Mary was more than a sense of dislocation inspired by the landscaping. It wasn't just the world around her, though if she were asked she would have to say that the world seemed to her to be different these last few weeks in some indefinable manner. It was not only that she felt very unlike herself.

To accentuate the feeling as she walked up the driveway—looking, in sweats and a t-shirt, lazy, ugly and extraordinarily unfit for socializing beyond the immediate family—the driver's door of Michael's car, parked in her old spot on the driveway, opened.

And it wasn't Michael stepping out. Her brother's legs weren't that long. It was a guy who was lighting up a cigarette. And Mary couldn't even think of anyone Michael knew who would a) smoke and b) do so in plain view where Melinda would spot him and impale him, except for that old dirt bag guitar player Michael used to hang out with at the club when he was younger. Michael's friend Billy. And she knew it wasn't him, this was definitely not Billy, unless he had dropped 25 years, grown an ass and come back from the dead.

The stranger turned around to see who was coming.

And Mary realized it was Jack.

"Jesus," was what she said under her breath. Maybe she hadn't even seen him from behind before.

51

It was the only sound she heard as she stopped in her place.

The whole world went pin-drop silent. The sound of cars in the distance quieted, the birds were no longer singing and up the street a dog stopped barking as Jack looked her way. Mary's face flushed because she was sure that the image he had of her in his mind was the image she had in hers—lying on her back, staring at herself in the mirror above his bed, her knees bouncing near her ears, grunting appreciatively and sucking away on her thumb as he fucked her thoroughly and well.

She had cut her nails down to nubs as soon as she'd gotten home that night.

"Hey," he said, real casual. Like that was an appropriate greeting for someone he'd never bothered to call. "What are you doing here?"

"Jack, hi," she said. Equally lame. And then with a little composure, "I'm slumming." The best course was to ignore the situation. Pretend he wasn't there. So she started walking again, thinking she would go right past him and into the house and try not to act too familiar at all. It wasn't like she had ever heard from him again. Or had expected to. Once she was going again, moving up the walkway, she felt more confident. "Just to clarify, you're not some obsessive, are you? Following me around? Hoping to infiltrate my life?"

"I was just going to ask you the same." He paused before saying, in a far less casual tone, "I actually came here hoping to see you. Six weeks is a long time."

"You're lying," she said, and this came out perhaps a little too flirtatious. She was looking a little too laid back for that today. But she turned around part way to see if he were lying.

"You're right," he said. He dragged on his cigarette. He wasn't even looking at her. "Mike invited me over here for Easter dinner."

This took a minute to sink in. "Michael. Of course." She didn't bother saying anything else. She let herself into the house as if all were good and normal.

The slamming of the front door heralded Mary's arrival. Laura, sitting in the kitchen, could hear Mary's voice through the wall, saying in a low voice, "Oh no, oh no, I need a minute. I need a minute," even as Michael, who was playing Nintendo with Max and Lorraine in the den, yelled out "Mary's home! Let's go see if she wants to count your boogers!"

This was followed by the children's high-pitched screams, shrieks, and squeals. And the noise of their little feet stamp-stamping in the hallway.

There was more stomping and giggling, until Laura heard Michael's muffled voice saying, "Hey, where'd she go? Do you think she's hiding?"

Max said, "Maybe she's counting the pimples on her butt," which set them all to giggling.

Then there was the sound of pattering, squeaking feet again, this time into the hall and up the stairs.

The door into the dining room opened behind her. Mary came in on tiptoes, closed the door behind her and leaned against it. "Aren't the parents always somewhere like this? Safe where they can't reach you? With food for comfort and company?"

"This tends to be a somewhat child-free zone until dinner is served," Laura said. "Sit down, you're safe. Neither Max nor Lorraine have mastered doorknobs yet." She thought Mary looked wonderful. Her face had just the right amount of color. And her hair was shorter, showing off those cheekbones, Melinda's cheekbones.

Mary slid into the booth. She had something on her mind, Laura could see, but she wasn't going to let it get in the way of family time. She just shook it off, and then she smiled. "I won't be safe here for long."

Somewhere impossibly far off on the second floor, Michael said, "Hey. Did you guys hear that?"

"You look wonderful, Mary."

"You don't know how much I've missed hearing someone say that."

"The club is monopolizing all of my time lately . . ."

The front door opened and closed again. Mary's eyes narrowed momentarily.

". . . Is something wrong?"

"I don't want to talk about it here. Life just isn't normal anymore."

"Welcome to life. It just gets more complicated and then you're old."

"Flatter me again?"

53

"Did you lose weight?"

"Oh thank you thank you thank you." Mary hugged Laura, dropped a kiss on her cheek, and raced for the door at the other side of the kitchen. "Where's Mom?"

"She said she wanted some flowers for the dinner table."

"Is she . . . you know . . . being okay?"

The door Mary entered through opened again. By the time Laura looked there and back Mary had vanished and Max and Lorraine were stampeding past, with Michael not two steps behind them.

"Hi, Mom."

"Mommy."

Michael had a tennis racket and the kids were holding ping-pong paddles. Max stumbled halfway through the kitchen, falling and banging his head on a chair. It looked painful, and he did let out a gasp, as did Michael and Laura. It looked like it must have hurt. It looked like he might cry. But then, realizing there were better things to do, he righted himself, rubbed his head once or twice, and raced after his sister to the next door.

"Takes a licking," Michael said as he turned the handle, and they ran through, waving their paddles in the air.

"It's in his blood."

He closed the door behind him and the kitchen was once again quiet.

The same door opened again.

"Isn't this wonderful?" Melinda practically bounded in with an armful of flowers. She set them on the kitchen table. With a quick appraisal of the room, she saw that Laura had been working on the salad. "You don't have to worry about that. Why don't you find some vases for the flowers, instead?" There was a worried look on her face for a moment. It quickly disappeared behind her bright smile and she hurried back out of the kitchen.

By the time Laura had located the vases and climbed down from the counter, Melinda had been out and in with two more loads of flowers. "That should do, don't you think?"

"There are enough flowers for a wedding," Laura said.

Melinda looked at Laura. Again there was that smile. She nodded toward the pile of flowers, as if to tell Laura to begin arranging the flowers. Then she walked over to the cutting boards, and continued the work Laura had started there. "How is everything?"

"Fine," Laura said. "I've accepted exhaustion as a constant in my life."

"You've been having trouble sleeping, too?"

"No. Just working too hard at the club. It's great having something to invest myself in this way . . . I love that. But it's been grueling. And, you know, the kids are bearing the brunt of it, in terms of my time, but they're doing okay. They've always been my best barometer."

"Of course," Melinda said. She dropped the knife. And then she picked up slices of carrots, tomatoes and eggs and dropped them into the salad bowl. She covered the bowl, opened the fridge and looked for a place to put it. There was some doubt as to the outcome. The fridge was already packed full. Casserole dishes filled with mashed potatoes and vegetables, jello molds in different colors, and all kinds of appetizers. In quick order, Melinda pulled five or six things out, and then put everything right back in, salad bowl included.

"You're just bouncing all over, I see," Laura said.

This brought Melinda to the chair beside Laura. "I can't find my tranquilizers anywhere," she said in a low voice with a hint of knowing amusement in her eyes. "They've been trying to work out my dosages. The Pelosic for my cholesterol is an upper, which nearly anyone would say is the last thing a person like me needs in my bloodstream, so they've got me on Lacator to sort of bring me down. Really balmy, sort of dreamy sensation comes with that if I overdo it. So I take red red blue in the morning and red blue at night and vary the afternoon red and blue depending on the day of the week. It's been a trick figuring out the combination of dosages that keeps me someplace level. And now I can't find the Lacator." She grabbed a handful of flowers, pushed them roughly into a vase. And once she had pushed and pulled them a bit, they looked good, like a real arrangement; Laura had been carefully trying to stick them in one by one and they looked droopy. "I was having terrible nightmares for a while. I was anxious just at the thought of going to bed."

"Nightmares about what?"

"Oh, horrible things. Little girls dying of starvation and disease, children being beaten and drowned, just horrible images. Things it's better not to think about if I want to be able to function in the world."

Laura wanted to ask her sister-in-law where she thought such anxieties were coming from, but restrained herself. There was a barrier there, and had always been, because Laura was very close to Eli. Laura knew that Eli could be impatient with the interests his wife sometimes pursued, and Laura had proven historically to be not always sure what slip of the tongue might set her brother off.

"I think someone must have hidden the bottle from me," Melinda said. She passed her vase to Laura, took the one Laura was working on and started primping it into shape. "Don't they smell wonderful? Municipal Services came and trimmed up the street. They were just lying up and down the block in heaps, and they still looked so unbelievably fresh, so I picked the best of them before the clean-up crew came along. And if I don't put them out now they'll . . . well, they're dead anyway." Before Laura could respond Melinda stood up, opened the cupboard, and pulled out two boxes of crackers. These she arranged in a circle on a plate beside a slab of cheese, and carried it out to the patio.

"Someone's trying to kill us with food," she heard Grand Auntie Dee yell out.

Grand Uncle Obe was laughing outside and she could hear Eli doing the same. If Joel were here, he would have been out with them, falling asleep in the deck chair next to Eli's. Joel had always gotten along well with her brother and his family, especially Melinda, which had always made the get-togethers easy for everyone.

Melinda came back into the kitchen with an empty platter. "Well, the deviled eggs are gone. Licked the plate clean," she said. And she showed Laura the plate. "They did." She set the plate in the sink, ran water in it, grabbed a towel, dried it off, replaced it in the cupboard and seated herself at the table again. As if she had been following Laura's train of thought, she asked, "Where is Joel this year?"

Laura set her first arrangement aside. It could go in the corner, behind Melinda's. She started filling another. "Arizona. With the wife and the new baby."

"Is he planning on spending any time with Max and Lorraine?"

"You know, it's the first summer none of the three has mentioned it? Not a phone call from him, not a query from them. I haven't quite been sure how far to push it. Is it my responsibility? I'm going to let the next few months slide and then see how June starts to shape up. Maybe they're all ready to move on."

"You mean not see each other? They should see their father."

"I mean not pretend it's the most pressing concern that's arisen since the divorce."

Laura asked her how many vases she thought they needed for one dinner table. They had already filled five, more than would fit beside the feast awaiting them.

Melinda ignored her. She pulled out a still-closed white rose from the bunch in front of her and started picking the thorns from the stem. "We used to do this when we were teenagers," she said. "And after the thorns were gone we would drip wax on it, or better yet, we'd dip the petals in cups of melted wax. I always burned my fingertips doing that. Sometimes I would set my nails on fire. We did that at our sweet sixteens, so that we could keep them forever." Melinda nodded at the thought, still smiling. "That's a nice memory now, isn't it? Nothing to be afraid of there."

It seemed to Melinda that she was being mocked. They were trying to act like nothing was wrong with anyone but her. They were trying to act like it was all in her imagination. Just to shut her up.

She hadn't even realized Mary was in the house until all the guests began taking their seats around the table and her daughter sauntered into the room. That was a statement about the lengths she'd been going to to avoid her own mother.

Mary caught her attention, and immediately pulled Melinda aside. She said in a very low voice, "Just keep it down, and keep it to yourself. I can see it in your eyes. No one wants to hear crazy tonight."

57

Would this have upset her more or less were she not on medication? She wasn't sure she remembered. Perhaps, though, it wasn't out of the range of her daughter's behavior to speak with her so. She was more intrigued by the insight that Mary seemed to be experiencing some inner turmoil of her own. There was a greenness to her daughter's presence, a turgid green. Her energy was agitated, frustrated, almost trapped. Although, and Melinda couldn't understand it, there was also an occasional blue sparkle, a flash, that seemed to brighten every so often. It had the effect of softening the overall sense of turmoil. It was a calming thing. What could that be?

Perhaps it was the medication which had her thinking this way. Earlier she had been imagining there were red sparks of light shooting from her sister-in-law's forehead and racing frenetically about her. She'd asked Laura about Joel, because that had seemed polite. What Melinda had wanted to ask was if there was someone new Laura was seeing.

During the meal, they all did their best to look away from Melinda, as if there were something there at her end of the table they did not wish to see. Were they trying to pretend she was not there? Or that she could not see right through them? Still it gave her the opportunity to observe them.

The roast beef is great, they said.

"I hope I cooked it enough," Melinda said.

It was a group production. The entire cast looked at her at once, smiled, and nodded in unison. There was no song; she would have preferred a song.

"It's divine," Laura said.

"Divine," Melinda repeated. And she nodded a few times for punctuation.

They were all but transparent. What she realized sitting there near silently was the power of silence. Talking must interfere with listening; she hadn't realized the clarity that came when she listened with all of her senses.

Michael, for example, well, her mind was eased by his presence today. She'd been overjoyed when he returned home. She'd admitted to Eli that if she'd been able to will it to happen, she would have. And to have him around the house, doing nothing but reconnecting with himself, that had been a throwback to his high school years, and a great pleasure for her.

In the months since he'd been working at the club, much of that had changed. He kept odd hours, moved into Mary's old room and used the outside door to come and go rather than the front door. Lately, he'd been eating his meals standing up in front of the television.

She blamed herself for driving him into isolation.

Michael, seeing she was watching him, reached over, and patted her on the hand while he chatted with Mary and his guest. "Dinner's great, Mom."

Otherwise, he was doing well. And still a good son.

Mary, on the other hand, looked like a cinder girl. She was dressed in rags. Big, bulky clothes that made her look fat and sloppy. And it was all because she was lazy. She could have been modeling by now. With a little effort, she could still get a career going, certainly live more comfortably instead of getting by cutting people's hair. If she would just get her act together. Stop worrying about boys so much. Those kind of things tended to take care of themselves better when they weren't the sole focus of a girl's attention.

Melinda had hoped to get Michael to encourage Mary to better herself. Michael had refused. No one listened to her.

In response to a question from Eli that Melinda hadn't quite heard, Mary said, clearly for the benefit of Max and Lorraine, "Oh, I told the munchkins what happens to kids who wander off into the hills."

Max said, "Coyotes." He wasn't following all the way.

But wide-eyed Lorraine was. She said, "Hill People."

Michael, in a raspy voice, repeated, "Hill People."

"You two are terrible," Laura said.

"No, Mommy. It's true. People live in the hills."

"That's not true. Michael, Mary, you two are terrible. Tell them the truth."

Mary said, "The truth is, don't get lost in the hills at night."

Michael said, "Or the Hill People will get you, duh." He snickered. The kids both laughed.

"Michael." Laura was exasperated.

"It's good advice. Ask anyone."

59

"You come pick them up tonight when they wake up crying." Laura turned to Eli. "Turned on the television the other night and there was Jaegar, going crazy."

"He got drunk, came by the house to see Andrina. She had a 'houseguest' apparently, and Jaeger walked in on them, turned around, grabbed a gun from his stash, and opened fire on her paramour's car, which was parked in the driveway."

Melinda said, "Oh, it was terrible. People up and down the street were finding bullets in their walls and hiding behind garbage cans to avoid getting hit. That's right." Just another sure sign of the impending Armageddon, Melinda thought. For some of us, it will mean the beginning of a new world. A better world. You've got to believe all this happens for reason.

Laura asked, "And what happened to Jaeger??"

"He's in jail." Eli shrugged. Eli was always shrugging. "Bill's due in town soon; I have a feeling he'll do what, if anything, can be done." The three of them were college friends: Eli, currently a lobbyist, Jaegar, a former civil rights activist, and Bill Clayton, state congressional representative. Eli was part of the Old Boys' Network, whether he admitted it or not. And his faith in it was firm.

"Bill's coming. Well, that's interesting." Laura's eyes glittered. "It's true then, isn't it? They're going to close Marble Canyon Road?"

"It looks like it."

"Any remarks on his candidacy?"

"No comment."

She smiled. Melinda watched as red sparks shot into the air over her head. "That road brings a lot of traffic past the club. It would be nice if they could get the job done quickly. That's all I ask."

"As long as they do it right."

Melinda didn't know what had gotten into Laura.

"You look absolutely radiant, Laura," Eli was in fact saying. "Doesn't she, Melinda?"

"Radiant," Melinda said. She winked at Laura.

"Thank you," Laura sparkled back. "Things have really been clicking at the club. You should come down some time, Melinda. Before the big re-opening. I'll treat you to lunch."

"Anyway," Eli said, "it looks like Jaegar's gone and screwed himself. Some guy spent the night with his ex-wife; for whatever reason, of all the indignities and injustices Jaegar has endured over the last thirty years, this one thing is what puts him over the edge."

Obe asked, "Is it that bad?"

"Oh, it's worse than that." Eli shrugged again. "Once upon a time, he was a rebel hero to a lot of people. He challenged powerful people, and then he dared them to find a way to stop him. And they couldn't, because in his heart and in his conduct, he was an upright man. Even in the worst of situations, he always had control of himself." Eli threw his hands up in mock exasperation. "And then he screws up like this. He goes and digs potholes in his front yard, wielding an unregistered firearm. So now," he said "who knows?"

"And there's nothing you can do?" Obe asked.

Melinda leaned over toward Mary. "Tonight," she told her in her lowest voice, "you can clean the ashes out of the fireplace. You're certainly dressed for the job."

"There's obviously one remaining thing to be done," Mary said. She grabbed Melinda's glass of wine right out from under her, and held it up in the air in front of Melinda's face. "You don't need this," she said curtly out of the side of her mouth.

Melinda reached for the wine glass in front of Mary's plate, but stopped herself when she saw it had already been drained.

"To the family dinner," Mary said.

Michael and Eli both said, "Here, here," and clinked their glasses.

Mary didn't thank her when she polished off Melinda's wine. Instead, she stared across the table at Jack, shamelessly flirting with him.

Melinda watched Mary a moment. Was this the man who had her tied in knots? She looked back and forth from Mary to Jack and then to Laura. When Melinda turned to look at Jack again, she found that Jack was staring back at her. What was their connection? And what was his connection to Michael? Was he the reason Michael's behavior had been so odd lately? And then again, as she had earlier with Mary, Melinda looked at her husband's sister, and felt as if she

61

were seeing her clearly. For once. She was in love. But surely it wasn't with this young man, who Melinda was not sure she liked at all. He might very well be the devil, with all the fireworks going off around here. It took a moment before Melinda realized she was still staring at him, and that the table had grown silent. It was another moment before she realized that Jack had continued to hold her stare the entire time; which, realizing this, she found very unsettling. It very nearly made her angry.

Before that happened, Melinda stood, and excused herself. She wouldn't sit long for being mocked in her own home.

Leave it to mom, Mary thought.

Apparently unable to sit so long in one place without acting up, midway through the meal she'd stood up, lifted her plate as if she were going to carry it into the kitchen, and, glaring at Jack—of all the people in the room she had to choose from—set the plate back down on the table hard enough to make her silverware jump. "Excuse me," she said.

And with that, she left the room.

Everyone looked up at her, and waited a moment.

The sense of relief in the room once it was clear she was gone was almost palpable. Mary felt it, too, though when she saw how much everyone else in the room brightened up she immediately felt a twinge of guilt, and began to resent the rest of them for their lack of insight into all her mother was putting herself through. Not that any of them had any idea. Not even know-it-all Michael.

Her father—who had put up with more than any of them, Mary included—thought it was a combination of empty nest syndrome and the onset of menopause, and therefore somehow beyond the domain of his influence, something to be dealt with by doctors and pharmacists and women support groups and a lot of extra time at the office.

But it wasn't going to go away just like that.

Her mother had, in fact, managed to control herself pretty well during the meal, considering her ruffled attitude at the start. Mary had waited and waited for her mom to break out with one mad rant or another. But beyond the potshots at her appearance, the time had never come.

It certainly wasn't fair for any of the rest of them to judge her.

That was Mary's job.

At the least, Mary thought, her mother was still trying to get better.

An hour later, after her second or third drink, Mary sat in the leather recliner at the edge of the Scrabble board thumbing through a magazine and reconsidering her plan of action with Jack. He was a tasty treat for the eyes. And he was sort of dry and understated, and funny. And he was naughty. Maybe there wouldn't be any harm in the two of the them having a little more fun.

"So," Mary asked, "what happened to the foliage up and down the block?"

Instantly, Michael was exasperated. But he kept his voice low. "You can guess what happened. Guess *who* happened. Guess who sent an angry chain of letters to Municipal Services because a couple of trees had grown, in her best estimate, too close to the telephone and power lines? Guess who threatened to hold them liable if any of the overgrown greenery up and down the block caused a smidgen of property damage on her watch?"

"Oh, not really," Mary said, looking around for another magazine.

"Oh, it'll grow back," Melinda said as she passed by on her way into the laundry room with a stack of dishes.

Laura and her father were in the den, talking with the television on. They were going to talk and talk like they always did, so the evening was fast going nowhere.

Mary wondered: Why isn't she doing the dishes in the kitchen?

Michael lowered his voice and leaned in. Mary knew Jack was listening, though he was trying to look otherwise occupied with her dad's music collection.

"What happened at that flipping therapy session, Mary? She's been crawling out of her skin for weeks now. You know, Dad's the one who made her go back to their old doctor."

Mary started to answer, but stopped herself when she felt her stomach do a sudden turn.

"Hold that thought," she said as she stood and moved for the bathroom.

She managed to maintain her composure until the bathroom door was locked behind her, but that was as far as she would be able to make it. The distance to the toilet seeming insurmountable, she threw up into the sink, and then didn't stop until her stomach was emptied.

"My mom has been real quirky lately," Michael said quietly later, as he closed the front door. They'd been waiting, but Mary never made it back from the bathroom.

"Lately?"

"Yeah, okay. Point." Michael saw something moving up the street. It was dark, and it took him a minute to see it was Mr. Green walking up the block. "And there's the perfect example. See that guy there? We call him Mr. Green."

"Because he has a green jacket?"

"Exactly. He's a well-known walker in Cheronkin. All of my life that I can remember, I can remember seeing Mr. Green out walking. He doesn't stick to the same route, as far as I know, because I've seen him in just about every part of town at one time or another in my life, just marching along."

And it was almost a march, Michael thought: big, steady, assertive steps, his body leaned just a small bit forward. It was a determined walk, like he had to be somewhere soon, except that it seemed like where he had to be was marching up another street somewhere else. He had dark, reddish-brown hair, cut nearly in a bowl-cut, wore dark-rimmed glasses, and everyone agreed it was most likely a nebbishly short-sleeved white dress shirt under his Members-Only jacket.

"My mom doesn't believe he's a real person. She doesn't think Mr. Green has aged enough for all the years she's seen him walking around, and she's never spoken to a person who knew the slightest details of his life. My mom's always had about two degrees of separation between her and anyone else in town. And the fact that she'd never been able to track him down pretty much convinced her he either wasn't real or else he was some sort of artificial life, i.e., a robot."

"That's what you're calling 'quirky'? Your mom thinks Mr. Green is a robot?"

"Exactly."

Jack didn't say anything else on the subject, which Michael appreciated.

Just beyond the range of the streetlight, Jack pulled a couple pills out of his jacket pocket, and popped them into his mouth. He saw Michael watching. "They're prescription. They'll help me sleep later," he explained.

"There's something going around, I guess. My mom's on stuff like that night and day. I guess the side effects don't seem as bad to me until someone outside the family sees her. We're all used to her."

"Has she been like that a long time?"

"It's gotten worse."

"Everyone's a freak show one way or another."

"Yeah, right. I'm not. You're not."

Jack didn't say anything.

"I mean, like, compared to other guys." Michael tried to backpedal. "Well . . . yeah. Fine. Freak shows, all of us."

"Thanks for having me over. Nice old family time. Feels like I know everybody already."

"Pretty bad, yeah?"

"Family is family."

"You didn't get to meet my dogs. They're the most normal ones here. Toro and Riles. They're Doberman Pincers. They're really my parents' dogs, but they like me better. Especially since they've become backyard dogs; they were exiled when my niece Lorraine was born. I let them sleep in my room at night."

Jack was not big on dog stories. He let Michael finish, though. "You're headed to the club again?"

"Yeah. Not to work. I want to check out this guy who's playing tonight. I've heard good things."

"Will you take me by there? I'll find myself a ride home later. You don't have to gopher me around everywhere."

"It's no problem. I wouldn't be doing much otherwise. If I walk in with you, it's almost like I have a social life." As they were getting into his car, Michael asked. "Didn't you get a rental? Where's your rental?"

"I'm going to need to get another one. The first one's all fucked up already."

"What's wrong with it?"

"Some guy filled it full of lead the other day."

Michael snorted. "You mean the wrong gasoline? I didn't know they even sold leaded anymore."

"Not gasoline. Bullets. It hasn't driven for shit since then."

Long after Michael and Jack's voices had faded, and her mother's repeated crossings through the living room to the dining room and back to the laundry had ceased, Mary sat in the guest bathroom, recovering from her bout of vomiting.

Her hands were trembling as she splashed water on her face. She'd never thrown up like that before. She felt fine, she felt okay now, except . . .

When she finally poked her head out, she heard her father and Aunt Laura were comparing their football pool successes. They could talk about nothing for hours, giggling and laughing the whole time like they were little kids still. Everyone else was gone.

Mary sighed, relieved.

She looked down at her stomach.

She'd had a round of eating disorders when she was younger, from self-induced vomiting to overdoing the diet pills to just eating like crap, she'd done the whole thing.

This was not like that, she was sure. This was something else. She could feel it.

Something unexpected. Something for which she was so poorly prepared that she wasn't yet going to let the reality of it truly sink in.

She rubbed her hand slowly up and down her stomach, thinking, *Oh my god, no.*

Melinda did not come out from the back of the house until everyone else had gone to bed. Eli wouldn't notice because she'd been sleeping in the guestroom since he returned from his last trip to D.C. She'd only be keeping him awake with her fretting, and he'd gotten so angry on his last visit home when she'd woken him to see if he could hear as clearly as she the sound of the scraping of the leaves as the vines spread through the pipes. He hadn't been able to hear anything, of course.

She'd been more restless than usual.

Because of the medication, she told herself.

Now that we're all home, she thought, we can take a proper family portrait. That's something to look into.

The embers were still popping in the fireplace, although the flames had mostly gone out.

At the least they could have blown the candles out.

If the house were on fire, she'd be the one who'd go first. She was here more than anyone else. Had anyone else thought of that? She thought maybe they had. Maybe they'd even taken a silent vote on it after she'd left the table.

Melinda needed to be alone right now. She needed to get control of herself. She couldn't seem to do that around the rest of them. She had to be a mother and a wife when they were around. And yet, for the lack of control, she always wanted to surround herself with them, to be occupied by them. But it was too hard trying to accomplish anything for herself while she was pretending everything was all right, when it was not. She needed to get her head together. She wanted that so badly.

She'd heard that Dr. Wen's condition continued to improve from what apparently had been a heart attack in combination with a mild stroke. He was looking at some time in rehabilitative therapy, and his doctors were impressed with his improvements.

Compared to that, the issues Melinda found herself confronting day to day as a result of the hypnotherapy session seemed minor in comparison. Bits and pieces of what she had experienced during the session continued to dribble out, and there were times, when she was tired, that she could become confused by the sight of something as common as the back of her hand and think that it belonged to someone else—someone she'd been in another life—or that she was seeing it through someone else's eyes.

She feared the memories of those previous lives might be bleeding into her mind.

She had been to the airport earlier in the week to pick up Eli, back from supposedly the last such business trip of the calendar year. He'd been gone for nearly two weeks. Though she had been looking forward to his return, she had also dreaded resuming the mask of normalcy—or the best she had managed to develop over the years of their marriage—that his presence demanded. Eli had very little patience with these things these days.

There had been hardly any other people at the airport, normal for the winter holidays. Summer was their only truly busy season. In the winter, the population might dwindle to as small as 10,000 in all of Cheronkin; in the summer it might be 7 or 8 times that amount. The no-growth movement she led so passionately fifteen years before had placed on the southern portion of Cheronkin County the burden and the blessing of one of the strictest moratoriums on new housing in the state.

Melinda was early, as usual. There were three men in blue airport maintenance jumpsuits tidying up the area when she arrived, and there were three other women on the far side of the lobby. They were behind a white column; she could not see them, but she could hear their voices. Two of them were apparently at the airport to pick up the third, who had just arrived through the gate. Melinda watched out the window as the small Cessna the arriving woman must have just flown in on, pulled out onto the runway. They were talking much too loudly for Melinda not to have overheard their exchanged greetings.

"It's so good to see you again."

"Welcome to the land of cow flatulence, the realm of enchantment . . ."

"Those shitty, tiny airplanes! Little winged coffins."

"Look at your hair!"

"And what kind of rat hole have you brought me to now?"

"It won't be but for six months . . . there's already so much going on. You can feel it in the air!"

"Six fucking months? Are you kidding?"

"As it is, it is beyond my control. It takes its own time."

"It is so good to see you again. Oh, Cam . . ."

She did not hear the rest of what was said after hearing that name. Her heart trembled. She simply had to move a few steps forward, and turn to look at the three of them across the room.

Facing her direction was a striking young black woman, really a beautiful girl, with long dark hair. To her right stood a statuesque, older woman, who she could see only in profile. But it was the one with her back turned to Melinda that made her heart jump; the very sight of her mane of shoulder-length bright orange hair was enough to make her feel light-headed.

This was the one who had been haunting Melinda since her hypnotherapy session.

The three of them were all smiling, pretending innocence.

They all had their hands around each other's backs.

In her mind's eye, Melinda could see the blade slicing into Dr. Wen's neck. And although she had explained some of it to Mary during her last hair appointment, she hadn't stated what she believed—that what had befallen Dr. Wen in her hypnotized state had caused his heart attack in the real world. When Mary described the way the doctor had grabbed his neck, it had affirmed Melinda's belief.

All three women hugged each other. And Melinda immediately became self-conscious. She had been openly staring at them, practically inviting their attention, which was the last thing she was prepared to deal with at this point.

So she had walked toward a seat where she wouldn't be able to see them, or they, her.

If it had, indeed, been the girl in her dreams. Melinda hadn't seen this girl's face, after all.

When she had seated herself, she heard the three of them laughing.

It was, surprisingly, a wonderful sound; friendly laughter early on a morning echoing across the lobby, and it had sounded exactly the way Melinda wished she felt.

But the sound of the laughter quickly changed. It became more shrill, a higher-pitched sound, as if the acoustics of the lobby were warping the noise. Melinda suddenly didn't like the sound of it; it made her wince in nearly the same way nails on a chalkboard did. It was cold and wicked and brimming with treacle, raising the hair on the back of her neck.

And then, as it dissolved, it sounded more like the squeals of little girls at play. She rose from her seat, and looked over her shoulder, toward the three, just to see just what exactly was going on. Although she could still hear the echo of their voices, no one else was there in the lobby with her.

She was all alone.

IN THE NEWS
West Coast Regional Reporter, **May 1**

The State Senate yesterday approved a 24-million-dollar road improvement package for Cheronkin County as part of a settlement with the families of 14 residents killed in accidents in the last six months on a stretch of road maintained by the state as an access route to the former Point Soledad Naval Station. The legislation, sponsored by Senator William Clayton (R-Thousand Oaks), a one-time Cheronkin resident, came in response to a 237-million-dollar class action suit filed late last month against the state. Clayton, one of a field of Republicans being considered for the gubernatorial, promised to travel to Cheronkin to oversee the closure of Marble Canyon Road personally.

5

Cheronkin County
Spring

Damn it. Hiccups, again.

Mary wasn't prepared for any great changes. She wasn't ready for her friends to marry or move away or find their life's calling; she didn't want Marcus scouting for new locations for the salon and she didn't want to think about the possibility of her parents' marriage collapsing. Not that there was any evidence of the last one happening, but there was no denying it wouldn't be a surprise, with her mother losing her mind and all. Her father simply didn't know how bad it was, both because he had been away so frequently and for so long each time since the start of the war and because Melinda masked it well when he was home.

Mary couldn't handle Melinda right now.

And if they did divorce, Melinda would never leave her alone.

So. Nothing else changes.

This was more than a resolution. This was a way of life, preserving what is, and she would simply refuse to budge in the face of potentially life-altering decisions, turning down job offers, travel opportunities, and marriage proposals alike. For now.

She liked her life. She liked her work, money wasn't a great concern, she dated good men who liked her more than she liked them, which was the way to do it, and she had a few good friends she knew she could count on. She was happy.

She'd found a moment in her life when she was content and at the same time everything wasn't out-of-control topsy-turvy. She had tomatoes and herbs and spices and little chili peppers growing in her kitchen like milkweed, and up until three weeks ago, that had been the craziest, most abnormal thing in her life.

She took the growth of those plants as a sign she was doing something right.

She was usually very adept at overcoming challenges, a trait that had been nurtured from birth by the queen of getting things done her way. For instance, her mother hadn't approved of Mary going to cosmetology school rather

71

than college; Mary credited her mother's stiff opposition for giving her the nerve to go through with it.

Mary had gone through a whole life inventory thing after breaking up with her last serious boyfriend, Shaun. Shaun, really fun, just a great person to be around, was never going to be able to shoulder a wife, a mortgage, and kids. She'd have to handle all the heavy responsibilities. This was not the way she wanted it. She needed someone who would be able to shoulder at least his part of the load.

Yet, she did feel like she was a long way from where she should be. She should be married, she should be planning for a family, shopping for a house, and after four years with a guy where that was the supposed promise at the end of the rainbow, she wasn't ready to start over again. She didn't want to end up chasing around desperately instead of enjoying life.

As far as the kid thing, she'd felt there was still time if the urge struck, although she'd never really felt that particular calling beyond the competitive pressure placed by its prominent place on most girls' to-do list. That was not to say she wouldn't change her mind for the right person; she knew lots of women who overnight went from faint interest to obsessed, be it for a man, a baby, or an inheritance. Regardless, her options were open, assuming her body was capable of breeding. It was left for fate to decide what the salon chemicals and the birth control and the diet pills and the bouts of bingeing and purging might have done to the system.

Mary was done chasing after things. She spent her free time with different men she liked for different reasons, all of whom treated her well. She was in her thirties, and finally feeling like her own woman. She had Carina, who had a mindset similar to her own. Of course, Carina's fantasy dream ending would be to marry off really well and just disappear out of town for a decade before returning a dramatically changed and wealthy woman. Mary told her she was pulling for her, and it wasn't a lie—it was easy to tell Carina it could happen. But really, Carina was too much fun for her to lose.

What would she do without Carina?

She felt herself choking up with unwanted emotion.

Damn. It.

At first, waking up didn't feel like a dream. Waking up felt like it was real. Waking up because she'd just heard the sound of someone walking in the leaves outside. Lots of someones. Making so much noise that she had to know they were there.

Then she woke up again. She remembered it was spring and that the ranch house was surrounded by pine trees and concrete—there weren't any leaves. And that's where she was, in one of the upstairs bedrooms in the guest house at the ranch house compound; she was at Uncle Bill's place, in the hills west and north of town, up a seven-mile long driveway that hadn't yet been repaved after the winter storms, and the property was surrounded by walls. Someone would have to be twelve feet tall to be peeking in at her.

She was going to look out the window to confirm that no one was really there, but it was dark still and she thought: What if she didn't like what she saw looking back in at her?

Then she thought that she was wrong in thinking that she had woken up at all. Maybe this was all a dream, and she was still asleep? That feeling didn't fade away.

She thought, maybe the weeks before had never happened.

Maybe it was all a dream.

That moment in the guest bathroom at Mom and Dad's when she just knew she was pregnant. The blur of three weeks of denial during which she spent too much time around styling chemicals and second-hand smoke for anyone who might be pregnant.

Truly, at that moment, those last three weeks seemed as if they could have been a wild and deceiving dream that had simply swept her along in its long and tiring current. Where did it start? Getting out of her car at her parents' house and seeing Jack there? For a moment, it was possible that none of it had been real, and it was still winter and none of it had been real. Or what passed as winter here.

It confused her now, the pregnancy thing. It might confuse her forever.

What she noticed first after deciding not to look out the window of the ranch house was the scent that clung to her. A thick, wet smell. She was wearing her flannel pajama top, the bottom buttons of which she'd left unbuttoned to make room for her growing belly, and she sat up, aching a bit in that belly, and then that smell overcame her and she thought: What is that wonderful, wonderful, new smell? She moved her legs a little, to test how

73

much of her was sore, and realized she wasn't wearing any sort of bottoms—underwear or pajamas. There were some wet spots on the bed. She didn't ask herself why. It was all very dreamy. It didn't matter. Apparently, the hidden side of pregnancy was all about crap like that, mysterious aches and secretions and spotting. She just sat there, feeling really worked and out of it, drinking in the smell of pine and that doughy mystery scent.

And that lasted for what seemed like hours, until she woke up yet again and was somehow in another room, on the second floor of the house; it was the living room and she was on the couch facing the stairs that she would have had to sleepwalk down to get there from the bedroom. What woke her up again had to do with there being people outside. She dreamed there were eyes and noses and mouths pressed up against the ranch house windows as people outside in the dark looked in at her. Like a zombie movie. They could see her, but not vice versa.

You can't see into the dark from the light.

She was like a blind lady in a zombie movie.

Again, there was no one looking in when she woke up. Being at ground level, she looked out the window this time, and she realized how different the yard around the house looked than she remembered it. In her dream, it was like Hansel and Gretel's house, small and isolated by the woods around it, pine trees tapping on the windows; in reality, however dense the growth outside the walls that surrounded the ranch house, inside the only trees that dotted the manicured lawn were fruit trees—oranges, avocados, apples, and lemons by the bushel.

But was what she was seeing real? Was she awake?

Turning back to the room, she sniffed the air hopefully, but instead of the cookie smell, she smelled something just awful, like poop and vomit, and she wondered if she had just dreamed that sweet smell before. And when she turned on the light on the bookshelf, well, it was horrific. There was a dark, wet, bloody pile on the carpet at the top of the stairs, which she could see from the couch. First, she wondered if it was crap, then she wondered if it were hers, then she thought it smelled too bad and looked too fleshy to be crap, like road kill without fur.

It was just so horrifying and overwhelming. She sat there frozen. She wondered what it could be and she wondered how it got there and where it came from but she wasn't going to go any closer to find out.

And then she noticed the blood on the stairwell carpeting. There was a bloodied sheet at the top of the stairs. And that was where most of the blood was, at the top of the stairs, though there were spots all the way down. She thought about going upstairs for a moment, but the idea kind of scared her.

She looked down at herself. There was blood all over her. Was it her blood that was all over everything? Where was it coming from? She felt around her stomach, where the blood was worst, and then checked herself out all over. But there was nothing. Her abdomen was a little sore? Was she bleeding? Her pajama blouse was unbuttoned from the top, and her nipple was engorged.. They were both like that—these alien little nubs that didn't belong to her.

Maybe it was the baby, a stray thought came.

Her heartbeat sped up.

The baby? Was the baby even real?

Maybe she had miscarried.

She didn't even want to think about what that might mean the clump at the top of the stairs was . . .

She gasped. Among the spatters and spots, there were also what looked like small footprints mixed in the stains on her pajama bottoms. There were similar marks in this room, on the wood floor. They were harder to see against the wood. She didn't notice them until she stood up from the couch, and just that sudden movement made her woozy. She had to steady herself for a moment before she regained her equilibrium.

Did people faint in their dreams?

The trail led to the downstairs staircase.

Being three weeks late in conjunction with some nausea wasn't enough to put Mary on edge about being pregnant. She didn't believe it could be true because she was very careful. And she'd never been regular enough to keep a calendar of the event. There had been unexplained times when it just hadn't shown up, sometimes for months, and there had been other pregnancy fears that had never panned out.

The fact that she hadn't thrown up again after the bout at her mother's supported this reasoning, or so she told herself when she was trying to deny what she also knew to be true. It could just have been a combination of nerves and too much rich food.

She made a point of avoiding alcohol, cigarettes— either her own or other people's—and had not had Regina, the salon assistant, apply any color that exposed her to too many fumes. The whole concept of being pregnant was sort of beyond her. Where did a person start? She couldn't see or imagine how that would play out. How would she handle it if she were pregnant?

She spent some time considering who the father of such a pregnancy might be: There were two possible men, she believed. Depending on her timeline, and assuming it was still the first month. Six weeks, maybe? She'd had her rebound thing with Shaun, and then there was Jack. Things never went that far with Dr. Todd, thank goodness. So it was Shaun or Jack. An ex or a one-night stand who was also her brother's new friend.

What set Mary into a true panic was the bump on her belly staring up at her when she was in the shower looking down after yoga class.

She screamed. It was almost a pouch.

She would have cancelled her appointments right then and there, except that it was a long-time client's wedding she was working the next day and that wasn't the sort of thing she did professionally, backing out at the last minute. She called around to find someone to cover, but everyone was already booked. So she dressed to conceal, and told herself she could settle it all after the wedding. She could make an appointment, and it could be settled. It was still early.

By the afternoon she was taking breaks to throw up as quietly as possible in the church bathroom, and to place calls to her Saturday afternoon appointments to cancel or reschedule. After she finished arranging the flower girls' hair, she called the salon receptionist to do the same with all of her clients for the week. She found a glass ashtray filled with chalky butter mint candies in the choir director's inbox, and used these to combat the taste of bile in her breath, which in very little time left her with a case of heartburn.

By early evening, despite a day of vomiting, the bump had grown. On her way back to her apartment, she called Nigel, the salon manager, to explain that she was taking a few days off for health reasons and that she would send him the rent check for her chair shortly. And then she left a message at her "Uncle" Bill's office that she was planning on going to the ranch house over the weekend, and for him to call her if that interfered with any of his plans.

She sat at the kitchen table in her apartment for an hour. Her back was sore, her feet aching, her stomach rumbling and her refrigerator and cupboards were nearly bare. She had tomatoes and herbs and spices and what she wanted was a burger, fries, and a double chocolate shake.

Oh, my god. I am so not ready for this.

"You're much further along than I expected from our conversation," Dr Rhandi told her the following morning. Her regular doctor was on safari. Dr. Rhandi was the attending.

When Mary didn't know how to respond—not the typical reaction but among the range of responses he was prepared to deal with—the doctor softened his demeanor and assured her by promising that the ultrasound would tell them how far along she really was—all she had to do was schedule an appointment with the receptionist.

"When does the ultrasound typically happen?"

"Usually about fourteen weeks. You might be there already. We'll have to see."

"Could I actually be that pregnant? I'm so irregular," she said lamely, overwhelmed. "I thought I was much less pregnant than this. I mean, I haven't even been living as if I were pregnant. I just had no idea. Shit."

"Would you like to listen to the heartbeat?"

"It has a heartbeat already?"

"Of course. There are home monitors that stick right to your belly. Ask the nurse up front. You can listen whenever you want to."

All of this, she needed a minute to absorb. "You know what? Let's wait on that. I'm still catching up to this."

Two hours later, her car winding up the last stretch of road at the northwestern edge of Cheronkin, she felt even further away from dealing with this as reality. Two months, three months, who knew? Not that it added significantly to the pool of potential fathers, but it did make her wonder where she'd been while all this was going on—shouldn't her body have done something else to let her know? Hadn't she had a period somewhere along the line? As if the memory would be enough to invalidate the doctor's opinion.

The abortion option seemed less appealing now. In her opinion, the further along she was, the better the reason she'd need for going that route. Fear of parenthood wasn't a good enough reason. She had some financial stability. She'd chosen her career path and as far as she knew, this was what she'd always be doing. She liked her job, and there was some flexibility, for example being able to cancel a week's worth of appointments when you've suddenly discovered you're pregnant.

She had a strong family, though god only knew what her mother would be like as an expectant grandma.

What she needed now was time to plan. Who to tell, when to tell, how to tell, how to figure out what she needed to figure out next. Pregnancy wasn't something she'd put a lot of thought into. She'd never been one of those girls who spent a lot of time picturing herself as a mom. Her visions of motherhood generally had included a nanny or governess who took care of the really trying stuff.

Mary enjoyed the unencumbered life. If things had worked out with Shaun, she was sure she would have enjoyed being married to him. But from the start of her life after the relationship (and after the back slip) she'd enjoyed herself too much to think about going back into a relationship and possibly having less good a time. She'd dated a number of men in the last few years, each of whom had brought great things into her life, and each of whom offered many drawbacks. The more successful they were, the less they were around. The more attractive they were, the more they liked to be seen.

It was a small social scene, even considering this and every adjacent county. There were just a handful of places—restaurants, clubs, bars—that were considered the best, and it was not uncommon to run into someone she'd dated before while on a date. Mary and Carina had adopted a simple rule not to date a man who had more exes running around a given room than either of them did.

Dr. Rhandi had said something in his office earlier in the day about how "this little girl"—meaning the baby in her belly—"can't wait to get out into the world." It was ringing in her head now. What would her name be? It was time to start thinking about these things. There was a sort of clarity of thought Mary could achieve when she was behind the wheel of the car. Driving just peeled it all away.

Shortly, she realized Dr. Rhandi was wrong. It was going to be a boy.

Likely she was going to just go ahead and have it.

The steps were wet in spots. She held her nose and she averted her eyes from the pile at the top.

It was her placenta? Carina once said that her hippie aunt cooked and ate hers after her cousin was born and the thought of that alone meant Mary couldn't look at it or she would throw up.

She was barefoot because she didn't want to look for her shoes. She didn't want to go anywhere she didn't have to. She was freaked out.

She really wanted to stay where she was until she woke up at sunrise. But then, she thought, the dream wouldn't go anywhere if she didn't move. She could have run out the door on the second floor, but how far could she get on foot? It was the middle of the night, she was miles of winding road from town and more than that from the nearest neighbors. Her car keys were on the kitchen counter downstairs. All the house phones were off because she didn't book in advance. And Cheronkin's cell phone dead zone extended out here, too.

It wasn't blood; it smelled like it could be pee. She wondered if maybe an animal or some animals had taken up residence while the house was sitting empty . . . one of several scenarios running through her head.

And what? It grabbed her miscarried mess and dragged it down here?

She went carefully down the steps, leaning down as she passed between floors to try to get a view. The position caused a sharp pain in her lower back. She was sore there. She thought even then she was starting to get an inkling of why she was sore and what had happened, but in a weird sort of way the realization wasn't coming to her fully.

There was a light on in the corner of the room, just out of view from the stairs.

She inched down another step, and another, and peeked carefully out.

The refrigerator door was open. There was a little boy right there, three or four years old—close to Max's size—munching on a sour pickle. There were cheerios all over the floor. They were stale, she would bet. That he would be alone seemed odd to her, so she

79

continued to scan the room for another person who might be lurking about.

From the side, he had the same wavy dark hair as her nephew Max. He had a blanket wrapped around him. It was cold down here, and he didn't seem to be wearing a shirt. He was so absorbed in his food search that he was totally unaware of her presence.

She positioned herself so he would have to get past her to get to the door, and then she cleared her throat. "Who are you?"

The boy gasped, jumped, and froze. He looked at her, eyes so filled with fright that she instantly felt guilty for scaring him so and then for laughing at how much she'd scared him. Tears welled up in his eyes just as quickly.

"No, don't cry. I'm sorry. I didn't mean to scare you . . . but that's what you get for breaking into people's houses . . . "

He was so very familiar that he seemed like he must have been someone she once knew who she was now forgetting. She stared and stared. Why did seeing his tears make her heart ache?

"Who are you?"

He leaped at her, and she thought he was going to try to bolt. He left the blanket in a pile on the floor spotlighted by the light in the refrigerator and just raced his naked little body toward the door. She scooted over to block him.

But he wasn't trying to get past her. He was running right to her, arms outstretched.

He jumped into her arms, nearly knocking her backward, and gripped her around her neck. The smell of him overpowered all of her senses. This was all a dream, she thought, it had to be. This was the cookie-dough smell, and it smelled even better this time.

When had she held him in her arms before?

She pulled him away long enough to stare at his face, to see herself clearly in it. And Jack. This was clearly Jack's son. Those eyes were his. Those ears were his. And all that hair. Like a little wolf boy. And then he hugged her again and she closed her eyes and she drank it in. This is what it was all about, she thought. This must be the part that makes all the other parts worthwhile.

She set him down, grabbed the blanket and wrapped him in it.

"You've got to keep warm."

Then she fainted. She knew it was going to happen before it did happen, but she'd never fainted before in a dream. She was sure when she woke up, she would find herself elsewhere in the house.

When Mary opened her eyes again, the first light of day was showing. The boy was over her face, staring at her. Did he look older? He was a little boy! How did she have a little boy already? Where had all the time gone? She thought back over the rush of the night before, the labor, the delivery . . . was she still dreaming now? Or did that happen years ago? She must be back in her dream: He might already be six.

"I'm okay. I just . . . I don't know." She laughed, but wasn't sure why. "Who the hell are you?"

He stared at her, confused.

Something surged pleasantly inside her just looking at him. She felt it deep in her body.

He tapped on her head with his forefinger.

"Stop that. I want to think a minute."

He shrugged.

She didn't know what to say.

He can't really know anything, can he? Words probably meant nothing to him.

"I'm sorry, now I need more than a minute." There was dried blood on her shirt. This boy needed clothes.

There was no way this was her kid. Forget the placenta at the top of the staircase.

Still, she felt calm. Was it the hormone bath from the pregnancy just making her dream crazy?

"You know what? Let's get dressed. After that, we can go for a walk or something. I need to think and being outside seems to help me with that."

He had no idea what she meant, but it made her feel better to talk.

So, to start with, that was what she did. As she led him upstairs, she asked him questions, which he didn't answer and which she didn't expect him to answer. As she searched the drawers and closets in the bedrooms, she talked, in very general terms, about her job, her family, her apartment, and the small garden in her kitchen, what she liked to eat. Even in her dreams, talking was comforting for her.

Meanwhile, he was jumping down the steps near the bottom of the staircase onto the floor of the bottom level. He started from the first step, a small jump down to the floor. Then from the second, which he did over and over again, then

81

the third. He worked himself up to the sixth step, but he needed to hold the banisters and swing to cross the distance to the bottom.

She wondered if she should take him someplace, to a doctor, a hospital, to her apartment?

To meet Mom?

She snorted.

That's just not going to happen. Not even in a dream.

They took the walkway to the back of the compound—it was a straight, short path that led to a gate through the walls. It was still more dark than light out, although that was changing quickly. Outside the gate was national parkland property; the path they picked up there ran under a lane of oak trees and would eventually cross a stream that would take them to the summit point with a 360 degree view that included all of Cheronkin, as well as a glimpse of the ocean.

As the gate opened, Mary waited for Zane—that was the name she'd always favored for a boy—to catch up and to walk through ahead of her. He was Lorraine's age, which, once she'd thought about it, made it easier on her. She could do this because she knew how to handle Max and Lorraine.

When Zane stepped through the gate, there was a tremendous commotion in the nearby underbrush, like a family of raccoons racing away. Mary got in front of him, remembering Michael's story about the stuff going on around him while he was tending to that dog in the hills. As the gate closed she tried to catch a glimpse of what it was that had been startled away. The memory of the sound of them was already fading; with the breeze erasing the last sounds that hinted of their presence. Whatever it was, it/they were gone.

Mary remembered those faces pressed against her window.

Were they going to come back tonight?

The gate latch clicked. Mary jumped at the noise and bumped her head on a bird feeder hanging from a tree branch.

Zane liked that. He laughed and laughed about it and reenacted it as they walked up the path.

The first part of the walk, to the river, was the happiest time she could remember. She talked and he ran and frolicked through a landscape more green and lush than she ever remembered it being here. There were rocks to climb around on. Pinecones and pebbles to throw at tree trunks. They came across fruit—wild strawberries, blueberries, grapes, and nuts, and saw deer and raccoons and all kinds of birds.

He was silly and continually trying to hold her attention. He would cross the path in front of her, yelling and then disappearing behind some bush or tree trunk before emerging again, yelling and racing down the path after her.

Whenever she stopped talking, even the silence was weirdly perfect and enjoyable. She didn't let that happen a lot, but instead felt that she needed to keep the conversation going, because he needed to be acquiring his speaking skills from her. She talked about the family more, told him about Carina, about Cheronkin. She told him about his Uncle Michael, what a good, kind, loving person he was. And then she went into a short biography of her brother, ending with the thought that Michael would be really freaked out by this.

He's not going to believe it, she thought.

Zane was totally comfortable outside, just the way she would want her little boy to be. He was not at all timid. Everything fascinated him, especially if it moved. If he stubbed his toe, or tripped, or got scratched, he just soldiered on. His scratches lasted only minutes before they faded away.

And he was growing up before her eyes.

Literally. He was inches taller just a half hour into the walk.

Mary had a vast conversational repertoire to draw upon. Beyond her own experiences, she had a thousand good stories she'd heard from clients over the years, material she could easily recall in detail. Once she got rolling, she sprinkled her monologue with songs she knew from babysitting, like the alphabet song, do-re-mi, every song she could remember from Schoolhouse Rock and then every cartoon theme song she could recall, which really weren't very many.

In and between all that, he picked up something. It was more like he was learning a second language than a first. She had been jabbering on about the different kinds of wildlife she had encountered and he had been listening intently, wiggling his lips and moving his tongue as he tried to imitate her, and she had told him about a family of deer she and Carina had seen. He asked her if they were young or old, and she said young, and he asked if they were babies and then they both looked at each other as they realized he was talking, and then she squealed and hugged him while he babbled on about understanding her and using words.

She was so proud of him after that. He was going to be brilliant.

"It's kind of smelly in that house. And I didn't know what the glowing things were."

"The glowing things? I don't know what you're talking about. Do I want to know? You can show me when we get back."

All she had been able to find in the house in terms of clothes had been the random old clothes in the drawers left behind by thirty years of visitors in the spare room. Mostly jackets, gloves, boots, and hats, but there were a few teenage boy shirts that were big on Zane and a pair of men's shorts she cinched with a tie; she settled on a little green Lacoste shirt with an alligator on the lapel, because it reminded her of Michael when he was little.

She'd worn her fanny pack, and had packed inside one of the sodas she'd brought along for the weekend away. With the house keys and the trail mix and the water—the last two for Zane, because she knew he'd be hungry before long—the fanny pack didn't quite zip all the way closed.

She saw Zane eyeing the shiny soda can. She pulled it out, cracked it open and offered him a sip. And then she told him about the time she made a midnight run to the store for toilet paper and a six-pack of her favorite brand and was actually grabbed by a guy in the parking lot who seemed like he was going to try to either hurt her or take her money.

"What did you do?"

"It's one of the reasons I swear by my soda. I had the six-pack double-bagged and I just started whaling on him with it. Knocked him out cold. It made a big mess because some of the cans cracked open, but the store comped me and gave me a new pack."

He thought that was a cool story, which, as it had when she told Max, made her feel cool. Of course, there was no knowing if he understood any of it.

But he didn't like the taste. Crinkled his nose at it. "What did they do to it? It tastes like it's dead." Then he started in: What is a store? What kind of a store was it? What does comp mean? What is a six-pack? What did she do with the six-pack again? Did she get to drink any of it afterward? Tell me the story again. What was the man grabbing you for? And after she answered all the questions she felt appropriate to answer, he asked her to tell him the story again and again until it had all apparently sunk in.

They rested at the river. They both sat down and in a moment he was leaning against her, and in another moment his eyes were closed and he was asleep. Then she moved him so his head was in her lap, and sat back in the lazy sun and wondered if it were possible that life could get better than it was for her at that moment in time.

She didn't fall asleep again, but was in an almost trance-like daze when Zane suddenly opened his eyes and sat up. He looked at his hands, felt them, then at his arms, then, to see if she were watching, he looked at Mary.

She smiled at him.

He smiled back, but shyly. There was a hint of something troubling in his eyes.

"Did you have a dream?"

"I saw things happening. They seemed real. But now they're gone. Where did they go?"

"They do seem real. What did you see happening?"

"I got old. This place turned into a dark forest. And then I turned into something else. And you were just like you are now, and you said that I was like an egg, incubating, and that when I got old I would hatch. You said Grandma told you I wasn't safe. And then we had to hide from Grandma because she wanted to kill me and you. She said we'd stolen part of her soul and she needed it back to move on."

"Yikes. Was I being mean? Was I joking?"

"No. Yes. You were scared of me."

"I'm not scared of you now, am I?"

"But I am getting older faster than you, aren't I?"

"Yeah, you noticed that?"

"Yeah."

"I don't know what that's all about, either. I'm just sort of going with it. If you think anything is lacking, or you want to do something else, I'm open to suggestions."

She stood up, he followed suit, and they continued the hike up to the summit.

Without Zane, it was a thirty-minute hike, walking at a brisk pace. With Zane, it seemed like they might never get there. It was a surprisingly scenic hike, past unexpectedly lush, thriving, blooming vegetation such as Mary had never seen in Cheronkin.

This new cycle of weather that had set upon Cheronkin, where the sky rained for an hour every day in the afternoon, and then cleared to become warm and humid, was apparently having a big effect out here in the hills.

Mary stopped herself. Was that real or had she just dreamed it? Had the weather really changed in Cheronkin? Maybe it had. Had she noticed it before? How could it be a dream, when all of her senses told her the lushness of her surroundings was real? And yet, why wouldn't it be a dream, when nothing about it resembled what she had known so well for so long?

She showed him how to skip rocks on the river, and they made crowns for themselves from twigs and vines and stems and flowers they plucked as they hiked. This was a time-honored activity she and Carina engaged in whenever they hiked together.

At one point, he threw a rock and hit a bird as it was taking off. It crashed to the ground, and as they ran closer, they could see it pivoting around on its broken wing. Its head looked a little mashed in, and it seemed a little stunned. It was about the same size as a wadded-up sock.

"Why did you do that?"

The look on his face was of genuine remorse. "I didn't mean to. I didn't see it until after I threw it."

They both stared at it.

"Should we do something for it?"

"Put it out of its misery?"

"Mom."

And then, Mary wasn't sure, but then it seemed like maybe it wasn't in such bad shape. Its head looked a little better, a little less dented. Its wing seemed a little straighter.

It stopped flailing and sat, its broken wing askew, the other folded flat. And then it lifted the broken wing and folded it in.

With that, it seemed like it was better.

It hopped to its feet, and flew away.

"Wow. Just like Michael's dog."

Zane sort of zoomed around, stopped here to look at a new thing, stopped there to pee behind a bush, to count pebbles. He found a place on the edge of an ivy bed where there was an abundance of ladybugs emerging from their eggs, and a hole in a tree from which it seemed that a horde of butterflies were similarly erupting from their cocoons.

Twice she became so absorbed in the scenery she lost track of him; both times, she backtracked to find him wandering through the bushes. Not just wandering, but actually looking sort of like he was in a trance, his eyes rolled up a little, his nose tilted upward as if he was smelling something, his head swaying slightly side to side.

The first time this happened, he responded to the sound of Mary calling his name. His eyes snapped back, he smiled, he sneezed, and came running back to her. The second time, to see how far he would go, and to see what he was doing, she just waited until he finished, which entailed him walking through the entirety of the spot of brush he was in. She couldn't figure out what he was doing, what he was getting out of it. The leaves rubbed against him very slowly as he walked through, against his nose, his cheeks, the arms at his side. And when he stepped out of the other side of the bush, he did as he had when she'd broken the trance: His eyes returned to normal, he sneezed, and then he came running to her.

"What was that?"

"I dunno. I forgot."

"You forgot pretty fast."

He shrugged and walked back to the path.

His appearance changed from moment to moment, although she was strangely calm and unconcerned by this. Was this part of parenting? This attitude of "Oh well, that's apparently who he is. Born and dead in the lifespan of a fly."

It was a gruesome thought, true, but she allowed herself it. This was a dream, whatever her senses might be telling her. It might very well be a delirium resulting from blood loss from a miscarriage. Although why her subconscious mind would put a child at the top of her list was beyond her.

She might simply be snoring away with a brain tumor that might be making her see things, or, worse, she might be wandering outside right now, having this adventure all alone, accompanied by her own mental delusion. She considered the possibility: what if she were sleepwalking right now, in the middle of the night?

The truth about Zane: His childhood was almost over. He was about the size of a twelve-year-old. He'd had to remove his shirt before he either busted a seam or cut off his circulation. The shorts were not so bad. They'd started out extra baggy and cinched super-tight at the waist. On Zane now they went to his knees and the cinch was much loosened. He still had that little boy slim waist.

His hair was getting long, but not so much that it looked overgrown. That part of him seemed to grow at a slower rate than the rest.

Should she feel guilty? If this were going to be all of his life, was this the right way to be spending it? Shouldn't she at least take him to meet her family? She'd been doing the math: driving out just to meet Mom would be a minimum hour-and-a-half excursion. That would be four, five years of his life? Was that worth it? And probably add half an hour for each additional person she introduced him to, like Michael and Carina? Then she could have witnesses she could trust. Would she then ask Michael where she could find Jack?

And that wasn't counting all the time they would have to spend dealing with the hysteria related to his very existence. Or else she would have to spend all of her free time lying about it. Either of those would be an entertaining scene to see, but not one to be part of.

Could she handle watching time eat him up while they were racing through the hills back to town? The sun was out but still low in the sky. He was a little funny-looking because of his hair and his jean shorts and because he was so lanky.

"Come on, Jethro."

He would be a cutie once she cut his hair.

88

Their path took them by a lookout point from which the curve of the ocean shoreline was visible over the farthest hillsides. Turning around, all of Cheronkin was visible, ringed by mountains, cleaved into quarters by the six-lane highway and the four lanes of Marble Canyon Road that intersected it.

"Your grandma lives down that way," she said, pointing east. "My place is on the other side of the freeway."

The land the ranch house was on was the oldest part of Cheronkin, mostly undeveloped land, but where it had been developed, it was used for farmed orchards.

Zane's interest in the view didn't last as long as the explanation. Almost before she was done speaking, he was calling out for her to come see something else.

She ignored him a minute, during which he called out to her six times, with increasing frustration. "Fine. I'm coming. I'm coming."

She walked over to the place he was standing, under the tree cover but at the edge of the trailhead. The landscape on the other side of the trailhead was more familiar, more like the dry hills she remembered. The land was not nearly as lush or overgrown. There was no tree cover, just individual trees that looked like they needed a good soak.

The object of Zane's interest was an arbor, with an arch just a little bit wider than the size of an average doorway. It was beautifully decorated with wildflowers.

"Oh! It's beautiful! I wonder what it's doing here?"

Zane walked underneath, turned, and bowed, as if to an invisible spirit.

At first glance, Mary thought it must be a leftover from some sort of bridal photo shoot. Or maybe it was for a wedding that hadn't happened yet. It was out of place. She realized she could see roots on both sides of the arbor. The plants were real.

Maybe she was going to be getting married later in this dream.

Oh, goody.

"Mom, look." Zane picked a yellow daisy from the ground. He pressed the stem into a branch on the arbor. He held it there for half a minute and let go of the flower. It remained in place on the plant.

"I don't . . ."

89

"Mom, you know, you talk a lot. Look." He pulled on the daisy. It wouldn't let go. She gasped. The flower's stem had grown into the branch. The flower hung there, its bloom unaffected.

"That's weird." That would explain the fifty different kinds of flowers blooming on one bush.

Zane, on the trailhead, came scurrying back. He ran around the arbor and hid behind her. To see what he was dodging, she stepped underneath the arch and through.

She paused; she thought about the tomato plant on her kitchen sink, now bearing fruit; she thought about the forested look of the neighborhoods around her mother's street after her mother had ordered the whole block pruned and trimmed. What was going on here?

There was an old man coming along the trail, from the opposite direction they'd come. She smiled and held up her hand to wave. Standard trail greetings, and then just move on. He had the look of a homeless person, but he was also familiar. It took her only a second to place him as someone she'd seen asking for handouts around town in years past. She thought maybe he was the guy Carina had once considered buying mushrooms from. He sort of acknowledged Mary, kind of tilting his head at her, but as he approached the arbor, he seemed more wary of it than interested in her. That changed when he was passing by her. At that point, he was openly staring at her.

It took her only a minute or two more to connect the guy who once sold mushrooms to the guy Michael was talking about who was selling acid outside the Hat years ago, the same one who dosed Michael at the beach. His "lots-of-dots" guy. Was that who this was? He was old and wiry-looking, skinny arms, gaunt cheeks, but not at all frightening. His teeth still looked okay. At the very least, he was the mushroom guy, which meant he'd been a vagrant here for ten or more years.

He startled her by speaking. He said, "So there's two of you here, are there? A regular nest."

This *was* Michael's Dot Guy, Mary thought. She assumed he was referring to Zane and herself.

"The one at the beach is your brother, is that right?"

That threw her off. She felt as if he'd read her mind. How did he know that?

He laughed. It wasn't mean or menacing—it actually was the kind of laugh that made her want to laugh along, very good-natured. He said, "Is your mother dead, then? Is that why you're both still around and all grown up? Otherwise, you know, she's going to be coming for you."

Zane popped out right beside Mary, slipping under her arm for protection while staring fiercely at the man. What, Mary wondered, did Melinda have to do with any of this? This was the second time in one afternoon that Melinda and murder had been part of the same sentence.

The man sputtered at the sight of Zane, and took a step back. He stared and even when it appeared he'd decided to say something, he still didn't.

"I guess," she said, stepping back, "we're going to go."

"Well, that's a puzzle," he said. "I didn't think you or your brother would be possible"—he gestured at Mary—"and that almost makes him the child of a paradox. Is there a word for that? I'll have to change it in my notes." He looked directly at Mary. "If he weren't a child, I'd be curious to see what would happen to him outside the green zone there." He gestured across the road, where the landscape was dry and parched, typical of the hills of Cheronkin as she remembered it—and not at all like the canopy of green at her back. The old man turned to point at the arbor. "There's a number of them around the hills, in an oval shape, all along the perimeter. Best keep him inside that zone there," he said, and it sounded weird and paranoid, but she thought it was advice. "Someone put these up to mark the boundaries. Just because he's alive in there doesn't mean he'll stay that way out here."

And then he turned in the direction he'd originally been headed, and walked away.

Mary said, "'Bye," sarcastically.

Zane nudged her.

The man stopped, but without turning around he yelled over his shoulder, "He isn't supposed to be here, and you know it, too! Was it because of you, or was it the father?"

And then he was over the next ridge and gone.

By the time they returned to the house, Zane had outgrown his clothes and was walking with the picnic blanket around his waist. It was red, white, and blue, and made him look like a rock star. He would have been just as happy walking around naked—but she'd insisted on his covering up. It was public land. She didn't know how she'd respond to being seen roaming the property with a naked 20-year-old who was also her son.

He was better-looking than his father, and that was saying something. Lean, on his way to being a handsome man. She'd expected no less of herself—if she did breed, she had always known she would do it well. Though she had always pictured it would be with a blond boy.

On the last portion of the hike, she'd started to think about the fact that he was probably going to die before her. Maybe before morning. It wasn't something she dwelled on; that line of thinking led only to a vast yawning pit of sadness in which she would soon be overwhelmed and drowned. Yet it was hard not to keep coming back to it.

This wasn't fair. Hesitancy or not on her part, that still didn't mean that the concept of having a child hadn't been with her for her entire life, whether she'd ever liked the idea or not. One day and it's over? One day?

"What's wrong, Mom?"

"It's going much too fast." A tear ran down her cheek. "I feel sad for all the things you've already missed! Birthday parties, first crush, ice cream, time with grandma and grandpa, making friends. And your father. I'm supposed to be married and set up before you get here, so I can do everything to make sure you get to have all those things. And what about everything else? The rest of your life? Which is going to be gone just as fast. This might be your only walk outdoors . . ."

She stopped herself. There was too much to get sucked into there, and none of it would make anything better. She saw the worry on his face. Not for himself, but for her.

"You know what? I'm going to start up a bath for you, like you're still my little boy. A bubble bath. You are still my little boy. I think there's bigger boy clothes in there. I mean, there's grown-up clothes that will fit you. You deserve at least one bubble bath in your life. And I'll give you a haircut while it fills—the tub is one of those huge old claw foot tubs and it takes forever to get filled. So I'll cut your hair and you can see what your mother does for work."

"I'm glad this day is with you. I'll remember it forever."

She snorted, wiped away the moisture from her cheek.

"There is a reason it's like this," he said, already sounding much too old. "You have to know it. I know it. You can't argue with what it is. There is a reason for it."

"That doesn't mean it isn't worth being pissed off about."

Once she had him seated on one of the dining room chair, sheet around his neck, hair pinned back from his face, sheers plugged in, she was ready to go. It took a while to get there, to sort of re-arrange her head, and while that had been happening, she'd asked him to help clean up. The afterbirth at the top of the stairs had aged much as Zane had. At twenty-some years, it looked like a flattened, shriveled cow patty, and she made him sweep it up and bury it in under a rose bush in the front yard,

With his hair back, he looked like Mary in a way, and like Mary's father.

"I once pledged to breed only with blondes to preserve the blue-blonde gene, and here I am with a dark-haired offspring. With dark eyes. Shudders. Just like your father."

Definitely, Jack was the father.

This was her element. Some of her customers likened an appointment with her to a visit to a therapist. She knew how to prod along a conversation, how to talk about herself in a way that drew people out to talk about themselves. And if they never talked, she was comfortable just chatting up a storm on her own. It didn't matter if she'd shared the same personal story with thirty people that day; each client felt as if she were opening up to them, and they tended to respond. For all her talk, that she was also a good listener made just as good an impression.

"Tell me about my grandma again."

"Your grandma, not your dad?"

"You said he's like me. I know me."

"You know what? I have pictures in my wallet. You have two grandmas that I know of, but I can only speak for my family. My mom, Grandma Melinda—see, she would probably shorten that given the chance, like Grandma Lynn, or Mylin—she's pretty intimidating. She's a great mom. She's really intense and focused, and sees a lot of things as being clearly right and wrong and goes around trying to fix everything according to the way she sees it."

None of that meant anything to him. She showed him a picture of Melinda and Eli from their 40th anniversary party.

"She's done cool things. Lots of big, complicated things, like raising money for all the public schools Michael and I went to, helping out charities, sort of being a pain in the butt with the city and county and state and federal officials for the benefit of the town. And lots of cool small things, too, like making your favorite meal on your birthday every year. Mine was smothered chicken, with mushrooms from a can, which was gross, but I loved it. She once let me ditch school to shop for a prom dress and then lied to the principal when they called to check on me. Slipped me cash when I first moved out. Dad—your grandpa—did that too, almost every time I visited. They both pretended it was urgent that the other didn't know. Every time I came over, I had to keep straight whose money went into each pocket, you know, like Dad in the right, Mom in the left?"

"And my Grandpa?"

"Gosh, I think he'd just love being called that. That might be enough to make him want to retire. He's great. I wish you could meet him, too. You look a little like him. Your forehead and your chin. All my friends growing up used to say how nice my father was. But he won't be back until next week, and that'll be too . . ." She stopped herself.

He ignored this, nodding at her to continue.

"He is a lobbyist," she continued. "Which means he spends a lot of time trying to influence the people who make the laws, or the rules that we all have to follow. Let's not get into that, it's really annoying . . . He is a really wonderful man, and he works in Washington DC, which is a long way away, so he spends a lot of time out of town. He used to work closer, which was much better, but for the last few years, since about a year after the first war started, he's been doing this."

"The war?"

"Yes. Supposedly. People fighting against each other. For it to be a 'war' there's got to be a reason, right? So they're fighting . . . well, we're fighting . . . but I don't think anyone could tell you why or what it is for. Someone attacked our country, and we attacked them back, and then while we were there fighting those people, we started fighting their neighbors and other countries attacked us and honestly, it's been going on two-thirds of my life. A couple times, it seemed like it was going to be over, but then it turned out we were still fighting, we were just doing it in secret. Every time one fight with one country is settled, the fighting just moves on. And then, to make things worse, about ten years ago, two other big countries started fighting in their own wars with different countries in different parts of the world and it doesn't seem like any of those fights are going to end soon. It's a lot of people fighting, and sometimes it seems like it's everywhere but here.

"It's been going on so long that people don't talk about it much anymore. It's like old news, even though I know a couple of my clients have relatives who just shipped out. It's happening far away from here. Stupid men. Sometimes, someone from nearby dies and that makes the headlines, but then it just recedes again. My dad says it'll end, but this feels different. Like it's just going to go on and on."

He was quiet while he thought about that. Then he said, "You're right. It won't stop. It's going to keep spreading slowly."

"I think so, too," she said, "It feels like it's about something bigger than a war. It's feels like someone's plan." Then she shifted gears. "Your Uncle Mike is the one I want you to meet the most. He's friends with your dad, too, I guess. I tortured my brother a lot growing up, but he's all right. He just moved back home; he broke up with his girlfriend, who I liked, but who I also thought was kind of tacky because she used to go around the house without underwear on. Yuck! One time, before Michael was allowed to drive by himself, I went to pick them up at the movie theater and there was this couple that was totally . . . you know, kissing . . . right in front of the theater's front doors. I couldn't even look at them, it was so overboard, her tight, tacky, cheap leather skirt, practically humping against the wall. And I went inside, and I looked all around and couldn't find them, and then I came back outside, and that couple was still going at the, you know, kissing. And then I notice the girl's shoes look familiar, and then I realize, oh my god, it's Michael and his girlfriend . . ."

Zane laughed, but only because of the silly voice she used. "What were they doing?"

"It was just tacky."

It was the better part of an hour before she was done with his hair; it was doubly strange for her because it not only looked like he'd matured—the result of the haircut—but he also seemed as if he had aged significantly.

He looked in the mirror briefly; with no real reaction.

What does he know about haircuts?

"If my clients' hair grew as slow as yours, I wouldn't be able to support myself."

This meant nothing to him. He only smiled because she did.

She considered giving him a few suggestions about masturbation when she sent him up to the tub to soak. Even if it were inappropriate, she thought he deserved at least that—especially since that was as close as he was going to get to getting any in his lifetime. She wasn't sure how the whole "awakening" thing went for boys. He was a guy, and she wasn't sure a guy could fully understand what that meant without the sexual component.

Isn't propagation what the male species is all about?

But then it seemed too dicey in the end. Let him find what he finds. Over the course of her lifetime she'd known too many boys who lost the ability to think rationally once that part of their physiology had come into play. And really, it might just give him another thing to be sad about, what with his lifespan being what it was.

He would be gone for a good hour.

During that time, she used the downstairs bathroom, where she discovered a pile of cans had been stashed away—insect repellant, hair spray, wood polish, cooking spray.

Zane came down the stairs dressed in the clothes she'd put out for him, a polo shirt and a pair of shorts she'd found in the bedroom closet. The sight of him sort of took her breath away. He was her age now, maybe a bit older. He was a little small for Uncle's Bill's clothes, but he still filled them out well. He was a handsome man, and he really resembled his father. Maybe this was what Jack was going to start looking like. The hair had grown in some, but to a length that was hip for his age.

"So, how was that?"

He smiled. "Good. I liked it."

Mary thought, what if you could just grow your man like this? Bring him home from the store, sprinkle a little water on the seed, and then raise him and mold him over the course of an afternoon to be the perfect mate? You could keep him away from all that other male crap and mother crap that messes them up so much, teach them how you want them to act and have an acceptable partner by mid-afternoon?

The thought of him growing so fast made her think of the plants in her kitchen, which had done just the same.

Should it seem obvious to her that those things could be related?

There wasn't much food left in the house, but by putting everything out on the table and combining it with the fruit and nuts and berries they had collected, it looked like a feast. He wouldn't touch the cheese in a can, the soft drinks, or the microwavable mac and cheese, though he did allow her to light the stove to cook the brown rice she found in the pantry. He stuck to the organics. Nothing processed.

"I was thinking," he said.

"Yes?"

"You don't live very healthy. None of that stuff is really what your body wants."

"Oh, really? I eat healthy, Mr. Know-it-all. But I also like to treat myself once in a while to something that isn't good for me."

"Like death in a can."

"Fine. Anything else?"

"It's all these pollutants. Like those chemicals from where you work? Even though I bet you haven't been there a for a while, I can smell them. They're in your skin. That's not good for you. And all the things you do to upset grandma, even if she drives you crazy, it just ties things up inside you."

"Wow. I don't like this at all. You're taking the side of someone you don't even know against me. Your grandmother over your mother. Then again, it does make a little more sense. While I was setting the table, I ventured into the bathroom and found all the stuff you put in there."

"What stuff?"

"Aerosols, bugs sprays, Pam, WD40."

He wrinkled his nose. "Stinky. Stinking poisons. I did that when I was little. I was in this room in the dark, staring at the glowing stuff . . ."

"What glowing stuff?"

"I didn't know what it was. But I understand now. It is the power lines for the house. They run under the ground from the east and then spread the electricity around the house in wires, yes?"

"Yeah, I mean, I guess so."

"Well, my eyes were different. In the dark, the lines in the wall hummed and glowed. And it smelled like poison in the room, and I kept finding stinky cans and kept moving them to the bathroom so I could close the door on them and stop the smell. I could smell it in the air. There's a lot of poisons all around. That couch right there? Just from lying on it you've breathed whatever's in the foam into your body."

"Well, you'd just be sick if you saw the city. This is nothing."

"That's what was wrong with the ground on the outside of the arch. All of the poisons of people living here have made things dull. It has seeped out of them and into the ground."

"And inside the arch?"

"It's not the same. It's another place, like another world."

"So how long have you been worried about my health?"

"It's true, though. You've got all these poisons covering you up—foundation, base, powder, eye makeup; you've got all these poisons that you use to "clean." And you work in a place with hair poisons. You eat really bad foods . . ."

Mary was not enjoying this.

"You need to purify, Mom. Purify what you put into yourself. Purify what you allow to come out of your mouth. Purify your thoughts. You need to get back to your natural self and get away from these harmful behaviors."

"For what purpose? To live a 'good' life?"

"No. To be strong for what is going to happen."

"What is going to happen?"

"It's happening already."

"You mean the plants outside? The whole nature-gone-wild thing?"

"I think there is more than that."

"I don't understand. And when did all of this occur to you?"

"It was so quiet in the bathroom I was finally able to think." Definitely a jab at her being talkative.

This was how kids talked to their parents. For some reason, it made Mary feel good to be spoken to like a parent.

"I'm pretty certain I'm not supposed to be here," he continued, "and yet, look at me: here I am. And if I'm not supposed to be here, then neither are you, since you created the possibility that makes me possible."

"I'm not supposed to be here? What about your father? Maybe he's the one who shouldn't be here . . . who should have . . . maybe he's the impossibility."

"Look at me, Mother."

She stared at him. There were silver hairs on his temples.

"Clearly, this is not normal. In some strange way, many things are clearer to me as the day has gone by . . ."

"Do you mean the things you see, like when you did that trance thing in the brush?"

"Yes."

"What do they mean? What did you see?"

"I need to pee," he said.

And then she realized: There were things he was not telling her. There were things he had not been telling her all morning! How could that be? When did that start? When she'd been here for nearly everything?

He rose, and started to leave the room, and then stopped himself, returned to her, and crouched down to talk to her. It was done with a very paternal air. She tried not to project her resentment.

"Listen," he said, "I want to explain what I've been thinking. When I had that dream by the river, I saw a lot of pictures of things in my head that I've just started to understand. There is so much energy loose all around here that the air is almost vibrating; the energy is coming up from the ground and it's healing things, and it's making things live. Even when maybe they shouldn't.

"Think about when you lit the pilot light on the stove earlier: the first match seemed like it was going to catch, and it flared up, but then it fizzled out. That was supposed to be my life. I wasn't supposed to be. But this energy in the air is stretching out a moment that was only supposed to be a flash. This is sort of the compromise. My life in a day."

"Geez, Zane, you're kind of crushing the vibe in here. I've tried to avoid lingering in this neighborhood of thought. Should I spend the rest of your life crying?"

"I think that old man we saw was right. He knew. He saw."

"Oh, he was a crazy old man . . ."

Zane walked over to the bookshelf and picked up a tin container with pencils in it. He rattled the pencils around in a circle, then reached into the tin to pull out a piece of chalk. Then he drew a circle on the wood floor around the chair Mary sat in.

"What are you doing?"

"At the end of my dream, I was very old. And I shed my skin. And I became something frightening that wasn't like me at all. If I come back, and I've turned into a monster, then you'll be safe from me in there."

"Oh, I don't like this." She felt a little punchy, a little giggly. "And then you're going off to the bathroom to pee? You're going to have to hold it." She held onto his hand. It was like her dad's hand, maybe even a bit older. The skin was soft, and thinner than her father's.

"No, really, I have to go." He pulled his hand.

She didn't let go. She giggled. "I'm not going to let you go. Not after you just said that to me."

Her giggling was a bit infectious. And he got the bug. He laughed. "But I have to go."

"Well, you shouldn't have said that first. 'I might turn into a horrible monster of which you should be so afraid that you'll remain in a chalk . . .'" She giggle-snorted. "'Chalk ring.' How's that going to help me?" She giggled again. "I'm having too much fun, Zane; I'm not going to let this turn into some horrible nightmare, because then I'm going to make myself wake up and I might never see you again."

100

They stared and stared at each other, the grins frozen on their faces.

"I love you, Mom."

"Oh, I don't like this at all. And then I'm just supposed to stay here while you're gone? And then, what? A scratch at the window, a creaking on the downstairs staircase, a mysterious thud in the bathroom? And you're no longer answering? Sorry, I can't risk it." Despite that, she let go of his hand. "If this is really a dream, then I'll be able to fly away if I need to. So, fine, you go pee." She picked up one of the old magazines in the rack beside the chair.

Zane stared at her a moment. He turned, took a step, and then promptly tripped on the Ottoman behind him. She realized it was happening only as he was falling. His knee hit the floor first. She heard the crack in the bone. His right hand hit next and there was another sharp crack. She started to shriek as his head went into the floor. The expression on his face was pure surprise. There was a noise like an egg breaking, the sound of the pieces of shell scratching against each other as they fell away, and lots of other snaps and pops.

Yet, because it evoked what Zane had just said about shedding his skin, she remained inside the circle he had drawn. What if this was his shell breaking?

When he slumped flat, there was a noise, softer than a crack, and he broke apart, broke into feathery pieces that looked more cotton than flesh, and the pieces spilled across the floorboards even as they were breaking apart into dust. That same mix of dust and filament poured out from his shirt sleeves, from the legs of his pants.

His head was just . . . gone.

Mary screamed again. But she also waited inside the circle until everything had settled. She watched the scattered remains fearfully, anxiously, crying all the while, until nothing new presented itself.

When she did step out of the circle, and she touched his shirt, there was nothing of him left but dust.

Mary didn't know how long she sat there, staring at nothing. Crying, staring, not believing, waiting for the dream to end, waiting to wake up. Finally, she looked around herself, for evidence that he had been here with her in this dream. She looked at the stairs from the bedroom, which had been spattered with blood when she last looked at them in the night. There were spots there, and they might have been blood, but they looked more like old dirt stains, and when she patted at one, it blew away.

The house was a mess, and though it would seem there could be no clearer evidence than that and her own memories, she wanted something more.

The bedroom upstairs offered more support. The sheets on the bed, which had been terribly stained the last time she'd seen them were now covered with an ash-like powder. She knew it was his blood, and that it had aged as fast as he had, and that it was going to be nothing but dust once she shook them in the wind.

This will be the only child she would ever have, she felt with certainty. This will never happen again.

She was ready for this dream to end and wondered, since it hadn't, what might be coming next. She lay her head on the pillow and told herself she was going to be waking up soon, and hoped, if she didn't wake up, that she might be able to sleep more and then think about all of this tomorrow. Maybe there would be time for that wedding dream.

But she couldn't sleep that night.

Over and over and over, while she missed him and ached in her heart, she realized and pondered and promised herself: Things in her life were going to have to change.

6

The Grand Reopening

The back room of the warehouse where hard-working, hard-drinking men once met regularly for cards by candlelight had transformed in the following seventy years, from a nondescript, geographically isolated property boundary marker to a site that boasted the status of being the unofficial hub of the musical—and, some music fans would argue, cultural—activity of the semi-rural region that surrounded it.

The wood plank structure attached to the side of a warehouse used for agricultural storage had been built by farm hands caught one too many times in the coastal storms that moved through the canyons and drenched the area with hardly any notice. They'd added on to it little by little over the years. At some point, the warehouse became a metal smith and potter's shop, and, in the course of a conversation over a game of seven-card stud, the storage building became a Thursday-night speakeasy. From speakeasy to saloon a year later, when a flush beat four-of-a-kind in the final hand of a game of winner takes all, a hat trick for the winner, who then hammered a hole through the wall facing the street to open things up to the public.

The Hat Trick had been a pool hall, a poker hall, a meeting hall, a choir hall, a diner, and a restaurant, depending on the time of the week and the season of the year, all the while attracting and building a clientele of loners who looked forward to the break it provided from the endless and harrowing drive of the two-lane, unpaved highway that curved through the area and led eventually to the city of harbors up north. Other businesses sprang up along on the same road, which was eventually repaved into a two-line Interstate highway, and a record company man, Murray Topplestein, who stumbled across the place, decided he had the makings of a performance space before him.

Murray's Hat developed a reputation for featuring bands and players who for one reason or another—age, color, gender, notorious behavior—weren't getting work anyplace else. It was never a first-run club, and didn't aspire to be; that had always been part of its appeal.

Like most things American, it seemed the club had seen its finest days by the early '70s. The owners allowed the facade of the building to fall into greater disrepair, both through their contracting of a management company that invested in only the minimal level of care, and by milking as much money from the enterprise as there was to get.

Its reputation for music never suffered because there was usually someone on hand in a position that mattered who cared a lot about that aspect of the club's existence. As the succeeding generations of patrons never had a clue that it had ever been any different, the point was moot; their memories of a weathered club would be as fondly held as their parents' rememberings of earlier incarnations.

Michael looked at his watch. People were going to be streaming in constantly, but that was the mass of them right there. No one else that mattered was going to show up until later. This was the invitation crowd. He thought he'd be more useful inside.

He was about to let himself in through the front doors when he stopped to survey the momentary quiet that overtook the street front. It wasn't that he was disappointed Talia wasn't there; for some reason, he had been sure she would be coming. He was still sure she would be there before the club closed.

There was a momentary feeling that he was waiting for something that wasn't going to happen—like sitting at the bus stop, not sure if he'd missed the last bus of the day, or waiting anywhere for someone to pick him up and they'd forgotten again. Quick as that thought came, it was immediately pushed out by another as a little breeze kicked up along the sidewalk that led from the parking lot to the front doors of the club.

She's here now.

He looked up the sidewalk: No one there. He looked the other way, toward a path which began as a paved walkway but then turned into a graveled walkway that ran along the side of the club to the employee parking lot, where there was also a dirt lot—an area that was popular with the smokers, stoners and, later in the evening, lovebirds out for necking.

There was a cat sitting in the middle of the sidewalk that way, watching him. Watching to see what he was going to do.

He felt something on the back of his neck, and looked again up the sidewalk at the same time Talia stepped around the corner, the breeze flicking up the hem of her skirt.

And there she is, he thought.

She didn't see him, notice him, anything him as she approached, and when she did acknowledge his presence with a glance, she clearly did not recognize him from their roadside meet.

Still, she was here because of him. And she was going to walk right by without recognizing him if he didn't say something. "Hi."

"Hello."

"Are you going to perform tonight, or are you attending as a guest, or both?"

She noticed him. She stopped and looked at him. "Do you think I can find my way around inside?"

"There's a door to the left, just inside the entrance—that'll take you backstage. It's all the same back there. The interior has kind of been, I don't know, dipped in shiny. It might be a good time to look around, because there's not that many people yet—and there's only a couple performances going on, but you can see the stages. It's all going to be going on later tonight."

She didn't say anything.

"Do you mind my asking where your friend is this evening?"

"Pardon?"

"Your friend from the beach? The redhead? I was figuring you were going to be bringing her along for support."

"From the beach. And you thought you would be seeing me with her here tonight?" She stared at him, visibly taken aback. Then perplexed. He managed not to break the stare before she did. She averted her eyes from his, looked over his shoulder. "She's really not a people person."

Now she looked at him closely. Now she thought about it minute. Surely, she remembered him; it was dark, but was he really that forgettable?

Her eyes were piercing as she studied him silently. He focused again mentally on her forehead.

Finally, she said, "I'm not really sure what to think about you."

"That's all right. I'm not sure what to make of myself. Maybe that's why I'm the doorman tonight."

She flashed a grin for a brief second. If it were possible, she looked more beautiful than he'd ever seen her. Almost radiant. And again, she was looking over his shoulder.

He turned, and saw she was staring at the cat. It was on the edge of the circle of light cast by the nearest lamppost.

"Great minds think alike," he said. "The food is good, the crowd is a show in itself, and the music rocks. It's where all the cool cats hang out." This went by her without a glimmer of response. More sincerely: "You should do us all the favor of singing tonight."

The door creaked open. It was Gilbert, one of the cooks.

"Mike, they need you in the office." The door closed.

"Office?"

"I just look like I'm a doorman. Nothing here is really what it seems." He didn't know why he said that. "I also answer phones, which is probably what they need me for now that you're here and the door-opening part is done."

Talia looked at the cat, and said hello.

Michael paused at the door and watched as she crouched and walked slowly toward it, trying not to startle it. She looked rather awkward, and it occurred to him that she was not the animal person she thought herself to be.

Sure enough, the cat perked up, tensed, prepared to flee.

Talia froze.

And then the cat just sort of shrugged, or what looked like a shrug, and out from its sides unfolded these long, magnificent wings. Talia gasped. The movement startled both of them.

It leapt into the air.

It was an owl. Not a cat. And in an instant it had disappeared into the night sky.

Talia turned and looked at him, again with that confused look.

He nodded. "That was weird. Did that cat just turn into a bird?"

She nodded yes, and they both laughed.

"Nothing here is what it seems to be." He didn't know why he said it again. "I'll see you inside, yes?"

She nodded yes. She didn't seem to be inclined to follow him in at that moment, so he closed the door behind him.

This was, as Aunt Laura described it to her assembled managers earlier in the afternoon, a community kiss-up event. A chance to remind them how good it is to have the club around. The real party would be later, and only a handful of those in attendance now would remain through the night. These were well-heeled patrons of the club and responsible citizens of Cheronkin, the sort of people the club had to avoid offending if it wished to remain in business. The goal wasn't to woo or to wow; their job tonight was to remind them of the club's role in the city's early development, its reputation as both a local and regional gathering place, and to stoke their memories of their own personal histories with the club.

As the event progressed, Michael found he could not pass by his aunt without being sucked into her schmoozing. She would spot him across the room, pull him over and into her conversation without introducing him, and then start handing him post-its and business cards. In the few conversations he had so witnessed, she had agreed to host a business group breakfast meeting on alternating Tuesdays and to work with the Cheronkin Teacher's Alumni group on creating a series of kid-friendly musical slash cultural events on Saturday mornings once a month. She had turned down the idea of holding Sunday morning services for the Holy Ghost Church (Sunday brunch was a moneymaker for the club), which had burned down on the night of the now-infamous Fandango beach party, but she did agree in concept to sponsor a benefit to raise funds to rebuild the church in the upcoming months. She crossed back and forth over the floor painted with the outline of a mid-twentieth century map of Cheronkin County, wheeling and dealing and having the time of her life. After a third conversation about someone's bountiful garden, she started talking up the idea of having a farmer's market in the parking lot one morning of the week

107

twice a month. She toyed with the idea as she continued to work the crowd, and it gave her a conversational focus to draw people in. She would say: "Let me ask you, how would you feel about the idea of starting a weekly farmer's market that is sponsored by the community?" And after talking about what a good growing season it was—because it seemed like everybody had a tale of bountiful fruits or vegetables to share—people enjoyed being involved in the idea. There was a guy with a print shop and fourteen fruiting avocado trees who would help with the advertising; there was a teacher with an herb garden who would volunteer students to help with setting up and parking; and, there was someone who wanted to do a bake sale with "all the organics we have going on here."

Jack's presence was a comfort for Michael. The misery emanating from him, as this was his big night—his artwork unveiled! All eyes upon him!—was highly amusing. He was hiding out, chain-smoking, and playing pinball in the game room.

Earlier in the day, Jack had had a loud argument with one of the restaurant floor managers while he was doing his set-up, during which he loudly complimented the manager's time management skills for his being able to find time to fuck around with one of the bus girls on his shift and to spend an hour on the phone every day with whoever else it was beside his wife that he was screwing.

True or not, everyone within listening range winced, and the floor manager had gone into the kitchen afterward and had not yet come out again. It was a common practice that it was best to stay out of Jack's way when he was at work, as he had had similar meltdowns in the process of setting up the displays. None of it did a lot to endear him to the rest of the staff.

"You're not up to basking in the adulation? Listening to the critiques?"

"Last time I looked, there are like five ladies I've sexed up out there and not a lot of crowd to get lost in. I'm gonna wait until the room fills a little more. Or else empties out a bit. What's up with you? Is that look on your face love struck or lovelorn?"

"A little bit of both. My ex called today."

"How was that?"

"It took about ten seconds of silence to realize I didn't really want to talk to her at all. It's not about not picking at the scab. It's more like, well, that door is closed."

"Hello?"

"Hi," she said. "It's me."

Once her voice had been very familiar. She'd expected him to recognize it. He had to search his memory. "Hello?" *Stalling her, looking for more.*

"Michael?"

It was Danielle.

"I can't believe you've already forgotten the sound of my voice."

He couldn't believe it, either. How long had it been since he'd thought of her? How long had it been since he wished he could stop thinking about her?

"You were out late night last night?"

"Yeah. I was working late last night."

"Doing?"

"I'm helping my aunt out at the club."

"Oh, right. I heard. Figures. Perfect for you."

"Yeah, it is. Right now it is."

Any questions he once upon a time might have wondered about were done and gone. He would really have to think about it to get the details of it together, even to feel about it again. And he wasn't going there.

And they all lived happily ever after.

"What's up with you?"

"I was thinking about you, Michael."

"Remembering the good old days? Starting to forget the bad ones?"

"You're working at the grand opening party tonight? My parents are going."

"Yeah. There's going to be a lot of old-timey staff. They put out an open invitation for former employees to sign on for shifts. It was kind of for PR purposes, but a lot of people responded. I'll just be one of many riding herd."

He was slightly nervous as the thought occurred she might be calling to say she would be there, too. He hadn't thought of that. He didn't want to see her again. Maybe ever. At least for now. That would be fine. "Why, are you going to be in town?"

109

"I can't make it. That would be great. I mean, to see you."
"Yeah, that's too bad . . . um, listen . . ."
"Oh."
A silent moment. Ten seconds long.
"That's the way? You're already a different person?"
"For me it is, Danielle."
"Really. Really, this is it?"
"No. That was it last time, and I told you that. This is my reaffirmation."
"Fine."

"It was lame." Michael sighed. "You know, it's not bad being single. Would be better if I were dating, but if I were dating I'd be neglecting the relationship because of work. Sex is what I want, not just fucking jerking off on the nights I'm not too exhausted . . ."

"What's it take if you're focused on the effort—five minutes?" He chuckled.

Michael laughed, but didn't let Jack interrupt the thought, ". . . Those are the nights when I sometimes miss Danielle. But not even as a person, as Danielle. I just miss that particular relationship benefit—fairly regular sex, no matter how many late hours you work."

Jack smiled. "The lad is looking to get laid tonight, is he?"

At the back of the game room was a door that Michael had never seen open. He'd even wondered if it was a faux door. But there it was: With a quiet click, the door opened, and into the game room marched a small, formal-looking crowd of people. Two guys in suits—security guards—two middle-aged men in suits, a woman in a more formal dress gown and a woman in a dress suit, a photographer, and the subject of his attention: A tall, handsome, older man in a suit, wearing a bolo tie. Next to and slightly behind him was a gray-haired and somewhat older, bespeckled gentleman, also dressed in business attire. Behind these two followed another photographer, and a man and a woman closer to Michael's age, but dressed in a manner similar to their bosses, in a suit and a pants suit, and two security guards at the rear.

They marched in and crossed through the room, heading purposefully for the main floor. The man in the bolo tie lifted his sunglasses and looked Michael's way. He smiled and nodded at Michael.

Jack had stopped playing pinball while the group passed. He looked at Michael curiously.

"That's my 'Uncle' Bill. Not really my uncle. My dad's best friend. My family ties to Cheronkin County go back."

"That a big posse he's got."

"My dad thinks my uncle is gearing up to run for governor," Michael said.

"I know that for almost any issue that the community faces, sides are quickly drawn and a healthy debate can always be counted on to ensue. There are a few issues on which we can reach easy consensus, but I think we are all in agreement that Marble Canyon Road here is not a safe road, and that it needs to be repaired."

There were a lot of people present, many of whom Michael had never seen in the club before, day or night. Having lived with the ongoing refurbishment, this new incarnation of their landmark would seem to have offered few surprises for the locals beyond a particularly strong musical lineup and the promise of appearances by some additional house favorites from the past. None of which had ever before drawn them out in force.

The draw was Senator Bill Clayton, who had the power to fill seats on his own.

"I'm here to tell you that an agreement has been reached in the Legislature and will soon be signed by the Governor; that all parties and all claims related to the tragic accidents on Marble Canyon Road have been settled, and that repair work on the road will begin shortly. Additionally, upon completion of repairs, the state has agreed to place the custodianship of the road—and of the parkland reserves that surround Marble Canyon Road—in the hands of the people of Cheronkin County."

Loud applause echoed through the room.

The senator was in full gear by the time Laura had made her way up front. Clapping along, Laura surveyed the room. She was nervous.

Long before tonight's announcement, there had been much discussion about the impact of the road repairs on the local service economy. It may have been a year of the most beautiful, temperate weather in Cheronkin history as well as along the whole Pacific shoreline, but it wouldn't matter if there weren't any people passing through town on their way to enjoy it. Conventional wisdom in these previously hypothetical debates (and amongst those businesses with their eyes on tapping into their share of the state's anticipated settlement to buffer against losses) had one in three businesses closing their doors by the end of summer thanks to the road work.

Fandango was relatively secure in terms of traffic, due to its proximity to the freeway and a dearth of upscale food establishments in the area.

This dire financial outlook impacted very few of the current attendees. Come the new century, the area known as old Cheronkin County was a well-heeled community of independent wealth. There were more than a few residents who would not only never feel the negative effects of the road closure, but who might even have hoped for such an event because it would both stem the always increasing flux of people into the area, and make the locale generally more exclusive.

A middle-aged rhythm-and-blues singer, a woman who played guitar and piano, was getting her set started up. The hanging monitors began to flicker on throughout the club, each one filled with her image. People were moving comfortably throughout the club, to the bar, to the pool tables, walking among the art pieces and inspecting just what had been done to the place overall. There were even a few people out on the dance floor, already swaying to the music.

Laura had tried to impart a sense of her understanding of the true spirit of the space into the redesign. The interior had been detailed with decorative and architectural flourishes in homage to the history of the club. Old photos, old furniture, old arcade games. She had been able to track down items from several different eras in the club's history by studying old photographs that had been pinned to the walls outside the restroom, and by picking the minds of the old-timers who clustered around the bar in the afternoon. Still, Laura thought, something wasn't right. The place was more polished and finished than anyone might have ever intended it to be. Was it too shiny?

Laura would have preferred to have kept all of the old wood in the downstairs lounge, with decades' worth of etchings and engravings, for instance, but the dry rot and the termite infestations had made that impossible. The banks of lights and the monitors that lined the ceilings gave the interior a tad too technological of a look. It was modern.

It was state-of-the art. It had never been like that before.

Jack's art pieces seemed in sync with the club, both old and new. Clear glass sculpture work in abstract shapes that, from a distance and bathed by the color-tinted lights overhead, resembled the bubbles that stacked themselves in lava lamps. Up close, they lent themselves to interpretation as to what they depicted, but people seemed to be having a good time discussing and debating what it was they were seeing.

When Michael ran into his aunt again, he was surprised to find her talking to his mother and standing not far from his Uncle Bill.

"Mom!"

"Hi, hon."

The senator was speaking to a gray-haired woman Michael didn't recognize. It wasn't the same woman he'd entered the building with. There was something about her—perhaps the lack of makeup—that made him think she must be a local. She was a tall woman, with a long, sharp face, with pointed features and shiny skin.

As if she felt him looking at her, she turned while she was speaking and stared back at Michael with startlingly blue eyes.

He looked away immediately.

Michael viewed his mother's presence with some ambivalence. His pleasure at seeing her out in public again was tempered by the realization this might just be too much for her. The last thing they needed was a meltdown. Gone was the unstoppable woman who once would have been eagerly charging through the crowd, calling out the names of the people she intended to corner for a donation or a contribution to whatever cause she was involved with at the time. Tonight, the tentativeness of her gestures, the anxious way she seemed to be looking around the club, as if someone were about to jump her, made Michael want to squirm.

"I don't think I've seen you since Easter," Laura was saying to Melinda. He decided to linger, thinking his aunt would have more slips of paper to pass to him.

"Oh, my goodness, is that true?" His mother leaned in and kissed Michael on the cheek while squeezing his arm. "Then I owe you a double apology, because I was not myself."

"As always, you were the perfect hostess. I had no idea anything was wrong—I think you said you were having trouble sleeping. And I can see by how fabulous you look that it isn't an issue anymore, am I right?"

"You do look great, Mom," Michael said.

That seemed to catch Melinda off guard. She looked for a moment as if she were trying to remember something. And then she shook her head, as if it were something she wanted to forget.

"Having a lot of prescriptions filled, is what it was. I had to . . . switch doctors unexpectedly and somehow wound up in the hands of Dr. Prozac. I've since given up on the modern pharmaceutical industry. At dinner that night, I was at the end of my wits because I couldn't find my pills, my damn pills. It still bothers me, wondering where they went, but thank goodness I lost them that night. That's not to say I've solved all the issues I was concerned about, health-wise. But I think things are moving forward."

"Well, you look marvelous. Best I've seen you in ages."

"I feel like I'm a hundred years old."

"I wouldn't judge myself by anyone in this crowd. Honestly. We've known some of these women going on twenty years now. They should be ashamed of themselves. That Kathy Anders planted a big wet kiss on my cheek with lips that just this afternoon she'd had pumped full with fat from her ass . . ."

"Laura!"

Michael saw some sort of signal go between Laura, Uncle Bill, and the man who continually whispered in Uncle Bill's ear. He said to the older woman in front of him that she should "speak to Jacob, and he'll talk you through it." Then he shook her hand.

Laura said, "I wanted to have a frank discussion with our dear friend, the Senator, about the importance of getting Marble Canyon Road fixed in a timely manner."

His aunt leaned in and excused herself, and when his mom turned to see what she had missed she wound up looking right into Uncle Bill's face. They exchanged quick, warm greetings, without the familiar hug that would follow if they were not in public.

Laura emptied her glass, set it on one of the tables, and stared at it for a moment as if she were wondering how long she was going to have to make herself wait before having her next. It was early yet, but clearly, Michael thought, she was going to be drunk by the end of the night.

And the next wave of people was starting to arrive in a strong, steady flow.

Michael leaned in toward his mom. "I'm going to go do a couple things, then I'll come back to check on you."

"Don't worry about me."

He thought about it a moment. "Is Dad here?"

"Yes, someplace. Scoot along."

As he walked away, the silver-haired lady was approaching his mother with a thoughtful look on her face. A few minutes later, when he was pulled into the kitchen by one of the chefs, he saw Talia walking up to the two women, saying hello, and kissing the gray-haired woman on the cheek.

By the time he returned, his mother and the silver-haired lady were gone. Talia remained, staring at one of Jack's sculptures. When he approached her on the pretext of wanting to find his mother, she looked up at him, and it was apparent by her expression that something had changed.

He tried not to look dismayed. There was no telling what Melinda might have said. "I guess I've lost the edge I had with mystique on my side," he said.

And she actually smiled at that. "Once you meet the mom, the mystery is gone."

He looked at her a moment, unable to interpret the look in her eyes; was it interest or was it pity or was it attraction or was it sympathy? Even if it were nothing like the heart-gripping rush of feeling that took him over, he knew there was something there that she felt for him.

115

He sighed. That was enough for him for now. He turned to survey the room, which was getting noisier, and she turned, too, so that they were standing side by side.

"Did you get a time slot to sing?"

"Somewhere at the end of a long line at the end of the night," she said, "if I stay that long. The lounge stage."

"That's exactly where you should be. Little lounge, little bar, it's practically a grotto. It's a great-sounding room. That'll be great. If you stay that long." He heard someone call his name. It was a familiar voice. He couldn't focus on it enough to figure out who it belonged to.

Talia heard it, too. "I'm going to go look around some more," she said.

"Good. Take your time." Take a good long time, he thought as he watched her go.

"Is that your dream girl? Michael! She's black! What would your mother say?"

It was Mary's best friend, Carina. The only one of Mary's friends who wasn't worthless. "I wondered about that myself. I think there's a possibility it would be something Melinda would wear like a badge of honor."

Carina was kooky, but in an endearing way. Tonight she seemed especially so. She'd always been able to make Michael laugh. "You're probably right. Didn't you have three kids from the projects live with you when you were younger?"

"For, like, a year," he shrugged.

"I always admired that about your family." A pause. "When I first met Mary and I thought your family was so much better than mine, I used to like to imagine I was that little girl living in your guestroom."

"You're kidding, right?"

"That's goofier than you imagining introducing 'Ms. All That' to your mother."

"I think they just met about ten minutes ago."

"Not really."

"Yeah. And I have no idea what happened or what was said."

"Double ouch."

"And I think it's okay for me to talk to her now, should I choose to approach her."

"Really. Did you get some signal about that?"

116

"Yes. And it's because of her talking to Mom."

"Really?"

"I think so." When Talia was out of view, he turned to Carina. She was eating from a plate of complimentary hors d'ouerves.

"Love the free food," she said. "I can't do happy hour anymore because I'm on the road, usually up north, and all I want is to get home. I miss the free appetizers at happy hour. Of course, it's not really free: I just spent fifteen dollars on Listerine in the ladies' room. That lady is making, like, a hundred-fifty percent markup."

"I'm afraid to ask about the mouthwash."

"Oh, I had an interview today after work. I'm trying to sort of change my workload around so I can work on my Masters—"

"Your Masters degree?"

"Yes. Don't smirk. And I'm doing it the real way. Not phoning or mailing it in, you know. Anyway, I want to cut back on my hours at the office and balance it out by working another job later in the evening. So, I went on this interview right after work, and I was really hungry, and it was with this sweet old lady with no teeth and she was really, really moving slowly when she went upstairs to get her paperwork. And there was this bowl of nuts on the desk. I don't know what they were—shelled almonds or cashews—but they were right there on the end table next to the couch. So I had one, and it wasn't wax, so I had another, and I had another and finally, she was gone so long, I ate all of them."

"Oh. That's not good."

"She came back, finally, and I apologized right away: 'I'm so sorry, I was so hungry, they were so tasty,' and on and on until she stops me. She says, 'Don't worry, honey. I can't eat those anyway with my teeth . . .'

"'Still,' I say, 'I'm sorry.' Well, she put her hand on mine to stop me, and she said, 'My grandkids send me the chocolates for the holidays each year. I can't eat the nuts inside, but I suck off the chocolate and put the nuts in that bowl. I'm glad to see them not go to waste.'"

Michael was still laughing five minutes later as they crossed the lobby, until Carina stopped him with her arm and pointed at Mary, who was studying either the positioning of the sculptures or else the map of Cheronkin County proper, old parts and new etched into the floor beneath them.

"I was just going to ask you," Carina said, "when you finished laughing at me, where your sister has been hiding."

Though he wasn't with her constantly over the next few hours, Michael was with Mary enough, and had seen in Carina's body language toward Mary enough to know that his sister was not at all herself. Something had been different about his brief contacts with her the last few weeks, although up until now he'd been able to dismiss it as a result of both of them having busy schedules.

But this was the sort of event on which her life did normally thrive, especially in light of the close connection she enjoyed with the club's latest owner. She had the home field advantage working for her in so many ways that this should have been her personal playground this evening.

And yet, she was somewhat detached from the proceedings. It didn't matter to her how many good-looking guys there were in the room, or whether any of them had in even the slightest way noticed her. She hadn't dressed to attract their attention, eschewing the revealing attire favored during this most tropical of winters for a more conservative look. She wasn't touching alcohol, hadn't yet perused the banquet fare, and, uncharacteristically entertained herself by browsing the sculptures, listening to the music, and taking a slow tour through the club to witness the changes, rather than frittering the time away from a perch from which she could check out the crowd and search for that person or persons who may or may not have been eyeing her.

As the hours passed, the club grew more chaotic. Things were flowing as far as Michael could see. Tables were turning over in the dining room, the crowd was moving and mixing and drinking, and all the music was top notch. When Michael found Mary, she was seated at a table near the C stage, where a band called the Vulgars was playing their reggae-accented surf tunes.

"Do you remember them?"

"From high school. Yeah. It was one of my theme groups when I was learning to surf. I came here with a fake ID to hear them play and was so proud when I left with all these different guys' phone numbers. Of course, as soon as I was legal, then all the Cheronkin nightspots suddenly became too back-country for us, remember?, and 'clubbing' meant heading out looking for men in the city."

Carina returned to the table carrying two drinks.

"Cosmo for me. Arnold Palmer for you."

Just hearing their particular sound brought Mary back to days of simpler pleasures. She asked, "Have you seen Jack?"

"He's around here somewhere. Suddenly Casanova's all shy. What do you think of the art?"

"I don't know yet. They're almost like optical illusions, aren't they? I was just staring at that one in the lobby, just trying to absorb the kaleidoscopic effect of all the reflective surfaces, to see it for what it was. It was almost like looking at an extreme Cubist painting, or a trick three-dimensional photograph, and I was getting so frustrated when I saw—I just saw it—there were three women I was staring at, all standing back to back in a circle, with their long, exaggerated arms raised high above their heads. And now that I've been looking at them a while, I think they're really amazing. Once I could see what it was, all the detail that was there became obvious."

"The detail! They're a bunch of blobs. I could do that myself if I knew how to work with glass." Carina smiled at them. "I thought they were plants at first because the bottoms of the first ones I saw looked like roots." A stocky guy passing by Carina touched her arm, and when she looked at him they both smiled and gave each other an awkward hug.

Michael turned to his sister. "You're not drinking?"

"I know," Mary said. "Unusual. I'm sort of experimenting with the idea of trying to sort of, I don't know, de-toxify myself."

"What inspired this?"

"Someone convinced me I might benefit from living a purer existence."

"How's it going?"

"Surprisingly well. I feel better. We'll see how it is when it has set in a little."

Michael could see there was something going on inside her, and that she wasn't going to talk about it.

She nodded at seeing his accepting that. "There's a good vibe in here tonight, so it's fun. We'll see how it is when Carina is puking out in the parking lot and I'm dead sober."

And like that, Carina was back. "You're not trying to grow back your virginity," she said, "are you?"

Both girls laughed.

Someone touched Michael's elbow. It was a busboy, Juan. Michael excused himself and followed him to the lounge downstairs.

Eli Phillips stood in Fandango's back doorway unnoticed, admiring his sister's handiwork.

When he was younger—when he was half his current age, in fact—there was a bar he used to frequent whenever he happened to be in the area. He went to college at the state university, and it happened that he knew quite a few people who lived in the general vicinity of Cheronkin.

This bar he went to was a little place, sandwiched between a bakery and a drugstore. This place was the worst. A dive. It was dark and smelled of mildew, and everything inside looked cracked or out of order. The tables all had matchbooks under the legs, there were knife carvings all over the walls and all the drapes were torn and ragged.

It looked like some kind of sleazy strip joint from the sidewalk. There would be loud, live music, sometimes good, sometimes great, and all that was visible from the street was this dimly lit hallway that turned right sharply, at the end. The kind of hallway a wise person should always feel half nervous about walking down for fear of what was waiting at the other end.

Eli was never sure what was going to happen in that place. The owner was a seedy guy who had a lot of connections in the music industry and always had these exceptional blues and jazz acts scheduled. He and Bill Clayton would take a table in the corner during the day, and they would play chess in the afternoon, and shoot the breeze with whoever happened to be in a talking mood. There were fights, there were arguments, there were scenes, and sometimes there were even stars popping in for a chat and a drink.

That place was Murray's Hat.

Fandango wasn't Murray's Hat. At least not on the surface. Mirrors and lightshows, coordinated pastel decor, a copper bar top, plants and pedestals all over the place. Glitzy and sparkly. Designed with inspiration and flair. That was what he had judged it by, the few times he'd been able to stop by.

But after having the chance to stroll around, without Laura as an escort, he could see that his sister had managed to preserve something of the old Hat. There were pool tables and pinball machines set up in the wing where the Hallmark shop used to be. They had always wanted a pool table at Murray's. And he could see that the kids who came in were still playing board games, backgammon and checkers. And the music, if the tail end of the last show was any indication, was still top of the line.

Laura had done a great job. Enough for his chest to swell some with pride.

He wished he had arrived early enough to see Bill. He'd meant to be on time. But there was no cutting down on the drive in from the airport. And, figuring Melinda was already on her way home, as long as Eli was there in time to help Laura into her office or back to her house to sleep her liquor off, he was right on time.

He concluded his tour and walked up to the balcony. The patio was quiet, all but vacated, except for a group of four or five kids goofing around one of the heat lamps. The lighting wasn't good enough to be sure, but from the sound of their voices and laughter, they were all happy and smashed.

Who was he to begrudge them this? Was it his job to remind them all of what was going on in the world outside? As far as it was from the war front to the East coast, it was even farther to California. And the people in Washington were no longer in touch with the realities of war; they had for so long been more concerned with maintaining the illusion of inevitable victory at home that they had come to accept that illusion as the reality they had to work with. But out here, it was much worse. No one wanted to hear about the war. Everybody knew the war was there and had been in one form or another for two decades, yet very few seemed aware that life here couldn't continue the way it was. To them, this pocket of the world was safe. There was a clear feeling among them that it would never really affect them.

Was it his job to tell them the truth? That as the days and weeks and months and years passed, and the war continued, it *was* going to affect them, and more and more, until, quite possibly, it would swallow their lives.

When Michael returned, both Mary and Carina were seated, gabbing and laughing away.

Mary said, "That guy she was talking to? She dated him seven years ago."

"Yuck," Carina said. She seemed embarrassed and slightly drunk.

Mary laughed and clapped her hands. "He just told her that after they broke up he bought a poodle and named her Carina because he liked saying her name so much." Mary laughed and laughed. "She sleeps under the covers in bed with him and licks his toes to wake him up in the morning!" She couldn't stop laughing.

Carina asked, "Where'd you go?"

"Oh, there was a couple having sex in the men's bathroom. The attendant stepped out for some reason and they slipped right in, so to speak. It was an Australian couple—have you seen them? I think there's a group of them renting a house for the summer on Vista."

"Oh, I saw them making out in a booth earlier."

"Yeah, I guess they couldn't wait. A nine-year-old boy walked in on them because he was worried about all the noises he was hearing from the stall."

"Really? What did you do?"

"I didn't shake his hand when he exited the bathroom and offered his apology. But what could I do?"

They were all quiet.

Carina said, "Everybody's letting their hair down tonight."

Mary turned to Michael. "I have a few questions for you. About Jack."

Michael looked surprised. "What do you want to know? And why don't you ask Jack?"

"What's his story?"

"I don't know. He doesn't talk about it much. He says he has amnesia—that he can't remember a lot of things before, like, six months ago. I'm not sure if he's pulling my leg or not, but I sort of believe him."

"Not really."

"Yeah, that's what I thought, too."

122

"Was he in an accident?"

"Yes. In Texas, a building collapsed on him. He's said a couple of things about knowing about things that had happened to him only because other people had told him about those things. I guess I sort of think it's true now."

"Is he doing anything to help himself? Like medicine, therapy, hypnosis?"

"He said the doctors he's seen have told him it might come back, or it might not."

Michael saw the two of them settling in for some feminine analysis. He knew he wouldn't be able to answer any probing questions they might ask on the matter, because he didn't spend his time with Jack asking such things. It was probably better not to know, especially for occasions such as this. He stood and excused himself. "I'll be back." He was pleased to have given them some good gossip to play with.

Michael sat at what he considered the best seat in the house, the second booth from the stage in the lounge, a position he had claimed mentally the night before while closing out and which he had staked out with a reserved sign an hour before.

Once the indoor show started, it was immediately worth the wait, as he'd known it would be. For this event alone, this night was a dream come true for Michael. Here he was, some sort of insider, with close familial connections to the head of the house, and all night long as he'd been moving back and forth throughout the club, he'd had a ringside seat to a roll call of some of the most notable artists who had graced the performance stages in the last forty years. He was bumping into them in the backstage areas, seeing them warming up, watching them getting excited about some of the other people they were going to be seeing. Some were still recording today, some had long since faded into obscurity. Many he had seen perform at the club before, others he'd only wished he'd had the chance to see.

No one gave their stories because the sets were short and packed tight together. Two or three songs for most acts. Michael probably would have stayed up for three days if that was what it took to hear everyone's stories since they'd last played the club. He could have sat happy as all get out in that booth through a weeklong festival to hear it all.

123

Plus, there was a sense of house pride in his chest as he surveyed the crowd. It was good to see the place packed again, to have it filled with energy, to see the club living up once again to its promise.

A door across the lounge swung open, and Michael saw his aunt standing just outside, her head rocking backward in laughter that echoed off the walls until the door closed. Although she didn't drink often, when she did she was a high-functioning drunk, albeit too ready with a raunchy joke and a bit loud.

Michael looked around him as the band took their positions. Everybody was just letting go all over the place. Was it worse than usual? He wasn't ready to say that—he didn't know what was usual for a crowd like this. But on top of all the people who were dancing and talking and eating and drinking, there were drugs being smoked and inhaled in every bathroom and in a corner of every outdoor patio; there was a lot of promiscuous behavior, chest flashing, lip-mashing, couples making out, feeling each other up to the point of that's enough, and most of these people were just getting started drinking.

The minute Talia stepped on the small stage and started singing, most of them stopped what they were doing and listened. Or else he just blocked them all out and he thought they did, too. Talia had wrangled herself a piano player from another band that had already played. She didn't even need him. She could have sung a cappella. She sang two songs he'd never heard of, one an old-fashioned-sounding blues tune "Things Are Gonna Change for the Better," and the other was almost like a hip-hop torch song, "You Treated Me Wrong."

"Isn't she a pistol?" he heard someone nearby say.

"She's incredible."

" . . . Wow."

Michael was near bursting with satisfaction. He knew she would slay them all. Her voice was incredibly full, though not controlled enough to be considered polished. She was not comfortable at all onstage, but that worked fine. It added a weird sort of tension. The discomfort softened the defiance she exuded. By the sneer nearly omnipresent on her lips, it might seem that she really didn't care about these

124

people at all, and yet she was afraid of them, and yet singing for them was all she wanted to do.

There was no denying it. He was falling in love with her.

The club was indeed nearly out of control when Michael slipped out of the lounge after Talia's set. People were dancing on tables in the restaurant portion of the club—the sound from the main stage was being pumped across the whole floor of the club. An Asian/Latin fusion band was playing. He thought for a minute that perhaps he should do something about the people on the tables; but then, he didn't want to spend the rest of the evening chasing people from tabletops. Instead, he headed back to the table upstairs, hoping Mary and Carina would still be around.

They waved at him.

"How was your dream girl?"

"Awesome. She has a great voice."

"And a great body."

Carina said, "I'm going to the bathroom."

He asked Mary, "So you did see her?"

"I peeked in. I think she's kind of off-putting. There was something about her, the way she looked between songs, that seemed to look as if she were somehow bored by the crowd."

"Yeah, I see that. It's weird, but I guess that kind of turns me on about her."

"You did look a little droolly in there."

Michael stood and looked over the edge of the railing, at the field that stretched out beside the club. Were there that many trees there, really? Or were there people out there, too? It wasn't a serious thought at first. But he kept looking, and then, he wasn't sure.

"Hey," he started to say, turning before he realized Mary was standing right next to him. "Oh, hi."

The door opened below them and Talia emerged, pulling her wrap around her as she moved away at a good pace. Her posture as she moved was more relaxed. Even carefree. She looked lighter than before. It had been good for her to do this.

Mary was watching him. "She's way out of your league."

"She's way out of my universe. It's still cool that I've gotten to meet her. I know it's not going to get me any action tonight."

"Or any night soon. What, you're desperate to score?"

"Otherwise, I'm afraid I'm going to find myself driving an hour and a half just to get laid by my lonely ex-girlfriend."

"You should just go home with Carina." Mary giggled. "She's easy and available. And fun, from what I've heard."

"Right," he said. Carina was, actually, the best-looking of Mary's friends. And his favorite. As a teenager, she had been one of the girls on his unattainable list: Greatly desired but just beyond reach.

"She's been raving about you all night . . ."

"It's this haircut. People can't resist it."

"I know, it's a great cut," she said with professional admiration, running her fingers through the hair above his ear.

They were both quiet. Michael stared at something he was sure was a person. Just standing there, watching the club. Maybe watching the two of them.

He looked at his sister. "Are you okay?"

"I'm working on it. It's getting better. My new purity living thing is actually helping."

"If you ever . . ."

"Not about this. Not ever. But it will be fine."

Quiet again.

Finally, not really expecting an answer, and, at least, expecting to have to go into an explanation of what he was referring to, he said, "What do you think they're doing out there?" He was talking about the Hill People. He was sure they were out in that field, watching the club. Watching Mary and himself. "I feel like they're popping up more and more." He didn't think she would know what he was talking about. He wasn't sure he wanted to talk about it with her. He thought she would just make fun.

"I don't know. Something in the air is drawing them here and drawing them out. We can't feel it, but they can."

"We're talking about the people . . . out there?"

"That's what I'm talking about, Michael. We're talking about the same thing, yes?"

"Yes."

"They're watching us now," she said. "Not just us, though. Everyone out here."

Carina called out her name from the line leading into the women's bathroom, and Mary smiled at him. "I'm gonna go wait in line with her." She squeezed his arm as she stood up and left.

Sometime before two, the crowd had noticeably thinned without losing any of its enthusiasm. Much of the club had been cleaned up and put away—the kitchen was closed—and so the folks still dancing on the tables and canoodling in the booths and smoking around the bar were doing so in an atmosphere that seemed very much post-party. Michael was watching the band Boondoggle on the main stage when a bolt of electricity flashed on the stage mid-song, mid-beat, and the lights went out throughout the club. Some club employee kept his head among the momentary confusion marked by the shocked screams of several females and the drunken laughter at the surprise of darkness. That employee clicked on his lighter, and in just a few minutes employees were lighting candles across the club. Very drunk and having problems with the intercom system on her first attempts, Aunt Laura's voice piped out of the vintage grilles which had been left in place throughout the club in another decorative tribute to the past.

"Thank you for sharing with us the official re-opening of Club Fandango, open for breakfast, lunch, and dinner every day of the week and offering the region's best musical lineups every Wednesday through Saturday night. If you need help exiting the club, please ask anyone armed with a candle for assistance."

Then, weirdly enough, after a bit of confusion and jostling, a majority of the attendees quietly and calmly gathered their things and exited the building as candles continued to be lit throughout the interior. A strange and respectful hush gripped a room that was rocking minutes before. The candlelight danced and sparkled on the reflective surfaces of the sculptures, and people laughed and talked in low voices as they exited. It gave Fandango an almost churchlike quality.

Michael seated himself among the last callers at the bar, asked for a beer and received with a nod of acknowledgment a pitcher from the bartender, Matt, another old-timer who was just in to help out for the night. Michael downed it gradually as the bar crowd thinned and the caterers cleaned by candlelight.

Jack appeared from the darkness at some point, sat down next to Michael and ordered a line of five tequila shots. He passed one to Michael, and they both downed a glassful.

Michael poured him a glass of beer. "So what's the plan?"

"I was thinking of getting a cab to the city."

"Not really. You don't want a booty call that comes with that much baggage. This is the part of the evening where you're just supposed to wait until you're so drunk that you're no longer that particular and neither is the other person."

"Yeah. We all don't have the same process here."

Jack smiled. He waited until Janet had moved down the bar to wash some glasses, and then leaned in closer to Michael. The whisper of Jack's voice sent a chill down his back. "Mike, I'm ready to go. I've been drinking all night. I'm long past not feeling all that particular."

Michael chuckled at that a little bit, until he sat back and saw Jack was expecting a response. Jack was picking up on him? Was that what had just happened? He looked around, suddenly feeling conspicuous, and was relieved there was no one nearby to overhear them. "I didn't know you did that."

"I don't, usually. I don't have a strict policy. As far as I can remember."

"Look at that, man, and you're so smooth with it," Michael said, impressed. "That makes me wonder if the amnesia thing is really just an angle."

There wasn't the least bit of embarrassment about Jack's manner as he downed another shot. It was all very low-key, a throw-away pickup, and brazen at the same time. Jack grinned. "That said . . ."

Without really thinking what he was doing, Michael stood, and pulled on his jacket.

Jack, surprised, waited a minute, then did the same.

They started walking toward the front. Michael thought, I'm not going anywhere with him. Not like that. I'm just going back to my car to pass out. Am I doing this?

Michael looked around one last time as he walked toward the door. Was anybody watching? Only Janet. She waved at him, and he waved back, feeling embarrassed in a way he never had before. And then he was outside, and all he was really sure of in the state he was in—and he was, really, too drunk even to fuck, or to make decisions about fucking, wasn't he?—all he was really sure of was that he didn't want to go home alone tonight.

7

The Grand Reopening
Same Night, Different Perspective

"You know, honey," an older woman's voice said from nearby, "you can let go of a lot of it. Most of it. The more black junk you drain out of yourself, the more sinks down into Mother Earth. She takes all of our pains in. She makes them her own."

Melinda, not sure that it was she being addressed, didn't look to find the speaker for two reasons.

The first had to do with a strange occurrence a few hours earlier, at home, when she'd been preparing herself for tonight. Eli had called to tell her he would be meeting her at the club instead of coming home first. His flight had been delayed and then rerouted north, blah blah blah, so he'd be meeting her at the club instead of driving with her.

Before he'd called, she'd been in her slip, applying eye makeup and feeling distressed by the amount of hair she was seeing in the sink on a daily basis. More hair there than there should have been unless she was having an issue or some prescriptive drug side effect. She just couldn't understand it, how much hair she seemed to be losing every day. Already her face seemed wider and longer.

That was the excuse she was looking for to not go to the club. Sudden onset thinning of the hair, and wigs were no longer in fashion. She wasn't going to go, she decided, though she kept putting on her mascara. It was a bad idea.

As she was thinking this thought, a voice on the radio said, very clearly, and seemingly directly to her: "It's important that you go to the club." It was a man's voice, deep, and it was gone as quickly as she realized what had been said. And when she turned to the radio, it wasn't even on. Eli liked to listen while he primped, not her.

And so she didn't wish to turn to find the owner of the voice at the club in case that there really wasn't anyone there.

"Once the Earth takes in our worst stuff," the older woman's voice continued, "it goes through something like a mulching process inside her. The iron heart of the world, the womb itself, heats it and the skin on top helps it cook. The good news is the black junk comes out of the process in the form of energy that feeds our bodies and our spirits and our minds. This is one of the ways our souls gather energy from the Earth and it is also how the womb feeds and lives. And the good news is, the more junk you give to Mother Earth, the more good stuff you have coming back in the form of energy to feed your soul."

The other reason Melinda didn't want to look was because she knew somewhere inside that she was going to turn and find herself face to face with one of the three women she had thought she had seen at the airport. Likely the older one.

She turned, and, indeed, it was the older woman. Melinda surprised herself by drawing up the nerve that had gotten her through years of community activism, and she smiled. She heard herself saying, "That sounds familiar, like something I might have studied in school. Is it Buddhist?"

The older woman's eyes sparkled at Melinda. "I've heard it many places, and repeated it so many times I don't know where I heard it first, but I always found it reassuring that someone was benefiting from my pain, much less the entire planet."

"My name is Melinda Phillips," she said, detaching from herself as she watched her hand shake the other woman's hand. It was comforting to find the woman to be tangible, that she didn't vanish into the air. That her hand didn't pass right through her. Ever the knee-jerk ambassador, she heard herself saying, "I'm a longtime resident of Cheronkin, and I feel like I could tell you who just about anyone in the room is." She released the hand, then pressed her hand against the woman's arm. "And even though I would say you do look familiar, I don't believe we've met."

"My name is Elena. Elena Altman." Her aura sparkled as brightly as her eyes, casting white clusters of light in all directions around her.

"Altman? Not of Altman Holdings." Altman had always been about growth limits, property development limits. Not kids in need, nor community. She had filed them under Environmental/Growth issues.

131

"Yes, dear, that's one of my accounts. How do you know that name?"

"Oh," she said, "I have been very involved in community events for many years. Your company was one I often turned to for support. For those times you lent it, thank you. You helped us with the Marble Canyon Road issue."

"I think I recognize your name, Melinda. You were involved with something else, a community event."

"The Harvest Ball. Yes, I used to be very involved."

"I haven't heard anything about it this year."

"Oh, I don't think it will be happening this year. That event had its day when the last local farm closed. This will have to do. This club's been here longer than all of us."

"Than I'm glad I came. I told my niece I was feeling that it was important that I be here."

Melinda considered for a moment sharing her own experience earlier in the day, when the voice from the radio had said the very same thing, but stopped herself.

Elena saw in her expression an opening, and made her move. "I don't want to be too . . ." she started to say, but then stopped herself, as if she couldn't get the words out of her mouth. This irritated her, but she began again. "When I first saw you this evening, I saw a look on your face and in your eyes that I believe I recognized from . . . personal experience. I've been in that place and it would have been good for me if someone in the know had had the nerve to say something to me."

"I don't know . . ." Melinda stammered, more off guard than she would have expected. She looked around for an exit from the conversation, flight instinct kicking into gear, and saw then the beautiful black girl approaching them, who had also been at the airport that afternoon. So that hadn't been her imagination, either. This was her niece?

"The therapies used for so-called 'past regression' can leave a person terribly confused. Do you find yourself catching yourself mid-sentence and remembering something that never happened to you in your life? Do you dream about places you've never been, remember names of towns and streets and the look of landscapes you've never visited or seen? It's enough to make a person think there is a reason the human mind chooses not to remember—it isn't equipped to deal with the enormity of it." She smiled at Melinda's astonished

132

expression. "But really, a doctor won't be able to lead you through it. Especially not a man. I know you'll find your way, honey. You can find me if you need to talk. There is a new reality coming. The signs are all around us. You know it, honey. Believe me, you'll be better off for having opened the doors you're opening here and now. And remember, you're not alone. There are others just like you, and they've come out the other side of what you're going through—and it is a tough road, I know from my own experience—and they've all come to understand that it is a blessing."

Elena touched the back of Melinda's hand as she turned to greet her visitor, and although the gesture was meant to be comforting, Melinda felt a chill. When Elena had said the words "new reality," an image flashed behind her eyes: the streets of Cheronkin derelict and overgrown, houses crumbling in the midst of an encroaching forest. Her children God knew where, if God hadn't given up on the whole experiment by now.

Elena held out and squeezed the younger girl's hand.

"Hi, Auntie," Melinda heard the younger girl say, "checking out the artwork?"

"I was about to—I've been chatting instead. Talia, this is Melinda Phillips."

Talia looked at her carefully, then extended her hand. If there was any real recognition, Melinda didn't sense it. She relaxed a little. She wasn't sure what she'd seen at the airport that day, exactly. And she had been a bit overwrought. It could have been a little bit of reality mixed with overall exhaustion and too much time with the Pill Doctor.

"Nice to meet you," Melinda said.

"Pleasure."

They all three stared at the piece of sculpture before them.

Elena said, "It reminds me of that young fellow, the boy who became a writer. It was the Arthur family next door when I first moved in. Richard Arthur. Dick Arthur was his published name."

"I know that name from my children's school. Both of my children had to do the same unit on notables from the community."

"He was the boy who lived next door when I first moved here," Elena said.

"Which was when?"

"Fifty years ago. Although I do travel quite a bit, this place is the touchstone I always return to. I thought it was my calling to be here. To be a sentry, waiting for this day to come, and hoping to be able to witness it. I'd had a vision that I was to be a part of something here, that I was to play a role. I was lonely. There was so much pain I'd left behind me. And this neighbor boy was lonely because his parents neglected him. It was a time when I'd just recently been thinking that I'd wanted a child and I was starting to accept the notion that I wasn't going to have one. And there he was on the other side of the fence ready to chat . . ."

("Your hair is so white," he said. "Are you an angel?"

"Certainly not."

"Are you a witch?"

"Perhaps I am, but not the way you mean it."

"Who is the man who follows you around? Is that your husband?"

"There's no man here."

"Yes, there is, I've seen him many times. A sad-looking man who loves you very much. He follows you around wherever you go.")

Elena's eyes were focused on the past for a moment, and she paused and cleared her throat before speaking again. "One night, for about an hour under the moon, I told him all sorts of tales."

"This was here in Cheronkin?"

"Yes, dear. Well, fifteen years later, what I hear is that there is a book out by this young man. He'd grown up, yes." She laughed. "And one of the stories in his book described that night, and whatever stories I had spun, he far outdid me. He'd blown them up even more . . . turned me into a night enchantress! I can't remember . . ." Elena lost her train of thought. The glow around her softened a little and then returned, although there was a slight scowl that appeared in her voice. "These statues remind me of that story—the way he described the fairy spirits he'd imagined when hearing my stories . . ."

In the end, it didn't sound to Melinda like the fond association Elena had been making when the story started.

Melinda wasn't sure if Elena were done, and she held on the elder woman's last word, waiting. She looked at Talia; for all her impassiveness, she sensed the younger girl was a little thrown by her aunt's behavior.

". . . You know, Melinda, there is one thing I discovered in uncovering my past lives. This is where all those many paths were leading me. In every life, this is where I always wanted to be. This is when and where I've been living my lives to be." She stopped herself and said, "My, I'm talkative tonight . . ." One look at her "niece" confirmed this fact and then she stopped herself, searched around the room a moment, her glance fluttering to the ceiling and flitting through the crowd while she clucked her tongue quietly against her gums.

And then her eyes settled on the statue before them. The white aura around her popped and sizzled. She scanned the room. Was she looking at the other sculptures, or was she looking for their creator? And then, abruptly, "Melinda, will you please excuse me?" And then, to Talia: "Will you please walk me to the car, dear?" Talia nodded. "I want to talk to you more, but this isn't . . ." And again, whatever it was she was going to say, whatever excuse she was going to make, she couldn't get it out. "We'll have to figure out a way to talk about this more in depth."

They left quickly. Melinda watched them go without moving.

A couple moved into the spot Elena and Talia had abandoned.

"To me, the Eve piece from the side looks like an innocent girl plucking an apple from a tree limb, childish in a way," the man, probably in his thirties, said to his companion. "Innocent young girl. Nubile young girl."

"I think it's weird you keep seeing 'young girls,'" she responded. "That's not what I'm seeing at all. It's kind of creepy."

"I thought there was intent, anger, and defiance in the face," he said, "like she knew exactly the import of what she was doing. Bordering on contemptuous."

"I just don't want to listen to you for a while," his companion said with resignation in her voice. "Just think it, and we'll talk about it on the drive home if it still feels necessary to say."

135

Melinda took a step away from them, and then, in an awkward shuffle through the growing crowd, nearly bumped into a pedestal on which another sculpture resided.

It was titled The Rose. It was all glass, with odd facets and strange protrusions. It did not look like a rose, though it was roundish in shape. And then she thought one cylindrical shape might be a leg, and then she saw an arm and another leg and a face, a woman's face, a woman lying on her back facing up as if in a yoga pose, with her feet tucked behind her head. And then, the image seemed to fill itself in in her head and she realized she was looking at something quite obscene. Her pose wasn't a stretch and at the place where her legs met, where many of the glass corners intersected, there was a cluster of faceted glass that almost certainly resembled a flower bud.

She blinked her eyes. Looked at it again. What was she thinking? Where did that come from? It was lumps of glass.

And indeed, when she studied it again, whatever it was she had thought she had seen was hard to find. She closed her eyes, held them closed, then opened them again to take another look.

It looked like a face.

For a moment, she thought it looked like Mary.

Melinda had worked very hard at the roles assigned her by life: mother, wife, friend, neighbor, and community activist. She was open-minded, willing to listen to new ideas that challenged her understanding of the world, ready to invest her energy in those things she believed in.

Or rather, she had been.

A few years back, when Michael was in college, that had abruptly ended.

The change had been gradual and the effects had only become more pronounced since Michael had returned. But then, maybe she'd been worse than she'd thought and having Michael at home meant she had to put a little more effort into masking the fact that she might be having some kind of nervous breakdown.

Eli had been traveling more, and it was true that Melinda had been spending a lot of time alone. She'd withdrawn from every one of her social and community obligations, from most if not all of her social obligations, and kept to herself even when she did go out to eat or to a movie or to a museum. It became easier because she didn't have to make excuses to herself for her feeling of numbed detachment from the world around her. It just didn't feel like the real world anymore. There had to be something more.

Seeing Bill Clayton announce the closure of Marble Canyon Road was seeing the marked ending of her activist life. The canyon had been the last issue with which she had been involved. She'd pushed for Marble Canyon Road to be repaired since the eighth accident and the tenth death. She'd worked with the families involved to gather signatures, to pressure town leaders, and to file the lawsuits that got the state legislators' attention. She'd been to the state capital, done the whole bit, gone from one assembly member's office to the next.

There was a certain amount of satisfaction in that, Melinda thought, although she was not feeling satisfied at all.

If Melinda went back far enough to explain her inner turmoil, she tended to think this transition had begun with the start of the war. It had been a mental strain on her from the start. It had been going on so long that no one talked about it in day-to-day life anymore, unlike when it started, when war had been on everybody's lips. In the line at the post office, she'd talked to people who didn't realize it was still going on. That it had never ended.

Her feeling in general was that war was wrong, although, at times, necessary. But she felt this war from the beginning was especially wrong. Even when the idea of it had seemed to be lurking in the distance she had been against it. At the time, Eli had told her, "It's coming. There's no way to stop it now."

The war had meant a dramatic change of course for Eli. His work, once steeped in altruistic ideals, had long since drifted to more practical concerns. He'd drifted for twenty years even further, to the point he would no longer discuss the morality of his work. He worked to support his country. He told himself he was looking at a bigger picture than she was. He did what he had to do as long as it wasn't something that would keep him awake nights. He did things for his friends, for future favors, for the government, and for the country.

He'd become absorbed in policy and personality. Their relationship, which had always been rock solid, and unquestionably so, was still that, and yet, at the same time, it would only remain that way if she'd didn't question it and he didn't see her falling into pieces.

War was just one of the many things from which Melinda simply disconnected; the horror of it had become so incomprehensible that the fact of its existence—when truly there seemed to be no need for it—created a paradox that she couldn't get past. Why was such destruction ingrained in our history? How could it be that the need for war never ended? Could one ever truly find peace again, or were all chances of that dashed the first time two peoples raised arms against each other?

Was war a method of population control? Was it naturally occurring as a part of our evolution into a higher form? Was war a necessity in our development? Was it possible that the human race would be "better" without so many people? Wasn't that somewhere at the core of what so many believed their "new realities" were about? Getting rid of all of the "other" people? Getting rid of some of the people? Most of them?

She knew people who thought the world would be a better place with less people, but she didn't know many who would see the sense in giving up a loved one, or many loved ones, to make the world a better place. The whole scenario of cleansing the world only worked for people who were sure they wouldn't be included themselves.

Speaking with Elena had brought out in Melinda a motherly, protective sensibility toward her chosen hometown. Her chosen people.

Melinda was convinced that something was suspicious about Elena Altman, and that she was not a person with kind intentions. Something was wrong about the whole thing, She hoped that she hadn't been used as a tool by Altman Holdings in the canyon effort. What might be the benefit to them of closing the canyon?

And yet. And yet.

There was the radio at home this morning. The timing that enabled her to meet Elena and Talia, who, up until then, she'd not really been sure existed.

And where was the third one? The redhead? Was she real or not?

As she had done many a time in her years, Melinda asked herself who she had on her side.

Even as she had been walking out the door of the club that night, she was mentally running down the names on the old community phone tree. She'd started that list when Mary was in elementary school, as a way of keeping in touch with the parents of the kids in Mary's school social group, but it had grown over the next two decades to a widely-cast web of contacts throughout the county.

Whatever Elena was up to, it was likely already underway. Had she or Altman donated to the Clayton campaign, too, to encourage the closure of Marble Canyon Road? Was Elena simply new-agey and rich and reclusive? Melinda thought there was more to it than that. Was she part of a cult? Was she harmless, or did she mean Melinda harm?

Melinda didn't think of Eli, or the fact that she hadn't waited at the club to see him, until she'd pulled her car into the driveway at home fifteen minutes later.

Much to Eli's surprise and delight, Melinda sent him off to his golf club the next morning. She didn't know where Michael was. She hadn't heard him come home, seen him at breakfast, or heard him leave for work. He was grown, and responsible, and it wasn't her business to knock on his door to see if he had overslept, or to call the club to see if he'd slept in the office, or to chase down wherever else he might be . . . still, she was going to have to fish a little. He'd been home a while; by now, there had to be a girl or two who'd caught more than his passing interest.

She started her calls with Riza Koleman, who lived six houses down and who hadn't spoken to Melinda since Municipal Services had landscaped the area.

"Oh, gosh, Melinda," Riza said in her accented English, "did you have these unwanted visitors last night, too?"

"No, Riza, I don't know what you're talking about."

"Well, there were two men on my back porch last night. I woke up when Ahmet cried. My grandson, he is spending the night while Mehdi and her husband are in

Vegas. Well, crossing back through the living room from his room, I could see them right through the sliding glass door. I think they were men. And I stood there a moment, and I walked toward them because I thought I was mis-seeing what I was seeing. I mean, we have perimeter alarms and motion detectors."

"What were they doing?"

"Nothing! Just standing there with their backs to me. I got so mad I couldn't control myself. I started to yell, 'Get the hell out of here!'"

"You didn't."

"I did. As I yelled it, I picked up the phone and I went straight for the light switch. And at the sound of my voice they ran off like rabbits. They didn't even look to see where it was coming from. I was so angry, but it was just terrifying. I was glad they ran."

"I'm so sorry. And I'm concerned."

"I told Pavel I wanted him to shoot them next time. Oh, and Melinda, I want you to know. I did finally get into the *Home and Terrace*—"

"Congratulations!"

"Thank you . . . but it's all because of the clean-up on our street. They loved the tailored look against the wild backdrop. So I'm all done with that. Just don't do it again without telling me first, right?"

"Riza, I—"

"Oh, I'm sorry, there's someone coming now. I'm expecting the alarm company. I'm going to get lasers installed." There was a beeping noise in the background. "Oh, great, now it decides to come on . . ."

It was in character for Riza to hang up without saying goodbye.

She needed scratch paper. Melinda opened the secretary desk and pulled out a scratch pad and a pencil. Her eyes rested on a deck of playing cards tucked into the back of a slot. She stared at the pack a moment, then pulled them out before closing the desk up again. An airline deck of cards, wrapped in a rubber band. She removed the rubber band, fanned the deck open. The cards were new enough that they were still slippery to the touch.

An image of a card from another deck of cards, the Queen of Diamonds, rolled across her mind's eye. It was from a specific deck of cards, in which the queens had pointed chins. She was thinking of the deck of cards that were her "babies" when she was little. Each of whom, card by card, succumbed to terrible fates.

Melinda remembered her grandmother lecturing her on finding ways to entertain herself that weren't so morbid. Gran Nan gave her dolls to play with but couldn't get her to give up the cards. And she remembered going to a doctor who told her grandmother to let her granddaughter work through things in her own way.

Her card babies continued dying. It was a process that lasted many, many months. Usually, it was because the card was either tattered or ripped or written on. One baby drank poisoned water, several were drowned by their mothers or fathers, in rivers, lakes, oceans, and bathtubs; a few were smothered, one was set on fire, several died from diseases Melinda couldn't even pronounce correctly, some from hunger.

Her grandmother had thought it all a very grim process indeed, and looked forward to (and eventually celebrated) the day the last of the cards had been put to rest. But they'd never been put to rest. Melinda had continued at random times throughout her life to have dreams about the girls she named the cards after.

Playtime is over, she thought.

She set the cards beside the phone base, but couldn't find the rubber band.

Her next call was to Nancy, who worked for the Cheronkin Police Department. First, the formalities: They talked about their daughters and sons—Nancy had a matching pair the same ages as Melinda's who had been close with Mary and Michael as children, although the friendships hadn't lasted into adulthood. It did give her pause to wonder, while Nancy was describing her grandkids, about Mary's whereabouts. She had been checking in with Melinda by phone, but hadn't put in time for a visit at home for a while. Which usually meant Mary wasn't up to looking Melinda in the eyes because of something Mary was trying to hide from her. Something she didn't want her mother to know.

Nancy told Melinda that there had been more than twenty reported incidents that matched Riza's, all of them in the older parts of Cheronkin. The working police theory was that immigrant workers, probably here illegally, were living in the hills and in the gorges around Cheronkin, and, like mountain lions and bears and coyotes, were venturing more brazenly into local neighborhoods. Increased enforcement of immigration laws had made it as difficult to live here as it was to leave. Decreased funding for police services meant the problem was likely too big for local authorities to do more than chase around after reports of people who had long since vanished into the night.

Erin Marks, whose face was on every bus stop bench and grocery cart in town, let Melinda know that real estate in the area was not moving, so much so that she had been working out of a neighboring office in the next county. "I really don't see the end of it, not until the canyon road opens again. It's killed the summer rental market, which means the market to own rentals is dead. It's really thrown me for a loop. This was a great rental market, and it was mine. But people interested in this area are paying for coastal access, unfortunately, and without Marble Canyon Road, Cheronkin no longer has it."

When Melinda asked her if she'd heard about people coming into people's yards at night, Veronica let out an exasperated gasp. "No, thank goodness. You're not going to start something, are you? It's the last thing the area market needs. Don't you like your home values, hon?"

"Well, I'm not sure how to respond to that."

"Oh, great. Well, I love you lots, Melinda. I'm at my stop. I'll call you in a bit. I've gotta go."

And so went the morning. She felt a rush of satisfaction after each successful call. She was reminded not only in the activity of talking to old friends, but in the reactions of the women she was speaking with—for the first time, some of them, in years—that she had been well liked and respected by her peers. She'd lost sight of the formidable person she had been. It was nice to be reminded not only of how much they had done, but also how much there was in their power to still accomplish.

She wasn't able to get hold of Karen Walker or Emily Watkins, but she did finally speak to Gretchen Solkitz, grandmother to Andrina Sorenson, who let her know that the Walkers had recently moved away from Cheronkin, and Emily Watkins was now Emily Sutterno. Her ex, Eric

Watkins, was now married to their former maid, now Daisy Watkins, and they had a big place on the north side.

Gretchen worked in the city records department, and was able to tell Melinda that Altman Holdings owned quite a bit of land on the southern side of town. The company has purchased fifty-four properties in the last thirty years, most of them with homes on them, although a few were undeveloped lots in the hills that were about to be opened to development. On the properties that did have houses at the time of purchase, the company pulled down the structures, planted trees, and then left the property undeveloped.

"Some of those places," Gretchen said, "you might have seen a hundred times, a great big empty lot left among a block of houses, and said to yourself, thank goodness that hasn't been developed—well, it's probably one of Altman's lots. Some of them have been donated for use as national parkland. Which means the land's off limits until the government is able to vet it for quote security and safety efficiencies unquote before they let the park service do what they have to do."

"Isn't it odd that this company would have so much invested in the area and then just give it away or plow it into the ground?"

"It's different, yes. They might have settled tax issues with the government with the donations. Sometimes people are waiting for the markets to get better, or for development rules to change or for water rights to be acquired. Maybe these people just want to give it back to the wilderness."

"That's admirable if it's true. Until they want to clear the lot your house is on."

"You can understand the appeal that way. They're unhappy with the population growing and they have the money to make an effort to mitigate it, or the other way, if they're buying up everything to turn it back into one giant, sprawling ranch, like it was in the olden days."

"Or one giant cookie-cutter mall, just like the present."

They chatted on for another twenty minutes.

"Gretchen, I have to tell you, I was just beginning to feel like it's only been a few days since we've spoken and not months or years. Just hearing your voice is comforting."

143

"Just hearing you've got something you're planning is comforting to me. Did you really call about Altman, or are you calling about the Hill People?"

Melinda almost gasped. "Oh, my goodness, no one I've spoken to has called them that. I didn't make that connection! Is that who you think it is? That's the children's boogeyman tale."

"I tell you, I don't know who they could be. They're not immigrant workers. Or illegals. And I'm sure if you're talking to them, everybody's told you stories about people in their backyards, am I right? Everyone I talk to has a story or knows someone else close by who does . . ."

Melinda happened to be at a window with a view of the street. There was Mr. Green, on the sidewalk straight across the street, walking purposefully up the block, as he had nearly daily for all the years she'd lived in Cheronkin. And he was still as stocky as he'd ever been, and his appearance was the same in dress, in hairstyling—red hair parted on the left and combed to the right— and in posture as it had ever been. For the last several years, as time continued to pass and Mr. Green continued to remain unchanged in either appearance or posture or pace or walking routine, she'd started to feel there was something unnatural about him. She had even wondered once or twice if he were real—as in not a real person at all.

He's a robot, she thought. Her kids knew that was what she thought.

She watched him for a minute as he trudged on down the block. When she turned away from him, a bright flash of orange at the opposite end of the block, on the street outside Riza's, caught her attention.

Gretchen said, "I tell you, closing the canyon road was a terrible mistake. I know we disagree on this, but it's going to turn Cheronkin into one big cul-de-sac, a dead end. Closing off Marble Canyon Road is just like giving the canyon to them."

"To the developers."

"To the Hill People."

The orange burst was moving, bouncing down the sidewalk.

Melinda said, "I don't like the thought of going up against an urban legend."

144

"Anyway, Melinda, if you're forming a committee, you sign me up. They're not getting past my dogs, but that doesn't mean I like them lurking about."

It *was* a girl. And with that hair, it had to be her.

Melinda's eyes widened, her neck straightened to alert. She grit her teeth and began to feel anxious. "Who is she?"

Gretchen asked, "Who is who?"

"Oh, I'm sorry, Gretchen, I'm watching this girl I don't recognize walking up the street right now. She looks very out of place. She paused. "You know," Melinda continued a beat later, "that isn't really true. She looks like someone I saw in a dream a few weeks back . . ."

"Melinda, are you okay?"

"Oh, yes, thank you, Gretchen. I think I'm going to have to go talk to her, see what her story is."

"Thatta girl."

"It's the neighborly thing to do."

"It's the Neighborhood Watch thing to do. Good for you. Glad you're back on the beat. Give me a call whenever you're ready to get together."

Melinda was hardly listening. She hung up the phone and watched with fascination and dread as the girl approached.

It was her.

And Melinda knew her name: Cameron.

Melinda stared with a growing disbelief as the girl continued up the block, closer and closer to her house. She stared, that is, until the girl turned her head toward Melinda's house, and seemingly met her stare from a couple hundred yards away.

Melinda stepped back from the window. But it wasn't far enough to take her out of the girl's view, so Melinda went into Mary's old room, and peeked out through the blinds, her heart hammering.

"What am I scared of?"

She waited and waited for Cameron to come into view again. The new position gave her a more limited view. All of a sudden, there she was, and when she came fully into view it was only a moment before she again met Melinda's stare.

And by then, she had reached the sidewalk nearly across the street. She stepped into the street straight out in front of the house. Melinda ran to the window at the top of the stairs, which had gauzy white curtains, through which she saw the girl start walking up Melinda's driveway.

Melinda gasped. Was the front door locked? It was hardly ever locked in the daytime if she was home. Could she get there in time to lock it? She raced to the stairs, desperate to make the attempt, but stopped herself . . . when she heard the lever on the door handle click.

Her heart froze in her chest.

Melinda hurried to the hall window again. Of course, the girl wasn't there. She was walking into the front hall downstairs.

Melinda heard the creak that the front door made when it was about three-quarters of the way open, a sound that came just before it bounced off the door jamb. And then she heard the bounce. She stole into the kids' old bathroom, and closed and locked the door soundlessly by twisting the handle and pushing the lock as she swung the door shut, and then releasing the lock and carefully releasing the handle.

She listened at the door a moment. The stairs had just been redone and recarpeted. Cameron wasn't going to make a sound coming up them.

What was Melinda doing? This was a girl less than half her age, a spindly little nothing younger than her daughter. Melinda should be able to take her apart.

And yet.

Melinda stepped into the shower, again trying to close the door noiselessly behind her, but getting a shucking noise as the rubber seal on the door closed.

"Melinda."

Melinda almost screamed when she heard that voice. It was so clear that it might have come from right behind her, or right outside the door.

"Melinda," the voice said, "I'm very hurt that you haven't acknowledged me, that you don't recognize me. We have a very long history, you and I. I've been waiting on the edges of your dreams since the night I realized it was you, waiting for you to remember me."

"Is it the children? Most of us are blessed with an inability to breed, but there are stories. They tell us that each child takes with them a sliver of the eternal soul, making it that much harder for the spirit to awaken and

146

remember in the lives that follow. You're not all there anymore, are you? But that's just one of the reasons you haven't woken up. You've built so many walls."

"Melinda," she continued, her voice low, gravelly, and controlled, seeming to float in the air as it came closer, until it seemed like it was right outside the bathroom door. "Melinda. Your home can't possibly hide you. It can't protect you from a single thing that's going to happen. Not your gates or your locks or your alarms, not dogs or doormen, not the lights you leave burning every night and day and certainly not any of your toys. I can see you through your walls," she said, "I can hear you through your doors. There isn't any place where you can hide."

Melinda closed her eyes, covered her ears with her hands and trembled.

"The two of us," Cameron said, "are going to have so much fun together. Once you get past this part of it, you'll thank me."

And then, for thirty seconds, nothing. Melinda waited for the bathroom door to open. She looked at the glass shower door. She would see the edge of the door if it opened more than a couple inches.

A gray spot appeared in the middle of the shower door; it seemed to be a reflection in the mirror outside the shower, but warped by the glass. After she noticed it, the spot grew darker—and for a moment, it looked almost like a bird was racing toward the glass. And when it hit the glass . . .

The door's glass pane cracked. Melinda jumped back as the beveled glass was instantly covered with dark fracture lines. The lines then spread beyond the glass, climbing across the tiles and up the walls. Everything around her was cracking. If the ground were shaking, she would have believed it was an earthquake.

But instead, it was as if she had been unknowingly living inside a shell, where the inside walls of that shell were painted with the scenes of her reality, in this case, her children's bathroom. And now the shell was collapsing around her. She cowered while it all came down, and she covered her ears and screamed. She didn't know why she yelled. Maybe it was deafening. Maybe there was no noise at all. And then the world had turned to darkness all around her. Was it night?

147

She was afraid to look. She knew where she was, and she knew it by the strange thrill this place brought to her heart. She was back where she'd first seen Cameron. She was in that ancient forest of towering trees, and it was the dead of night.

She wasn't alone. It wasn't quiet, as it had been in her therapy session. There were other people in the forest around her; they were waiting for her.

Melinda's eyes were still closed, she realized. She'd closed them when it all fell down. This was not what she wanted to see. She was not ready for this yet.

When she opened her eyes a few minutes later, she found she hadn't gone anywhere. She was still huddled in the shower.

Reality, as it were, was still together.

What the hell was that?

She still waited well over an hour before she rose and stepped as silently as possible from the shower. It was another forty-five minutes before she could summon the nerve to quietly open the door, not knowing who or what she would be faced with when she stepped outside or downstairs, but there was no sign of Cameron anywhere. Melinda's phone list was still on the table beside the notes from her calls, and beside the phone was the deck of cards, rubber band affixed. The furniture, the room, everything looked the same.

Melinda was glad when Eli returned home from playing golf, a short while after she'd made it down the staircase. The two of them hardly exchanged a word, but having another breathing human being in the house made her feel less vulnerable. What's more, things like what had happened this afternoon generally didn't happen when Eli was around.

Although he had apparently had more than a few drinks at the club bar, Eli seemed sincerely interested when he asked her if everything had gone okay with her planning. She didn't discuss Hill People, because without seeing it himself, he'd dismiss it as urban myth. She didn't discuss Altman Holdings—that would involve too many topics she couldn't broach with him, from regression session to hypnotherapist to airport hallucinations. And, finally, she didn't tell him about the intruder this afternoon—he'd have her in therapy, or committed, if she told him she'd spent two

148

hours cowering in the shower, afraid of a twenty-year-old redhead.

This, apparently, was to be her sole strategy for keeping her marriage intact. To keep from him all the crazy stuff so he wouldn't leave her—that way, she wouldn't have to face it alone. A fine strategy.

She told him everything went well, that it had been good to discover her old phone network was still around. She said, "There's a lot to do, and not a lot of time."

Eli said, "Isn't that the story of the world?"

Later, after dinner was cooked and served and then the remains cleaned away, and after Eli had gone to his desk to read work-related material, Melinda, in the upstairs bathroom, washed the last of the soap from her face. When she had dried herself off, she saw the follicles of hair in the sink—again, more than there should have been—and she sighed. It was definitely happening faster. None of the hair medicines seemed to have an effect. It was all still concealable, but for how much longer?

Again, the thought: She needed help.

You can't do it alone, she thought. But, if Elena intends harm—for she likely wouldn't care if the entire population were gone from the valley—then you will have to have help to stop her.

You will have a town meeting, she told herself, You will make the phone calls tomorrow to get it started. You will get out the flyer paper and your stencil and you will get everybody's help. There isn't any need to do this alone. You know you aren't capable of doing this alone. Drawing the community together has always been your strength. Like you, they will do just about anything to protect their families and their homes when they are threatened.

As for the matter of the hair, she would ask Mary in the morning what to do. Melinda would have a chance to find out what her daughter had been up to, and maybe try to get an idea what it was Mary was hiding from her. And after that, she was going to figure out where the kids' school books were sequestered away. She was certain all those boxes were still on the premises. She wanted to know more about the writer Elena had referred to: Dick Arthur.

IN THE NEWS
West Coast Regional Reporter, **May 1:**
Over the protests of attendees at a Cheronkin City Council meeting, city council members voted to extend tree maintenance intervals to 10 years from the current 5, citing the high cost of "keeping everyone's hedges neatly trimmed." City tree services remain months behind in dealing with an explosion of growth thought to have resulted from heavy winter rains followed by early tropical spring weather. Lower than usual tax collections have forced city managers to make cutbacks in many city services.

West Coast Regional Reporter, **May 2:**
Four area hospitals have agreed to pool their resources to try to determine what exactly it is they are doing right. Southern Counties Mercy Grace Hospital, Cheronkin Hills Hospital, the Oaks Emergent Care Hospital, and the Northern Valley Health Services Center have agreed to share information with a committee to review the remarkable improvement in treatment for patients across the medical spectrum.

"Really, what we have here in terms of positive outcomes is unprecedented, and has been reflected in every patient case reviewed for the last six months. For the last couple weeks, because we've freed up beds, we've been able to admit long-term care patients from hospitals outside our region, and even they are doing better here."

The committee will examine six factors in patient care: clinical effectiveness, safety, patient centeredness, production efficiency, staff orientation, and responsive governance.

8
End of Spring

"It wouldn't really take me long to go down the blame chain to be able to saddle my mother with responsibility for the fact that I'm standing here in the Fandango parking lot at seven-thirty on a Saturday morning," Mary said.

"I work here," Michael said. "I was told to be here. What possible excuse could you or mom have for being here?"

"Carina and I try to hit all the town events, big and small."

Carina added, without sarcasm, "We're big community boosters. The big M.P. trained us well. That's your mom."

"I know," Michael said.

"Carina secretly wished she could have the initials M.P., too."

"I always thought it was cool. You guys were more than a family. You were a secret initials club. Melinda, Mary, Michael."

"Anyway, Carina calls me up and says things like 'the big Cheronkin Orchard Pick is coming up on Saturday, and we go do it.'" Mary thought about it. "Mom did train us well."

It was a recent Cheronkin tradition that spring ended with a parade. It was really more of a local car rally than a parade, and it was a budget affair, and it was never held on the last day of spring because June tended to be one of the hotter months. It definitely had a small-town feel to it, with townspeople and members of various community organizations—anyone with a car who wanted to participate, really—driving the main thoroughfare in cars decorated with whatever materials were available.

Another product of another committee chaired by Melinda Phillips, the parade was originally intended as a north/south, old Cheronkin/new Cheronkin event, an attempt to bridge some of the distance between the two sides of town. Marble Canyon Road was the only choice for a route; it was the only roadway that ran through both sides of town.

But the whole idea never worked out as planned.

Marble Canyon Road on the northern side of the interstate was lined with apartment buildings, fast food restaurants, gas stations, banks, strip malls, boutiques and salons. On the south side, Marble Canyon Road was a winding, scenic drive along which only a handful of human structures were visible. Little would a person suspect there were hundreds of homes tucked among the hills and knolls off either side of the road.

Much to Melinda's chagrin, the parade watchers had all lined up, from the first installment of the parade, on the southern portion of the road. Many of the people driving the "floats," after spending two hours in stop-and-go traffic on the south side of the road, bailed out of the parade when the freeway overpass came into view, unwilling to drive the last two miles of Marble Canyon Road, under the freeway and into the north side of town. By year four, most of the businesses on the north side of the road had dropped out of the parade; and in that and the following years it became an event held by the people of old Cheronkin for the entertainment of the people of old Cheronkin. One of Melinda's protégés on the committee would later develop the concepts for the community barbecue and crafts fair that followed later renditions of the rally.

At some point in the parade's history, the car rally became a water fight. Generally, those in the parade were armed with water weapons including hoses, balloons, and buckets, while other Cheronkin denizens, similarly armed, hid out in the brush along the hillsides. Nearly the whole of the driving portion was a running water battle.

Murray's Hat ran a vintage fire engine that when not in use for the parade was housed in the county volunteer fire department and visited frequently by elementary and pre school age children. It had two water tanks, two hoses, and a water cannon, all of which had added to the float's general appeal to Michael in his younger days. There it would be, year after year, coming down the boulevard while the crowd cheered, boom box playing, loaded with Murphy's insiders, soaking the crowds up and down both sides of the street.

"I can't believe we're going to get to ride on the fire engine!" Michael was like a child in his excitement. "Uhm . . . where's our nephew?"

"And it's the first time we've gotten to ride this thing without having to sleep with anyone," Carina giggled, at which Mary rolled her eyes.

Then she thought about it. "God, was I that much of a slut?" Mary asked, sure that she was feeling less amused than she once would have been by the thought.

"No, that's not how it was. We always prided ourselves on not being sluttier."

"Laura should be dropping Max off any time," Mary said.

"Are we loaded up on balloons?" Michael wanted to be prepared. "That old fire station fart is driving."

"Why does he always drive?"

"Walter has to drive. He's the only person insured to drive it. He's not going to let us go crazy with the water cannon. He already said he thought it had all gotten to be too much. He has an override switch for the hose up there."

"Isn't that weird? That it's our float this year?"

"Best perk so far," Michael said. "I haven't been a part of the parade, or even a spectator, for years."

"I love that your brother gets to play with us all the time now," Carina said.

Mary eyed him. "You slept at the club last night, didn't you?"

"Yeah, I've been known to do that. There's a great couch in Aunt Laura's office."

"Is that so you can avoid Mom?"

"No. I like Mom when Dad's around. It was a late night last night. Fridays and Saturdays are always late nights."

"Are you hiding something? Is that why you're avoiding her?"

"If you're trying to remind me of what it's like having dinner with her," Michael said, "you're succeeding. I can't take all the digging."

So, she thought, he is hiding something. Had he hooked up with someone? The singer?

"Anyway, Mary, I've seen her enough that I know that she thinks *you've* been trying to conceal something."

They both eyed each other suspiciously, he more playfully than her.

"As a matter of fact, I, too, have seen Mom, to work on her hair in the last couple weeks. She just hasn't been happy with how it's been coming . . . out." Mary thought about that. Shrugged. "She thinks you're hiding something, too. A girlfriend. I didn't tell her about the singer girl, because I didn't think it counted.

"Anyway, dear brother, all I was going to suggest was that you think about finding an apartment or a townhouse or a condo. Then you might actually *want* to go home at night." Mary was happy to be spending more time with her brother. She'd been keeping her distance for some time now, and it was wearing thin with everybody, particularly as it was all without explanation. Being out with Michael and Carina felt safe for her. Like baby steps. "Seriously, I mean, what are your plans? Are you going to stay? Are you just taking a year off from life?"

Michael cut it short. "I don't have any answers prepared. So. Why don't you tell me what it is that you've been up to?"

Mary rolled with it. "Lots of stuff. Mostly self stuff. Good for me, good to me. I gave notice at the salon."

"Really?"

"It was time. I just . . . there's so many chemicals there, in the air, on my skin . . . there's just got to be a better way to do it."

Carina was listening, too. "So what are you going to do? Who's supposed to cut my hair now, when you've been doing it for twenty years?"

"I'll always cut your hair . . . I've been doing some research. I'm thinking of opening an organic, all-natural salon. I still need to find a place, but I don't have money to go on forever waiting to do this."

"Where would your shop be?"

"Well, ideal would be if Auntie was able to redevelop the shops around the club, but now that all the businesses around here are suffering because of the canyon road being closed, I don't think I can wait for that to happen. So someplace on the other side of the freeway. If our beloved and departed dog Lamont had a better name, I would have named it after her. But I think I might call if Purity," Mary said, without a touch of irony.

154

The End of Spring Parade was not a well-choreographed event, and never had been. In places, Marble Canyon Road was too narrow to handle parked cars, pedestrians, and vehicles like the fire engine doing three-point turns in the midst of the congestion. In previous years, before Marble Canyon Road's closure, there had also been through-traffic on the road during the parade, which had added an air of energy to the event, not all of it good. Though there were exceptions, most people cruising inland through the canyon to the interstate after a drive up the coast weren't happy to get caught behind a forty-car line-up or to be the targets of the locals' water balloons.

This year, because Marble Canyon Road was closed, the planners reversed the route. Cars first lined up in the Fandango parking lot and then rallied to the last turnoff before Marble Canyon Road ended at the concrete slabs marking the closed portion of the highway.

"It's going to be a tough ride," Michael said as the fire engine rumbled out onto the street. "Look how many people there are lined up on that hilltop, and then right below it. They're just waiting for their first target." Unconsciously, he was clenching and unclenching the fists at his sides. "I hope this doesn't send out the wrong message, so many of our family members being onboard." Besides himself, his sister, and Carina, Max, his nephew, was also onboard. Max was hovering anxiously about his pail of water balloons.

"The club is a family enterprise now. It's a fact," Mary said. And there're other people on board. We didn't even get the good seats in the cab."

"That's why I gave up those seats. We don't need to rub the fact of family ownership in people's faces."

"Well, that's what I'm going to do," Mary said, standing up. "I'm claiming the water cannon."

Carina said, "I want one of the hoses. Wasn't Lamont your dog?"

"Yeah, remember her, Michael?"

"Of course." He was loading balloons into a food server's apron tied around his waist, with FANDANGO across the front. "Best. Dog. Ever."

"Mom wanted us to participate in this inner city after school program and we both refused because it was going to be like three hours of driving to the city, twice a week."

155

"After school." Michael shook his head, still incredulous.

"Of course, she bought the tickets anyway, but Michael and I went to the bowling alley and hid out there the morning we were supposed to go, so she went alone. And then she got lost in the bad part of downtown for nearly three hours before nearly hitting a stray puppy, which she then decided to bring home, and which she named after what she imagined might have been a student's name at the school she was looking for, if she had ever reached it. Not realizing that she'd brought home a female, not a male."

"Your mom's crazy."

Mary looked like she was almost getting misty. Michael nudged her.

"Lamont was a great dog," she said quietly.

Lamont was a black lab mix with big, amber eyes that always looked moist, as if she were about to cry. She'd been born on the streets, brought into a pound, adopted, then turned out on the streets when her new owner moved . . . this they knew because Lamont had been part of a generation of pound puppies implanted with tiny tracking chips in their necks.

Lamont was afraid of flashlights and chains and raised voices. She was a vegetarian—she just didn't want meat. She seemed to be sort of dainty for a big dog, in the way she nearly pranced when she walked. She had a deep growl and a rumbling bark for close, unidentifiable noises and for strangers at the door in uniforms, but otherwise she was a very peaceful, calm dog, and she made you feel that way, too, just by being nearby.

"So I was thinking about Lamont," Mary said, "and how good and sweet and pure she was and how she was quietly very smart and observant, and I had this weird flash of insight that, like, for just a second, made the whole thing clear to me. What I was after."

Carina was game. "What are you after?"

"Purity. More than just going natural and getting organic; it's about being outside and breathing clean air, being honest, not putting energy into people and things that aren't worth it, getting the chemicals out of me, exercising, drinking water, being with people I love, getting rid of the negativity, getting rid of the things that burden me, eating only food that is good for me and drinking things that are good for me . . ."

Michael surveyed the stocks of balloons. "I think we left a bucket of balloons behind. And I don't think I heard you say 'develop harmonious relationship with honored mother.' That's got to able to drain some toxins out of your gut."

Mary thought about it. "Is she going to be here today?"

"I don't know. I haven't talked to her about it because I assumed she would be here, naturally. She's been doing her shut-in thing again lately. Just asks me out the window to pick up milk or eggs or steak or potatoes at the market. I'm glad Dad's back again. And even with him here, I've still hardly seen her."

"What does Dad say?"

"She's been busy with a project."

"Oh, groan."

The fire engine had driven maybe three hundred yards along the parade route when they came to the first group of bystanders, many of whom, despite the mostly clear and cloudless day, were holding umbrellas. Immediately, the first wave of water balloons were launched from the trees above and behind the spectators, and a cheer went up all around. Michael told everyone to save their balloons until farther up the road, when the trees would be over the vehicle, and most everyone listened. Because the best attack positions were a distance from the road, most balloons missed the fire truck altogether and/or landed on the spectators, but one got through and popped on the back of Max's head.

He burst into tears.

For the following slow section of the five-mile-per-hour stop-and-go crawl, Max cried, Mary tried to comfort, Michael hosed down both attackers and sweaty spectators with water and Carina and the other staffers on board vigorously fought back against the dousing they were receiving with waves of balloons and blasts of the water cannon. Michael saw the spot on the sidelines staked out by Aunt Laura and his parents coming up. Aunt Laura and his dad were there, and with them Lorraine, who was trying to stand on roller skates too big for her small feet. He saw his mom farther back in the crowd, making her rounds of hellos.

"We're coming up on Aunt Laura, Mary."

157

Mary knelt next to their nephew. "Max, do you want to climb off with your mom and keep crying or do you want to stop crying, have some fun, throw a few balloons at other people, and ride with us to the end?"

A balloon smashed into the fire truck just beside Max's head, and they both flinched. Max screamed with renewed vigor.

"Okay, okay. Yell for Steamboat Willie up there to stop for a minute."

The truck stopped, although none too soon. Mary got off carrying Max, who was still sobbing, and then it crawled onward. Michael and Carina waved sadly at her. She gave them the thumbs up, but Michael could see disappointment in her eyes.

"Well, that's a bummer," Carina said. "I don't think she finished the Lamont story."

"She'll meet up with us at the barbecue."

"At least we still have each other," Carina said in her ditsiest voice, "my hero, Michael."

It was an act he'd seen a dozen times; however, but when she touched his hand while she fluttered her eyes and smiled at him, a surprising blush rose to his cheeks, and the humor in her eyes gave way to surprise at his expression which gave way to a blush in her own cheeks.

He stepped back from her like he'd been burned by a match.

"Sorry, Michael."

"Don't be . . . it's not . . . it's fine. It's fine."

It wasn't long before the fire truck reached a stretch in the route where the trees were just off the shoulder on either side of the road, and the branches had grown long enough to form an arch over the two-lane Marble Canyon Road, a canopy that had recently grown so thick that it felt like driving into a tunnel.

The younger guys from the club took possession of the water cannon and someone else figured out how to manually pump an extra hose, but the fire truck was basically being pummeled the moment they passed under the arched branches, and it wasn't long before everyone was running for cover.

Laughing and squealing, Michael and Carina took refuge under a clear plastic dome in the middle of the truck, hidden from view from the sides of the road.

"Geez," Carina said, "look how overgrown it is."

"Yeah, it's like a jungle."

Some of the people lobbing balloons at them were climbing on or hanging from branches nearly directly overhead. Most of them were teenage kids, out having the time of their lives.

Carina pulled a joint out of a pocket, and a lighter out of the other.

"Too bad Mary isn't here. She'd like this. All we need is some Hendrix while they're bombing away."

"I miss her, too."

"What do you think has been up with her?" Carina took a drag, and passed him the joint. "What do you know?"

"I don't know. Has she said something to you?"

"Nothing. Not much."

"Do you think she's okay?" Michael watched Carina's reaction carefully, and was relieved by what he saw before Carina even spoke. Carina knew pretty well what was going on with Mary most of the time.

"She's getting better, whatever it was. She's good at finding ways to do that."

They heard a noise coming from a car or two back that sounded almost like a loose tailpipe dragging on the asphalt.

Michael passed the joint back to Carina. Someone overhead smelled the scent of the cannabis as he was moving by, and gave them a thumbs up.

Carina stared at the joint. "I'm dating a guy who likes to smoke. I finally learned how to roll a joint."

He took another hit. Breathed out low, so the smoke went into the bottom of the compartment they were in before it started to filter out. He wondered if people in the crowd could smell it. And if it made them all wish they had some.

The harsh scratching noise seemed to be coming closer. It sounded like something metal was dragging and bouncing on the asphalt.

They each had another drag when someone at the back of the truck said, "look, it's that Mary girl!"

Sure enough, it was Mary, wearing Danielle's cheap metal roller skates that scratched and screeched with each

159

small, quick, unsteady step she took. She was slowly passing by the white pickup decorated with a unicorn horn that was driving behind them.

It was a very un-Mary picture. She looked uncoordinated and awkward, not to mention overdressed, but she also looked determined.

Everybody onboard clapped their hands and cheered as she approached. Water balloons rained down around her from trees. Walter honked the horn and slowed a bit, and then blasts of water from soaker guns and hoses at the sides of the road rained down on Mary. She threw the bucket of balloons they'd left behind into the back of the truck and then grabbed the handle at the back and jumped.

But she missed the step. Maybe it was because of the condition of the roller skates. Regardless, she managed to hold onto the truck and to hold herself up. If she'd slipped a bit more, or lost her grip, Michael thought, she'd probably be hurt or dead now. Or lying in the road waiting for the next car in the procession to roll over her.

Not for the first time, Michael wondered if his sister were crazy.

Another hurried, not-quite-but-nearly-panicked jump, and she was onboard.

Applause and cheers followed from on board and from the spectators. But the water attacks from the trees only intensified. Mary hurried for cover. She didn't see Michael or Carina, or hear them calling her name, and she was hit by a couple of balloons, an atomic water gun, and a garden hose before she found them huddled under their dome.

She took one look at them, and then at him, and Michael automatically started making room for her, which basically meant him getting out from under the cover so she could get in. Mary then climbed under and Michael crouched low and covered his head.

It was about forty-five seconds later that the fire truck finally drove out of the trees. The creek came right up to the road, and the tree line was pushed to the other side of the creek, which meant the opposition was limited to the one side of the road where the trees were still over the road. And the sun was coming through.

The shoulder off the road at that point was wide enough that it made a great spot for spectators, and, accordingly, people had spread out their blankets and set up their umbrellas and folding chairs and now sat clapping and cheering as each vehicle cruised by. Michael saw scores of kids on the other side of the road, racing around on the ground behind the trees.

The crew jumped up all over the fire engine when the barrage ended. They grabbed their water weapons of choice and started fighting back again. The kids who were out there fighting them seemed to like that even better than simply pummeling the fire truck. They were doing Indian cries and plotting attacks and yelling out commands dramatically at every swing of the water cannon.

It was an okay crowd of people. Not the most Michael had seen at this event, but a lot compared to what he'd expected, what with all the stories he'd been hearing of people leaving town. There were many faces in the crowd that were familiar from his entire life of growing up in Cheronkin. People he knew as kids who were now grown up also, parents of his high school friends, former teachers, store clerks, people from Mary's different salons, and, of course, many, many faces he knew from hanging out at the Hat.

There was someone ahead who caught his eye, someone who was looking right at him. Michael's heart jumped. It was a man, dressed in black, and he stood out from the more colorfully and casually attired parade watchers. For a weird, disorienting moment, he thought it looked like his friend Billy, who died when Michael was in college. And when he thought that it was Billy, and that Billy was looking up at the fire engine full of Laura's family, Michael imagined there was nothing but scorn in his eyes.

Billy had believed that the early '70s were the heyday for both Cheronkin and the Hat. When he was in one of his frequent funks about not being able to find work, this was just the kind of event he would have sneered at, along with the community of wealth Cheronkin had become. Filled with people who drove the best cars and had the best schools, people who got a kick out of dressing down into their rattiest kum-bye-ya clothes, plunking beach chairs by the side of the road, trying to pretend they were a hippy version of the average American.

And it was true, Cheronkin wasn't the backyard for white trash it had once been. It had lost its tarnish. And everyone here who wasn't a kid was probably feeling that doing something like this did somehow make them more like the average joe.

But it wasn't Billy, he saw as he got closer.

He looked so familiar.

The man watched as recognition dawned on Michael's face. Vagrant. Drug peddler. It was the lot-of-dots guy. He tipped his hat at Michael right before a water balloon hit Michael square in the chest.

When Michael looked for him again, the fire truck was rolling past the spot where he'd been standing. There was a clearing in the crowd where he had been moments before, but the lots-of-dots guy was gone.

After the barricades on Marble Canyon Road came into sight, the line of cars veered off it and onto a route that after a short distance toward the hills led to the community center, where a big grill in the parking lot already sizzled and smoked, laden with hot dogs and tofu and chicken. There were craft stands set up along the sloping hillside behind the center, and families pitching blankets throughout the lightly wooded areas that dotted the landscape. At the top of the hill was a long, flat plateau that on all other sides overlooked a steep drop into one of the canyon's valleys. That top section, which had been a multi-sport playing field in Michael's youth, was surrounded by a metal fence which people routinely scaled for stargazing and other purposes

Cheronkin County's community roots were more apparent here than at the opening night at the club. They were, for the most part, a bunch of former hippies, and kids of former hippies. Many of them, like Michael's father, were in jobs totally antithetical to everything they had believed decades before, living lives not all that different than the lives their parents led, except now they had so much more of everything.

And yet, surveying the scene, Michael felt almost like he was walking into a historical reenactment. Everything looked exactly the same as it had been the last time he attended, years and years before. But here they were, the same middle-aged guys (now post-middle-age) milling around at the sidelines in their faded Tie Dyed T-shirts and bandannas. And there it was, the same aged, faded peace sign

162

banner unfurled on the back wall of the community center, the same feeling of entering the lunch area at a hippie-themed fairground.

It all looked so dated, and yet, it had always looked dated to Michael, even when he was a kid. It looked the same to him as it always had. It had always had the air of a sincere historical reenactment. The Tie Dye, the headbands, the sarongs, the incense odor, the guitar circles, the petitions and the protest sessions—it had always seemed like an idealized homage to the sizable portion of the population with ties to and/or fond memories of the movements of the era. It was, in fact, the one time of the year when a lot of the funkier hair and beard styles found adorning the older generation of Cheronkin seemed totally in place.

The most notable difference Michael could see from past renditions were the number of updated anti-war signs, t-shirts and other paraphernalia on display, as well as peace signs and rainbows and yin and yang symbols. It was a sentiment totally in character with the theme of the event; however, in the past, the signs had all been vintage items used as props, and had referred to wars in the past. It was new for anyone to be talking about the war in the present.

Michael could remember being admonished by an event coordinator for bringing his water gun in from the car rally: This community event in particular is about peace, not conflict.

Back in the city, when he'd been with Danielle, they'd known a number of people who were passionate about the war, some in support of it, most against it. But here, except for family dinners when his father was in town, it often felt as if it wasn't a part of anyone else's existence.

Michael found Mary being introduced by Carina to an older woman named Barbara. Her black t-shirt read EAT THE RICH across her chest.

"Remember that time, like eight years ago, the doctor's son, Allan, had us dog sit and house sit for him? And we did mushrooms that one day . . ."

"Oh, my gosh!" Mary laughed. "We shaved Allan's dog because it was too furry. Shampooing and conditioning only made it poofier."

"Right. It turned out that it looked like a rat underneath the fur. And we went for a nature walk in his back yard? And we ended up at this spot where we could see right into one of the neighbors' houses?"

Mary remembered. "There were two naked people with long silver hair dancing and bouncing and shimmying around on a bed?"

Michael was incredulous as he watched both of their faces, and the woman's, who was just as amused as they were.

"Mary, this is Barbara. I just met her in the Andy Gump line and started chatting, found out she lived up by Allan, and told her about our adventure because there was nothing else to talk about in line, and guess what? She and her husband are the naked shimmying people."

"No way!"

Their laughter came out in shrieks.

"My husband and I dropped acid that day," old Barbara said. "I don't remember what we were celebrating. Maybe we were celebrating having acid again. We were bouncing on the bed naked, that I do know. And I was jiggling, I'm sure, not shimmying. Old people jiggle."

None of them wanted to linger long. Michael had a tofu dog while they looked at the beads and the bongs and the braided bracelets and the driftwood art. Each of them ran into familiar faces and used the other two as an excuse to exit the conversation.

"So," Mary asked, "where's your friend Jack?"

"I haven't seen him for weeks, since a couple days after the big party at Fandango. I think he said that Uncle Bill commissioned a couple of pieces for Aunt Meg. I think he's been working on that—he hasn't been around the club much since his art went on display."

"Do you still think that whole amnesia thing is true?"

"Maybe. I don't know. All I've really heard him say about it was that he wondered if he had a family, a wife and kids, and if one day he'd gone out to rent a movie and just never come home."

"Weird."

"Yeah. And I saw his place for the first time, and that made it easier to believe. He has like four pairs of pants, three shirts, a jacket, and a pair of shoes. No furniture other than his art table and the bed. No TV. No food or drinks other than a water jug on the floor in the kitchen. No refrigerator. He has nothing."

"Where is his place?"

"A studio backhouse on Coburn. He liked it because the owner told him that a serial killer—long since jailed and executed—had once stayed there overnight."

"Did you tell him everyone says that here?"

"No. I didn't want to ruin his fun." Michael was feeling the call of the club. He was due on soon. "I'm going to get a ride over to the club. My shift starts soon. There's a promotion going on tonight for KKCC."

"You love your job, don't you?"

He smiled. "Don't pinch me, but it feels like a dream. I always wanted to be a club insider. I'm going to keep doing this for a while if I have a choice. Not forever. Not for permanent, I don't think. It's really good experience for a résumé. I do feel like I'm playing hooky and getting paid for it. I feel like I'm supposed to be here in Cheronkin right now, and I'm feeling really lucky that I've found something so great to do while I'm here. But I don't want to jinx it."

"You feel like you're here because of Mom?"

"Yeah, a little. It's weird. I don't really want to spend that much time there with her, but I don't want to be so far away, either."

"It's not that weird. I feel that way, too. She's probably figured out a way to brainwave us into staying close by. Listen," Mary said, reminded of something. "Another subject now: Do you know who painted that map on the floor of the club? Was that part of the renovation?"

"No, that's always been there. From the days of the Hat. How come?"

"I was wondering how accurate it was. And, you know, what year in Cheronkin was represented by the map."

"I don't know. It's been there as long as I can remember."

They walked down the hill, stopping in front of the peace banner.

"It was nice hanging out with you, little brother." Mary gave him an uncharacteristically long and warm hug, followed by a kiss on the cheek.

"Is this part of the new Mary?"

He listened as Mary and Carina walked away. Mary was saying, "It's about being kind, being humble, being appreciative, being true and trustworthy, and all of that was connected to living more cleanly, eating natural food and drinking natural water, exercising . . ."

Carina said, "You're crediting your dog for a diet plan?"

"It's not a diet plan," Mary said, "it is a life plan. And my dog inspired it with her amazingly good and pure heart and her ability to be in tune with the world. I'll never be that pure, but this is my way of worshipping at her altar."

Michael called out, "'Bye, sister. I love you, pure or not."

"I love you, too, Michael."

The closing of the canyon road had been a boon to the club, and to business north of the highway, in terms of customers from the interstate, although Michael suspected the gain had been offset somewhat by a drop in the number of locals who frequented the club. There were just less people around town as summer approached.

For travelers, there was nowhere else to go when a person exited the freeway who would otherwise have stopped off for food and gas before heading toward the coast. Cheronkin was the last stop for an hour if that same person were headed north. All the signs on the south detoured back to the freeway, bypassing Fandango on the way in and the way out. And there was the fact that the club was the only upscale destination in the area.

In the long run, it wouldn't be enough without the tourists and beachgoers who would normally already be filling up the rentals on both sides of the freeway. The effects of losing those customers were just going to impact the club more and more as summer wore on.

When he arrived at the employee entrance, he saw the bulletin board had been papered over with a bright new flyer. It took only a moment to recognize his mother's handiwork. "TOWN MEETING! Join us at the Isla Jordan Auditorium to discuss Community Concerns.

He'd only seen his parents a couple times in the last few weeks, but he still considered it odd that his mom hadn't mentioned anything about this. Unless this was something she wanted to keep on the down low.

His dad must be leaving town again, he thought. And she must be keeping this covert, setting things up under his radar, and waiting until he was gone to raise her next ruckus.

There was a peculiar property of Jack's sculpture work that Michael wanted to mention to Jack when he saw him again. The sculptures appeared not only to vibrate with the music playing in the club, as Michael had already observed on many occasions, but also seemed to be broadcasting the sound as well. It wasn't an echo of the sound, because there wasn't a delay in between. In certain spots in the club, where more than one of the sculptures were positioned closely together, the acoustics would sometime seem to warp, as if each of their vibrational fields were interacting with the others'. In those zones, all the general sounds of the club were greatly muted, and instead what was clear was a low and constant hum that was accompanied, very clearly, by whatever live music was at the time playing in the club.

He discussed it at some point in the evening with one of the waitresses.

"I usually only notice it if I'm talking while I pass through," she said. "It's a tiny little zone on the floor. I think the humming noise is the sound of the sculpture vibrating. And you don't have to be in one of the zones to hear the vibrating. They're practically humming along. They all do it. And I like it. I just think this weird sound thing happens in some places because they're all vibrating so close together. If there's three bands playing through the place and I'm standing in one of the places, all the music tangles together."

The radio station event was done by eleven, and a comforting sort of normalness crept back into the place as the radio revelers—really a much different crowd than regularly hit the club—slowly drifted out and away. Aaron appeared when the kitchen was no longer serving anything but desserts and coffee and the only music in the place was the band playing the stage in the back room.

Michael automatically adjusted his course and went to look for Aaron's paycheck. Was it payday already again?

Aaron saw him going. "No hurries for me. On your schedule, O Captain. I'll be at the bar with my girl, Janet."

He winked at the eternally middle-aged, kinky-haired, leather-skinned bartender, and Janet grinned back and let out a throaty chuckle, then set to work mixing him a drink.

"Hard stuff tonight."

Janet grabbed the vodka without missing a beat. When Michael reemerged from the office, Aaron was still staring in Michael's direction, but his eyes were glazed over.

Janet gave him his drink, and Michael heard her ask Aaron, "What's up with you?"

"I went out hunting last night. With Esposito."

"Oh, now, why'd you go and do that? You know he's not a hunter. He's a gun lover. He's a gun-shooting lover. He's a lover of the act of holding and shooting a gun."

"It wasn't like that. I thought he might be all psycho. But it was fun. It was more like he was Militia Man. Ready to find his spot and just sit there for hours. I don't even think he wants to shoot something. He just wants them to walk on by him so he can surprise 'em, just for the laugh. I think he just wants the gun to be able to protect himself if the animal gets pissed."

"Did you shoot anything?"

"Well, we were looking for pigs. Wild pigs. What we finally got, after lying on our stomachs for hours, was a pack of coyotes. Six of 'em just wandered by. You know, it's pretty overgrown out there; you can hide out pretty good."

"I hate coyotes. Ate both of my cats. If you're going to shoot anything, that's a good choice."

"It's illegal to kill them. But I agree. I wanted to shoot one."

"You know, come to think of it, I haven't seen 'em around here as much as I used to."

"Well, I can tell you why." He paused, but Michael didn't think it was for dramatic effect. He seemed not to want to think about what he was about to say. That did not stop him. "I thought Esposito was going to try to pop one of them. He hates the coyotes. But before anything could happen, this guy I didn't see at all just steps out from behind a tree on the other side of the coyotes from us. A tall guy. I think it was a guy. And real fast he grabs one of the coyotes by its legs. They don't even see him coming 'til he's got one. He picks it up by its hind legs like it's a chicken's legs he's holding. The rest of the pack just, like, takes off whimpering. And the coyote he's caught is shrieking and thrashing and yipping like crazy.

"Well, this guy swings the coyote around and smashes the thing against a tree trunk, once and twice. Sickening noise. I might never forget it. And then he swings the body—which is just, like, it's dead—over his shoulder, and starts to walk off.

"And Esposito and I are just, like, holding our breaths, because it's unbelievable and it's shocking and it's all happening in, like, sixty seconds. Like, it's happening so fast that I haven't even reached the point of hoping he doesn't notice us there. And he's walking off in the opposite direction, and he stops."

"Oh, shit."

"He looks right at where we are hiding."

"What did he look like?"

"It was too dark. It was like watching moving shadows. But he was looking right at us, and he was either trying to scare us or trying to let us know it could just as easily have been one of us over his shoulder . . . and then he just walked off and disappeared into the trees."

"What about your guns?"

"I'm so glad Esposito didn't go Rambo. I thanked him. I think we'd be dead, too, if he had."

"You know," Janet said, "Esposito is from the suburbs. He's a militiaman only in his head."

"No kidding. On the way back, he was even more freaked out when I told him I thought it might have been one of the Hill People. He'd never heard of them, and he thought I was making a racial slur about immigrants. And when I told him a couple of Hill People stories, he was like, 'What the fuck? There's people living in the hills around us? And everybody knows about it?' He said, 'If it's a crazy mountain man, I can handle that. If it's a colony, I'm fucking out of here.'"

"Really?" Michael tried not to sound disconcerted. He disliked job interviewing, and was sure Laura would make him take care of Esposito's replacement.

"What do you think it was?"

"Oh, it was a man, maybe a homeless person. Maybe a Hill person."

Janet said, "One of the waitresses said that she'd heard stories that the immigrants, legal and otherwise, anyone who was living outdoors or in their cars, have left the valley because of the other people in the hills. That's what they said in the kitchen, too: Arturo called them 'the other people in the hills.'"

"So I wouldn't be surprised if Esposito doesn't come back. He was pretty freaked."

And that was where it started, the topic of conversation that would rule the rest of the evening at the bar. It was to Michael's great surprise that so many had stories about encounters in their yards or in their driveways. Several had been taking measures to protect themselves, from purchasing fancier security in their homes, to taking self-defense classes, to buying guns and stocking pepper spray to carry, to not going out alone late at night.

"I remember the start of the Hill People stories," Mitch offered, an older guy who came by the bar three times a week after playing golf and stayed long into the afternoon. "It was about seven years after the southern ranch property was sold and that whole area was cut up into lots. A lot of people who had been essentially squatting with the ranch owners' permission were forced out, and some of them moved into the hills to try to stay. Same thing happened when the Taymor farm closed. Well, six years go by, and there's a fire out in the hills. And after the fire is out, folks start worrying about landslides when the rains come, so they set about to clear the rivers of debris and they find a massive outdoor campsite, with about eighteen different camps all set up alongside the river, tapped into municipal power by miles-long cables, filtering and using water from the river.

"There was a big back-and-forth about it when the photographs of the people and their living conditions got out. This being Cheronkin, half of the town sympathized with them and was trying to plan "camp-ins" to keep the authorities from clearing the squatters out, which of course, it being the 'fifties, the authorities did before anyone had time to form the ACLU. One of the papers might have called them Hill People in their coverage."

"I didn't know it was a real story they were based on. They were kind of like our boogeyman. I've always heard there were people who lived in the hills like that," Michael

170

said. "My dad always told me that if I did see people in the hills, I shouldn't be afraid of them because they were people who were down on their luck."

"See, I don't think that's true anymore," Janet said.

Donna, a single mom nursing a drink and picking at a cheesecake at the end of her shift in the restaurant, shared her tale: Two nights before she had run into someone unidentified while taking out her trash at home after dark. Although the fellow had run at the sight of her, she was concerned enough about her son's safety that she was thinking of moving to an apartment on the other side of the town, where a homeowner was more likely to run into a coyote than someone from out of the hills.

Michael looked away from Donna to the front door, and there she was, across the room, looking his way. Talia. Instead of surprise, he felt relief. Whether she knew it or not, she liked him. He knew that just like he'd known she would be back. And then, day after day, she didn't show up and he thought maybe he'd been very wrong about it all. He'd been sure she'd be back. If not for him, then for the club. But then, even if it were for the club, he would believe it was also because of him.

"Hi. Good to see you here today," he said, too much the restaurant Michael.

"I'm not supposed to be here," Talia returned, eyes twinkling, but sounding a little torn.

She was dressed down, the way she was when he saw her on the road. Hair in a pony tail, sweats, and a t-shirt. He didn't know which way he liked her better. He did know her smile was so perfect that he had to look away before he got lost in the way it completed her beauty . . . "Why shouldn't you be here?" . . . and he ended up staring at her beautiful hands and her long fingers.

"My aunt warned me away. She thinks there's a spell on this place that makes people speak the truth. She thinks the artist put it into the sculptures." Talia thought about what she's just said, then smiled broadly. She was more relaxed than he'd seen her before. "See, that's wild. I don't know whether or not I would normally have bothered to answer your question. Or said it just that way." She smiled again. "Or that, either."

"Does your aunt have a guilty conscience?"

"Don't all the really rich old white people?"

"But not you."

"Not yet. I think I'd put on a pretty good show if people knew to ask the right questions. Truth is truth. Can't always avoid it."

"Is she really your aunt?"

"She's more like a mentor. She recognized something in me that reminded her of herself, and took it upon herself to offer me the sort of guidance she thought she could have benefited from when she was younger. And she was right, really, She's my family now—" She stopped herself and smiled, but the smile showed a little wariness.

He could see she wasn't comfortable sharing information about herself. "Well, I feel I'd be wrong to not ask. Mom's always finding new interests to pursue, and she usually hooks into people who have, should I say, alternative interests? What is your aunt into, some sort of new agey . . ."

"She—" She stopped this answer from leaving her mouth, too. And she mulled on it a second. "She's into the whole past lives thing."

"Really."

"Yeah."

"Oh, well . . . that's not so bad, right?" He laughed. "I mean, it's sort of in the neighborhood of the things she's dabbled in." Talia didn't laugh. She was watching his reaction closely. "What about you," he asked, "do you believe in that stuff, too? Before I say anything that offends you?"

"I'm not so much into the *past* part of it. There are aspects about what it means to my present—those are what seem most relevant if any of it is true. It has everything to do with who I am now and why I'm here in this town now." She thought about what she'd just said.

"The 'great change' mom always talks about. That's happening now, I guess? It would explain a lot of things, wouldn't it?"

"It's funny. I've been friends with Elena for so long, and she has these things she is involved in which I am not as involved in as she is. And she is very enthusiastic, and she shares these wild and very eccentric stories and visions that a normal person would have to think are wacky, and then

172

something happens that makes me think: What if she's right?

"So she invited me to come to Cheronkin to share in this, and I figured I couldn't lose either way, right or wrong. And it turns out that it is everything that she said. And more. And how great is that? I have renewed my faith that the world is going to change in ways that are better for us, and we are going to change in ways that are better for the Earth."

He thought about it. "You said something bad was coming, that I had come to the wrong place to be safe."

She gasped. "I did, didn't I?" She started to volunteer something about that, but stopped herself. Then she looked almost afraid to speak. Had he been too sarcastic? "Things have changed, I guess. I look at it differently now. It's different to be here and to see it and to feel it happening around me."

"Listen, you didn't come here to debate me. You want to talk to Marko about doing a set?" She nodded. "It's the same guy from the grand opening night. It's good that you came in instead of calling. He does all the bookings."

Michael lingered by the bar, waiting for her to return. A couple of guys in their late thirties were talking about the time, fifteen years before, when they rolled their car up in the hills. One guy got part of his ear cut off, and the other had to go for help. The one who stayed was pinned in the car and couldn't move. He said it was about half an hour of waiting when he heard the sound of feet shuffling around the car, but he couldn't see anything that was going on outside. He called out to them, but whoever it was didn't answer. But after a few minutes he heard them taking parts and pieces off his car, he heard banging and scraping and things coming free, and the noise didn't stop until the far-off siren started coming closer.

Michael was listening closer than he thought. He didn't see Talia until she was standing a few feet away from him. "Were you able to set something up with Marko?"

"I was. I did."

"Excellent." Michael noticed Janet and others at the bar watching him. "And, for the record, what do you think they are? The people in the hills."

173

She thought about it. "They're waiting to be found, and to be brought home. And something about this locality is calling them here from all over. They used to be people, but they're not quite that anymore because people had no room for them." She smiled awkwardly, afraid to look and see who might be listening.

"Hmm." He didn't know what to say about that. "That's different."

"New World. I've got to go."

"I'll walk you out."

"Thank you."

Her bike was outside the door, against the wall. He pointed at the basket. "What's in there?"

She smiled at him as she pulled the bike around. She wasn't going to answer, but then she changed her mind. She lifted the lid. The bottom third of the basket was filled with seeds of varying size, shape, and color. When she spoke, she spoke slowly and carefully, as if she were guarding her words.

"When I first met Elena, years ago, she helped me to remember that I had collected these seeds over many years and then hidden them away, and forgotten they existed. Even after I found it, I didn't know what to do with them, so the seeds have been stored away again even though it took me so long to find them. Elena has a very good heart, and for as long as I've known her she's been waiting for some sign that her "better world" is coming, and living her life in expectation. So when she called and said this was 'it,' I brought the box along, and I've been planting the seeds here and there to see what happens. You know," she said when she was finished, "you're sworn to secrecy. There's a code."

"I won't say anything."

"I've got to go now. 'Bye."

"'Bye."

And she rode off into the night.

Laura Hollins had originally come to Cheronkin County on a whim. She had intended neither to stay for long nor to ever return. During his college years, her brother Eli had spent several summers with a dorm pal in Cheronkin. At the end of Eli's junior year, when she was nineteen years old, she had followed him there, hoping to have some fun away from all the intrusion and clutter of life at home with the parents.

She'd had so much confidence when she arrived. And she'd lost nearly all of it by that summer's end.

The moment she realized her whole life's plan had changed she had been seated on a stool in a bar called Murray's Hat in Cheronkin's meager downtown. No one had asked to see her ID, and there she had been, sipping at a giant blue margarita, feeling as if her insides had been twisted all around. After she had dropped Eli off at the condo, she had come to Murray's, thinking a drink might help her regain her bearings. Her stomach had churned. Her heart had raced, and she had felt the blood drain out of her face. She was sickened by the feeling that possessed her—and nearly trembling at what she was considering doing about it.

She'd just met Bill Clayton for the very first time, and that experience had affected her profoundly. After years of hearing her brother mention the name in connection with his life at school, meeting Bill had overwhelmed her. He was, for all appearances, everything she had ever wanted in a man. She had known from the moment she looked in his eyes that there was to be something between them.

The margaritas at Murray's had been to shore up the confidence which had suddenly altogether abandoned her.

From the beginning, a drink had always helped her with Bill.

Soon after, she had parked her old car in the driveway outside the Clayton family ranch house, walked in through the front door of the main house, through the house, to the master bedroom, where she had found Bill waiting for her.

Theirs hadn't been the most successful of relationships. Even then, Bill had been doing well politically. He had already been involved in regional issues when she met him. People seemed to believe even then that he was going places. Laura, suddenly vulnerable and needy, learned a lot fast, and soon felt neglected. She was often left behind and alone with the liquor cabinet at the ranch house, waiting for his phone calls.

It wasn't long until it became too pathetic even for her. She'd kept all but a whiff of the relationship from her brother; he'd never known how serious it had been. She'd had

175

to leave town to make it stick, and to make sure it didn't ruin Eli's relationship with Bill.

A note was all she'd left behind. He probably hadn't seen it until weeks afterward. He never mentioned it to Eli. And she had not seen him again.

He never tried to stop her. She thought that was the classiest thing he'd done, letting her leave. It was also what had hurt the most.

And then she had spent twenty years trying to convince herself that she'd changed.

That she had learned from the mistakes she'd made.

He'd married and she'd married.

He was still married. He would always be married.

The rest of the staff had gone. She walked around the doors to make sure they were locked. She walked through the kitchen, taking mental notes on what hadn't been done right during closing duties. She double-checked the notes for the morning delivery.

Walking out of the kitchen, she found herself, interestingly enough, feeling somewhat uncomfortable with the artwork. It was her guilt, she told herself, making her feel she could see the disapproval in faces that weren't even really there. She did not like to stare at them for too long; neither did she like to have them staring at her.

The artwork had helped her achieve the look she wanted. What she had tried to capture was the spirit of that place and time.

It turned out she had built herself the most splendid of cages.

Twenty years have passed, Laura thought, and this was where I ended up. The only thing changed was that the rent had gone up. And for the most part, what she still felt was anger. At herself. For all the time she had wasted. For letting herself get lost in Bill. Every dream she'd ever had came out of the time she first spent in Cheronkin. And now, suddenly, her head was nearly spinning again as she was finding that the world did turn full circle and maybe dreams did have a chance of coming true.

When she heard the knock, she walked across the dance floor to Fandango's back doors, which opened onto the patio. She pushed them open.

Bill was there on the other side. In his old leather jacket, a familiar smile on his face. "Hi," he said.

"Hi yourself."

Twenty years.

This was what life did to a person who never learned her lesson.

IN THE NEWS

West Coast Regional Reporter, May 21:

Trippin' Out: Police in Cheronkin County admitted they may have picked up and escorted to the county line a man suspected of selling LSD- and marijuana-laced cigarettes to attendees at a beach barbecue in early January.

The officers reportedly discovered a man asleep on a bench outside Hoffman Hills Abbey, once the site of a monastery and now a bakery, and assumed he was a transient. Cheronkin County is one of several California counties that enforces strict ordinances against transients.

"Our policy is to escort all transients to the county line and to promise to promptly arrest them should they return," said David Long, the department's press liaison. According to Long, the officers had second thoughts after dropping the suspect off. They returned to the Abbey and discovered a methamphetamine still in a wooded section of the K.D. Land Cemetery, which is adjacent to the Abbey.

West Coast Regional Reporter, May 23:

Coleman Canyon Park rangers closed down the popular campground in central California and conducted campsite-to-campsite searches after a 6-year-old boy, Sonny Fuentes, disappeared while playing in a dry creek bed next to the family's campsite. Fuentes is the seventh child to disappear under similar circumstances in central California over the last nineteen months. No connection to those earlier disappearances has been established.

9

An excerpt from Dick Arthur's unpublished manuscript,
Who's Been Sleeping In My Head?

A NOTE FROM THE AUTHOR

A brief history might be necessary here for those under the age of fifteen today, who were not yet alive when the Wave Event occurred:

To visualize the beginning of the Wave Event, imagine a pinpoint poked through a piece of paper; that is how the Wave began, as a pinpoint in the sky above the Earth. For those who saw it in its first moments, it looked like a star twinkling with uncharacteristic brightness in the early afternoon. And then it was an expanding flash of light detected by astronomers across half the globe, brighter than the light of day.

Satellites confirm that the Wave Event began as a point of light 12,000 miles from the surface of the earth. In seconds, the pinpoint-sized object expanded into a disc of light thousands of miles in diameter, and it seemed to be moving toward the planet. It continued to grow as it sped toward the Earth, which, revolving gracefully around the Sun and yet spinning a bit wobbly on its axis, moved into and through what was, by the time of contact, a circle of white light many times wider than the diameter of the planet. The disc of light, the edges of which could not be seen from the Earth's surface, continued to grow as the entirety of the planet passed through it.

Below is a drawing:

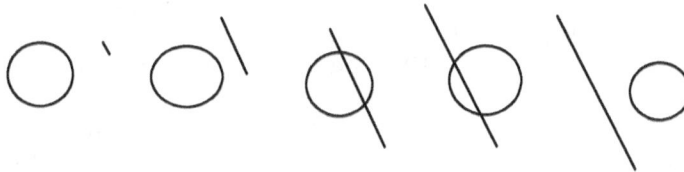

Standing on the ground, looking up at the sky, the typical human being would have seen a point of light that rapidly grew into a round, flat, white circle in the sky. After a moment, it might have appeared that a giant finger had poked a hole in the sky, revealing only bright light underneath, like a tear in a lampshade. It might also have appeared that the rip was spreading, and that as it did so it was eating up the sky. Very soon, the object had spread wider and farther than the visible horizon. It *was* the sky. And the whole of this new sky glowed an ambient white, like a ceiling made of neon, and it would have also seemed to be closing in on wherever it was on the planet that person watching it was standing.

You would have looked up and seen a wall of white approaching. You might have tried to duck or crouch or hide under a table, but before you could act, it was upon you. There was no time to run or even to think, so quickly did it wash over you, through you, past you, and then in no time at all again your head and eyes were on the other side of it and the rest of your body emerged from it and you were whole and you were standing exactly in the same spot in which you had been standing during the timeframe of the event. Everything around you looked the same, but it felt like a different world.

As you came out on the other side of the light, you realized it was a wave of light and that there was another side to it. You watched the wall of white roll on and away from you and you wondered what the hell was it? Some new kind of bomb?

As it rolled away from you, you would have seen trees, houses, streetlamps, streets, all the physical world emerged from the Wave, and the world was reset as it was before. You would have then realized that you had not emerged in another world after all; it was not another reality, and you were not dead. (Or so it seemed. Or so you wanted to pretend it seemed. Even though you knew everything was different. This was part of the new reality.) You were standing exactly where you'd been moments before and everything was the same.

And then, in the distance, coming from more than one direction, and headed in more than one direction, you heard sirens, a sound that would be common for many days to come.

The Wave Event lasted only minutes, but its devastating after-effects lingered. It soon became apparent that not all of the human (or animal) population had emerged from the other side of that wall of light. In fact, the Wave had exacted a terrible toll on the human race.

For, in fact, the Wave swept over some people and animals, and it swept them away. They never emerged from the other side of the light. When the event was complete, there were 600-800 million people fewer people on the planet. No estimate of animal deaths has been compiled, as most of the information was anecdotal. Many millions more people died in the aftermath, as a direct result of the absence of those who had vanished. There were cars, for example, and trucks and buses, suddenly rendered driverless, that caused a horrific toll in property damage, fires, and loss of life; there were people who performed duties vital to the societies in which they lived—for example, air traffic controllers—who disappeared in the middle of performing those valuable tasks. Wherever the Wave had caught them—in bed, at work, in a bar, guarding a prison, sitting in a cell—the individuals were no more when the Wave rolled on. (And it seems now, twenty years later, that they won't be coming back, or that they haven't yet). Surviving this mass loss required the efforts of all who remained. It must be made clear in any discussion that the cooperation exhibited in the immediate post-Wave environment cannot be overstated or overvalued. Those who were left clearly understood that a judgment had been rendered, and they understood it fell to the good to step in to get the work done.

The disappeared came from all backgrounds and occupations; however, certain identifiable segments of the world's societies were more likely to have disappeared in the wake of the Wave: these included violent criminals, both incarcerated and on the streets, security personnel, military combatants, and religious and political leaders. There was much debate over the moral component implicit in any conclusions drawn about the vanished, though it is even now taboo to express the sentiment—the general, unspoken consensus has long been that a lot of bad people were suddenly gone from the world, and to the betterment of all who remained.

As one might hope to be the case in a universe supposed by the majority to be overseen by some kind of a loving god, the vanished tended to be violent and vicious, hateful and cruel, or the sorts of people who knowingly employed the violent or vicious or hateful or cruel for their own benefit. The range of individuals involved, in terms of income, race, occupation, and location, was remarkably well distributed when adjustments were made to certain population studies data for the presence of prisons—where percentages of the vanished were much higher than in the general population—and for Wave-related deaths taking place in the arenas of war or other armed conflict. Initially, individual cases were highlighted in the media that showcased people who had disappeared who had not seemed to fit the sociopathic profile attributed to those taken by the Wave; but generally, on closer investigation, the judgment borne out was invariably proven correct. It is an apparent lesson now that many of the world's evils were often lurking not more than a few doors down the street, if not next door.

An International Day of Mourning was offered up at the end of that first week. The people of the world took it a step further, and in the streets, in the fields, in the empty palaces of vanished tyrants, they danced and celebrated the freedom of their continued existence.

Perhaps no other aspect of life in this age of humanity was more affected by the Wave Event than religious identity. None of it was covered in any basic religious text. Yes, the evil among us had been vanquished, but no one was clear, in those first years, what rubric had been used to decide who was bad and who was not. And the form of this cleansing, the Wave itself, seemed futuristic, possibly a product of a more scientifically advanced technology, perhaps even an alien culture. It did not seem this would be the sort of tech or methodology wielded by the ancient and monotheistic gods worshipped by mankind. And too, every faith suffered deaths among its leadership, and losses among its followers. None, it seemed, had the words to articulate an explanation for what had occurred that did not sound antiquated and quaint.

Two upstart "religious" groups appeared to capitalize on the shift in mainstream religious thought brought on by the Wave. It is likely a significant matter that one of these groups does not identify itself as a religion but rather as a corporation, and the other exists as the stuff of speculation, elevated but a step above urban legend.

The first of these groups, the so-called Framework, posits the theory of human life as a sort of Petri-dish experiment conducted by aliens on a planet altered to be suitable for such work. The Framework viewpoint aligns surprisingly well with fundamentalist interpretations of the first book of the Bible, wherein Yahweh creates all in seven days. Supporters believe that aliens established on the planet Earth a controlled environment within which they were able to speed the natural processes of evolution in order to develop the hominid species that now dominates the planet. They find that alien scientists were not only responsible for the creation of man, but also for many creatures now regarded as mythic, such as the chimera, the unicorn, and the dragon. They place the blame for the splitting of Pangaea and the great floods that destroyed the majority of life on the planet on a conflict between these alien scientists who settled on the planet and another group of aliens who wanted the Earth for their own.

To what purpose the aliens' experiment, the Framework suggests the experiment was the purpose, as has been the case with much of humankind's study of space.

In regards to the Wave, the Framework posits the event as a sort of cosmic inoculation of the planetary body by those who are monitoring our development. As a doctor would administer a shot to a sick patient so did the aliens administer medicine into that controlled environment, a light-based vaccine which killed off those parts of the collective human body which were not contributing to our overall growth and development.

Absent the marketing flair of the Framework for selling its shamelessly branded ideology, the second group, the antithesis of the first, did not enter mainstream thought until the latter part of the decade following the Wave Event, although the movement has existed, according to followers, since the birth of the planet.

Core to the faith this group holds is the belief that life existed on the planet prior to the arrival of humans, in the form of highly developed and immortal spirit beings, exclusively female in gender, who were bonded with the soul

183

of the planet and freely roamed its surface. The evolution of these first spirits is a convoluted history from there, and one with many parallels to the world's existing creation myths, to early books of the Bible, and to the mythologies of the ancient Greeks. That history ends with a punishment meted out to these powerful, earthly, chthonic spirits: ever before free, they would ever forward be bound to the female descendants of sons and daughters of humankind.

So it follows, according to their history, they have been bound to humanity ever since. Each spirit is born into the body of a human female, living the life of that female until such a time as the spirit is able to awaken again and resume its prior life. She will live in that form for an extended period of time, often more than a hundred years, longer than the average woman, until the form dies, and then after an unspecified time she will be born again into another human female baby, and begin the process again.

Typically, a woman so possessed will realize her inner connection to the channeled spirit in her twenties, and will immediately sever all ties to the life she has led up until that moment. Then she will attempt to pick up on the life she had been living when last she lived and died, and in doing so, she will vanish from her former life.

There is a paucity of documentation available on this new religious movement, and yet, despite the lack of a billboard-style campaign such as that currently waged by the Framework, knowledge of the first spirits is widespread in many communities worldwide, communities which embrace the concept of a coming world wherein all are clothed and fed and sheltered. Many theories mild and outrageous have been postulated, from suggestions that involve both notable historical figures—from the Virgin Mary to Catherine the Great—to more credible connections posited to many of the goddess movements that have mysteriously risen and just as mysteriously disappeared over the history of humankind, to the Lilith movement, to the Eleusian mysteries, to the Daughters of Eve.

The central goal of adherents is to right the wrongs visited upon themselves and upon the planet, which they view as their godhead. By their tradition, Mother Earth has for millennium been recovering from the damage done by a terrible conflict with the early ancestors of modern man, and this task has been made more difficult by the ongoing damage inflicted by their seed. They believe mankind has already begun dividing into factions, each governed by a great power that wishes to establish control over the world. They believe these factions will become embroiled in a growing conflict which, through mutual death and destruction, will create the opportunity for these first spirits to reassert their dominance over the competing factions and to restore the planet.

They believe that a series of seven events will occur as the planet gathers her forces and raises her own army. The last event in this series will signal the turning of the world and the emergence of a new reality which very much resembles an Eden-like world and which will contain only a small remainder of the totality of humankind. By their reckoning, the Wave Event was the fifth event, with the previous having occurred in Cheronkin County, California; Lillian, Germany; Durham, North Carolina; and Cozi, Peru; each event more costly in terms of human life than the previous, each occurring in the twenty years preceding the Wave Event.

What appeal this belief system holds for its followers is difficult to fathom, but they would hardly be the first in history to firmly hold faith in the idea that decimating mankind is the only hope for the future; just as faithfully they assume they will be among the survivors of such an unimaginable horror—as if survival of such a holocaust in itself might not present an equal horror.

All involved directly are sworn to secrecy. It is part of their credo to leave nothing behind them when they awaken in their new host bodies, and that none should witness their sacred rites and live. And yet, it seems, over the millennia, there have been those here and there who have survived to tell a snippet of the tale. And so it is that our present society is awash in conjecture about their agenda, if no longer their very existence.

Among the conjecture, none of it supported by hard evidence:
• That among the followers of this and related Goddess/Earth based groups, there is generally one woman, and occasionally two or three, regarded as the vessel(s) of a first spirit, and whose advice on future events is often sought.

185

- That followers practice forms of witchcraft
- That the first spirit incarnations are generally unable to conceive or bear children. That in the exceptions to this rule, the children are generally killed during the awakening phase. ~~The children who survive into adulthood are infertile.~~
- That the movement encourages women to leave their husbands and become lesbians
- That they kidnap children and eat them
- That they are part of a terrorist plot to undermine our democracy
- That they have the power to influence ordinary human minds, to plant suggestions and affect behavior in others

This group was brought to my attention more than half a century ago. Had I mentioned it then, I would have been institutionalized. Had I mentioned this thirty years ago, I would likely have been out of my university job by the end of my shift. And then, of course, the world changed. Had I written these words ten years ago, I would have been regarded with suspicion but also with interest from a society still reeling from the Wave and still open to suggestions. This afternoon, I spoke on the subject before a sold-out audience at a campus theatre, and I anticipate doing media interviews for the next three days. Their secret is out. Now we must find a way to stop them.

None of the story that follows was intended for human consumption, or to ever be recorded or written or read. Although it is a fiction, it describes secret histories, hidden rites and traditions, and the future of the planet as it is anticipated to unfold by these first spirits. When I first realized the extent of the information provided to me, I was afraid to share it, for fear they would seek to destroy me. That has proved to be true, even before I was aware that what I was publishing might have any basis in reality, and they have been after me since; and that is why, and after such an illustrious opening to my career, I lived half of my life in hiding.

I've been asked many times over the last decade what I believe initiated the Wave Event. What I believe happened is that somewhere in the world, five seconds before the Wave began, a small child was witness to a battle, a riot, a bombing, a rape, a beating, and that child—who was just about to be swallowed by the violence he or she had witnessed—that child cried out to the world, to the universe, to whatever powers might have been listening. And what the child wanted was not only salvation, but also retribution. Not just for it to stop; but for it to never happen again.

And that is how the believer in the first spirits views the whole of human history, and this is the view which they ascribe to their Goddess Earth, and this is their fervent wish for the last battle mankind wages against itself: grant us salvation from humankind, and help us to make them pay for what they've done to this world. Although not necessarily in that order.

10

Mid-June

"This is the problem with living in paradise, and the weather is unrelentingly perfect, including the regular bouts of tropical rain. It's hard to get anything productive done." Carina was spread eagle on the other side of the stream that bubbled out of the crevice at the top of the giant rock shelf on which she and Mary were lying. "People who aren't from here think it's apathy and self-centeredness, but it's simple things like this kind of day that are what life is all about. All the stuff they think is really important for us to fill our days and our brains with just takes us further away from this."

The stream ran down its worn path in the stone, past an outcropping of rocks on which sat a length of rope, to the edge of the shelf, where it dropped twenty feet to the next terrace of rocks below.

"Then again, tanning time is productive time. The body needs regular doses of sunlight. And when do I ever get to tan? Anyway: Wouldn't it be great if Michael and I started dating? I'd be such a great sister-in-law, and so would you. And I love Michael, and I'd treat him better than that pig Danielle ever did . . ."

Mary laughed. Carina apparently thought there had been a moment with Michael at the Fandango grand reopening and then another one during the car rally that indicated a window of opportunity existed.

"You know what? I'm all for it, even though I'm sure it would be weird. I mean, I love him, but it's been hard to forget things like him taking my teenage sex diary and reading it to his little rat friends."

"You can't oppose a marriage because of something someone did when he was in junior high. He thought he was being cool, not exposing the neighborhood ho."

"That was when I was with Spencer. Total first-time experimentation on a big scale, and I thought it was important enough to chronicle in writing. We had sex like ten times a week, in every position a horny seventeen-year-old boy could imagine, in every place that was accessible to us. I was so dumb, too. Thank God for the clinic at the Holiday House, or I would have been a mother by my junior year, Spencer being a firm advocate of the withdrawal method of contraception. After a while, I totally forgot about the calendar. I forgot I had stashed it away in my bedroom, I forgot to write in it, I forgot that it existed. And then I come around the corner and he's showing it to his friends."

"You know what? It was just a location-situation-type thing, Mary. It's not like we've even talked."

"It doesn't have as much to do with the calendar that he isn't trustworthy or anything like that. He's my brother. What if something went wrong?"

"I can't believe you've spent time thinking about it like that."

"So he hasn't called you? That's just the type of thing I don't want to know."

"You know what? We never talked about anyone calling anyone. I told him I have a boyfriend."

"Why?"

"I thought he would think it was unfeminine that I know how to roll my own joints."

"Are you kidding?"

"Fine, Mary, That's a deal. I won't say a word to you about Michael or vice versa. Except maybe in the case that I do want you to go beat him up, which at this point I can't perceive happening. How about instead you can tell me about Doctor Todd."

A rubber ball, only partially inflated, came sailing from below and dropped down in the pool of running water next to their towels, splashing water all over them.

"Sorry!" a voice called from below.

Carina reached out, plucked the ball from the water, and tossed it back down.

Mary, self-conscious about her minimal state of dress, quickly pulled on a t-shirt. It wasn't that there was any evidence of what she'd been through, at least physically. It was that she'd had dreams where her abdomen and vagina had been more adversely affected by the birthing than she had at first realized and so everything was protruding more than it should. She also believed the dreams were tied to a deep-seated feeling that her body wasn't going to let her

189

have another child. She was never meant to deliver a child in the first place.

"Maybe that's a hint we should head back."

"I'm done, if you are," and with that Carina went about packing up their stuff. "I ran into him at the movies. That doctor you went out with. Dr. Todd."

"Really."

"I couldn't remember how that one ended. He was cute and flirty."

Mary didn't answer as she dropped the rope and they climbed down from the stony perch at the top of the waterfall. There was a party of four, two guys and two girls, all in their early twenties, who had set up their base on the next terrace down, which was surrounded by shallow pools populated by the occasional salamander. With the girls there, the guys wouldn't be spending too much time staring at their butts while they climbed down.

Always a nice way to meet people.

She hadn't expected they would run into anyone on a weekday. It was a long hike in from the nearest parking. She and Carina had been willing to make a day of it to come back to one of their favorite spots from high school, one of the few waterfalls in the hills and the only one with enough space to spread out a towel on.

The guys were cute. One had a T-shirt that said I LIKE SOCCER MOMS. Not that, at this point in her life, she had any time or use for them.

One of the guys offered that they had passed some pretty spectacular flowers on the way up, and a really amazing arbor. Before Carina could point out that Mary, too, had mentioned seeing a spectacular arbor in the hills, Mary jumped in and asked him if he had taken the Two Pines path or Marble Head, a test to determine if these were locals or out-of-towners. He knew exactly what she was talking about, and told her where she could find the flowers and the arbor near the Joshua tree that was off the Marble Head walk, which was the way they'd planned on going back to their cars anyway.

As they walked off, Mary thought her heart might be fluttering. Of course she had said something to Michael and Carina about the arbor. But it kept her thinking about the whole . . . incident at the ranch house. She was still trying to convince herself it had all been a dream. Because otherwise, what the hell had it been?

Carina stopped from time to time to pick wildflowers, stem and all, which she started weaving into a circle in her hands; she was making a crown. Mary immediately began to do the same, and they walked in silence until they were out of earshot of the other hikers.

"Jeffrey Todd," Mary said, "was a big, dirty swinger. Without me knowing anything was going on, he invited me to his house for a party with his doctor and nurse friends. Uchh, I was totally overdressed. What a waste of looking too good. It was like a frat party, dancing, drinking, taking Jacuzzis, and playing a loud game of croquet. There was Thai food and frozen yogurt, and they'd gone through bottles and bottles of wine by the time I got there. There were a couple funny jokes here and there, and the little wine I had didn't go the distance of making me feel more comfortable.

"So I'm sitting next to Jeffrey's best friend, Alex, behind this big glass table Jeffrey has in his living room. There are three other girls, all trainee nurses who don't know how to wear their makeup, sitting on each side of the table, all of them leaning in while Alex breaks out his stash of coke. A couple people have long since disappeared to the back of the house, my guess was to have sex. And Alex is telling us a story while he cuts up the coke. A story about one of his lovers who suggested he consider using deodorant.

"'American women,' he said, 'as a group of women, are so concerned with hygiene. They're always worried about how they smell. I told her that, and I told her maybe she should consider using some pussy powder.'"

"Eww," Carina said.

"The coke was good, so I figured that was why we gave him the benefit of a laugh. Which shows what I know. Because, when I lick my finger and start to run it across the tabletop, you know, picking up the bits and particles so I can do a freeze, I can see through the glass table that one of the girls has moved her hand into Alex's lap, where she is playing with the head of his uncircumcised penis, this hooded and bent purple knob that is just popping out behind the elastic. She is just fondling away, for all of us to see."

"Oh, my goodness!"

191

Mary laughed. "I'll say. I swear, I don't have anything against the uncircumcised and I think all the myths are over exaggerated, but there was dried smegma on it . . ." Mary couldn't continue.

"It was dirty?"

"Like he hadn't washed it since the last time."

Both girls laughed. Mary waved her hand in a circle as if she were erasing the memory, as if that would help her to finish the story. "It was so gross. And I didn't know what to say. So, as soon as I saw it, I just sort of backed up and away from the table, maintaining eye contact the whole time."

"With him, the girls, or the penis?"

"With him. Right. Suddenly, it's a porno. And I look over at Jeffrey, to get him to come to my rescue, and I see that he is dancing very slowly, cheek to cheek with this cheap little coked-up nurse, and both of them are staring at me. And I can just tell that he's completely excited by all of this, which means he probably did this all the time, and the nurse looks like she's ready to start undressing him.

"I think they've been watching the whole scene with Alex, and I'm having trouble figuring out why any of that would turn them on when I feel these hands that smell like rose-scented lotion brushing lightly up over my shoulders and playing with my hair."

"No way. Don't tell me it was Alex."

"No. It's this Rebecca chick, another nurse, who is suddenly standing behind me. It was so bizarre. I felt like I was the only person in the room who hadn't been bitten by the vampire. I headed for the front door. And then I walked home to my place at about three in the morning. Ah, now I remember why I didn't feel like mentioning it to anybody." It had bothered her once, she realized, and it didn't at all anymore. It was too long ago, long before other things that matter more.

"I'm so sorry to bring up a bad memory." They came upon the Joshua Tree, and followed a narrow trail beside it over a couple of small hills. "Look." Carina slipped her crown on her head.

"Lovely." Mary did the same.

"Oooh. Nice use of mustard."

"Oh, I was sorry, too. Better to know, though. Watch out for him."

192

Carina stopped in her tracks. "Oh."

"What?"

"Look."

And there it was.

Mary's heart jumped again. It was real.

And exactly where the guy had said, and formed exactly as the other one had been. An archway made by two trees growing five or so feet apart, decorated up and down with a wild array of flowers. This one was more grown in than the other, the flowers further into their bloom, the buds swollen and open wide, looking almost as if their time was about to end. As if the petals might begin to drop any time now.

"You think it's for a wedding?"

"The one I saw was in the hills by the ranch house. It would be a mighty big reception."

"Not that there's any place around here for a ceremony. Is there? Maybe some hiking thing, or moutainbiking, or for horse people?"

"No."

"Well, let's put something on it. I want to contribute."

Mary lifted off her crown.

"Perfect." Carina did the same, and they both found places on either side of the arch to hang their hats.

After Mary had let go of the crown, she stared at the vines. "Now let's see." This is real. This is not a dream. And if this was not a dream, then the other one was not a dream. *What really happened to me?*

"What are we watching for?"

Nothing was happening. Mary had expected the crowns to slowly blend into the greenery, and for the flower buds they'd picked, which had already started to wilt, to began to open again.

"I guess nothing," Mary said after a minute more. She reached for her crown, in the process bumping a rose bloom, sending red petals to the ground. When she lifted the crown she felt some resistance.

"Look!"

"What?"

There were three strands of vines that had grown into the crown from the arbor.

"It's growing together. Look how fast that happened. Yours is probably attached, too."

"Not really." Carina tested her crown by picking it up as Mary had. It, too, had several small, thin vines attached to it from the arbor. "Wow. What do you think it is? Venus flytrap vine?"

"I don't know. Look, it's not growing around the crown. It's growing into it."

"Creepy. Wouldn't want to fall asleep against that by accident."

"What do you think it means?" Mary was thinking of Zane when she said it. Was she always going to miss him?

"I haven't got a clue," Carina said. "You know that."

They studied it a while longer, trying to brainstorm the name of someone they knew who they could mention the arbors to who might find the information meaningful, then, failing that, turned to leave, and were soon back on the main trail. The walk to the parking lot from this trail involved a lot of switchbacks, but it was a fun path to take because of the way the area had grown in. It was almost like being in the mountains. They walked and Carina regaled Mary with stories about her own father's weirdness, which soon had Mary in stitches.

Halfway down the section of switchbacks, Mary became convinced she was seeing something ahead of them, on or off the path she couldn't tell, something that looked like it could be person or animal. It would disappear from view at some points along the path, and at others come close enough for her to believe that it was human. She pointed it out to Carina, who started scanning the horizon. Mary didn't think it was on the same path as them; it seemed to be moving more parallel to their position, which meant it was just cutting through the forest. Maybe it was an animal.

The hike back to the car, as a result, passed quickly, as they hurried their pace to advance on whatever it was Mary thought she was seeing. The only thing both girls would say for certain was that at some point, as they were coming to the clearing in the trees that would lead to the parking lot, the sun reflected off something in the area they believed the person to be. Carina wouldn't have been willing to wager on what it was at that point, but to Mary there was no doubt that it was someone's head of red hair.

"Okay," Mary said, "I have a strange story I haven't shared. On Tuesday, I took my mother to the space I'm thinking of renting for the new boutique, and she told me these kind of weird stories about this girl she keeps having 'encounters' with—"

"Ooh, sounds either sexy or uncomfortable or both. Is it a red-haired girl?"

"Yes."

"Chills. Really. That just gave me the chills. Is she from around here? I don't know anyone with hair like that—"

"No. Mom didn't, either. And you know my mother can remember the names and faces of the parents of every one of my elementary-school classmates, and she could probably tell you what nearly every one of them is up to today, or, if she couldn't, she would know someone she could check with who would know. You know her. Do you think she could possibly forget that hair color if she'd ever seen it around town?"

"Doubtful. What kind of 'encounters'?"

"Melinda saw them at the airport when she was picking up my dad a couple months ago. She says this redhead was with two other women, one of them Michael's singer girl and the other some rich old Cheronkin lady—can't remember the name."

"She's friends with Michael's wannabe girlfriend? My competition?"

"Mom was freaked out by some vibe she got from them, but wasn't sure it wasn't some hallucinatory side effect of her meds. Then I guess she ran into the other two women at the club opening."

"The singer and the older woman? I saw the end of that."

"But not the redhead, right?"

"Not that red hair," Carina said, pointing ahead of them, "no. We both would have remembered."

"I think so, too. And then, according to Mom, about a month ago—"

"What? You're kidding. Wait." Carina held out her hand, gesturing for Mary to stop. She looked closely at Mary's face. "You're leaving something out. I can tell you are. You've been doing that a while now, not sharing the full story. And isn't that what I'm here for? I count on you for that."

"I almost don't want to tell you. It was the first time she saw this girl. It's so funky. I thought it was too funky at the time. A while ago, before the whole airport sighting incident, my mom went to this, what's it called, regression therapy."

"Oh, your mom is so wild."

"Yeah, right. Well, I went along with her to sort of keep an eye on things."

"I always thought that would be fun. I mean, wouldn't it be a trip, if it were at all true?"

"Yeah, well. While under hypnosis, Mom had some kind of disturbing dream slash memory, which included in its cast of characters the same red-haired girl she saw at the airport."

"The same girl?"

"Yes, but before she'd ever seen her. Before the airport. Before she'd ever seen the girl or known she was a real person."

"Oh, weird."

"And then, last month, Mom nearly had a nervous . . . breakdown? I don't know what to call it other than that, brought on by some anxiety attack that started because she thought the girl was trying to invade the house. For whatever reason. I don't know why she would want to invade our house. Melinda says the redhead walked into our house through the front door, talking crap at her and promising to 'get her.'"

"Yikes."

"Note, though, as Mom did when sharing the story, that afterward there was no sign that anyone had been home that afternoon but her."

"Still, way yikes. Time to upgrade the security system. Do you think it is just the power of suggestion?"

"What is?"

"That you thought you saw red hair up ahead?"

"I would if you hadn't seen it, too."

Carina was slow to process this. "Right, right," she said after a minute.

Mary was uncharacteristically quiet as she ate her salad later at Fandango. She was trying to imagine what that particular girl might be doing up in the woods.

"Something in me has changed, Michael. And it's not like Mom, where all of a sudden and for a short span of time I'm completely interested in something and then it's over. This is it. I mean, since I've been cutting hair, I've known I would be doing this my entire life. It's just one of the things I do, and I'm good at it. And I've always had a steady income. But it's going to be totally organic from here on in."

"How are you paying for it?"

"I sold Dad on it. He's going to co-sign for the small business loan."

"Cool for you. Do you think that means I can ask him to help me with a new car?"

"You know, this is going to work. Especially here. The product is out there—I've already found a bunch of alternatives I can work with and even sell. There are still some of the processes that I haven't worked out or I just haven't had any experience with . . . and I think I found a place on the other side of the freeway, of course, because even if prices are dropping, I can't make the rent over here."

"So you're serious."

"Thinking seriously. But I'm also still taking time off. I've never done this before, for this length of time. I've been working since I was fourteen. It's kind of fun."

"Well, you look great, sister."

"I have this tomato plant at home. At one point, it was, or seemed like it was dead. And then, it's like I turned into a green thumb, and it started growing. Little cherry tomatoes, I love them. And then I thought I would test my green thumb, so I planted all these herbs in the window planter, and filled all the vases around my kitchen. There is so much light in there. And now my kitchen is like a garden. It smells so good, and there are peppers and tomatoes and onions and garlic. I've even got these three beautiful, fat carrots growing in the window box now . . . It all goes along with my new clean-living pledge. I am a green thumb now, do you hear, can you believe it?"

Before she left the club, Mary had another look at the map on the floor in the front lobby of the club. She could easily identify the general areas of the two arbors she had seen, one to the north, one to the west. What did those areas have in common? Were there really others? And where should she look to find them?

197

As had been their tradition since junior high school, on the last day before the County Fair picked up from its site on the edge of the state campus outside of Cheronkin and moved its sprawl down south, Mary and Carina made their tour of a scene that in times past had yielded a steady supply of available collegiate men.

Carina brought a flask of rice wine, figuring it was organic enough to be acceptable to Mary's new palate; Mary acquiesced because she understood her friend needed that from her once in a while and, besides, she couldn't counter the "organic" argument. They emptied it as they toured the animal nursery.

The rides were rickety and stomach-churning, which Mary still had a penchant for, though generally they went on for too long; the food was fast and greasy; and the only guys who looked good enough to flirt with also happened to look like the guys most likely to be out on parole. The college boys, not for the first time in recent years, seemed too young, too scrubbed up, too clean, too new. The best-looking guys were the ones who were there with their wives and their kids.

Carina and Mary found their greatest amusement in watching one trashy blond-haired woman's drunken flirtations with seedy-looking scumbag ride operators in an attempt to make her pig boyfriend jealous. At some point, the girl saw she was amusing Carina and actually called the two of them lushes. Carina heard the word *luscious* and spent a few minutes doing faux modeling poses as the girl and the boyfriend walked away, him watching Carina with a look of bewilderment.

Finally, though, enough was enough. After they each had their own cotton candy, Mary and Carina agreed to stay to ride the Ferris wheel as a last hurrah for the evening. Happily playing with their treats with sticky red fingers, they watched silently as a cute couple in their twenties boarded the Ferris wheel ahead of them.

It took some time to unload and load all the seats. And they waited in the cold, shivering as they looked out over the ocean. Mary was very soon nauseous. She closed her eyes, leaned against Carina, and started worrying about her family again.

Carina, seemingly reading her mind, asked Mary if she had seen the family units lately.

"I saw my brother for lunch. And my mom, for a little bit."

"They're doing okay?"

"Just don't tell me my brother is a babe."

"He is these days."

Mary gave Carina an irritated look. "Mom asked me about Dick Arthur. Do you remember that name?"

"Dick Arthur?" Carina hadn't the slightest.

"Some writer," Mary said. "He wrote a story about Cheronkin that Michael says contains the only reference in a major fiction novel to the existence of our town. And my mother mentioned something she heard from that Elena Altman at the Fandango opening—"

"Oh, yeah, I remember her. I was thinking about her. The one who was with Talia."

"Yes, exactly. Elena is Talia's 'Auntie.' And you know what? You are spending too much time thinking about my brother and his life. You used to have other prospective boyfriends."

"I know." Carina hung her head in mock shame. "It's like a sickness."

"Elena told my mother that she was the character in Dick Arthur's story, so she's been trying to find my old school copy of the book. I guess it's out of print now, and hard to find. She asked Michael for his, but he left his copy behind after the break-up with Danielle."

"You and Michael both had copies of the same book?"

"Yes. And you probably do, too. We had to read his stories, I guess, in our lit class. Because he was a writer who lived in our community."

Carina didn't get it. "He was in our class?"

"Never mind," Mary said, giving up.

"And how about Melinda otherwise? Is she still out keeping the order?" Mary gave her a look. "What?"

"Just to give you an idea what my mom is like, Carina, without really getting into it. When I dropped by to visit her today, I noticed there were all these people all over the place, on the sidewalk up and down the block, sitting in their cars with binoculars, in the trees with cameras, even up on one of the lampposts. I asked one of the neighbors how long these people have been camped outside. She tells me a week now."

"There were a lot of them?"

"About thirty people that I saw. Carina, they're Bird Society members. My mom won't admit she's the one who filed the report, but she won't deny it, either."

"What report?"

"The one that cites the sighting of some centuries-long-extinct owl hanging around in the trees behind our house. Because she had a dream about it. Or she thinks she had a dream about it but isn't sure. As if a lack of admission on her part was enough to raise doubt about her doing it. And then Melinda's got that whole town meeting thing coming up—"

Carina gasped suddenly and squeezed Mary's hand. They were at the top of the wheel, moving forward over the top and down, looking at the back of the cute couple's chair and the backs of their heads for the briefest of seconds before their seat dropped beneath them.

"Did you see? Did you see?"

Of course Mary hadn't. "What was it?"

Carina squeezed Mary's hand again to shush her.

When they reached the top of the wheel again, the couple were kissing very passionately when the backs of their heads came into view again. The girl raised her hand straight up, and some stray light caught and glinted off of something on her finger.

Carina started screaming, "They're engaged! They're engaged!"

She was so enthusiastic Mary would have thought Carina knew them. But apparently, everybody was really happy for them. Mary included, for a short while. People were laughing and shrieking and congratulating them, but the driver gave them an extra long ride, and six more passes left her feeling sick again. It was when people started being off-loaded that Mary started to feel some sadness.

She hadn't gotten her period back yet. It had been two months. But there was something more to it. Her body felt different, like it was done with that. Mary was comfortable with the knowledge she would just have to make do with Max and Lorraine and the children of whoever it was Michael eventually managed to marry and impregnate.

It was like a door that she'd just noticed was cracked open. And whenever she took the time to truly think about all the implications, she'd push the door open wider and realize just how much of an effect this was going to have on her pursuit of life and love and happiness as she had always anticipated it. Where was she going to find those things, when it felt like all the parts of her that were needed in the search had been birthed out of her already and then turned to dust?

Carina read the strange look on Mary's face and pulled her back from that abyss. She leaned over and said to Mary, "We should just try to enjoy the moment. This is the closest I have ever been to a man offering a ring and the promise of eternal love."

As the last few seats before theirs were emptied and refilled, they both sat silently watching the crowd. A familiar piece of fabric caught Mary's eye, a scrap of a dress showing underneath a cape worn by a woman in a hat holding a cup of coffee. A breeze lifted the cape enough for Mary to see the bottom of the dress and to recognize it as being similar to a dress her Aunt Laura had worn at a family dinner before, a dress that Mary had always loved. A closer look and she was sure that it was her aunt standing there. Mary scanned the crowd, looking for the kids. The wheel turned a seat more, the happy couple were unloaded, and the two headed off for wedded bliss and eternal love.

She pointed Laura out to Carina. "Is that . . .?"

"It is, isn't it? And who is she with?"

It wasn't the kids or the nanny who walked up beside her aunt, took her hand, and kissed her romantically on the lips. Even bundled up as much as he was, Mary recognized him in a second. What did they think they were, in disguise? Why wouldn't they just get a room?

"That's my 'Uncle' Bill."

Mary was late getting started on her hike, but the approach of the solstice meant she had enough daylight, by her estimation, to be back at her car by dusk. She'd set this as one of her tasks for the week, but everything else on her list had taken precedence, and she'd had to postpone until a last-minute hair coloring cancellation gave her an opening.

She had accomplished a lot, including testing out some of the new hair product on family and friends, and even with the time available, she could have put this hike off until the following week, but she also felt the time outdoors alone would be good for her.

She hadn't dealt with her aunt's affair in any way at all. It was the Aunt Rachel/Uncle Stan thing all over again. Bunch of cheaters in the family. Mary didn't want to tell her father. She was sure that talking to Aunt Laura about it would be mortifying. So she hadn't done anything. Yet.

She had taken the existence of such a relationship as a further signal that nothing was what it seemed, and no one was quite as good a person as you thought him or her to be. Mary didn't particularly care for Mrs. Bill Clayton, but she also didn't like the thought of her aunt, who she'd always admired for her openness and directness, having a cheap little affair with a married man. Even if they had once dated a million years ago. "Aunt" Meg, Bill's wife, had been with him for thirty years.

Mary had actually kind of admired her, too, even though Meg was kind of scary, in a take-no-shit sort of way. Very straightforward, very no nonsense. Expected eye contact and direct answers. The type of person who called you on evasive answers right in front of everybody. Mary had been fortunate to have always avoided being the focus of her attention, but she had seen Meg make people squirm.

Mary remembered Meg joking to her at her parents' twentieth anniversary party about how bad the press was to candidates' wives if those wives happened to have opinions or businesses of their own, both of which applied to Meg.

To illustrate her point, Meg had said, "I look great, don't I?"

And that night she did. Very elegant. Much slimmed down. Haircut good, not great—better than average for a fifty-some-year-old woman.

Mary had nodded.

"Well, if I died tonight," Meg said, "I guarantee you the picture they would print would be from some event where I weigh thirty pounds more and I'm in a pantsuit, big glasses, very little makeup and I've got a drink in one hand and a drumstick in the other."

Tonight, as Mary walked toward the top of a mountain, she was thinking maybe there were a lot of things she couldn't imagine being true that were true.

She'd not been able, at first, from the map on the floor of Fandango, to determine a pattern to where the arbors were set, other than that they were in the zone where all the plants were growing like crazy. She'd realized by studying a street map that the hike behind the ranch house ended at a spot that butted up against parkland, and that there was a parking lot and trailhead—technically in the next county, and not part of Cheronkin—not too far from where the arbor had been erected. And that was true of the other arbor she'd seen—not too far off the trailhead, and only a moderate hike in from the parking lot.

Whoever had placed them had carried them in from their cars. It made sense that there was only so far they would be able to get carrying the weight of the lumber.

There were three other trailheads with parking lots in the greened-over areas. Since she'd already found arbors north and west of town, she'd chosen from those three candidates a trailhead to the south to hike. And if Marble Canyon Road had been open, she would have been able to drive a few quick miles into the canyon, make a turn, and drive another ten minutes to get to the parking lot that marked the start of the trail. Instead, she had to reach that same parking lot from the other direction, taking the longest way around, a twenty-mile journey that started with the freeway and ended on that same turn-off on the same road.

The trail climbed easily through some pretty forest scenery before turning into a set of tedious switchbacks that took her back and forth across several sloping hillsides. There was ivy growing over the fallen trunks and branches strewn between the trees on either side of the trail, and wildflowers, and poppies. It was a challenging hike, much of it decorated by a sprinkling of four-foot tall saplings of a variety of trees, plants which Mary was sure hadn't been there the last time she'd made this climb. Spread out as they were, and so close in height, they seemed to have been planted together, so as to one day form a grove over the switchbacks. Or maybe, she thought, that was the day the growing thing started here. She wondered if that was the same night Michael's dog "died"?

203

At the end of the last switchback, the trail led her through areas she had hiked many times in her life, and which looked nothing like they ever had before. Everything was gorgeously green. Areas which she remembered in previous summers as being fields filled with long, dry, golden grass and the sounds of crickets and birds—those were gone. In their place were green, flower-filled pastures hidden behind the curtains of ivy that draped over the surrounding trees. There were animals everywhere, and the air was filled with the songs of birds. She saw squirrels and rabbits and even a deer, the first she had seen in the hills in over twenty years.

Her reward, near the top of the highest hilltop in the vicinity, was another arbor, nearly exactly the same as the others, but even deeper into its blooming. So many petals had fallen that they covered the ground around it, and although the arbor was still covered with a few fat, non-matching wild blooms, it didn't look like it was going to be growing anything new soon. She stared at the arbor, and realized she'd left her camera in the car.

She asked herself: What if she cast away her preconceived notions and assumed not only that her mother were right, that there was something going on in town that they should be concerned about, some big, New Agey, world-changing event, but also that she was being haunted by this woman, this girl, or at least she was trying to make Melinda feel that way. What would she be, and by extension the other two? Part of some kind of witchy cult?

What if the canyon accidents were tied together? What if someone wanted to cut the town off from civilization? Drive people away. Why was everybody talking about the Hill People now—what had changed that had stirred everything up? The stories about them had been part of her childhood. They had been, literally, the local bogeymen, the ones adults snickered slightly about when putting a fright into their kids. And her Dad always had said there was no such thing. Just a handful of homeless people and mentally unhealthy people who live outdoors and who find the warmer coastal climate better for that lifestyle.

That was just obviously no longer the case, she thought. It wasn't a handful anymore. It was more like every societal fringe dweller for a thousand miles around was gathered here.

Now, even the cashier at the grocery store was talking about them as if they were an accepted part of their lives. Were the Hill People acting up because of the same thing that Melinda thought was happening? Were they waiting for something to happen? Were they causing what was happening? Did they put up the arbors?

The arbors weren't Hill People handiwork. The Hill People were probably afraid of them—or else they'd have scavenged the arbors into pieces long before now.

Mary would bet the arbors were Cameron's work. Cameron had probably been tending to it on the same day she and Carina had been there.

When Mary finally left the arbor, she returned to the main trail feeling satisfied with her mission. It was later than she'd intended; dusk had overtaken the day. But she knew the path was straightforward, and that she could find her way back to her car however dark it was. Still, she didn't like being alone in the woods, and she kicked herself for not telling anyone she was out here and for leaving her pepper spray in the camera bag in her car.

Worse, even as she thought she should be feeling at ease, a cold discomfort set her on edge.

Mary stopped walking and looked around for a rock she could use as a defensive weapon. Her inner alarm bells were ringing; she fully expected to find herself at any moment standing face-to-face with a Hill person or a coyote or a bear. A cursory glance around her didn't reveal any sort of threat, but the feeling did not go away. She peered around a tree, looking into one of the overgrown meadows she'd passed on the way in.

Mary saw, about a hundred feet away from where she stood, the redheaded girl, naked, doing some kind of slow, ceremonial dance in the middle of the open field. She flowed from one pose to another, with much bowing of her head. There appeared to be a knife lying on the ground beside her. It might have been a short sword. Even in the dying light, there was no mistaking the piece of steel.

This was Cameron, her mother's harasser. Not a figment of Melinda's imagination. Mary watched silently.

The dance ended shortly thereafter, with Cameron lying prostrate on the ground, breathing heavily, saying something unintelligible.

Mary pulled back behind the tree. In the course of her movement, the tiniest piece of bark fell when she repositioned her hand on the tree, and, with the smallest of noises, landed nearly silently on the ground by her shoe.

It was nothing. It was only slightly louder than her own breathing.

And yet, when she looked around the tree again, Cameron was gone.

And in response to the question *Where did she go?*, Mary heard crashing and thrashing sounds in the brush nearby. Was there something coming through the undergrowth to get to her? She looked again into the meadow.

The knife was gone, too.

Oh, shit.

Mary ran. As she moved, she considered how much of the distance between the two Cameron could have covered. She plotted in her mind the straightest route to her car. Was she blowing any chance of cover by running wildly? Should she consider stealth instead of a sprint? Maybe the girl hadn't had a true idea where Mary was until Mary had gone into flight mode and set herself up as a moving target.

Maybe there's still time to stop and hide, she thought.

She tried to listen as she ran, but couldn't hear anything over her own breathing and the sound of her heart pumping and pounding in her ears. When she hit the switchbacks, she ignored the zigs and the zags and took a straight line down the hillside, like she would have as a kid. If you kept low, you could scoot under the trees and bushes on the paths worn through by wildlife—coyotes, boars, and foxes, mainly—and anything you couldn't scoot under you could leapfrog over. It wasn't a steep run, but, in places, as a kid, it had been a wild ride. She remembered it as a fun downhill run. Today it was hard on her back and the undergrowth was doing a number scratching up her legs. But she felt she was making time on her pursuer.

In fact, she thought she might have put some good distance between them by the time she reached the bottom of the hill. As she slid down a section of clay chips, she startled and set into the air a family of birds that scolded her for the interruption as they took to the air.

And in response, she heard something come crashing through the undergrowth on the hill behind her.

Her one advantage, she knew, was that even if Cameron were younger, and in great shape, Mary was at least her match in experience out here. This was her home ground.

What could this be all about? What had Cameron been doing? Praying? What were the chances she was going to run up with Mary's handmade flower crown, trying to return it? She'd been wishing all week that she'd kept it.

When she hit the last section of the trail, she felt a surge of adrenaline at the thought of reaching her car. She grabbed her keys from her fanny pack and gripped them in her hand, the ignition key ready for action.

She winced when the car beeped as she disarmed and unlocked it. Why not just signal her escape route to the whole world? But at least the sound came from closer than she'd thought it would be. In a moment, she could see the trailhead's end not more than two hundred yards away down a straight path.

And then, that crashing sound behind her again.

It was very close now. She reached into her fanny pack one more time and grabbed her soda. And then, behind her, the crazy girl, sword and all, was coming through the foliage onto the path behind her.

Mary shrieked and hurled the soda behind her without looking, and raced on.

She heard the girl curse as the soda can and the blade made contact, and the pop that followed and the spray, but she didn't allow herself to look back.

Seconds could make all the difference.

There were no other cars in the lot. Maybe Cameron had parked down on the main road?

And then Mary was in her car, and, seconds later, peeling out of the parking lot. She looked in her rear-view mirror, and didn't see any movement behind her as she raced off.

She didn't follow me into the parking lot.

She was even more confident in her car than she'd felt on foot, and she ignored the feeling that there was something she'd forgotten. It was that overconfidence that had her turning right when she sped out of the parking lot. She was so sure she could be on her front doorstep in less than fifteen minutes.

She'd been aware that by turning right, she was exposing herself to crossing paths again with Cameron, if Cameron had thought to head to the main road to try to cut Mary off. But in Mary's rush to escape, she headed toward Marble Canyon Road, a fact she only realized after a winding, five-minute drive that passed in a blur of anxiety. Her stomach turned a little when she saw the first of the neon pylons that marked the road closure ahead.

Going back did not seem to be an option. Mary was terrified of seeing Cameron again.

First there were cones, which she sped around, then there was gravel, for which she slowed, and, finally, a gate. Two giant metal yellow arms reached out from either side of the road, with a padlocked chain dangling between them.

She slowed, but did not stop all the way. She pressed the car forward, and the arms pushed back until the chain joining them was taut and she felt the resistance against the car. Then she slowly pushed forward, leaning into the chain, adding touches of gas, more than she thought she was going to have to. The left outside headlight popped. With a final, light rev, one of the links in the chain started to separate. She pushed the rest of the way through as it dropped to the ground, and turned right onto Marble Canyon Road.

The road was so familiar, she instantly felt that she was home free. She wanted to stop for a minute and catch her breath, and calm down, and stop shaking but felt that she wouldn't be able to do that safely until she was at the front desk inside the sheriff's station.

Oh my god oh my god what was that about?

There hadn't been another car. Where was Cameron's car? Was it because Mary had watched too many horror movies as a teen that she was convinced Cameron was going to pop up in front of her at any moment and try to chop her head off?

Cameron didn't have a car there and there hadn't been a car behind Mary on the road. There was no way she could be anywhere remotely close by . . .

And almost at the same time she thought about it, there *was* something ahead in the road. A person. Her heart leapt.

It was *her*. Was it her?

No. It was more than one person.

Mary slid into the left lane to avoid them. They, however, made no effort to get out of her way.

A lot more. She couldn't tell exactly how many. Unless the night and busted headlight were playing tricks on her, they were all over the road.

Hill People. The real thing. And they weren't trying to hide. They weren't running away. They were moving into the road, trying to block her way.

She sent them after me.

She couldn't escape the fact that they didn't appear to be monsters or half-human; as they flashed momentarily in her headlights, she could see they were just people. Or they had been once, when they had it together. Vagrant, filthy, unshaven, hopeless people, but people just the same. Mary thought she might be able to get past them until *thunk,* one walked into and bounced off the side of her car, making a sick thud and bump. She was only a couple of minutes from the start of town. She held onto control of the car and again thought she had a chance. She didn't scream until the third or fourth random bump, which broke off her side-view mirror. She tried not to think of them as people, but it wasn't possible. And she was going to have to drive through them if she wanted to make it home.

She did finally hit someone full on, with a bump on impact and a bounce as the car rolled over the body. There was a rattle afterward coming from underneath the car and the sound of something *tink-tinking* against the bottom of the car. Mary tried to avoid the next grouping, and then screamed again at the bone-breaking impacts that followed. The car bounced off a guardrail—which seemed to throw free everyone who'd still been holding onto the outside of the car—and then it spun in three complete circles through a curve without managing to go over the side of the road, but all the while plowing brutally through everybody in its path. As Mary struggled to regain control of the car, she hit a second guardrail, and then a third dead-on. It broke, and the car sailed through.

For a few seconds after the shocking impact of breaking through the guardrail, she saw the ground on the other side of the shallow gulch that ran beside this section of Marble Canyon Road racing toward her.

And then in a breathless moment there was white all around her and impact.

She opened her eyes moments later. There was still white all around her. White plastic?

This better not be heaven, she thought.

Mary was suspended and cocooned inside a cloud of airbags. She thought she hadn't moved far from her seat, but that her seat was now faced toward the ground. But instead of falling forward, she was just hanging there. Thankfully, her mother had kicked in for the deluxe airbag system. She smelled gas, oil, and fire.

She was alive!

"Yes!"

And then the car exploded.

11

Five days later

The fact that it was past two when Michael was getting home and all the house lights were on, and Carina's car was parked in the driveway, none of it was encouraging. His stomach felt cold and empty, even though he'd been grazing on food in the kitchen at Fandango all night. His stomach had been hurting for a few days already, but this hurting cold feeling now was much worse, and that was all he was feeling as he was parking the car.

Lying on the passenger seat was a large manila envelope that had arrived at Fandango earlier today. Inside was a copy of Dick Arthur's *Surreality Reigns,* which Michael had located at a used bookstore in Portland, Oregon, and which he'd planned to surprise his mother with. Having once been a Dick Arthur fan, he'd been troubled to realize he'd left his copies of Arthur's books back in the city, and glad to seek out a replacement copy of this title for his mom.

But now it seemed like it would be better if he waited to see why people were up.

If Mom and Dad were both out of town, this might be a good thing, potentially another memorable Mary party. But the fact that his mother was home and up late meant it was serious.

He couldn't imagine what it could be about, other than his father. Michael hoped he hadn't been in an accident. And why was Carina's car here and not Mary's? Likely they were out together and stopped by—or maybe they had talked to Mom and been told to come over?

Instead of retiring quietly to his room, per usual, he headed into the main house through the side door.

It was a silent, worried twosome that greeted him in the kitchen. It was overwhelmingly strange for Michael at first—he felt as if he'd stepped into a parallel universe, because both Carina and Mom had dramatically different haircuts than the last time he'd seen them. His mother had bangs and Carina's hair was shorter and much wavier. Their eyes were desperate, but their hairstyles were high fashion.

"What's going on? Where's Mary? Is she here?"

They looked at each other. Melinda spoke first.

"Michael, when was the last time you saw your sister?"

What followed was an excruciating evening. First, Michael joined up with them in what they had been doing for the last couple of hours. Eating, drinking, and following each other from room to room while rehashing all they'd done up to present time to track down Mary. He listened in for most of it, except when they wanted to grill him with questions. He didn't know anything. He'd only been back in town a short time. And in those relatively few months, he couldn't really say he knew all the things his sister was up to, who she saw, where she went. He hadn't been around her on a day-to-day basis for years, and he couldn't say whether or not this was normal behavior for Mary.

His mother kept repeating that she had completely avoided worrying until Mary missed her appointment to check up on her new hairstyle.

He drove to Mary's condo, which his mother and Carina had already done today on separate occasions. In the bright lights at night, the place seemed eerie, well decorated, and vacant.

The plants growing in the kitchen, though still alive and growing, were drying out and looking abandoned. The tomato plants, nearing the end of their cycles, looked like fruitless, fuzzy, flowerless weeds. There were herb plants the size of small tumbleweeds crowded together in the planter in the kitchen window. It smelled of Italian spices and mint.

The mail was piled up in the front hall below the drop slot. At the bottom of the pile was a housing association newsletter dated four days before. The last time Carina had said she saw Mary was five days before and Melinda the day before that, and for him, it had been ten days before, at the club. He tried to remember what it was they had been talking about. Her salon? Mom?

He wondered if they should file a missing persons report. His mother probably already had.

There were boxes of organic hair product in the spare bedroom, and there were a lot of business-looking papers on the table. Her car was gone, her purse was gone, her keys were gone, yet her toiletries and luggage remained. He knew his mother had interpreted that as evidence that a murderer/rapist/kidnapper drove off with her or her body.

There wasn't any sign of a struggle, and Mary wasn't the type to not struggle. That was something he could say to his mother when she broke out with her grim scenarios. He would also tell her there wasn't any evidence, far as he could see, of where she might have gone, or that she wasn't planning on coming home. And he would be sure to say to his mom—because he felt it was true and because she needed to hear it—that Mary was still alive. He knew she wasn't dead.

When Michael returned and shared the nothing new that he had learned, Melinda and Carina talked him through his entire visit to Mary's apartment: What he'd noticed, and what he did and did not check for. It was four-thirty in the morning. His mother told him she had a list of things she was going to try to locate the next day, when she was planning to drop by Mary's apartment again.

She also wanted to clean up the plants in the kitchen.

When Michael brought up the missing persons report, they told him that they had, of course, already taken care of it. Anything that they could have done, they had done.

Finally, he looked at them both and said, "This just isn't going to be solved before sunrise. Maybe we should all go to bed for an hour or two?" It was as if it hadn't occurred to them.

Carina slept in Mary's room because, she told Michael, she thought it smelled like Mary and it made her feel closer to Mary to be there.

The following days were hard on everyone. Going into the new workweek not knowing anything was terrible. By midweek, Michael had talked to his mother more than he had in the previous ten years combined, playing the part of sounding board as she worked her way through chasing down each friend, co-worker, and ex-boyfriend she had been able to remember and identify. She had gotten Mary's credit card reports, and identified as best she could any person at any store from which Mary had made a purchase on the last day the card was used, which was five days before they realized she was gone. Melinda also had Mary's phone statements, and had worked through every contact on the days in question and was working through the previous month's calls.

His mother thought it had something to do with the new business. The person Mary was going to rent from, the real-estate agent who showed her rental spaces, the hair product distributors, they were all suspects. She had spoken to them all by now, and followed up with some of them, and there'd been no one who stood out as suspicious.

Michael kept believing Mary was okay. That she was alive and going to come back to them. The only explanation he could think of was that she had left town unexpectedly and on short notice with a guy. Carina had half-heartedly allowed that she could consider it a possibility, but that she would have expected a call by now, regardless.

The idea of Mary up and leaving without a word was unfathomable to his mom. "Well, why would she do that? Why now of all times?"

Michael believed he would know if Mary were truly and completely gone. If she had died, he would know. Somehow. And he didn't think she was dead, which meant she had to be out there. Somewhere. The moments of doubt were the hardest, generally reinforced by the feeling that most people wanted him to give in and believe something he didn't think was true because it would be easier for everybody to start moving on.

Each day was a little worse. But the furthest he'd gone in that direction was sometimes catching himself wondering if he would know if she were really dead.

Why did he think he would know?

Everyone at the club had been going out of their way for both Michael and Laura, and picking up any slack that resulted when the police were there and when Melinda called time and again and when things just went on like the world had to and nothing else changed and they were all still too stunned to think clearly.

Aunt Laura had been the most comforting to be around, and the feeling seemed to be mutual. She and Michael had breakfast and lunch or lunch and dinner together every day, and it had been a good thing for him. Maybe partly it was because she and Mary had always been so close—it made Michael feel more like he was part of that special group.

Besides, Aunt Laura seemed to be the sanest family member right at the moment other than the kids.

Plus, he'd seen Max and Lorraine every day since everyone had realized Mary was missing. They were dropped off at the club in the afternoons after their summer camp, which had started just this week. That was when Mary had offered to look after them. The end result of having them there was constant distraction, but their appearance in the front lobby each day, although another reminder that it meant it had been another day that Mary wasn't there, was always a welcome sight, because he knew they were going to make him smile.

It was about eight, and Michael was on his way to the kitchen when Janet, on her way back to the bar with a box of straws and a terribly concerned look on her face, nearly bumped into him. She looked at him, and got flustered, so he waited for her to compose herself before he asked if she were okay. Her face grew even more morose. She handed him a note with his name on it.

He didn't open it immediately. "You read this?"

"I am so sorry that I did, but it was just sitting on the bar and I had to see what it was. I shouldn't have. And I'm sorry. And I won't say anything to anyone about it."

"What does it say?"

Janet looked down.

In a perfect, old-fashioned handwriting, the note read: *There is a car wreck in a ravine along Marble Canyon Road. It's south of the bike path about 2 miles in.*

It had to be from Talia.

He walked right over to Laura's office to show it to her. The kids were seated on the couch, watching cartoons. After she read it, she looked at him with a worried look on her face, He asked her to call his mom and dad and to tell them to call Carina.

"You're going to go out there now?"

"And the police. But call the police right before you leave. Give me a chance to get there first."

"I don't want you to go alone."

"I'll be fine."

"Where's Jack? I saw him around here somewhere. He's been working up at Bill's place, but Bill's just come back

215

into town and he doesn't want Jack around while he's doing campaign work. Look in the poolroom. Take Jack with you. And we're going to be coming right out behind you. I have to see if someone can watch Max and Lorraine."

Michael had just parked the car when everybody else started pulling in. He had spent his head start just getting onto Marble Canyon Road. He'd shoved around some of the barriers and Jack had picked the lock on the gates. The others had just cruised on through. His parents showed up first, then Carina, and then Aunt Laura, with Max and Lorraine in the back seat. They were watching a movie on a portable DVD player.

Michael crossed with Jack to the break in the guardrail while everyone was climbing out of their cars. It was too dark, and there were too many bushes to see much of anything from this position.

Jack signaled that he was going to have a look around below and walked about twenty feet down the road from the break, where the drop to the ground was shorter, and climbed over the guardrail. Michael turned around and met up with everybody else in the middle of the street.

Melinda was trying to read Michael's face from the moment he stepped close enough for her to see. Looking for what? The confirmation of all their worst fears?

"I just got here, Mom. I don't know what's what. Jack went down to have a look first."

"I don't trust Jack."

"Do you want to take the first look if it is her car?"

They walked to the break and looked over. They could see Jack climbing down. He disappeared and reappeared as he moved to a spot directly below the break. Michael's father tried to track his progress with his flashlight. Jack stopped and looked around and then saw something farther down, and started working down into the gorge beside the road.

His mother gasped and leaned on his Dad, who was wincing.

Carina said, "Oh no oh no oh no oh no."

He could also hear Aunt Laura telling Max and Lorraine to keep watching their movie.

"Don't touch anything," his dad called out, "not until the police come."

His mom gave Michael a nudge. In response, he yelled out to Jack, "I guess I'm going down there. Wait for me."

Michael walked to the spot Jack had climbed over. It was a short drop to a narrow path that curved down into the brush. He started climbing down, and then realized everyone but Max and Lorraine was following him. It was another minute before he realized that from this vantage point, he could see a spot straight down below the road where there was something in the gulch.

He couldn't help the choking sound that came out of him.

They all followed his gaze.

Carina said, "Oh no oh no oh no oh no."

And as they were watching, Jack appeared beside it.

Michael's voice cracked, "Is she there?"

Jack climbed on it, peering and poking. "No, she's not."

"She could have been thrown out," Carina said.

Melinda jumped on that. "Let's look around."

"Let's wait for the police," his father said.

That sounded sensible, but they all climbed down to the car, anyway. To walk around it. To start looking.

When they reached it, they saw that it didn't even look like an assembled car. The pieces of it were spread all over the place, covered with mud. Some of them looked burned. The cabin was in one smashed piece, lying about ten feet from the engine.

"Did her car just split apart?"

"That's what it was made to do in a serious collision. The pieces are meant to separate in a way that protects the driver and the cabin."

The tires were in tatters. The inside of the cabin was filled with deflated airbags that looked like burnt paper.

Everyone was quiet.

Michael had never felt so sad in his life.

"I don't see blood," Carina said.

"She's alive still. I can feel it," Melinda said. "You can feel it, can't you?" She looked at Michael. She knew he did. Before he could respond, she turned away from him to

217

face the hills, and yelled out, "MARY! MARY CAN YOU HEAR ME? MARY?"

His heart ached at the sound of his mother's wounded voice. Mary would answer that voice if she could . . .

They all waited a moment in silence.

The sound of a police siren starting up in the distance ended the moment.

"That must be the car they're sending out here." His Dad looked incredibly tired. "We should all step away from here. If she did get out, we could be trampling on footprints, we could be ruining evidence that might help them . . ."

Everyone but Melinda started moving. "We should start searching now. What if she's out there just holding on to hear us? Just waiting to be found."

"Don't do that," Aunt Laura said. "Let's just wait for the police to get us organized. They might see something here that we don't. And they'll help with setting up a search party."

"Mommy?" They all jumped at the sound of the voice, and then they all realized simultaneously it was Lorraine's voice, coming from the car up on the road. Laura started racing up the path toward the road.

They heard Lorraine call out, "Max?"

"Mommy's coming," Laura said. To herself, she said, "What was I thinking?" Then she yelled out, "Max, talk to your sister."

"Mommy?" Lorraine's voice rose a little.

"I'm coming, honey." Laura disappeared after she stepped back onto the road.

They had only a moment more to contemplate the wreckage before they heard Laura yelling out Max's name, panic in her voice.

"Max? Max! Answer me! Max, where are you? This isn't funny. This isn't the time for this! Answer me, Max!"

And then they were all hurrying back up to the road, his mother included. They could hear the sound of Laura's shoes clicking rapidly on the pavement. She appeared back at the guardrail.

"Max isn't in the car! I don't see him anywhere!"

Five minutes later, Michael, Carina, Jack, Melinda, and Eli stood in a circle around Laura's SUV, each of them facing outward, each one armed with a flashlight, and then each started walking in the direction he or she faced, calling out Max's name. Laura waited by the car with Lorraine for the police to come.

However they all felt about Mary, they also knew they couldn't help her at this instant in time. Max became the first and most immediate concern. There was no question in anyone's mind that they had to find him as soon as possible. If it helped to give them an excuse to start looking immediately for Mary, too, all the better.

Melinda was not going to be able to leave the site without making some effort to find her.

Jack ended up on the side of the road opposite the wreckage. He struggled to cross through the wildly overgrown brush on either side of the riverbed that ran beside the road, slipped and slid on loose, gravelly soil to get over a small mound that rose up behind the line of brush and, walking a bit, came upon a dirt road. Maybe it was a bike path.

When he looked down it, he thought it looked like it ran right beneath the road. He'd be willing to bet there was a path that led right up from the maintenance road to Marble Canyon Road. He could have just taken a straight walk out here if it hadn't been hidden from view by all the undergrowth.

He walked for about five more minutes before he noticed a small set of tennis-shoe prints in the dirt. Jack turned, looked back, and realized that for a bit now he'd been walking beside the tennis-shoe prints without even noticing.

Jack listened. He thought he could hear something other than crickets nearby. Not too close, but following him. Someone moving in the bushes, someone whispering, something that he was sure was in the air until, as he followed the footprints, he went around a bend in the road and saw Max ahead of him, slowly walking forward.

"Max!"

All the noises around him went silent. All the noises of the night went silent.

Although Max jumped at hearing his name, and spun around quickly in Jack's direction, his eyes were glassy.

"Hey, Max, what are you doing out here, buddy? You're not supposed to wander away from the car."

Max looked confused.

Jack heard noises again. Different noises. These were not shy or standoffish kinds of noises. He walked forward to take Max's hand, to get him moving quickly back to the cars and the bright headlights.

Jack said, "You must be a sleepwalker, Max. Does your mom tell you you walk in your sleep?" Max didn't answer. He looked a little bashful. "I'm not mad, Max, really. I'm just glad I found you." Max was disoriented and didn't quite get it all, but he seemed calmer when Jack spoke. He moved faster to keep up with Jack.

Jack finally picked him up and started jogging.

"You know, Max, I've gotten to the point where nothing in this world can surprise me. I believe that anything can and does happen. Most people are small and greedy and selfish and none of them understand that the world ends up giving them exactly what they deserve in the end anyway. There are nice people, honest people, people who have lived their lives sheltered enough for their ideals to remain intact, and they're always the ones who end up getting trampled first. They're the ones who least expect it. And that's why they've practically been asking for it. They're too damn trusting. And they never realize that they have to start taking for themselves until the day they wake up and realize that all they have left is a whole lot of nothing."

None of it meant anything to Max.

Not the words, not the sound of people racing through the brush around them.

They were only about halfway back to the car when they came across a cluster of rocks hidden among the trees. The noises that Jack had heard following them had grown more persistent, and also worrisome. They'd kept their distance, though, and Jack took advantage, finding a nook in among the rocks where a small boy could tuck himself in and not be found.

"Can you count to fifty?"

"One, two, three, four, five . . ."

"Good, good. Now this is the game. I'm going to hide and you're going to hide. We're both going to count to fifty, and as soon as we reach fifty, we're going to run that way." Jack pointed up the path toward Marble Canyon Road. "See the lights? It's not far. And when we get there, we'll get to see a police car, because the police are coming. Maybe they'll even let us sit inside it. Doesn't that sound great?

"Well, whoever gets someone's attention on the road first wins. You can yell, you can scream, you can make any noise you want to as you run to get their attention. And you know what? You have a special advantage, because your mom is up there. She'll be able to hear your voice better than anybody will be able to hear mine."

Max smiled.

"You understand?"

Max nodded.

"Okay. When I say go, you hide there and start counting, and then I'll hide over there and start counting. If you get a little head start, that will make it more fair, right?"

Max nodded.

"And when you reach fifty, you run, right? Don't wait for me or else I'm going to pass you and win, right? Just run. It might seem like a long way, but it's not. Really." Jack didn't know if Max really understood until he said, "Go!" and Max scrambled under the rock and started counting.

Counting along in his head, Jack moved off in the direction he'd found Max.

As soon as he stepped out from the rocks, he could hear them all about again. He sprinted down the bike path, away from the road, to put some distance between himself and Max. He didn't get very far before he was winded.

Damn cigarettes.

He wanted to go a bit farther, then loop back toward Marble Canyon Road. Jogging straight into wilderness was not going to save his skin.

Fifty.

He had reached the spot where he had found Max. There was a trail that headed off the bike path. Had this been where Max was headed? Should he go that way?

The question was answered a moment later for him, when he looked back the way he had just come, and saw the shapes of three people standing there. And then there were two stepping out on the side trail, and then there were more of them stepping onto the path ahead of him.

They were all around him, and the trees and the tall plants made it appear that maybe there were twice as many

221

as he could see. They stood shoulder to shoulder, tall shapes, short shapes, one missing an arm, all of them part of the night's shadows.

"Oh," Jack said.

The feeling that gripped his heart was disturbingly familiar, as if he had been through something like this before, although the memory seemed like it belonged to another person. He'd felt like this at least once before he forgot it all.

He wondered, not for the first time, how many times in this life had he been hunted? And for what crimes? He reached into his pocket and held the gun that had come into his possession in Texas—the last time things went out of order.

They were nearly silent as they watched him. And with every second that passed, it seemed as if there were more of them. The whole night behind them was filled with movement, with flickering streaks of black that shimmered and turned and then disappeared. As if a shadow could sparkle.

The moment Jack started to move, they rushed in at him.

Some of them had rocks, but no one was throwing anything yet. They wanted to cage him in or pin him down and they would stone him to reach that goal.

He just wanted to get past them.

One of them ripped the watch off his wrist as he was fighting through.

That watch was one of six things he'd had since before the Great Forgetting.

The next one who touched him after that, Jack shot point blank in the head. That scared them all back and almost got him clear of the group. When a handful of them started to scavenge from the fallen body, it gave him a few seconds more distraction. There were still many others to go after him.

The world became a different place once he was off the maintenance road. The undergrowth was dense and full of thorns, the grass in places was taller than the average person, and the oaks that huddled around the river tributaries were so immense that they looked like they must be prehistoric. All through these places he could hear the

222

sound of them chasing after him, crashing through the bramble and the tall green weeds, climbing down from the highest branches of the trees. They were all he could hear.

Jack ran as long and as hard and as fast as he could. He zigged and zagged among trees, scrambled over rocks, tried to take advantage of any kind of obstacle nature had provided to help him lose them. After a short bit of that, the sounds of pursuit had waned, and he thought he could tell that they were a bit behind him.

He dove into and under an imposing wall of bramble, and lay there perfectly still. On the other side was a small clearing around what must have been, at one time, a pond. There was only a shallow puddle of water in it.

He lay that way for a while, catching his breath, trying to get a sense of where he was and where town might be, ignoring the things he felt moving in the fertile soil against his skin. There was a flurry of movement as a group of his pursuers moved by him and onward without pausing.

For a few minutes, he heard nothing.

He closed his eyes and listened.

Nothing.

When Jack opened his eyes, there was a little girl standing there on the other side of the pond bed, looking at him. The sight of her made him jump. She was wearing a dress with stripes all over it. She had pigtails and glasses. "Hi," she said. "I'm Jenny Sayles."

Jack didn't say anything. He wasn't sure it was real.

"I'm Keith," a smaller, high-pitched voice closer to him said. The head of a little blond-haired boy peeked out from behind the girl. "We thought we were getting a new friend tonight."

"Quiet," Jack said. And he didn't move. He didn't know what to do. It wasn't right that the kids were there. They were part of this. He tightened his grip on the gun under the leaves, hoping he wouldn't have to shoot them, too.

"We're lost," Keith said, too cute and cheerful.

Jennifer said, "So is he, Keith."

"Quiet."

"You don't have to worry about that," Jennifer said. "They already know where you are."

Jack pushed himself up.

And a dark shape came crashing through the plants behind him, tackling him so hard it knocked him a distance and it made something crack somewhere around his ribcage. He was thrown over the little boy's head and into the pond bed, face down in the mud. The impact pushed the air out of him and before he could catch his breath, there was another body falling on top of the one who grabbed him first. And another body landed on top after that. And another, and another, each one smothering him a little more, pushing his face into the mud. The stink of them was thick in his nose, the stink of oil, of sweat, the smell of old, dry shit and mud made him want to gag. It felt almost like choking. His head started to spin.

It was already too late, he knew, when there was a light,

(feathery touch that caressed, a creamy smooth hand put gently on the back of his neck that stroked him, then not so gently grabbed him, nails digging into his flesh for a handhold to lift him out of the dirt. Bits and pebbles of sand and clay ran down the length of his body, underneath his clothes, coming out of his pant legs, some falling down into his socks and shoes while he was held off the ground. The sound when the pebbles hit the ground beneath him wasn't right. It was like the sound of a bird tapping on a window.

The person holding Jack shook him hard a few times, then threw him through the air like a toy. Jack found himself hoping for a tree or a bush, and not, with his luck, a rocky outcropping, to pad his landing. Instead, he hit something flat and solid, a wall that cracked when his head bashed into it. The ground was cold and smooth and hard.

He was in a room. A palatial room with glass walls and marble floors and a running backlit fountain out on the patio. There were fancy boxes, etched and painted, built into the ceilings. Jack knew it could not be where he really was. This was something they were making him see, like Mike said happened at the beach. Should have believed him. Thought the boy just couldn't handle his weed.

It might, in fact, have been the case that he was dying, that somehow he had withdrawn into his own imagination in the last instants before he died. There was an overwhelming desire inside him to believe his surroundings were real and that he was now safe from the Hill People. Through the glass ceiling Jack could see that there were stars in the sky overhead, but the view above was obscured by towering trees that surrounded the structure. It couldn't be Cheronkin, because the forest outside was ancient and towering and dark. The stars looked shinier and brighter, as if they were closer.

Before he could locate his attacker, he felt her hand settling around his neck again, grabbing hold of him by the throat. The fingers burned against his skin. He started to choke as he was lifted up again and slammed into the wall a couple of times, cracking the glass more each time. And then he was held there, like a painting in the middle of the wall.

He found himself staring into the deepest, greenest eyes.

Long, bright, orange hair. An oval face, the color of white porcelain, lightly freckled. There was a partially-healed cut on her forehead. Her breath smelled of flowers. Her nails sank like claws into his neck.

The heat from her hand made it feel as if her fingers were melting through his skin.

Was this death? Was this how he envisioned her? Was this her palace and he was here because he was dying?

"Please."

Her voice was unnaturally low. She sounded to be gleefully pleased with herself. "I don't know if you are an accidental devil, or one who is full of intent, I do admit that. But I do think you are a test. You are a test for me and that is why I keep running into you. First in Texas, now here. And my answer to that test, to be truthful, is that I don't think the end result is any different whichever you claim to be, man or devil. But I'm not accepting as coincidence your presence here in this place and at this time. You're not going to be ruining everything."

His voice sounded wrong, not at all like his own when he said, "What if I have no idea what you're talking about?"

She slammed him against the wall again.

"Who are you? Who sent you?"

And in Jack's mind's eye, he saw the clearest memory yet of what must have been his old life. It was a view of a place that looked like Hell—maybe Oklahoma or Arizona or Nevada or Kansas—with a 360-degree view of a nearly dead, nearly lifeless desert. The heat and the humidity were unbearable.

"I believe everyone in the world would be better off without you." Again a slam. "Who are you? What are you?"

225

In this memory, he told his wife that he was going out to the porch to have a smoke. She was a nasty bitch. She told him she hoped that the porch fell down on his head. Monster kids snickered, but only that, because they knew he would find them if they laughed too long and hard, memory or no memory.

This redhead knew right then something wasn't so right anymore. She had played with her meal for too long. She wanted to let go of Jack, but he grabbed her by the wrist and asked her, incredulously, "How long have I been this way?"

She shrieked in frustration and rage and pulled away from him. She called him something in a language he'd heard before, long ago: dog dog dog.

Jack thought, What was this place, inside these walls? It was like a pocket in the middle of reality.

He could still feel the burn of her hand on his throat. "Let sleeping dogs lie," he said. "And then don't invite them into your home."

Her words put him on four legs. She had turned him into an animal. And the fear instinct that filled him drove him to tuck tail and run, head straight for the door and the great wild forest outside. There was easier prey outside and more badness to come in here.

But he was awake enough now, animal or not, that he could taste the scent of her in the air, this woman, and her fear. Even as she laughed, it was her fear that guided her.

She clapped her hands, pleased with herself because she thought she had reduced him to a pet. He could see exactly what she was, that she was a child playing with her new toys.

A rush of fury washed over him.

He said her name—it was almost like a grunt—not the name she used now, but the name she spent part of every lifetime trying to remember and which in every lifetime was a little farther from her grasp. And even when she remembered it herself, how many times could she have heard someone else use it? It had to be hard to ignore.

The sound distracted her as he leapt for her throat. There was, indeed, a hint of wonder and confusion in her eyes. It was her true name. When his fangs sank into her warm skin, the madness of it all overwhelmed him.

She screamed, "Devil!", but all he heard was the echo of her laughter and the clapping of her hands)

226

Laura Hollins felt that losing Max was a warning for her.

Up until the last few months, she had been the sort of person who felt honored to be able to live the life she lived, to have her kids, to have Joel completely out of the picture, even to have been able to find some bit of joy in just about every day. And she'd let that life fade into distant memory. She had traveled so far off that road that the universe had had to deliver her this warning.

She promised herself while she was waiting for Max's return that she was going to stop drinking again, that she was going to rein in her hours, that she was going to stop hiring nannies and babysitters, and that she was going to stop seeing Bill, all because she needed to re-prioritize and rededicate herself to being a better mother to her kids. While they still were kids.

She waited in the car, listening to Lorraine breathing in her sleep. Carina came back and did not come to the car, but indicated from across the street that she'd come up empty-handed. The police arrived and Melinda and Eli and Michael returned to meet them. There was a lot of gesturing to the side of the road where Mary's car went over, and to Laura's car.

And then Max came running up from the side of the road. Laura shrieked his name and sprang out of the car to grab him in a tight hug. She whispered in his ear, "Where did you go?"

"Over there." He pointed in the direction he'd come from. "Jack found me."

"Jack? Where is Jack?"

"He's coming. We were racing. He let me have a head start. He told me not to wait."

"What does that mean?"

"I did just what he said. I covered my eyes and my ears without peeking, I counted to fifty, and then I ran toward your voices. It was a race."

Another police car arrived shortly after, and a tow truck. Max soon fell asleep beside her in the car.

Eli and Melinda watched from their car across the street.

Laura wasn't sure if she should wait or leave as plans progressed to pull up the car. A few officers were searching the immediate vicinity of the accident for signs of Mary and a fourth patrol car was driving slowly west on Marble Canyon

227

Road, its searchlights scouring the brush on either side of the road.

That police car was soon miles in, and she could only see it on certain curves, trudging along at a slow pace, searchlights scouring the sides of the road. And it kept going without stopping until it was completely out of view.

12

June 25

Laura awoke after only a few hours of sleep, and in quick order decided she was obligated to commit one violation of the vow she'd made the night before. It was, to her, the act necessary to consecrate the vow.

She hoped Melinda and Eli and Michael were at home, and that they were not still camped out on Marble Canyon Road, as she imagined they likely were. Later in the morning, she would pick up food from the club, track them down, and feed them.

Marko was going to open Fandango this morning, and either she or Michael would cover the afternoon/evening shift. She wasn't sure it was best for Michael, or if he could handle it, but if he thought he wanted to work she was going to let him.

There was likely going to be a search event in the hills before the day was over, and that was going to wreck Laura. The idea of Mary out there for days, in what kind of condition, was too ghastly for Laura to mull over for very long. Dwelling on it left her paralyzed with fear. It was too easy, as a mother, to put her own child in that scenario and wonder what she would do. She didn't want to do that and yet there was no way around it. Having Mary was, for so long, the closest thing in Laura's life to having her own child.

Melinda's town meeting had been scheduled for the morning. She'd had to book the school auditorium nearly a month in advance. Laura guessed Melinda would have brought it up the previous night if she'd remembered it, and she wasn't going to interrupt their grief to ask about it, so Laura had decided on her own to attend as a family representative.

Melinda had, of course, made arrangements for childcare for the meeting. Laura dropped off Max and Lorraine with promises to both of them to return after the meeting. Max seemed unfazed by his experience the night before—what he could remember of it—and Lorraine had awoken fully rested and surprisingly untroubled.

229

The fact that neither of the children asked about Mary struck Laura as odd, and she wondered if it was perhaps intentional on their parts. On some level, Laura thought, maybe they understood that they really didn't want to know.

There was no knowing if there would actually be a town meeting; either way, she was on limited time. Even if she were still mindful of the gathering, Melinda could go either way on attending. She had every right to forget the whole get-together, as Laura would were she in Melinda's position; yet, her sister-in-law was not one to miss out on her obligations—her sense of responsibility to the community was not something she carried lightly.

If Melinda didn't show, how much of a meeting would it be, anyway?

She thought she had time to get to Bill's ranch house and return, with time to spare, before the meeting ended.

"Ladies and gentlemen . . . ladies and gentlemen . . . ladies and gentleman, if I could have your attention up here onstage. My name is Gretchen Solkitz. Thank you. Everyone, Please listen. We've just had word early this morning that there's been another accident on Marble Canyon Road."

The crowd gasped. There was much shushing and whispering that followed, as many of them waited for the name and a handful of those in the know shared what information they had with their neighbors.

"The accident appears to have happened six days ago. The wreckage was found beside the road yesterday. It appears to have involved only one car and one occupant: Ms. Mary Phillips . . ."

Gretchen paused while the room chattered and shushed and whispered and hushed.

"Right now, the police have yet to locate Ms. Phillips' body, and their work overnight was hampered by a shortage of officers available to respond to the scene. There was no evidence of alcohol, and police are still trying to determine how Ms. Phillips accessed the Canyon road.

"Now, most of us here know Mary's mother, Melinda. It was she who planned today's town meeting, it was she who helped raise the funds that helped to build the auditorium we sit in. It was her intention that we would have an opportunity to voice our concerns about the recent goings-on in

230

this community. Melinda felt that her neighbors might be as worried about the state of the community as she was, and she is a great believer in the power of this community to achieve a goal when we work together. I also know she would hope that we would be able to get along without her if she gave us a time and place to meet.

"I know my spiel I'm supposed to give to get us started, but I can't stop thinking about and worrying about Melinda and her family. I'm sure they're out there on that road right now, and I know there are those among us here who can, tragically, understand exactly what the Phillips family might be feeling right now. And I keep wondering if maybe today might be one day where we have to focus on the one rather than the many ..."

The ranch house did not look as inviting as it once had to Laura. Not with the limousines and the cars, the van covered with antennas and satellite dishes, and the bodyguards stationed about and asking for her identification. It had gone from hideaway to headquarters.

The guards let her in after a little back-and-forth on their walkie-talkies, and as she parked her car and then handed her keys to the man in charge of the driveway, she felt relief that this wasn't going to be her life. She felt out of place. It no longer seemed to be a place she wanted to be. And the disconnection she felt from a place she had once so dearly loved left her a bit shaken.

She went straight to the main residence, to his office, and found him seated behind the desk. Bill was about to make a call—the phone was in his hand. His face was lined with concern, and she thought he was mentally rehearsing what he was about to say. He looked tired, and shaken, and she thought he might have already heard about Mary. He stopped when he saw her, examined the expression on her face with some curiosity, and in a quick motion with his free hand signaled his assistant to leave the room and close the door behind him, which the young man did without uttering a sound. Still, she stared at him, almost not recognizing him, and realized she had never seen him this way. He was worried.

Bill set down the phone.

"Hello, Ms Hollins. To what do I owe this unscheduled pleasure? I thought we had agreed scheduling was important."

She tried to look him in the eyes. She couldn't. Not at first. She gestured for him to stay seated. "Mary was apparently in a car accident. Her car went off a section of Marble Canyon Road, maybe earlier this week. We just found the wreckage last night. We went there last night. I was there past midnight. There's no body yet." Saying this, tears rolled down her cheeks.

"Not Mary," he said, truly shocked. "Oh, god. Not Mary. Damn it! I was just going to send her a housecleaning bill. The place smelled like hell when I got here, like rotten meat. She was the last one up here, a few months back."

"They're looking for her body now. On that road, Bill. Marble Canyon Road. Why isn't there any work being done on the road? Why does it look as if there's nothing but barriers blocking a road that isn't being repaired?"

"Of course there's no work being done on the road after midnight."

Her eyes narrowed. "I'll lose the club if that road doesn't reopen. This town is withering with that road closed."

"Financial ruin isn't in your cards or the cards of anyone else that matters in this town." On a desk to the left was an object covered with a familiar-looking piece of fabric. He followed her gaze. "It's the artist's work-in-progress," he said, following her gaze. "He said it was a portrait of public service. I think it looks like a paperweight blob. I cover it up because I feel like it's watching me, even though it doesn't even have eyes. To tell the truth, I hired him because I didn't want him lounging around the nightclub with nothing to do but make eyes at you."

"Should I be flattered by your insecurity?"

"Forget it," he said. "I don't know why I said that. A little too honest." He ran a hand through his hair, pushing it into place. "That seems to be my problem these days. I'm supposed to sit at this desk and make these calls, very important calls, every day, and they require a lot of bullshitting and I can't seem to finesse the bullshit."

Laura eyed the fabric-covered lump.

"Do you love me, Bill?"

232

"Yes."

"Would you leave Meg for me?"

He struggled with that one. It almost seemed like he wanted to say yes, or at least to not say no. But, finally, he said, "Would you want me to?"

"No," she said firmly.

"I don't see that in the cards, either. Does that surprise you?"

"Yesterday? Maybe. Right now, not at all. It was so easy, out of this context," she gestured to a stack of glossy campaign mailers on the desk, "to see everything in you that you used to be. To think that all of your public and political persona were just a shield. But you're not really the man you used to be. You know how to play that part still, but it's no longer you. I don't know why you would choose this for your life. This was the very last thing you wanted to be."

He shrugged. "It was the only way to get the things that I want. The things that the people who back me want. With the family background, and no other real prospects that appealed to me, it wasn't a hard decision."

She remained calm.

"Do you think people at the town meeting going on right now aren't discussing the canyon body count and wondering how it could possibly have happened again after—" Laura thought of Mary, and started crying once more. Bill started to stand, and she again gestured for him to stay as he was. "Do you think the police aren't going to start calling people involved with the road, if they haven't already? Just to ask if maybe they'd seen something?"

He stood up anyway. "Honey, there are a lot of people in this town who never want to see that road reopened. That's square one in the puzzle you're trying to assemble."

"There's nothing being done," she said. "I've been out there. How much of that money have you taken already? How long do you think you have before someone notices?"

"It's all going to be settled and the road's going to be repaired if there's still a will to repair it and the work will be fully funded and there's not going to be anything to notice. These things take time. Repairing a road like Marble Canyon takes time. People understand all of that. And if they don't, maybe there's enough money left that we can buy 'em all out. We can make this whole little suburb our home for a song.

Divide the land with the four billionaires in the area who would like nothing more than to see the town empty of everyone who isn't employed by them—"

"That's a nice narrative. Your party would be proud. Or better, how about this one? Candidate 'borrows' money from road repair fund; candidate's best friend's daughter dies on unrepaired road. It's clear and simple, and they'll use it against you for the rest of your career."

"I'll pencil it onto my growing list of concerns."

He feared this was true. She could see it in his eyes. And there wasn't any lingering concern she could see in them for Mary, or for Eli.

"I'm done. I don't want anything to do with this. I'm going to go now. I needed to be sure, and to be sure I needed to do this face-to-face. She turned and started toward the door. She wondered if she wanted him to try to talk her out of leaving. She didn't think so.

"Listen, Laura, I hear what you're telling me, and I respect your feelings on the matter of our involvement, but you leaving to return to the hub of community activity at this moment is not going to give me the time I still need—"

She didn't say a thing. She could see, out the window, her car being driven on the back of a flatbed truck down the driveway toward the street.

"I'm having a crisis with one of my local supporters; she no longer seems to be taking my calls, and I don't think having my name bandied about at a Cheronkin forum is going to help the situation. I've just heard a rumor she's on her way out of town, and I want to believe there's time to smooth it all out. Once that's settled, you'll be on your way. You'll see," he said, placidly ignoring the look of exasperation on her face, "everything is going to work out for the best."

Melinda and Eli spent the night at the side of the road. They stayed with the two officers who had first responded to the call, waited as other police cars and other officers arrived and then waited for the tow truck to arrive and then for it to slowly extract the car pieces from the gorge. Melinda had napped through the moment the car's "cage" had appeared behind the guardrail, but had awoken to see it on Marble Canyon Road, a smashed, crumpled, singed, and stained wreck being pulled onto the flatbed of a tow truck as the morning sun peeked out.

She wanted to cry. Eli sobbed behind his sunglasses. Melinda didn't cry.

She's not dead. Melinda thought. I would know if my firstborn child were dead. We have to find her before it's too late.

More officers arrived and the first two left. The new ones began reviewing the crash site. Melinda watched from the road as they picked through the debris that remained in the gorge. Broken glass, a car door, a side view mirror among the shrubbery. They marked a small perimeter area around the debris, and looked for something . . . what? A sign of where Mary might have gone? Her body? Some further clue in the wreckage?

Melinda would have gone down to join them, but they abruptly returned to the road. All the officers present regrouped, and then two began walking west down Marble Canyon Road, away from town. They did not go far before one of them stopped to point at something, something which he photographed and put into a plastic baggie. They continued to study the pavement, then walked on and studied more of it. They called over two other officers, and then all four of them spread out across the road and again began walking west, each of them stopping regularly to mark something in the street. They went quite some distance down the road before they turned around and walked back.

"You know what?" Melinda heard one of the officers saying into his walkie-talkie, "We're going to need more hands out here. The crime scene is too big for us to cover with a handful of us."

She stopped one of others. "Officer Marshall," she said slowly, reading his badge. "What's happening now?"

"Mr. and Mrs. Phillips, there's a great deal of blood out there on the road, going back a few hundred yards. We've found a couple of body parts, including a finger and part of an arm, and that was only a very quick walk-through."

"My god. A finger?"

"It doesn't look like a female's finger. It almost doesn't look like a human finger."

"What does it mean?"

235

"Possibly that your daughter's car hit someone or someones or something or somethings before it went off the road. We need to have the car looked at," Marshall said to another officer, "and we need more hands out here. The evidence has been out here in the sun for days now. Also, can we find out the name of the company doing the work on the road? They might have seen something."

And as they walked away from her to compare notes, Melinda had the distinct feeling that they were not going to be looking for Mary first. They were going to do other things while Mary was lost out there somewhere.

If they aren't going to start, she thought, I am.

She was mentally pushing her exhaustion aside, committing to that course of action as an older station wagon drove up and parked beside her car. It was Gretchen who emerged, a grim yet supportive look on her face.

For a short window of time that morning, the atmosphere lifted for Melinda, and alongside the dread of the situation, she felt an unusual level of appreciation for the good her fellow citizens were capable of without her having to play the role of taskmaster.

Melinda had completely forgotten it was the morning of the meeting, and she was tremendously touched by the gesture, although she felt more convinced as each new recruit arrived that it would amount to nothing.

Parked cars soon lined both sides of the street, and a steady stream of people came walking grim-faced and respectfully up to her to shake her hand or pat her shoulder and then moved toward Gretchen, who organized them into search teams to scour the areas where the wreck had been found and anywhere along her route that she might have been thrown from the car.

She's not here anymore, Melinda thought. No one will find anything.

For better or for worse, these were her people. This was their collective home. If she counted all the years she had known each and every familiar face and added those numbers together, the result would be a number in the thousands. This was old Cheronkin, from a time when it had been the only Cheronkin, and these were the people who had let her carve out her niche among them, had listened to her, helped her, and inspired her, and then followed her lead. And the fact that they could still come together like this, just like they would have in older days, proved they were a different lot than you'd find in most towns.

The area was bustling with activity for the next eight hours, when suddenly, over a very short time, the many elements involved concluded, one by one, that they'd done all they could and come up empty-handed, and they all went home.

By then, they police had offered Melinda and Eli a rough narrative: Mary had accessed Marble Canyon Road through a gate on an access road a few miles west. She'd been speeding. She ran into something, or somethings, at least one of which was human—they were going to need time for the lab to study the many, many samples they'd gathered before they could describe what had been hit—and at that point Mary lost control of the car and, after skidding through several turns, went over the side of the road, whereupon, despite the safety features built into the vehicle, the gas tank ruptured and exploded.

"That's what you think happened?"

"Yes, ma'am."

"Where is she now? Where's that part of the scenario?"

"Ma'am, that's the part that we don't know yet. Maybe we'll have a better picture when we get information back on the samples. We are going to keep looking for her."

Perhaps it was exhaustion that prevented her from pointing out the inadequacies in his answers. It was seemingly only a blink of an eye later and she and Eli were home, and, numb or not, they fell asleep on adjoining couches in their clothes, both of them hoping the world would be better when they woke up.

The sight of the pieces of Mary's broken car resting on the road hit Michael like a physical blow. A wave of sadness swallowed him whole. The sides of the doors and hood were painted with streaks of dark color that must have been blood. His knees wanted to fold.

He started to cry.

Mary, no. No.

Up until that point, he had been not only worried about Mary, but also about Jack. Where had he gone? Was he okay? He had been forgotten by everyone else in all the goings-on that followed with the arrival of the police and Max's reappearance at the side of the road. Although everyone was thankful that Jack had somehow gotten Max back to the road, his absence faded as an issue, even when Carina at some point asked, "Where do you think Jack went?" Everyone else was too wrapped up in Mary to try to answer.

Staring at Mary's car, so was Michael.

Mary's car was so much a part of her identity, it was impossible to see the damages it had sustained without feeling the same had been done to Mary. And it was so terrible to see her car battered like that. His head pounded, his arms felt numb, his heart hurt. And worse, after seeing the wreckage, and after it had been towed away, he couldn't find a way to keep the images out of his thoughts, of Mary's car and Mary broken up inside to fit the shape of what was left, and so he finally had to slip away quietly after catching his dad's eye.

In the morning, he rejoined his parents and took part in the early hours of the search, grateful that the community had come out to support them in such numbers. It felt like the only way to do a thorough search that would leave them satisfied that nothing had been missed. However, after the first few hours, the search had twice covered the area around the wreck, plus a good distance more, and it became apparent nothing would be found that was going to tell them what had happened to Mary.

Following that insight, at his first opportunity, he slipped into his car and drove to the club, where he sat in the parking lot for longer than he intended, sorting out his emotions, deciding if he really wanted to be at the club, or anywhere.

And then he walked to the front doors and let himself in.

It was quiet inside. The staff was busy doing side work as part of the transition from lunch to dinner. He was somewhat relieved as he joined them in changing out the lunch stations to see that no one else seemed to be aware of the news of another car crash. Everyone who knew was out at the site. It was one of those rare times when he could feel

238

thankful that cell phones didn't work inside the hills of Cheronkin. For a small window of time, it was like he had stepped into the eye of the hurricane, where all was still well and good. Weird as it was from his perspective, to everyone else, it was just a normal morning at Fandango. Janet had been good to her word, and hadn't said a thing.

He dreaded the moment the first whispers would be heard. He dreaded having to answer the phone, but start it did, with the first of the searchers who dropped by to offer him their personal condolences. It turned out it wasn't all that bad—in fact, it helped him cope a little better, and made him feel a bit calmer. He didn't speak of any of it to anyone else—explaining to anyone who asked that it would be too much, and that he likely would break down.

In the late afternoon, he received a call from the childcare service. Laura had dropped the kids off while she went to the town meeting and, Michael would have assumed, back out to the accident site. But looking back on the afternoon, he realized that he hadn't seen her there.

But then again, he hadn't been playing greeter. He'd been late getting there. He'd just assumed Laura was out there someplace and that Marko was running the club that morning and that there was a reason he didn't see her car parked anyplace nearby when he pulled in.

Aunt Laura hadn't returned to pick them up, and it was past time the caretakers wanted to be home. So Michael excused himself, with everyone now sympathetic to his obligations at the moment, and a short time later picked up a shell-shocked and worried pair of kids.

"Where's Mommy?"

"You know what? Your mommy said we could have a sleepover tonight. Do you want to go to Aunt Melinda's?"

"I want Mommy," Lorraine said.

Max was more compliant. "Can we have ice cream? And no tomatoes for dinner?"

"Sure. I guess." Michael thought about it. "Does Grandma M make you eat tomatoes?"

"All the time. And she knows I don't like them plain."

Poor kid, he thought. Because of Melinda, Max would never like tomatoes again. She had ruined broccoli for Michael the same way. "It's because she knows you don't like them. Just knowing you don't like them, it makes her want you to eat them—and like them—even more. You know that, right?" Michael asked. "She's kind of sick that way."

His mother and father were both asleep when Michael got home. Knocked out. They didn't stir when the three arrivals came in. It was left to Michael to get the kids into their pajamas and to get them to brush their teeth and wash their faces. As the sole overseer, he felt more than inept; for him, it had always been easier to interact with them as someone else's kids, and not to be the one worried about the nitty gritty of getting them to do useful things.

He let them watch television while he called around for Laura. He tried both her home numbers, and her office number, but beyond that, he had no idea where she might be. He saw in his mother's phonebook a number for ex-Uncle Joel, but didn't think the situation warranted calling him.

The woman Michael had worked with all these months was not a social animal, except at the club, and only as work required. Aunt Laura was usually either at the club or with the kids. She didn't hang out with people when she wasn't working and most of the socializing Michael saw her involved in was club-related and strictly during club hours. Even if she were dining on a business lunch, it was at the club. She wasn't dating anyone that he knew of, and he had no idea if she even had any friends in town that she spent personal time with. His impression had always been that outside of the club, it was family, family, family time— either with all of them, or with his dad, or with Mary. So he couldn't imagine where she might be, and he felt much more concerned in light of what had happened to Mary. This was totally out of character.

Later, he sat in the chair between the beds in the guestroom as both kids nodded off. He'd planned to stay for only a moment while they wound down. But as he listened to their breathing, and watched their little eyelids flutter, he knew he wouldn't be far behind.

He would leave all the new cans of worms for the morning. There was too much weighing on him to do anything other than pray that Aunt Laura and Mary were both all right.

Amen.

The first light of the day found Melinda driving past the crash site on Marble Canyon Road, past the neon caution pylons that followed a line around the curve beyond the crash site, to the maintenance road a few miles farther down. The gates were open, one side with a broken chain and padlock hanging from it.

Melinda had so many questions. Why would Mary have been out here? Hiking in the hills? Why would it have been so important to take this route home? Was she in such a hurry to get to town that it didn't matter? Was she low on gas?

Melinda was sure Mary knew the road was being repaired, and that it just wasn't safe. Mary might have believed her driving skills and her familiarity with the canyon would have prevented her from crashing under similar circumstances, but that confidence was countered by the fact that her daughter had known personally two people who had died in the canyon crashes.

It wouldn't make sense, forcing her way onto this road, knowing she would likely encounter another barrier farther down the road, unless there were something pushing her to do so. Getting home quickly just would not be enough motivation to drive her to do this. That alone wouldn't be the reason. Honestly, it sounded like one of the things one of the idiot boys she dated in high school would do.

A short time later, Melinda turned her car off the maintenance road and onto the driveway to the Morewill Park parking lot.

This is where she came from, obviously. She was hiking? Alone? Melinda hoped not alone. Maybe Mary had forgotten an appointment and was running late when she left, so she tried to take Marble Canyon Road?

Melinda approached the trailhead slowly. She and Eli had been here many times on hikes when they were younger. What she remembered were brush-covered hills.

This was a forest.

She told herself that whether or not Mary had been here, it would be a good thing for her to walk outdoors and try to order her thoughts. The scenery ahead was gorgeous, more so than Melinda had ever seen in this area, lush green hillside after lush green hillside.

She hadn't taken two steps down the trail when she caught a glint of sunlight reflected off something 100 feet down the path from the trailhead marker. Her heart jumped as she came closer.

It was half a diet soda can. Mary's brand. The other half lay nearby.

She picked up the pieces. There was no doubt in her mind that it was Mary's, with or without the lipstick.

Mary was here before the accident. And from here she'd taken the access road to Marble Canyon. Why? If she'd forgotten the road was closed and driven up to the gate, why wouldn't she turn around and take the road back? Wasn't that what Mary would have done?

Melinda could only imagine Mary taking Marble Canyon Road in an emergency. It had to have been an emergency, something that meant she had to get home and it was worth risking the closed Marble Canyon Road to get there. She didn't want to take the long way home, and going back wasn't an option? Why? Was she injured already? Maybe she picked up someone injured . . .

And the pieces of Mary's aluminum can were strange. Mary was not the type to litter. That wasn't her way. And how had the can been so neatly cut apart, and why?

She walked up the path from the trailhead, and was soon surrounded by the trees.

Since Mary's disappearance, a typical dream usually began with some specific memory Melinda held of Michael and Mary as children: playing in the bathtub or in the kitchen or in the middle of a department store. Something would distract her attention—a clock on the wall, a phone ringing, a teapot about to boil—and there would be a feeling of falling, falling into something black somewhere between the seconds of time, afraid she wouldn't be able to catch her next breath, spinning down a drain.

Her first thought would always be, "Where are the children?" Because they would be gone. But when she looked in the spot where they had all just been together, that was gone, too, and she was somewhere else, and she couldn't remember what it was she was trying to remember. And then she became someone else—in these dreams, Melinda was often a child, and not herself but someone else's child—and sometimes she would see short, vivid flashes of these other dream childrens' lives, and sometimes they were longer moments. And it seemed to Melinda at times as if they must have existed in the real world, and not only in her head. In her dreams, when she was one of these other children, she would often recognize people she never remembered meeting, and feel great joy or overwhelming sadness at seeing them again.

But there was a certain commonality to all of the dreams. These children she dreamed of being could find joy in the smallest of places, even when the adults around them acted as if they were insane. Some of the children in her dreams died, usually of disease or malnutrition or bad water at this age; one or two of the children she dreamed of were like her, without true families; one died in a fall and another was killed by her father, who spoke in a language Melinda didn't understand. But for the most part, even those who were doomed to die were eager to believe there were good things in life, and they were hungry to laugh and learn.

And there was something else these children she dreamed of all had in common, she was coming to believe: They had shared a common soul. Something that survived the whims of cruel and careless men and lived to try again. Their soul—Melinda's soul—had survived.

Why did that make her feel angry? Suffering for the whims of men.

And now, here, in this place, where the canopy was like a cathedral, Melinda stared at the grooves and twists in the bark of the trunk of an oak and thought she could see a face from her dreams. It was a girl, no older than four, dark-haired and smiling. In another, more slender tree, she saw the likeness of a darker-skinned girl, also with dark hair. She wondered if somewhere in the forest she would find the girl whose face she saw during her session with Dr. Wen.

Melinda thought: These are me. These were me. And these were the models for her childhood deck of playing cards, the only friends she had before she was rescued from her parents. She thought she must have been acting out unconsciously as a child, using the cards to live out her past-life memories. These were her memories of those who were forever imprinted on her soul.

They had died, each of them, while they were young.

In her mind's eye, Melinda saw another face, a girl who looked so familiar that Melinda felt she should be able to put a name to her. This one was on the verge of adolescence, intelligence in her eyes. She wouldn't make it to thirteen before being killed by her extended family for reasons having to do with misogyny and family honor. This had been the Queen of Spades in Melinda's deck of cards. Her name sounded like Luce, Melinda thought. Melinda's grandmother had been horrified at the sordid tale of Luce's death when it was recited by her young granddaughter. Dying, for this girl, had been a horrific event.

In her imaginings, the girl's face, peaceful, looked suddenly alert, as if responding to a noise.

Melinda stopped moving, and listened to the shuffle of something else moving under the trees. The faces in the trees vanished.

She was being watched.

When Melinda returned to the car some time later, she sat in the parking lot for a half hour, pondering her questions.

Finally, though, she had to leave.

She opened the car door, and stood up and faced toward the trailhead.

"If you've hurt her," she said, to no one specifically, but for all of them to hear—because she thought the people in the hills were cowardly and afraid of her, while she, strangely, felt unafraid of them. She thought that was why she herself hadn't experienced a sighting—they feared her.

But she didn't know what threat she could make.

"I want back whatever you have taken from us. From her. From me. You will pay if you've hurt her. I want it all back . . ."

There was no answer before she left.

The next morning's breakfast conversation with his father left Michael with a feeling of déjà vu. The players were different—Max and Lorraine were parked in front of morning cartoons with hot cereal—but the feeling of helplessness was much the same as it had been a week before with Mary's absence. Neither of them knew where Aunt Laura was. Neither of them had seen her since the night they'd found Mary's car. The last people who had seen her had been the daycare workers she'd dropped Max and Lorraine off with the morning before.

Michael's father was mad, impatient to find his daughter and his sister, and not used to having to wait for results. It was hard to talk through the matter in low tones while attending to the kids. They tried to work out a plan where Michael would be able to look after the club, his father would be able to search the streets, talk to his friends on the police force, do something to find her, and someone else would keep an eye on the houses in case Laura returned to either.

But every plan ran into the challenge of doing something with the kids.

"We can't lose her, too," Eli said.

"We haven't lost anyone, as far as I know. Hang in there. We'll find her. We'll find Mary, too," Melinda said as she joined them.

Michael was, for the first time in a long time, relieved at his mother's return. Again speaking in hushed tones, all three talked the matter out. Melinda explained her morning's investigations in very bare bones. She thought Mary had been up at Morewill Park before her accident. She wondered again why Mary would have driven home the way she did.

"It sounds like she was being chased," Michael said. "Or she was hurt. Like she had to get to help fast. I mean, she's a great driver. She did some kind of math in her head and decided that was the best way, and that she could manage it."

They all mulled that over in silent agreement.

Michael explained about picking up the kids, not having seen Aunt Laura the previous day, and his father described his failed attempts to reach Laura by phone.

"Well," Melinda said, "the kids are supposed to go to their camp this morning, so that would take care of them for the day. And Michael can go to the club, and Eli, you should go to her house. We have a copy of her house key hanging in the kitchen. I'm going to call Gretchen and see if they've found out anything more about Mary."

Michael smiled at his mother grimly, and got a blank, distant look in return, but felt comforted nonetheless. In a crisis, Melinda was always the best one to turn to for direction.

Melinda felt strangely detached as she moved back and forth through the empty house, clearing the clutter, taking and making phone calls. When she was sure Gretchen would be at her desk, she seated herself at the kitchen counter and gave her friend a call.

"Glory, Melinda," Gretchen said after their initial greetings, "something happened on that road and I can't quite imagine what. You know that just up from the accident site they found blood all over the road, and some body parts off the road."

"I heard it was a finger."

"It was more than that. Different body parts. And what they found is what was left after days out in the wild. There was more blood than they could properly deal with. There was so much they thought Mary might have hit an animal, or a pack of them, but then they found fingers and other things. And there's blood under the burn marks on the car. They're trying to match the blood from the car with blood on the street."

"So what's the theory?"

"No one's saying it, but it's got to be Hill People. She ran into a pack of 'em."

When Gretchen said the word "pack" Melinda had just then looked at the deck of cards on the counter near the phone cradle. It had been sitting next to the phone for something like weeks now.

Melinda left the question of where Mary might be now unspoken. She wasn't ready for Gretchen to be so straightforward. She wanted not to focus on the morbid, but rather on her sense that Mary was still alive.

As she wound up the conversation, and told Gretchen to keep her updated, she undid the rubber band around the pack, and flipped the first card. She gasped.

"You all right there?"

"Let's talk again later, okay, Gretchen?"

"Sure thing. Take heart, hon."

"I will. And thank you for everything."

She looked at the card. It was the three of diamonds. And on the card, in small writing that looked almost like charcoal, the word "Kristjiandottir"

And in her mind, she heard herself as a child saying, "This is Kristy Ann's daughter. She was three when she died."

She turned another card, the nine of spades. The writing on it read "Lute."

Melinda stared at the card. That was the girl's name. Lute.

When had she had these cards out? Just the other day. The day that Cameron was in the house.

Melinda flipped rapidly through the cards, and each had a name written on it. Many of them were familiar, and many were unreadable—many were written in other languages, with letterings she could not read, though at times, with particular cards, there was a name on the tip of her tongue that she could almost remember without being able to read it.

Had Cameron done this? For what reason?

And as she read the names and moved through the deck, she felt that each one touched her mind and her heart deeper. Each name connected her to every other name a little more closely. Even the unreadable ones resonated in her mind. Were these the names of the women she had been in her previous lives? The names of the girls in the trees? The names of the cards she'd carried as a child? Why else would they be familiar?

Melinda asked herself, Don't you understand? They all were you. They all are you.

There was a knock on the front door.

Melinda picked up the cards and the rubber band. As she walked to the door, she pulled the rubber band around the pack. She looked through the eyehole as she rested her hand on the doorknob.

It was Mr. Green. Cheronkin's long-time resident walker. She was so surprised to see that ruddy round face that she stopped for a moment and peered through the eyehole again to look at his face, which filled the lens. His red, neatly combed hair was streaked with gray, a sign that brought great comfort to Melinda because, for the twenty-plus years she'd been watching him on his daily walks around the area, he never seemed to have aged. Maybe he was human, after all. The gray-streaked red hair, combed neatly to the side, those frosty blue eyes. His eyes were striking, when she'd never been close enough to see anything more than the black-rimmed glasses he wore.

She'd never known him to stop walking, much less approach a residence.

But he wasn't there to stop. As she pulled the door open, he came in behind it and as she was backing away to give room for the door to swing open, he pushed forward, pushing the door into her, knocking her backward. He stepped up to her as she regained her balance and pushed her backward again. Then, with one hand, he grabbed her by her shirt as she fell away from him. The door slammed closed.

With his other hand he grabbed her neck and then he let go of her shirt. She fell backward onto the small, narrow-legged table tucked against the wall beneath the staircase in the hallway, where she often left her keys, the morning paper, and the mail. The hand on her neck did not tighten, but neither did it release her as she fell. He followed along with her, and so she was lying across the table and he was standing over her with both of his hands on her neck. She was lying on an oval-shaped porcelain dish that was typically the repository for her car keys. It dug into her shoulder blade as Mr. Green leaned into her, pushing her down. His glasses slid off his face and dropped to the ground.

She wondered if he were going to try to rape her or kill her or both and which it was going to be first. For a few precious seconds she flailed her arms helplessly, beating her hands ineffectually on his arms and his back. He was stocky and solid and she couldn't hurt him with her hands, She occasionally caught sight of his round, frosty-blue eyes as she wriggled and twisted to resist his tightening grip. His coarse breathing was all she could hear. For a moment, she thought she felt something there in the middle of his back, under the green jacket: two round furry posts . . . was it fur or feathers?

It was feathers. It was wings. He had wings.

She was being murdered by an angel.

When the pain in her shoulder blade sharpened, she shifted her weight on the table, and as he shifted himself to compensate for her movement, she kneed him as hard as she could between his legs and, instead of flailing her right arm uselessly, she stuck her fingers into his eyes. Whatever else he was, he had the same soft spots as any man. She pushed until her fingers were wet, although somehow he did not scream or let go of her neck.

With a sharp crack, the table collapsed, and she dropped to the floor. The weight of him on her as she fell onto the broken pieces of the table hurt terribly, but she focused herself through the pain. The dish, which survived the fall intact, broke as Melinda rolled over it.

Mr. Green's right hand slipped and then he struggled to regain his grip on her, punching her twice in the chin in the process. She ignored the pain, continued struggling away from him.

He said to her, "You've gone too far. There's nothing to do now but send you back where you came from."

She grasped a piece of wood, a table leg, as she fought to keep away from his free hand. She gasped for air as she hit the side of his head with it again, and again and again. It seemed not to hurt him. It seemed like a nuisance to him. But his face and his eyes were covered with blood, and apparently even angels needed to be able to see, for he started trying to wipe if off his eyes. She pulled herself farther out from under him. Frustrated, he struck her on the face again, a glancing blow this time, then tried to reestablish his grip on her. But she wasn't going to let that happen.

"You're too late," she said in a voice that she did not recognize. There was power in it, authority. Was this her true voice? The angel heard it, too. He paused and stared into her eyes.

How many lifetimes had that voice, her voice, been waiting for her to embrace it?

She said a word Melinda didn't recognize; it sounded like she was spitting out a curse.

The lights flickered. Pieces of furniture throughout the house—everything that wasn't nailed down—shifted, then jumped, some of it lifting a quarter of an inch off the ground before banging to the ground. Mr. Green looked away from her with a start at the sudden noise.

Grasping the table leg with both hands, and with a speed and ferocity that surprised even herself, she thrust the jagged end of the wood into his forehead.

And it hadn't been nature keeping her in check all this time; it had been men and perhaps it had even been the angels themselves keeping her down.

"You won't kill me again."

Mr. Green fell backward, cushioned by his wings, a gushing wound in the middle of his forehead. His widow's peak pointed to it. Writhing in pain, he did not make another noise for several moments.

Then, as she watched, his body started to fade. In only a few moments, he was gone.

Melinda waited a moment, breathing hard, assessing the broken table, the front door. It was too hard to tell how she felt at the moment, with her adrenaline pumping. Stunned? Frightened? Shocked? And thrilled. She wanted to cry.

She wondered where angels went when they died.

Still, the noise she made was almost a choking sound. Her hands were shaking and she raced into the kitchen, toward the sink, thinking she was going to throw up.

"Hunh. Uhhhh!" She didn't throw up. Her heart was racing. Was she going to faint? Was anyone going to believe her this time? Did she believe it? Should she take a picture of the broken table in the hallway?

She returned to the front door. Locked all seven locks, including the deadbolt. Not a lot of good any of that does, she thought.

The table was broken. Her body felt battered. That was real. She knew it was real.

Or was that a dream?

She had been so strong! Not weak. Afraid, but not weak. Thrilled like a ride down a rollercoaster and this was only the first drop of the ride. Even for a dream, this would be a great improvement on the usual fare. It was nice to win for once.

She paused. Had it been a dream? The table was broken. His blood on the carpet, like the blood on her hands, was gone. She looked in a mirror, and there was her proof.

Where his hands had been around her neck, her skin was red and bruised. It would be black and blue by morning.

Melinda cleaned up the mess in the front hall. She had recognized that without evidence, no one would believe she was attacked by an angel or that she had managed to fight him off. And then she had thought about the process of discovering no one believed her.

For instance, when Eli came home and asked her what had happened to the table and she explained about the angel. Bruise marks or no, he wouldn't believe it. He would *pooh pooh* it and in the state she was in she would likely have to kill him if he started minimizing this concern. As soon as anything too outrageous came out, he was more than likely going to look at her as a suspect, putting it all on her.

As if she would do this to herself.

In the process of tidying up, she recognized and felt, deep in her heart and soul, that the one item on the list of things that had to happen before the completion of this transformative event was that her family needed to gather.

That was the last piece to be assembled.

They needed to be together. She needed to call them together.

She would call a family meeting. That was at the top of tomorrow's To Do list. She wanted Mary to be there. Mary was supposed to be there, at the beginning of this new life, Melinda felt it in her heart. It was fate, it was destiny that her daughter be there. That was the picture at the start of the new world. The accident, Mary being gone, that was not the reality Melinda believed was going on here; that was a temporary diversion.

Mary was fine. Melinda thought she could wait for her, at least a bit longer.

But there was nothing to stop her from preparing. It was important to start preparing. She had to ask herself: What was important enough to her that she would want to try to save it? To take it with her?

Even as she started going through things, she repeatedly stopped herself. Why was she thinking about packing, taking stuff with her? Was it important that she be going someplace? Why had she gotten that feeling, so strong, that they were going to be leaving here? Was it because Mr. Green and whatever and whoever he was a part of had found her? Cameron knew where to find her, too. Apparently everyone who wanted to hurt her knew where to go.

If someone sent Mr. Green, they will send others, she thought. Maybe more of them this time. And probably sooner rather than later.

Without knowing it to be true, but feeling in her heart that it was, she continued her planning.

She thought the family meeting would have to take place the following night, at the latest.

That was very important.

Melinda wondered where they were. Why hadn't Mary shown up in some form yet? Why was she still hiding from them all? Was it just for attention? And what was Michael's excuse? Would she have to wait up tonight until he came home, and corner him to get him to commit? Would she have to hunt him down at the club and bring him home like he was a high school student out after curfew? She was actually beginning to feel angry at him for being away from the house so much during such a trying time. And at Eli, who was everywhere but here? Shouldn't he be here with her? Protecting her? But she felt less angry with Eli than she did with the kids. They were a part of her in a way Eli was not.

They should be with her when she needed them.

Spending the day at the club proved to be the better choice for Michael, rather than staying at home thinking about how bad everything has been. Mary was still with him all day, on his mind and in the faces of the employees he spoke with and in some of the customers' eyes. But there were all the things to do at the club that Aunt Laura would normally have taken care of, and he was able to distract himself with these tasks from one section of time to the next, one after the other, throughout the day, through dinner, and into closing.

It was two when he was finally ready to let himself out and turn off the last lights. Tempting as the couch had increasingly seemed as a place to crash, he knew he should go home just to be with what was left of the family.

As he stepped up to the doors, he saw someone approaching from the other side.

Talia.

He opened the door as she stopped just before the threshold. He held the door back, to invite her in, but she refused.

"Is your friend here?"

"Who, Jack?"

"Hm." There was something different about her voice. She was trying to cover it, but he could hear it. Almost like a cold. But she didn't look sick. She looked, if possible, more beautiful than before; almost radiant in the dark of the night. And yet, she also looked sad. And a little scared. He thought maybe she'd been crying. "I haven't seen him. My sister, Jack, my aunt. I haven't seen any of them. It's like ten little Indians around here." They were both quiet, until he asked, "Why do you look as sad as I feel? What happened"

"Cam's gone, too." She looked down at her feet, so he couldn't try to read her face.

"Oh, Yeah? Gone how? Where did she go?"

He thought he understood, from the look on her face, in her lack of response, that her friend was dead. It took him a moment more to realize it was significant that she had come to the club to share this news with him. "I'm sorry," he said. "What happened?"

"Elena and I both heard her screaming in the middle of the night two nights ago; the sound woke us both up from our sleep, but we couldn't figure out where the sound we'd heard came from."

"Was she outside? Do you think it was Hill People?"

"No, they're not . . . they're not an issue with us," she said. "Especially not her. And we don't know where she was when it happened."

"You think Jack knows something? He was with us two nights ago, looking for my sister. God, it feels like it's been a month."

"But you haven't seen him since."

"No." Michael shook his head.

She stared at him, examining his expression. For what? To see if he might be lying?

"What," he asked, "do you think happened?"

She thought about it a few moments before she answered. "I can't talk about it. I can't talk about any of this with you," she said with some frustration. "And now I'm afraid I'm next. That it's going to happen to me. This is all much more than I thought it was going to be. And I'm not ready to die for the cause; I just came to dip my toe in the water. So I'm going to be joining my aunt in the city tonight. And then we're going to fly out . . ." she stopped herself. "Yes, so, I wanted to thank you, and to say goodbye. I'm so sorry about that: I was expecting the beginning of something better."

"What about your big event? Don't you have some sort of cosmic harmonic convergence thing you're waiting for?"

"When it happens, Michael, it's going to be just like a window opening and closing—and then it's going to be over. It's possible it will happen so quietly that no one will see it. I came here planning to be on the lookout, so I didn't miss a thing. Believing that when it was over, the whole world would be on the road to something better. That's all I imagined. That a window would open on something, and then it would close, and the world would go on until the next one opened someplace else. Which could be next year or next century. Nothing would seem to have changed when it was done, and yet everything would have changed. But I would have known, or been that much more sure, because I was here. But I've gotten enough of a taste of it." The thought exasperated her almost to the point of tears. "And I've been so sure about it and felt so safe—partially because of Cam—but now I don't know what to expect."

It didn't make very much sense to Michael at all. He was never into the whole New-Agey drama. But he understood that she was doing her best to share something about herself with him. So he listened and stared at her and nodded. He thought he could learn to live with it if it came with the rest of the package.

As if she were reading his mind, she gave him a thrilling hint of a smile, then acted as if a great idea had just dawned on her. But it was clearly something she'd thought of earlier. "Why don't you come along with me? You could be my manager."

His heart skipped a beat. Not what he expected. "Wow. Is it that bad? You're expecting some sort of calamity?"

"Truth, I don't know what it is. And it's not like Elena hasn't thought something was going to happen before, and then it didn't. But clearly, this is different this time." An image popped into Michael's mind of Talia falling asleep while she waited by the side of the road for the Rapture to come, next to her bicycle and a suitcase. "I can't think about leaving right now. Someone's got to be the last little Indian.

Someone's got to be here when the rest of the tribe comes back. Man, I haven't even checked in with my mom all afternoon." He'd been feeling the impulse to call Melinda all day, but stronger than that had been a desire to establish distance from her. He didn't want to get sucked into her mourning craziness when he had found a kind of calm here at the club.

Up until that moment, Talia was relaxed. But at the mention of his mother, the look of worry appeared again in her eyes. She stepped back. "I've got to go, I think. I'm running late. Sure you don't want to go? You know what happens to the last little Indian, don't you? Same as all the rest."

"Thank you for telling me about the car. About Mary's car. I was planning on seeking you out to tell you that."

"I'm sorry about your sister. If it makes a difference, I think she's alive out there."

"I want to believe that. I'm sorry about . . . your friend."

"Everything turns out different than you would expect it to."

"That's true, too."

He watched her go, then closed the door, and found he was still standing inside the club. Finding himself strangely and intensely aroused only a few minutes after she'd left, he found a dark corner, dropped his pants, spit on his erection and jerked off. He noticed one of Jack's statues near him, a blob titled Diana. He imagined it was Talia's eager face.

After he finished, it took him half an hour to wipe it clean.

It was the kind of thing Jack would find either hilarious or sacrilegious.

When he was done, he crawled onto the couch in Laura's office and fell asleep.

Melinda waited in bed, awake, until 3:00 AM, listening for Michael's car, for Michael's door key in the lock to his room, or the sound of Michael's door closing.

Tomorrow, she promised herself, they were going to have the meeting, whether the rest of the family liked it or not. Tomorrow might be the last chance. It was going to be too

255

late if they waited any longer. This thing was going to happen and they needed to be on the same page.

Eli was going to be a problem. She'd always hidden the more alternative aspects of her life from him, because, really, he didn't want to hear about it. It hadn't even been about hiding. She'd just made a habit of pursuing those things during his times away, and if she ever did tell him about it, it was usually framed as something to do with her free time. Eli wasn't a subscriber to any kind of alternative reality, the idea that things weren't at all what they seemed. He'd never have left her over it, but he would have heaped on the scorn when he had the chance.

There had never been a need before like this for him to understand. Would that make a difference?

As for the kids, she would go to the club tomorrow and drag Michael home by the ear if that was what it took. As for Mary . . .

Melinda walked through the dark house to the kitchen, to the door to the back patio. When she stood on the back patio, she walked to the end of concrete, and looked about the yard. The night was silent, not even the sound of crickets. There were several of them here, still as could be. Hill People. She could not mistake that they were there. Or that, drawn as they were to the house and to all it promised, they were afraid of her now.

When she spoke, there was that sound again in her voice. Command, tension, anger, frustration were all in there, too. She did not yell, but even in a low voice she heard the authority resonating in her tone.

"Find my daughter," she told them, nearly in a fury at the thought that people like these might be holding her daughter. They backed away from her, but they did not run. "And bring her here to me."

13

June 26

Melinda was awake and dressed early again. She cut fruit for Eli and the kids to have with their cereal, and left a note propped up by the coffee machine for Eli to take Max and Lorraine to daycare.

Then, using directions from Gretchen, she drove to Elena Altman's property, a nearly block-long piece of land surrounded by a tall brick wall. There was a driveway, which led to a wrought-iron gate, which was closed.

It looked to be a property spread across four parcels of land.

Zoning laws Melinda had campaigned for wouldn't permit such a thing today. That effort had been necessary to keep Cheronkin from turning into an enclave of mansions.

Melinda stepped out of the car and walked to the gate. To the side of the driveway was an alcove built into the brick, with a mailbox and an intercom.

She pressed the button and looked around. There was no one about.

"Hello, Elena? I think this is Elena Altman's address. This is Melinda Phillips. I'm sorry for dropping by unannounced like this but I was hoping for a chance to talk with you . . ." She paused. She waited. Was Elena even home? There wasn't a car in sight. It was too early in the morning for there not to be someone home at a property this size.

"Honey, how can I help you?"

Melinda's heart jumped. It was Elena's voice. She felt a rush of gratitude.

"Hello, Elena? This is Melinda Phillips. We met at the Fandango club opening?"

"Yes, of course I remember you. I've been waiting to hear from you again."

"I'm sorry for calling on you so early. Do you have a moment, so that we could speak face to face?"

"I'm afraid I can't promise much, dear. Let's just do what we can. This little bit is going to be hard enough on a little old lady like me. We won't be able to meet again just yet. But don't worry—it's a marvelous spinning wheel we're on and everything comes around again."

"Please. Elena, my daughter has disappeared. Her car was found on the side of Marble Canyon Road. We don't know where she is or where her body is . . . I think she's alive, I feel she's alive; inside I feel her, and I know she's still out there . . ."

"Well, of course you do. A little part of you resides inside of her. If she were gone, it would have come back to you. That's what happens to people like us when we have children. They take a little part of us. Although I do sympathize for you. I've suffered a recent loss. In these situations, it is always best to trust your instincts."

"She is alive, isn't she?"

"You know the answer to that. That's not really why you're here, is it?"

"It is, actually, the reason I'm here. But it's also just the tip of the iceberg, isn't it Elena? I know there's something going on here, and that it's bigger than Mary. And I think it's about Marble Canyon, but then, it's bigger than that, too. I don't know what it is. Why did you support the effort to repair Marble Canyon Road? Personally, I was tired of people from the community losing their lives. Now I'm worried to death that it's all going to turn out to have been about real estate and money—that all these people are intended to suffer solely for the profit of a transnational business such as yours. That your plan all along has been to close the road, drive us out of our homes, and turn this into . . . what? I don't know what. I can't imagine what. I'm just sickened at the thought that my involvement with the road might have been the result of a manipulation, and that my actions might have in any way contributed to my daughter's accident.

"And you know what? I think I'd be better able to understand what you are up to except for the fact that I opened up a hole in my existence when I did that regression therapy. It's an endless distraction. And now I want it closed up. And here you are again, comfortably established at the nexus of my concerns. And I'm not sure of your motives.

"I'm not interested in what I was then or who I was. I don't want to be the person who has lived forever. I was imperfect before, yes, and that's why I started down this road. But I'd prefer imperfect over whatever this is now. I'd choose ignorance over insight. I want to be the Melinda Phillips I used to be. But I can't hold onto that person now for more than short periods of time. Other pieces—other selves?—keep intruding. I really need help understanding this—if I'm going to get it under control. Because you can help me with this, I think."

"Once you catch a glimpse of the magnitude," Elenna said, "it can be overwhelming. But it's only more challenging if you resist. And what is it you are resisting? Yourself? Whatever it is you're experiencing or remembering or reliving comes from inside of you, not from without. How can you deny what you already know simply because it's been revealed to you?"

Melinda waited.

The intercom was silent. She straightened herself up, wondering what she might look like to passerby, crouched anxiously at the front gate.

She waited.

"Melinda, do you remember, when we spoke at the club, we talked about the great change about to take place?"

"Yes. Yes, I do."

"Picture two circles, spinning or vibrating at a different rate right next to each other, and imagine that, for a moment in time, they overlap, that there is an area common to both."

"Okay," Melinda said.

"That is what is happening right now. There are different realities that exist, and two of them are slowly coming into alignment. They are not in alignment yet, but as they come closer to being so, there will be moments when they touch. In those places they touch, for whatever the window of time that the overlap exists, the rules aren't the same. That is where we are now. This is the first of those events. You are, Melinda, by my understanding, channeling a reincarnated spirit. Something has prevented that spirit from awakening in the last of your many lives."

"Apparently," Melinda said quietly, "I've died young many times."

"That would explain some things, yes. I think it might even have been possible for you to not have felt these stirrings in this lifetime, or ever again, because that spirit has been buried away for so long. But then this change in the air occurs here, and our reality is suddenly vibrating at a different speed, and that sleeping soul inside of you was drawn out."

"I don't know that I believe that's true," Melinda said, feeling the need to reject her words outright but wondering if they might be true. "I'm not sure what's real right now, or what I might be imagining. I mean, maybe I have a tumor my doctor can't find that's doing this to me. There are many things that you've said that ring true to me, but I'm finding it hard to accept anything you're saying outright because I don't understand your agenda."

"Honey, I've spent what feels like several lifetimes in this place. I love this land. My soul and my spirit have returned here whenever it has been possible. I have done everything in my power to protect our home. I don't want to see innocents hurt, whether or not that might seem to be forestalling the inevitable. I don't see a benefit to the planet in the loss of humankind that so many others profess to see.

"Do you know, at some point in time not too long ago, there were only about two thousand humans left on the planet? The icing over of the planet cornered every last living one of them on the African continent. Where would we be now if people hadn't made it past that point? We would have been erased along with them.

"You'll have to remember, dear, I didn't have an exact timetable for when this would occur, only an expectation. And from that expectation, I admit, I invested not only in your group, but also in your friend, the Senator, because I thought he would be able to close the canyon and I thought he was sympathetic toward the idea of slowing the growth of the community. Trust a man to be untrustworthy and that at least will make for a fair beginning and ending. He benefited greatly from the outcome, I assure you."

"Why?"

"To lessen the population at risk, dear. To keep them away. My thinking has been that if a window were to open and close, it would be to the benefit of all that no one were around to see it. Leaving no witnesses is one of the first tenets, you know.

"Melinda, I want to assure you that I understand the process you're going through; that it should be so hard I take

260

as a punishment of Nature itself for failing her. I've tried to help the younger ones I've chanced to encounter, to help them find their ways through this very transition that you're going through, and I think I've been successful in some cases, and less so in others. But a child who has been raised with alternative ideas is far more adaptable than a determined woman in her middle age who has a stricter view of the world. You have a lot of . . . barriers to overcome."

"I have barriers."

"Melinda, it is in some of our natures to return in each successive life. It is in our natures to die and to be reborn, and, as we live in our new lives and grow to maturity, to awaken again and resume where we left off before. Some, most, are enraged to realize we have ever been forced to sleep. The reawakening of your eternal soul can be most painful emotionally. I wish I could help you more. Simply know that the Mother Earth will consume all your pains. You'll see, dear. We'll talk more then." Elena said, quietly, "Melinda, you have seen the womb of the world? Have you been there? To the forest?"

Melinda knew Elena was referring to the place where she had dreamed herself to be during the regression therapy session, and again when Cameron was at the house.

"Yes, I think I know the place you're talking about."

"That is where She hides all that is precious to her. That's where the Deep Magic lies. That is the other spinning, vibrating sphere that is touching upon ours. That is what the window opens upon. That is what the world is going to become."

"What about the angel who tried to choke me in my home yesterday? Where does he fit into your big picture?"

Elena gasped, "Oh, dear." She paused. "I hope you're all right. That was my worst oversight. Not recognizing who was around us. It's easy to live in Cheronkin, tucked away from the world, and think you're living unnoticed; easy to forget the hierarchies of men who are watching for the same signs that we are, with agendas all their own. Trust that there will be more of them. And there are other players at work, too, apparently. That, I'm afraid, is why it's no longer safe to stay here, even if only to observe how it ends. It's a shame, when I've waited so long. But there's mischief afoot. And I've seen enough to know we should be on our way."

261

"He was my second uninvited intruder. The first being your red-headed friend."

"Cameron was a very troubled girl, dear. I didn't realize she had frightened you until after the fact. Believe it or not, she had your best interests at heart. She wanted to reach out to you. She believed you two shared a common history. I asked her to deliver a message, not throw a brick through your window. I didn't realize she'd made such a habit of acting out until it was too late."

"Your message was to frighten me?"

"She wanted to nudge you into awakening to the possibilities. We both thought such a message would help you."

"Help me? How? What am I supposed to do? What is it she wanted me to do?"

"What the butterfly does. Set yourself free. Until you do, you won't know where to go next. But once you have, your next step will become more clear. But dear, and this is important: whether or not you resolve this issue within yourself in the next few days. I urge you to leave town, if only for a short time. I don't believe it will be safe here again until this is over."

Melinda found she was once again leaning in close to the speaker. "What do you think will happen?"

Another voice broke in from somewhere else. "Excuse me?"

Melinda looked up with a start, and realized someone was standing inside the gate, and she was addressing Melinda.

"Excuse me? There's no one home. Mrs. Altman has gone on vacation."

"I was just speaking with her."

The woman stared at her a moment. "I heard your voice on the intercom inside the house. I am not to answer, but it seemed you were leaving a very long message. No one is home. And I am to be leaving shortly, as well. Is there someone else here with you, then?" She looked, saw no one, then shrugged at Melinda. Without another word, she turned and walked back to the house.

Melinda waited ten more minutes for the voice on the intercom to speak again before she left.

When Melinda returned home, her mind was clearer. Driving home from Elena's, she had debated whether or not she had just hallucinated a conversation in Elena's driveway, whether or not she believed the maid when she said Elena was not home, whether or not she had completely lost her grip on reality. It could be a textbook case of schizophrenia, but she didn't know if people under such a condition were capable of recognizing the possibility, as she was. But once home, she decided the heart of the matter, imagined conversation or not, was that she no longer felt safe in Cheronkin, and that they needed to leave—and sooner rather than later.

She went in through the front door, feeling a sliver of the absolutely crazed fear that she had felt when Mr. Green attacked her the evening before. Her bruises from that encounter were quickly fading. This morning, she'd pulled the broken pieces of the table from the trashcan and then stored them in a box. As proof, in case it came up later. It really wasn't enough evidence to convince anyone else that such a thing had happened, but at least she could confirm it for herself.

And had it happened?

She went back to getting things ready.

There were two messages on the machine, from her phone tree contacts, reporting sightings of Hill People in their yards the previous night. Eli received a call as she was getting ready to check in with Riza. He took the call at his desk upstairs, and a few moments later he was in the kitchen, his voice sounding lighter than it had in weeks.

"That was Bill. He says that Laura is at his house in the hills."

"What?"

"He said she showed up drunk late last night at his ranch house, that she was a wreck because of Mary."

"I thought she'd stopped that behavior. So she just abandoned the children? And where was she the night before?" Melinda stopped when she saw the flicker of irritation in Eli's eyes. The emotion was strong enough to penetrate the grayness that had hovered over his aura for so long now. Since long before Mary disappeared. Melinda imagined that the halls of the government buildings were filled with gray people. It was only when Eli was home for

263

an extended time that he began to lighten—but it had been years since that had happened.

"He has a press conference this morning up north, and he thinks it'll be easier for everybody if I pick her up. Bill said that if he didn't get back in time to meet us, he'd find a way to get in touch. I'm going to pick her up."

"That's going to take you hours. Maybe I should do it?"

"I'm going to take care of it."

"Fine. Do we know if she's all right?"

"I don't know anything other than that she's there."

As he picked up his keys, she thought to stop him. "Eli?"

"Yes?"

Should she tell him they would be leaving town in a hurry later tonight? Instead, she said, "I love you. I'm sorry you have to go through this." Because she understood, very clearly, that he would not be willing to leave Cheronkin. Neither, she thought, would the kids.

"I love you, too, Melin," he said quietly as he picked up his keys.

How could she leave all of these pieces of her to face whatever this was alone?

After Eli was gone, Melinda felt some relief. His absence eased some of the pressure. But there was also a little bit of confusion. Should she be concerned for Laura? Why wasn't she more so? Should she be more concerned for Max and Lorraine?

The phone rang.

It was Riza.

"Oh, Melinda. I'm so glad you're home. I don't feel like I can take this much longer, all these lurkers hanging about. The dogs have kept them away, but now they're out there barking all the time. It makes me feel like I'm under siege. I didn't move to California to feel under siege."

Michael woke on the couch huddled under the small throw blanket Laura kept on the couch purely for decoration. He was wearing his t-shirt from the night before and his pants were on the desk where he left them after he jerked off, an act for which, when he reflected upon it, he felt great chagrin and embarrassment, mostly resulting from the fear that the act was somehow inadvertently witnessed, recorded, transmitted and/or shared among the people who knew who he was.

Once he was dressed, the thought of heading out of the office into the bustle outside made him uncomfortable, too.

What if he left something incriminating out there?

Instead, he sat in the chair behind Laura's desk, writing down a list of checks that needed to be cut for the vendors. He was more tired than he ever remembered being. His head was buzzing a little, and he felt disoriented looking at the office from Laura's perspective. There was a lot to do.

He didn't want to be doing her job. He wanted Laura back.

The restaurant was probably nearing the end of the breakfast service. He listened to the murmurs and clinks of porcelain and glass and metal, and wondered at the fact the club just kept on running.

Nothing stopped this place.

He heard the bar TVs mention Uncle Bill holding a press conference, and decided to watch it before he went outside. Ten or fifteen minutes more, he thought. He turned on the television as an announcer on the morning news said, "Coming next, a senator is expected to announce his withdrawal from the race for governor."

The news program soon cut away to Santa Barbara, where, according to the announcer, it was anticipated that State Senator Bill Clayton was going to concede the race for governor, and urge his supporters to cast their votes for one of his former rivals.

There was a flash of cameras, and Uncle Bill stepped onstage and walked behind the podium with a manila folder in his hand. There was something weird about the way he looked, the expression on his face, like he had a sour taste in his mouth. It wasn't his best photo op. From his appearance, Michael would have guessed he'd had a couple rough days.

He looked to be not entirely sure about being there. He looked up at the camera from the podium, and promised not to waste too much more of anyone's time or money. Michael was sweeping the crumbs from whatever it was he ate the night before as a snack into the trashcan when he heard someone on the television scream. Michael thought he heard Uncle Bill say something odd, something like "The Earth takes all of

265

our pains and makes them her own." Michael looked up in time to see Uncle Bill holding a gun pointed to the side of his head. The camera jerked left and away from him before the gun popped.

He stood in one place for a few seconds, staring, stunned, as they replayed it.

Oh my God.

He heard other voices outside the locked door saying the same thing.

He picked up the phone and dialed Melinda. The line was busy.

Would she have been watching it? Would she have even known he was having a press conference? Did Dad see it?

He called the hostess stand at the front of the restaurant. It was Christie who answered. "Christie, it's Michael."

"Hi, Michael. Aren't you in the office?"

"I am. Is the bar TV on?" He knew it was, because he could hear it.

"It is."

"Any chance people will object if you turn it off?"

"Everybody is glued. Ready for a riot?"

"Okay. Just thought I'd check."

Listening to the local news broadcast as he drove to Bill's ranch house, Eli felt a numbing cold race through his bones. The audio was nearly a garble. Bill's voice was clear. He sounded defeated. There was a collective gasp from the crowd of reporters and the gunshot and the harried descriptions of the commentator trying to accurately and unemotionally report that the senator had just shot himself. Eli thought over and over again *Oh my God. I just talked to him.*

The report was clarified and cleaned up of emotion by a second journalist, who shortly afterward gave a third retelling of the incident in an even more abbreviated form, followed soon after by a condensed three-line summary by the news anchor. The threads of the story were still undetermined, but they would surely run with it. Eli could imagine tangents that would include a personal profile, a commentary on violent messages broadcast intentionally (or unintentionally) by the media and a brief discussion of his wife, Margaret. And then the couple's long presence on the state's political scene, and the Clayton family's even longer history with the state government.

The tangent they wouldn't cover, at least not yet, was his sister, who he was praying was okay as he raced toward Bill's ranch. Whoever investigated would want to talk to Eli if they had a list of Bill's morning's calls. Eli was certain he would be contacted in regards to the content of that conversation, and he knew it would soon be time to start considering his answers. He imagined there would be reporters driving this same route in less than twenty-four hours. He didn't have a complete picture, but instead two pieces that might be unrelated but likely were connected, simply by the coincidence of them occurring at the same time.

Once he was on the back road to Bill's house, he felt nearly overcome by the memories of forty years of driving that road to see his friend. This could very well be the last time for Eli—even if there was a reason to return, a central part of the equation and ritual and history was now gone.

It was Bill who had brought him to Cheronkin in the first place; it was vacationing with him that brought all the hidden charms of this place to life for Eli. If not for Bill, he and Melinda might very well have been East Coast suburban dwellers.

There was no point in blaming the place, Eli understood. But still, more and more he wished they'd chosen another option, that they'd ended up someplace where Mary would still be there with them, and so would Melinda—because he missed how she used to be—and Bill Clayton could choose to do whatever damned stupid thing he did in his life without Eli bearing any of the consequences. His sister, who he prayed was safe, would have gone to the East Coast to be with family just as surely as she had ended up here.

But this wasn't the place to blame.

If they'd stayed in the East, the lure of the different—in the form of Bill's campaign—would that have been enough to draw him away from his family? It was all hypothetical, and all of it about roads not taken. Maybe Eli would have ended up here regardless.

And yet . . . and yet . . . sitting on the airplane the last time, feeling like he wouldn't be able to mentally make that journey, east to west, work to home, politics to family, to love, to home, again—he had hoped, in the back of his mind and heart, that it would be someplace other than here that he landed. Because even though the skies were clear, life in Cheronkin was vexed and covered with clouds.

As always, he'd been relieved to be home once he was there.

How different would this ending be right now? Even if he'd resisted, he wouldn't have been able to resist for long. This war, he'd noted at the beginning from the sidelines, was slowly going to pull everyone into its orbit; years later, he'd begun to look at it as if he had done his time and now it was maybe time for someone else.

This was the next front anyway, the next nexus of need. It was easy to focus on work and to pay less attention to the overall discontent at home except for the main precept that home is supposedly what we are working to maintain. But if his own life was any evidence, home was a fast-crumbling sense of security in the notion that everything will at some point be all right again.

Maybe it won't. Ever. Be.

Eli nearly drove past the figure in the road without a second glance, near as he was to the ranch house. One of the roles he'd always played well was big brother. He'd been Laura's ride home countless times since he'd gotten his license; and maybe a dozen times he'd found her in questionable circumstances, some of which merited an explanation, some of which he hadn't cared to know the details of. It was a simple rule: If she called, and he could come get her, he would.

There was something about the figure, a woman dressed in baggy clothes and a baseball cap, that struck him as familiar; and she clearly recognized him, and then he realized it was his sister. He stopped beside her and she climbed in; she was disconsolate, her face streaked with tears.

"He's gone."

"I heard it. Are you okay?"

"Physically, yeah. The guards left the minute they heard about it. I don't know if my car is there locked up or if they towed it. Should we go look?"

"No. We're not going near there for a while. How many guards?"

"Four."

They were both quiet. There were going to be questions. He turned the car around. Ahead of them on the road, there was a van with cameras and a spotlight on its roof headed up the road in the direction Eli had been driving before.

"We're going to have to make some quick plans now, Laura."

When Michael answered the office phone and heard his father's voice, weakened and tired, he wanted to cry. It was almost like receiving permission to let a few tears run down his cheek. The way things had been, he'd half been expecting that his dad might disappear, too, and that he would never have the chance to speak to him again.

Hearing that Aunt Laura was okay was a relief. Still, he had to bite his tongue to keep from asking when she might be able to make it to the club.

Lunch was fast approaching, and there was sure to be a crowd because there was nowhere else for people to gather to talk about the senator's suicide. It was the topic on every staff member's lips, though it had cast a weird pall in the air. Michael finally had to exercise his authority and turn the TVs off to avoid the constant replay of the event.

"I think you should close the place down, right away, before you guys get overrun with media," was his father's message. Laura is with me and she agrees. Tell the staff they're going to get a few days off, and then lock the doors and the parking lot gates and head out."

"Seriously? Dad, the place hasn't been completely closed in, like, sixty plus years."

"Seriously. The sooner, the better. Otherwise, I promise, it's going to be a headache for you all."

"I can handle a headache. When will she be back? The money is all handled, the bookings are handled. I feel bad telling everybody to go home indefinitely. I mean, that is what you're saying? Should I ask them how they feel about it?"

"Michael, listen." Michael heard the tone that said these were orders. Was he ready to face the consequences for disobeying? "This is for family. We have to protect your aunt now, and this is one of the things we have to do. Do you understand?"

269

He felt bad for his father. His best friend, gone. His daughter, gone. His father had found his sister. And now he wanted to protect her. "I understand. I'll get it done."

When they both said goodbye, Michael started the effort: He closed down the inside eating areas, and had the staff covering those sections break down the settings and the tables and stack the chairs in the storage area. He had the kitchen staff, which had been preparing lunch, set up the buffet tables outside. What food could be stored in the refrigerator or freezer was packed up and put away, and what couldn't be stored was set on the patio. They ignored knocks on the front doors and waited for the last of the day's delivery trucks at the back entrance with apologies and bottles of wine provided on each order they refused.

Finally, he turned off the lighted sign out front, and turned out the CLOSED sign in the window. And then joined everyone on the patio for lunch. The phones were ringing a lot, as usual, but he stopped answering all but the office line.

When the closing work was nearly done, he gathered the staff on the patio. He first announced that he had heard from his father about his aunt, and that she had been found and was doing well, which everyone applauded, although he could see the trepidation on all their faces. None of this was normal operating procedure. He denied having any other details and thanked the Great Whatever for bringing her home safe, to which several answered, Amen.

Then he told them the club would be closing shortly after their meal, and that he didn't know when it would reopen—he said that he hoped it would be next week, but he also said that he didn't know for sure and he wasn't going to lie to them by making false promises.

The mood among the employees was remarkably calm and accepting, although, of course, some of them began worrying about money, about job-hunting, about what might happen next. Would Laura return to the club? It was assumed so, even by Michael. They were glad to hear she was okay, and curious about the details, and then there was the added layer of the weird residue from the Senator's suicide.

He okayed Janet to mix drinks for everyone, and for a while, with music courtesy of a piano and drum duo for whom the gig was their only show this month, they ate and drank and sang and danced, everybody sort of drifted in and around,

270

finishing up their closing chores, making phone calls for rides, some collecting their personal things from the staff lockers. And as they finished off the food and drink and cleaned away those dishes, they began to say their goodbyes and to drift out of the club. He promised each one a check in the mail, and a phone call to let them know what was going to be happening. He didn't know if he would be able to deliver. On her way out, Janet told him not to worry. The club, she said, would survive. It always had.

He believed it when she said it, but after everyone had left, he wondered if it were true.

It was the end for him. The end of Cheronkin. The end of the club. The end of this whole life. And what other life did he have outside these hills? A life he hadn't thought twice about since he left it. Where else would he go? Where would he want to go? He told himself he didn't want to be anywhere near Danielle, but he also felt sure that a timely call from her would seem like a life preserver right now.

The phone rang as he stepped into the office. He let the recorder pick up. It was, in fact, Danielle.

"Hi, Michael. It's me. I heard you might be there. I heard the news. I wanted to see how you were doing . . ."

He let her go on without picking up.

He was wrong. Going back wasn't an option.

He wanted to go home, but he didn't want to see his mother. He knew that she wanted him there; knowing this made him not want to be anywhere near home.

His dad called to make sure everything was done.

Michael asked if he had talked to mom.

"I have, but she said she was turning off the phone after we were done talking."

"She's probably getting calls about Uncle Bill."

"She said the phone's been ringing off the hook. She also said she was worried about you, and wanted me to tell you that it's time for you to come home or you're not getting dessert. I'll see you later. I'm on an errand that's going to take me a while."

"Okay. 'Bye, Dad. I love you."

"I love you, too, son."

Michael sighed. At least there was Talia. He'd gotten to meet her.

But now she was gone too. This was what it felt like to be left behind.

Maybe, if he continued working in clubs, he would see her again someday.

There was some promise of a possibility he could land a job in another club in the city based on his experience here.

But that sort of thinking underscored the truth: His time here really was over. And what a mess it was ending up. His sister was missing, the only friend he'd made in the last year had disappeared, his uncle was dead, his aunt was found, but too soon to make a difference in his effort to prove he was capable of doing his dream job . . . without the club, there was just about nothing here other than his mother and father; add to the mixture the fact that everything else that wasn't here any longer—like a friend, or a girlfriend, or a job—didn't exist for him anywhere else in the world, either.

How was it that after a year off he was by most counts and measures worse off than when he started?

He was still on that same track later, feeling bad for himself, when he was the only one left, but then was distracted by worries about the club. Did he need to think about extra protection for the premises? Should he use the chains and padlocks on the doors? Who else did he need to call? The bank, the promoter? Was it going to all be in his hands, or was it safe to assume his time as the responsible one was over? Or was he supposed to be simply waiting for his next instructions?

He stayed a little while longer with the Muzak playing, hiding out in the office and making phone calls. And that time passed all too fast, and the afternoon turned to evening as he straightened up the office again before he left, locking the door behind him when he left.

Maybe he was wrong; maybe he was just getting sucked into the depressing aura of the day, the week, the last month. Dad and Aunt Laura were going to be sad for a while, and Melinda, too, about Uncle Bill, with Mary as the foundation of their pain. Maybe what he needed to do was just stop fighting the impulse, to just go home and be there for them.

That would make Mom happy, he thought.

He knew she was likely worried, but that she also knew that he and dad had been in communication. He couldn't explain why the last thing he wanted to do was call her, or worse, to go home. It would be too down of an ending to an already sad ending.

When he turned to the front door, finally ready to exit, there she was again.

Talia.

Deja vu, And yet, he was so startled to see her, and she, apparently, to see him, that they both gasped.

"Scared me."

"Me, too. Sorry."

"Me, too. I thought I was too late. That you'd left already."

"No, that was you. Remember?" Two things flashed through his mind. The first was an image of himself in the midst of his indiscretion the previous evening, and what he had been thinking about doing with her. The second was: She liked him. Maybe she even loved him.

She smiled. "I had some . . ." She looked around the room. Was she worried someone else was there? "I'm glad you're here."

"No one's here. We closed for the day. Because . . . well, a number of reasons. It's a different kind of day. I was just going home to be with the family."

She nodded her head as if she understood. Did she know about his uncle? Had she returned to offer sympathies? There had to be something more.

She took a breath, and stepped over the threshold, into the club. "I don't have much time, Michael." Her voice sounded strange, a little throaty. Still, he liked the way his name sounded on her lips. "I shouldn't be here. I should be gone from here."

"Because the celestial alignment is an end-of-Cheronkin kind of thing?"

She said, "I don't know, but I wouldn't be sarcastic about it."

"Sarcasm is the only remaining defense."

"Literally, in the short time I've known you, I've seen this town changing into something else. It's not subtle; you people see it, and it affects you and it is a very different environment to be living in than it was a year ago, and still, it's like no one wants to wonder why it's that way. For everyone I see, it's just another thing to work around. As long as you've got your stuff to do and all that. Do your best to find a way to work around it so that nothing changes and everything stays the same, regardless of the fact that everything has changed. It makes me wonder if people can change." She scanned the inside of the club as she spoke. Watching the statues or worried about running into Jack?

"While you're sitting here, like any other human being, you're seeing and hearing what is happening—it's registering with you—but you're too busy dealing with life to want to believe it has anything to do with you. So you just go about your ways. As long as you can just go about your ways, it's all okay."

"I'm not understanding."

"It's starting now. It's started already. It's been going on since the night I met you. Whatever it is." She shook her head and chuckled. "I think my crazy old aunt is right about so many things. And I'm afraid she's right about the rest. Soon it is going to be over, and everything is going to continue after it's over—but nothing afterward is ever going to be the same. And there's only a handful of people who are even going to know it happened at all. People will one day look back and say, 'when did this start?', and no one will know. And this is it. This is when."

"What is it I'm missing? What's going to happen?"

She stopped. She looked at him crossly for asking a question. "I don't know what it's going to be."

He thought she was worried about the statues. She still believed there was something about them that compelled her to speak the truth. "My aunt believed, and believes, that the human race is about to undergo a great and transformative change."

"I told you, the idea isn't totally alien. My mom thinks like that, too."

This clearly, for some reason, distressed her more. "You have to understand that in my lifetime, I have experienced things that have convinced me she may be right, and I also have collected a lot of arguments about why she might be wrong. My aunt might just be a crazy old rich white lady. The idea that some great change is going to suddenly alleviate the problems of the world, make the world a better place for everyone left is a big one to swallow.

"But then I see what is happening here, and I think I can feel it happening, like it's happening under my skin, too, and I know now that she is right about some things both big and small, public and personal . . . I can feel the charge of something coming in the air, the energy of it building up in my blood. I can almost touch and taste and smell the world that is awakening here and I can also believe that I remember that scent in the deepest, oldest parts of my soul.

"And it starts here. Maybe tonight. In some way that I cannot imagine, in some form that I cannot predict, the planets are going to line up and it's going to happen. I thought we could come here and be witnesses, you know, watch it happen and have a view on something magnificent, the beginning of a new hope for the world. But there are no innocent bystanders here. Cameron showed me that. And that is why I had to leave and why I still have to leave."

Michael didn't say anything. He didn't know what to say. There was so much weighing on his heart, and he didn't have room for one more thing. Especially a big, crazy thing. So he said that.

This response angered her. "You can't just get on with living, Michael. Don't you understand? Do you remember the night we met? The dead dog lying in the hills? He was dead, Michael. Dead. And then he wasn't. It happened right in front of your eyes. And since then, everything has been different here."

He didn't say a word to the contrary, but she saw the resolute skepticism on his face.

"Michael."

"You sound like my mom. I've heard this all before."

"And that!" This exasperated her. Then she reestablished calm. "Michael. Call the local emergency room. Ask them how many people have died since the night we found that dog. They'll tell you not a one."

"Bill Clayton just shot himself dead this morning."

"A hundred miles north of here."

"Cameron."

"Not sure what happened, or where. She'll be back, anyway. Someday. I believe that, too."

He didn't have an argument to make. She would have a nonsensical answer for everything. He knew how this worked. He shrugged as if it didn't mean much to him one way or the other.

"I'm proving it to you by telling you this while standing in this room. This room where I cannot tell a lie . . ."

"But you can be selective about what you share . . ."

"True. Very true. I wouldn't have respected you if you hadn't seen that. It's my perogative. I'm not a criminal," she said, sounding mildly offended.

"Okay," he said.

"Close your eyes."

"Okay."

"Michael, think about what I'm saying to you. Nature run amok. Nothing dies. If what I'm telling you is true, if nothing dies while this is happening, then your sister is alive out there."

He opened his eyes before she was finished and stared back at her.

"What I'm saying is true. Do you know it is true?"

He knew it was true.

"Yes," he said.

"I can take you to where I think she might be. Where I think she is now. But we leave now."

He looked her in the eyes. "There's something you're not telling me. But I can't think of what question I might ask you to reveal it. And you're right, I don't want to interrogate you. But why do we have to leave now?"

She bit her lip. "I think your mother is going to be here in about six minutes."

He rolled his eyes. After all, shouldn't he wait for Melinda, to share the news? But then, he could think of a few reasons why it might not make for a good encounter. Worse, Talia might be wrong about Mary. He should know more before he said anything.

"You should have said that first."

His car was parked on the street behind the club parking lot. He wondered where her car was.

They exited out the back, him feeling a silly thrill at the idea of evading Melinda. And for the first time in weeks, he also felt hopeful.

14

Before the Dawn

Melinda navigated her car into the club's empty parking lot. She pulled up to the curb outside the front doors. The inside of the building was illuminated briefly by the headlights, which sparkled across Jack's sculptures, dusting the room with light, a display that continued for a few seconds after the headlights were off.

Shortly thereafter, Melinda knocked on the doors. That was followed by her calling out Michael's name. Try not to sound angry, she thought. She jiggled the door handles, pushed on the doors. They were locked. She stepped back a step. "Michael? Are you there?" What was she supposed to do?

The doors are open, she told herself.

She pushed the handle again. There was a smooth click, and she pulled the door open. Immediately, as she entered, she knew Michael had just been here, because there were traces of his bluish-green energy still lingering in the air, along with the residue of someone else's energy that was familiar but which she did not immediately recognize.

He was here. He should be here now.

"Michael? It's your mother."

She waited. Nothing.

"Michael? It's time to come home."

She had been waiting for Michael to come home since the early afternoon. After hearing from Eli about Laura, she'd felt that at last some of the pieces of her puzzle were starting to come together, and she'd felt the need to continue her preparations.

She had spent the morning surveying their home and their possessions, trying to determine what might be desirable to bring along with them if they were forced to leave, and what to leave behind. She'd started with rather high expectations of what she owned that was valuable. In each room, she set a basket that she quickly filled with various items—artwork, family photographs, clothes—and, after filling every basket at least partway, she just as quickly

277

started pulling items out that she had just put in. In the end, she had nearly decided that in the new world that was coming, their old possessions would be ballast; they might all be better off carrying less, and leaving more stuff behind. She settled for high-value, easy-to-carry: jewelry, all the money from the safe, passports, credit cards, checkbooks, a sheet of paper with every account in their names, car pink slip.

Mindful of the angel's attack, she had also developed a strategy that involved hiding weapons—knives, cutters, an axe—around the house, so she would be better prepared if there was a recurrence.

Not if, she reminded herself, but when.

She had disconnected the phones after speaking with Eli, thinking someone else might be listening in on her calls. It was a decision that added to the impatience with which she had endured the previous twelve hours, thinking her family would be home soon when no one was actually intending to be there on time.

"Michael, I know you were here. I can still feel you in the air."

No answer.

Her eyes settled on one of the sculptures. It was the piece she had been standing next to when Elena approached her the night of the opening. She'd thought it a rose, then a lewd sculpture of Mary, but now it seemed to be something entirely different. She stared at it, and it seemed like it was changing its shape in front her. And then she could see something else in it. It was a little girl, and her face was so familiar that it hurt to look at her. Her eyes were closed, her face distorted in pain.

Melinda gasped and drew away from the sculpture.

She looked at another piece, on a pedestal in a nearby alcove with two small tables, and it was the same: another girl, tears streaming down her eyes in sadness and despair, dying. These were not like the ones in the forest. These were suffering.

Then she knew they were all going to be the same. Each of these statues was going to show her another tortured part of herself that no longer existed. Why?

"Why, why, why?"

She clenched her fists, and steadied herself. She walked back to the first sculpture, and with careful, considered action, she pushed the glass to the edge of the pedestal, and then off.

After it hit the ground, it exploded into pieces, and Melinda felt a grim satisfaction. Flecks of glass bounced off her pants' legs. And, forgetting about Michael entirely, she walked through the club looking for more of the sculptures to include in the destruction.

She was going to smash them all.

As Melinda was stepping into Fandango, a shadow was slowly gathering in the parking lot behind the club. At first it would have seemed to be a cloud of gnats and flies, but gradually it darkened into a shadow. And then it coalesced into the shape of a man.

It was Jack.

He took two steps toward the club before the sound of glass shattering echoed outside the club walls. Seemingly in reaction to the sound of the breakage, he collapsed on his second step toward the club's front door. As Melinda continued her vandalism, Jack reacted to each sculpture being destroyed as if he were being dealt a body blow. His nose bled. Each crash slowed him a little more, and after he staggered past the valet section, he collapsed in a dark pile on the passenger side of Melinda's car. He curled up as he convulsed, panting from the effort even that small movement required.

By the time Melinda had destroyed what she believed to be the last sculpture—by climbing on a table and pushing it off a high pedestal with a broom—she was breathing heavily. She stood in the dark of the club's main hall for a few minutes, scanning the room to see if she had missed any.

She dropped the broom on the floor.

And then she was ready to leave.

When Melinda stepped out the front doors, she scanned the empty parking lot, wondering who was there—because she sensed another presence—but, not seeing anyone, she stepped into her car, closed the door, and drove off without looking back.

After Melinda left, a breeze started to pick up in the parking lot.

279

Jack slowly gathered himself together and, recovering bit by bit, stood and stumbled to the front doors of the club. His face was etched with signs of confusion and disbelief. There were cuts on his face and hands—all over his body, he realized. His strength gaining, he strode in through the darkness, stopping when he heard and felt the crunch of glass under his shoe.

He realized what had happened: All his work had been destroyed.

His eyes flashed angrily as he walked slowly around the club.

No souvenirs for the kids, he thought.

At the back of the club, to his surprise, he found one that had survived, on a shelf where its presence had likely been obscured by the leaves of a plant. It was titled FAT VENUS. He held it close to his chest. It vibrated in his hands, and as he listened closely he heard the faintest whisper of music. The shards and piles of crystal and glass were doing the same thing, reflecting back the vibrations in the air.

This was the Deep Magic coming.

If he listened too closely, he thought, he might lose himself in it.

And so it begins.

And he knew he should be on his way.

He turned to leave, moving for the front doors.

As he walked, the doors he passed unlocked themselves, and slowly swung open, allowing the breeze outside, steadily growing, to sweep into the club. Likewise, the windows he passed unlatched themselves and slid open, letting in crosscurrents of wind that ruffled papers and napkins across the club. Bits and pieces of glass and crystalline, powdered dust were kicked in puffs across the floor, out the door, and into the air outside.

With that little bit of help, in a very short time, Jack thought, everyone nearby would be able to hear it. Everyone would be able to see what was happening. They could all be a part of it. What was the point in throwing a party and not telling anybody about it? Why not include the community? Why not thank them for their warm reception? Why not give the world a hint of what's to come? If there was anyone left who was even paying attention. It was a sad day, he thought, when a guy like me is the one left in charge of the lighthouse.

At least I found a souvenir for the brats. For the woman, me coming home, that's going to have to be present enough. I'm sure they missed me as much as I missed them.

The wind gusted through the club as Jack strode out the front doors. Long before he reached the end of the lighted area of the parking lot, as the winds continued to rise and the trees swayed under the full moon, he had disappeared into the night.

That Talia was on edge became very apparent once they were in the car. As she fed Michael directions that had him headed down the back roads to the east of town, she continually checked the clock on the dashboard and the position of the moon peeking over the horizon ahead of them. At first, they hardly spoke otherwise.

He was overwhelmed by feelings of guilt for ditching his mother, if indeed she had just been about to show up at the club because she was so frustrated at his absence. And although Melinda was not the type to blow her top in an uncontrolled manner, he was sure she was furious with him for not checking in with her, for not being home. Somewhere in the back of his mind, he thought he could hear her saying *It's time to come home, Michael.*

Bringing Mary home would get him off the hook.

"What makes you think Mary's out here?"

"Because I know that man is out here. That crazy man. He'll know where she is if she's anywhere out here."

"How long have you thought this?"

"It's just come to my mind recently. I would have mentioned it last time I saw you, but I didn't think it would be right to raise your hopes if I wasn't sure."

This seemed evasive. He didn't want to imagine that it would make a difference to Mary, those last twenty-four hours or whenever it was the thought had occurred to Talia. Michael didn't want to think about Mary out there that much longer with some kook, just waiting to be found and saved. What mattered was that Talia had come back to tell him, when she clearly didn't want to be there.

"What makes you more sure now?"

"I have my ways."

He thought about it. He was willing to believe her. "Did you grow up here? Or have you just learned the back roads from riding around?"

"No," she said. "Turn left here. I grew up all over."

"I remember seeing you at the club."

"That was one of my first visits here. That was something Elena cooked up to win me over, because I told her I'd been a singer in the past, and she wanted me to see that I could be one again.

"The day I went to the Hat for the first time, I was so nervous. People I considered legendary had played there. But it was such a tough place, too, with all the bikers there in the day, and Cheronkin was such a white, white place back then.

"I dressed myself up in a poodle skirt, a cashmere sweater, big, fake pearls and high heels just because I wanted each and every person in the place to stare at me when Elena brought me in to introduce to me the manager. I wanted them to stare at me and I wanted to stare them down. And that was exactly what I did." She shook her head dismissively. "I thought I was It. Or soon to be It. It was all about being noticed for all the wrong things back then." She stared ahead, then indicated he should turn onto a maintenance road. "Elena helped me through confusing times and sort of showed me a way through."

Eli returned home after seven, and found Melinda preparing dinner. It was to be a family favorite, pork roast and potatoes. The house felt different from the moment he walked in, lighter, as if it had been thoroughly cleaned and all the excess clutter had been removed. There was the smell of dinner being prepared, and the dogs standing outside the sliding glass door barking happily at the sight of him entering the house.

For a few moments, it felt normal.

He enjoyed it for what it was before he sought out Melinda in the kitchen.

The expression on her face was inscrutable. He was struck, for a moment, at how beautiful she was. Her hair was pulled back from her face and tied up in a bun because she'd decided not to let anyone do her hair until Mary did it again for her. But pulling back her hair revealed how much hair she had lost in front, and her face looked like an oval rather than a circle. And still, she was stunning.

And she had probably popped a tranquilizer again. The truth? He wanted one, too.

Melinda asked where Laura was. Eli saw the phone cord had been disconnected. "We picked up the kids and then I put the three of them on a flight to Hawaii. It's just going to be a mess here, and she was a mess already. None of them needs to be part of this story."

"What was the story?"

"They've been having an affair for a time now, apparently." He looked at the table. It was set for four.

"Is that why he killed himself?"

He checked her expression, to see if that was some kind of jab. Because he was going to call her on it. But her expression was almost blank. "I don't know." Eli shrugged. "Doubtful. I didn't know him well enough to know he was cheating with my sister. Who knows what else there was? That might just be the tip of the iceberg. You never know what's hidden below."

"Well, you've done what you could, and you were there for your sister. You can rest now, knowing you've done what you could, and let someone else carry the burden."

Talia directed Michael to stop at the bottom of a hill formed of reddish rock, atop which sat a giant, light-colored boulder that looked exactly like an acorn lying on its side. The area behind was similarly covered with the red rock.

When he was in school, this was a place his classes came on field trips, to collect samples of the rock and to climb around on the red stone pedestals that dotted the terrain.

One thing that struck Michael before he got out of the car was that whatever it was that had affected the foliage in and around town had not spread this far. It was dry and parched, typical for that time of year, typical of Cheronkin, when the greens of spring were quickly burned into the yellows and golds of summer. It looked harsh and hot, but it also seemed a lot more like the home environment he remembered.

It couldn't be just one thing that brought this change to Cheronkin, could it? One thing that could deliver daily cloudbursts along one side of an invisible dividing line and none to the other; one power that made everything in a certain zone grow wildly out of control, one force that kept everything in that zone from dying. One force that had somehow and for some reason set Cheronkin in its sights. Was any of that possible?

Wasn't that what people said when disaster struck?

Why here? Why now? Why us?

The landscape ahead was barren but for the rocks. The trailhead was right behind the acorn rock. She gestured in that direction. He unlocked his seatbelt.

She opened her car door, and undid her seatbelt, but clearly wasn't planning on joining him on the trail. She said, "I told myself that I would do what I could to help you. Be safe now."

Michael got out, walked around the car, and started down the trail. After a few steps, although he thought he knew the answer, he turned to ask Talia if she was going to join him. Some small part of him was hoping he'd be bringing both Mary and Talia home later on.

He turned in time to watch Talia, now sitting in the driver's seat, pulling the passenger door closed with a bang as she pulled away in his car.

It was so . . . surprising. He stared at the dust she'd kicked up in her wake, with two questions in mind: Why did she do that? And, stupidly: Is she coming back?

He thought about it a minute longer, and again came to the conclusion that it was only going to matter if Mary wasn't there. And, despite the sudden swirl of confusion in his head and the sinking feeling in his heart and stomach that he might have been led on even more than he thought, he followed the trail across the red rock formations and then into the brush and up the hill.

At several of the trail intersections, he saw pennies scattered across the ground, and sticks of gum and other small trinkets, such as spinning tops and shiny buttons. In each case they were never on the main path; instead, they were always lying a few feet down an intersecting path.

At the top of the trail was an area that felt like an encampment. It was flat and snug against a tall rocky hillside, with a few eucalyptus trees growing in a cluster on one side and two oak trees growing on the left. There were rocks and boulders that created little nooks here and there, some of which looked like they were used for specific purposes. Michael passed a small little pocket of space with something in it that looked like pictures he had seen of a moonshine still. Another little cranny was packed with miniature wood barrels and old-fashioned dairy truck milk bottles.

Once he was closer to the hillside, Michael saw that the rock wall had shallow caves in it. There were hidey-holes all over the place.

He wondered if this was where the old man Talia was talking about lived. And was he here now?

Michael slowed down, suddenly a bit nervous. He realized he'd been too focused on the thought of finding Mary, not enough on his own safety. Who knew what Talia had really dropped him off here for? Maybe it wasn't going to be Mary at all.

As if in response to his nerves, he heard something coming. It was close and it was coming closer. He looked around for a place to hide and realized there weren't any, which was probably why this was the guy's chosen hideaway. Once someone was in, there was no place to hide.

He turned as the noise approached, ready to run.

Mary limped into view.

Oh, thank God.

"Michael?"

"Mary!"

"Oh, thank God," she said. "Thank God!"

Walking looked painful for her. He hurried to her and threw his arms around her, but tried not to jostle her too much, as she looked to be in pain. She had been hurt in the crash, obviously.

"What happened?"

"They're just starting to work again. My 'roommate' took off earlier, told me I'm on my own here on in."

"You wanted him to stay longer?"

"No, but he said it was up to me to be able to walk back to town on my own power. 'Town, or wherever you go next,'" is what he said. He couldn't risk bringing me in, and wouldn't risk even helping me get closer."

"Who was it?"

"Your lots-of-dots guy."

He thought about that. "Really."

285

She nodded. "He makes that stuff out here. And other places, too, I guess. He's been out here longer than we thought."

Michael looked around, again aware of the strangeness of their surroundings. Although Mary seemed somewhat at ease, it didn't feel safe to him.

He asked, "Can we go?"

"Um . . . yeah?"

"I mean, do you have all your stuff?"

"Are you kidding?"

Michael turned around, offered her his arm, and they started walking down the trail.

"Did he hurt you?"

"Surprisingly, no. I mean, he's got that whole demented street person thing going on, and that persona is probably a little part of the true picture, but I think he's mostly doing that to keep people away from him. He saved me. He pulled me out of my car, and I don't know why—he kept saying it was for research purposes—and he's been taking care of me while I healed. It has been so weird," she said, sounding a little down, "because I was improving and getting better and feeling better every day until we moved here yesterday. We're out of the healing zone. And I'm just not feeling as good today. Not like I'm dying or anything, just like I need to take it slower."

"Let's get out of here slowly then. It's creepy."

"Really? I guess I was getting used to it. My biggest complaint so far has been the lack of indoor plumbing." She pulled something off of her waist. It was a fanny pack with a notebook in it. She handed it to Michael.

"What's that?"

"His journal, I think. Or his *old* journal."

"He's not going to hunt me down to get this back?"

"He wanted me to read it. He said he has three other copies stashed around, in case something 'happens to him.' He said he wanted me to try to get it published. I told him I was a cosmetologist." She shrugged. "He didn't care."

Michael held it up to read the title: *Who's Been Sleeping In My Head?* By Dick Arthur. "Really? He's Dick Arthur?" He looked at her incredulously. He thought of the book in the manila envelope on the passenger seat floor in his car.

"For real? I don't know. He was very excited to know I recognized the name. But he could just as well be a delusional nutbag, too." She seemed to want to go along more cautiously than Michael, and this was in addition to the slow speed at which she was already moving.

He didn't say anything, but instead followed her lead. "Are you going to tell me what happened?"

"Geez, are you ever going to ask?"

"Really, Mary. Are you okay?"

"Michael, honestly, I'm better than I could have ever expected."

"What happened?"

"Well, I'm not clear on everything. Even some of what I was there and aware of I'm not clear on. I was hiking in the hills, looking for another one of those arbors, when I came across Cameron, who was, like, doing tai chi naked in the woods."

"This is how the story begins?"

"Right. I know. Well, she had a knife with her, and she chased after me. Maybe you can invite *them* over for the *next* family dinner."

"Was she naked while she chased you?"

"Did not look. Just ran. Got away from her, got to my car, went the wrong way home and ended up at the canyon. Thought I could get home safer that way, and I didn't want to drive back past the place that I just got away from. But then . . . well, the Hill People were out, and they, were, like blocking the road. I ran into them. A lot of them." Tears slid down her face. "I crashed. I think that is what happened.

"And then I woke up and I was—my body was, up to my neck—I had been buried up to my neck. I was in sort of a reclining position, like in a mud bath. Except it wasn't mud, it was just dirt."

"Yikes."

"Yeah, I was sort of in and out of awareness at that point, so I was weirdly calm; Richard—"

"Richard?"

"Right. Richard told me later that he'd given me some 'medicine' to lessen the pain. My legs were pretty chewed up, and I guess there were some burns. He buried me like that, I guess, well . . . I think it had to do with the thing that happened to the dog you found. He knew about it, too. Not the dog, but the healing thing."

Michael guessed that he was looking at her strangely.

She said, "What?"

"I never talked about a healing thing with you."

"I know. I saw a bird die and come back to life and, at the time, I related that to your dog tale. That was when I actually started to believe your dog-resurrection slash met-a-rock-star story. There is a healing thing going on in the hills around town. Richard thought it was coming up from the ground. Things aren't dying when they are supposed to die, things are living that aren't meant to live ..."

"Like your tomato plants."

"Exactly! I mean, I couldn't stand on my own four days ago. Most of my burns—at least the ones I can see—have, for the most part, peeled away. I was thinking about Mom's hypno-doctor the other day. I bet he's fully recovered now. I had a lot of time to spend thinking.

"He brought me water and crappy food—probably out of peoples' garbage cans. I didn't care. I think it was yesterday when he said we had to move to keep away from the Hill People. It must have been really hard for him to do, because even though I really felt up to it when we started, he basically had to carry me half the distance here."

"Why did you have to move?"

"I don't know. He actually blamed Mom."

"You mean our mom?"

"I think so. It was hard to understand it all. He was a crazy talker, and on top of that he kept me drugged to stop the pain. He was using less and less every day, but I think it was out of stinginess rather than him trying to wean me. Better net result for me, I guess . . . but I liked whatever he had me on."

"Did he know Mom?"

"I don't think so. It was sort of like a 'your momma' thing he did all the time. Mostly, it bugged me. That day, when he said we had to move and he dug me up, he said he thought Mom had sent them out hunting for me. He said that I wasn't going to like what she did to me once she had me back. She wasn't going to risk letting me go again. And for some reason, I thought it was funny. But it really wasn't

288

funny. It was just crazy. We'd heard the Hill People all through the time we were moving camps; they were here and there all around us and making all these weird noises...

"This morning, he said it was time for him to be going, and told me that 'fly, founder, or flounder, you're on your own.' He just up and left. And even though I didn't want to spend another night here, I thought that if I was all alone it wouldn't be at all safe. Limping like this, I'd be coyote bait out there. So I was going to leave in the morning and try to make it through the night and home without having to worry about the Hill People catching me."

"That sounds like a good plan. You should have mentioned it before I made us flee your camp."

She said, "Let's stick to the roads and we'll be okay. We'll try to make it to one of the squatter shacks. That's what I was going to do. We can block the door and spend the night there if we have to."

"Sounds like the beginning of a bad zombie movie. Let's stay outside for a while. It's all right, at least out here. It's a nice night. The moon's bright and it's just rising. It's good, just seeing you again. I mean, you're feeling okay, right?"

She nodded.

Something lying in the dirt caught his eye. It was another one of those piles. Three pennies, a purple, metallic piece of curly ribbon and a tiny silver dreidel.

"What is that?"

"That is one of the lures that Richard leaves out to draw the Hill People away from wherever he's sleeping. He sets them out in a way that he says distracts them and leads them away from wherever he is." She shrugged. "Because they can't resist shiny things."

"Okay. We have choices." Michael continued. "We can work back toward town. Or we could probably go to the highway and stay out of that green area entirely. It's a shorter walk to the highway than it is to go all the way back to town. Then maybe we can call for a ride. Mom will be so happy to know you're coming home."

Eli was asleep before he'd finished half his meal, courtesy of the mixture of tranquilizers in his drinks. Melinda left him slouched over his plate and hurried to finish. She knew—

without knowing how she knew—that in only a few more hours it would be too late for anyone to leave.

She took many of the items she had gathered in each room earlier and then decided to leave behind, and placed them in a pile, either on the carpet, in a cubby, or a drawer. Photographs mostly, things with her signature on them, personal papers, journals, the videotaped session with Dr. Wen. Some things went in the pile simply because she was convinced they were covered with her fingerprints. And then on each of these piles she poured something that she thought would burn well.

There were enough oils and perfumes in the bathrooms to take care of the rooms upstairs; downstairs, in the kitchen, and the garage, there was seemingly no end to the options for flammable liquids to choose among.

She felt some small regret about Eli each time she passed by his form. She straightened him, so it looked like he was resting his head in his arms. She couldn't bring herself to put him down the rest of the way.

And then there was nothing more she could do, and there was no more time to do it. She had money, the keys to the car, and some food and water. And pictures of both the kids, so she wouldn't forget what they looked like when one day she returned to hunt them down.

One day, they were all going to be together again.

They should have been at that table with their father.

Wherever there was a small pile to be burned, and there were a few, she placed a candle atop it, and lit it. And when that was done, she went to the stove in the kitchen, blew out the pilots, then turned on all six burners, which hissed out their fumes in harmony. In the living room, she turned on the gas in the fireplaces.

Out to the car in the driveway, and that, she thought to herself, was it for life in Cheronkin. There was an image of a place that had been forming in her mind. She thought it was on the coast, in Oregon. She hadn't been there in her life, but still she remembered it—and more, she thought she could find her way there.

Melinda drove off into the night. It was a new world.

As Michael knew they would, at some point he and Mary faced an awkward part of the conversation.

"How did you find me? How did you get here?"

"Talia dropped me off. Then she drove off in my car."

Mary stopped. "Again, are you kidding?"

"I'm just thankful she brought me to you. We can make it home."

"Not tonight, we can't."

"Should we go back to your old hideout? Wait until tomorrow morning?"

"She's one of them. Whatever they are. Some kind of cult. Some kind of witches."

"I don't know what they are. I like Talia."

"It's all weird. And my accident? That's just one night, and not mentioning all of the freaking weird stuff before and screwing around with Mom's head . . . I don't want to go there right now. I mean, what the hell is going on? Right before I saw Cameron in the woods, right before, I was telling myself to try to take a different point of view, to imagine that all the New-Agey everything Mom has been talking about forever is really happening."

"Talia said something like that tonight."

"Well, she's one of them, too. Whatever they are. Whatever they believe."

"She said Cameron was dead."

"Good. Now I'll just have to worry about redheads in my nightmares."

"When do you think it's going to happen?"

"What's going to happen?"

"Whatever it is. The start of the new age? What's it going to be? An earthquake? A meteor? An infestation?"

"I'm sure I don't know. Maybe it's not going to happen at all. People are wrong about that stuff all the time."

"Except . . ."

"Right. Except this and except that. I know what you're saying. Richard said that after one of his story collections was published, he started to feel like some of the people he wrote about wanted to kill him. For three years, while he published four more books, he said there were accidents and incidents happening all around him, many of which were nearly lethal to him; finally, he couldn't take it anymore and dropped out of sight. He came here because he was sure no one would recognize him and no one would think to look for him here.

"His stories were more paranoid with each book," Michael said. "He went from witches to ghost to aliens to all kinds of freaks living among ordinary folks, plotting to take over the planet."

She was quiet. "You know what's weird? I was ready to try to walk home a few times before this. You can imagine by how I'm doing now that I wouldn't have done better if I'd left before this. But every time I found myself feeling that way, it wasn't because I wanted to do it for me; it was because of Mom. I wanted to get back to her because I could feel how much she wanted me to come back. I probably would have ended up crawling, and I was still ready to go. It was almost like she was pulling me . . ."

It was getting windy. When a squatters' shack came into view, they both welcomed the sight.

Michael asked her, "Which one is it?"

The squatters' shacks around the area, which had been there since before the land was formally settled, were frequently used as playhouses by the area's teen- and college-aged kids.

"I think it's Big Water."

The name was a reference to the interior, where someone or someones had painted the walls in hues of blue, with sea plants and fish, supposedly in reference to what the entire valley was supposed to have looked like millions of years before, when it was underwater.

There was very little inside other than a cardboard box turned on its back for use as a table. There was a kids' telescope on top of the box, beside two candles and a book of Winnie-the-Pooh aphorisms.

They were still outside of the zone of green, although not by far: It wasn't too far down the road that they could see the first stands of trees. The treetops looked blue in the moonlight, and not as menacing as they would surely be on a darker night. Michael and Mary were both relieved not to have encountered anything—Hill person, coyote, or otherwise—but neither of them was up to continuing further at night if it risked catching the attention of anyone or anything that might have overlooked them before. And they both agreed that was more likely to happen if they were under the forest canopy, where it likely wouldn't be as clear and bright.

They decided not to light the candle—they really didn't need it under the light of the full moon, which illuminated the painted walls enough for them to be able to see the fine detail: the metallic hues in the fish scales, the segments of red in the beds of the seaweed, the sparkle in the shells in the oyster bed. They slept sitting up against the wall, next to each other, in that rectangular room.

Michael was feeling thankful as they drifted off to sleep.

"I knew you weren't dead," he said.

Who was it that heard the music first that night? The far-off and distant sound that rode in on the wind, stirring in every person within a certain radius enticing memories and dreams of fond and beloved things. Was there a late celebration going on in someone else's backyard? Was the sound echoing off the foothills? Was it coming from down the street or around the block, and why was the sound so clear?

It was different from the music from Fandango, which could occasionally be heard on those nights when the freeway wasn't busy. This sound didn't seem to be coming from any one place, any one direction; it seemed to be vibrating in the air.

Riza Koleman turned off her security system at five after one and stepped out onto the porch to investigate the sounds. She didn't notice the flicker of flame in an upstairs window at the Phillips' house up the block as she moved down the walkway to the street.

Gretchen and Martin Solkitz, who lived two miles north of Riza, and another two miles west, walked together through the front yard in their nightclothes, wondering what that wonderful sound might be and where it might be coming from.

Gretchen's niece, Andrina, who lived closer to the freeway, closed her three white terriers in the bedroom, because the sound of their barking was keeping her from figuring out what specific event it was the music reminded her of. The sound of it made her think contentedly of her childhood.

For everyone who awakened in their homes that night, and for all those who were awake already and had their attention captured, the youngest children slept through it as if it were a lullaby. While they dreamed, their parents and neighbors slowly made their way into their front yards, and into the streets.

They seemed to notice each other, but for the most part they did not interact. Each was caught up in the midst of their own reveries. Whatever they carried in their hands, they dropped and left to the wind. Purses and hats, wallets and keys. Whatever they wore, they started to remove. Shoes and socks, pants and dresses, nightgowns and robes.

Dogs bayed and howled. On a few streets there were groups of people on the sidewalks, all headed in one direction, moving in concert but seeming to be each in his or her own world. Many people were dancing, some moving rambunctiously to different rhythms and others gently swaying with the wind.

Was there magic in the wind? Did the air sparkle in places?

Not all were in the streets; others took to back trails and to worn paths through backyards and brush.

They marched and jumped and ran and frolicked in the moonlight up to Marble Canyon Road, then off down the trail that led to the plateau above and behind the Cheronkin Community Center. They climbed over the perimeter fence, or entered through holes cut in the metal links, until their combined weight knocked a section to the ground and opened up an entrance.

For a short while, there were throngs on the streets, moving in unison naturally, seemingly unencumbered by concern or self-consciousness.

And then the flow of people turned into a trickle, and then there were only a few stragglers left outside, and most everyone else was on their way up the hill.

Michael went outside to pee after a few hours of sleep. He wasn't accustomed to sleeping in a sitting position. Tired, leery of Hill People and other critters, he didn't want to go too far from the structure, so he took five steps and made that the spot. It was bright out, and the moon was full, and there were five bright stars in a line near the moon which he didn't think were usually there. Were those planets? Was one of them red? Was this the planetary alignment?

What he noticed first after the stars were the flashes of light in the air to the west. Sparkling, twinkling, jumping around on the wind like bursts from a sparkler. He went inside and grabbed the telescope, then returned to the spot. The telescope didn't help him to see anything other than that the flashes were small and bright and all over and seemingly random, and that, with the way the tree tops were shaking, the wind seemed to be howling that way, where here it was only a breeze.

Michael climbed to the roof, and gave it another try. What he noticed then were the people.

Miles away, he could see them up on the flat area on top of the hill behind the community center, which was at the base of two taller hills behind it. The relatively barren space was the size of a football field and lit like a stage by the moon, with the dark of dense forest defining its perimeter. Currently, it also seemed to be overrun by what looked like several hundred people.

Michael didn't see a band or speakers or a deejay, but he thought he could hear in the air snippets of some kind of music. People were spread across the whole space, and engaged in all kinds of random and seemingly unrelated activities, like the guy near the edge of the crowd who was doing tai chi while a woman standing next to him hopped in place with her hands at her side, and a second woman ran in circles around both of them. Overall, it looked like one mad, drugged romp in the night, and it took him back to his night at the beach party. Reinforcing that feeling a few moments later was the realization that people out there seemed not to be dressed.

He wondered: What if Dick Arthur spiked the local water supply with all of his leftover dots?

Mary limped out of the structure.

"What is it?"

"I don't know. It looks like the town is having some kind of pagan moon celebration. Come see. I'll help you up."

While she climbed up, he studied the whole arena before him. People were having all kinds of sex out there, on top of the wild dancing and the chasing and the running about that was going on in excess. He could also see people doing yoga, people jumping around like cheerleaders and crawling around like babies, people playing what looked like imaginary games of football and tennis, and people who looked like they were doing gymnastics or hoola hooping, or metal detecting for gold. The telescope wasn't powerful enough to provide detail like faces or clothes or body parts, but it did give a view of the overall tableau.

"Oh, my goodness," Mary said a few minutes later, when she was perched beside him and staring through the telescope. "It *is* a town orgy." She looked at Michael, annoyed. "Notice how it's always on nights when we're not around?"

A bright light flashed in the center of the field and then went out. A moment later, the air above the field erupted in flashes and sprays of glittering light. "Oooh. What was that?"

"The air was kind of sparkling like that before," he said. "Something in the air is reflecting the light from the ground, I think. You tell me, Mary. You have the eye piece."

They were staring in silence moments later when the center of the field changed color; a huge circle of black opened up where the middle of the crowd had been—and then those people who had been standing there were gone. People nearby backed away or ran frantically as the perimeter of the collapsed area quickly expanded. Others fell in. And while many in the crowd reacted to the commotion, there were also a number who continued whatever they were doing without reacting at all.

Mary said, "It's a sinkhole."

But it was more than that, because the forest around the hilltop had started to move, too. The wind blew fiercely, but it was more than the wind. The open, lighted area of the plateau was shrinking, as if the forest were advancing onto it.

The sinkhole grew in size and the crowd continued to pull back. People ran towards the trees, then stopped before they reached the trees, then moved just as quickly back in the direction of the sinkhole. It took Michael only a moment more to realize the dark boundary that surrounded the crowd was not made up of trees alone. It wasn't a forest at all. The whole hilltop area was surrounded by Hill People. Maybe thousands of them. And they were flooding onto the hilltop area, racing toward the hole in the ground.

"I can't watch this."

"Let me look."

296

"I hope Carina's not there," Mary said quietly as she passed the telescope to him.

When he'd focused on the hilltop, the scene was chaotic. People were running all over the place, but there was no place to run as they were being closed in on from all directions.

"Oh, no."

The townspeople were all being swept up and pushed into that dark crater by the hoards of onrushing bodies.

In the areas where people had some limited room to move about, they were running and being chased, defending themselves and being struck down, fighting and falling. The inexorable swell of Hill People pushed forward, dragging every one of them along as the Hill People swarmed toward the gaping hole in the Earth and flung themselves in.

It was not very long before the entire field was a mass of bodies, one indiscernible from the next, and it was impossible to tell where the hole began and ended. Well lit or not, it was hard to see anything clearly in that chaotic swarm. But then the flow of bodies from the hills slowed, and as the people who were already crowded on the field continued to fling themselves into the Earth—where they quickly disappeared from view—the mass of bodies on the hilltop just as quickly started to shrink in size.

And like a magic trick, the crater receded as their numbers diminished.

It was not long before there were maybe a hundred Hill People left, pushing into a circle in the center of the field, then fifty, then twenty in an even tighter circle, then four, then there wasn't a person to be seen on the whole football-field-sized area, and there was no evidence of any break in the ground. Everyone who had been there before had been swallowed up; the plateau was vacant and the night was once more given back to the wind and the moon and the stars, although the pops and flashes of light that had been going on throughout the event continued.

What was it his uncle had said before he shot himself? *The Earth takes in all our pains.*

This is why Talia dragged me out here and took away my car, Michael thought. She wanted to make sure I was safe from it.

He turned to Mary, too stunned to speak. There were tears running down her cheeks again. He gazed off toward the area where he thought their home was, and prayed his mother and father were okay. That they hadn't been up there on that hilltop. It was too far for Mary or him to make it home tonight to do anything about it. There was nothing they could do but be glad they at least had each other.

As he stared into the night, it was hard to tell at first that there was smoke rising into the sky.

Seeing the first tall licks of flame made it clearer: Something was on fire, and it seemed to be in the vicinity of their mother and father's house.

Epilogue

IN THE NEWS
West Coast Regional Reporter
Cheronkin County, California – Federal, state, and local authorities converged on this small liberal enclave on Wednesday to study a problem the likes of which none involved had ever before encountered: Where did half of the town's population go?

Officer Julio Gravez, responding to a pre-dawn phone call from an out-of-state relative of a Cheronkin resident worried that there might have been foul play, crossed under the Interstate and in short order discovered food, clothing, and personal items which had been discarded on residential streets throughout the town located in the foothills south of the Interstate freeway. Using identification on some found items, Gravez and his partner attempted to locate the owners at their home addresses and found that each of the houses were empty, and had been left unlocked, some with their doors open.

When they went to neighboring properties hoping to gather information, they found those houses vacant as well, and after the tenth house was found in a similar condition, the officers placed a call to their superiors to notify them of their discovery.

Firefighter Frank Welter was awakened in Fire Station 187 by an automatic message relayed by a high-altitude drone satellite, employed by the federal government as a security measure to monitor happenings on the ground. The aerial drone reported a fire in a neighborhood two miles west of the homes being searched by Officer Gravez. Although it was not unusual to receive a notice of visual confirmation from a drone, it was unusual for the report to have been received before a call from residents.

When Welter and crew arrived on the scene, they found one side of the street, with five houses on it, engulfed in flames. Says Welter, "What I was struck by first was not the size of the fire, it was the fact that there were no people out. In situations like this, generally there will be lots of crowd movement. People trying to get out of their burning houses, people watching from their own houses, that kind of thing. Pandemonium is normal, and this was nothing like normal. It was also unusual, for this area, for the fire to have progressed so far without our having been notified."

By the time the fire was under control, seven houses had been burned to the ground, and one death had resulted. "There was only one person in one of those seven houses at three a.m. Every other house, including the seven we saved on the other side of the street, was empty. There was no one there. The deceased has been identified as Eli Phillips, 54, a longtime Cheronkin resident."

By the next day, state and federal officials were knocking on doors throughout town and finding that except for a total of thirty-seven homes, no one was home. In those thirty-seven homes were found a total of sixty-four children under the age of eight, some of whom were outside their homes, trying to locate their parents, grandparents, and guardians. It would not be long before all the assembled authorities came to the conclusion that these children and a handful of adults who happened to be away from the area overnight were the only people remaining in this part of town. Everyone else was gone.

The children have since been relocated to extended families.

Nervous Neighbors
For those living on the other side of the Interstate that divides this town into northern and southern sections, the reaction has been one of fear mixed with curiosity. There are rumors of cults meeting in the hills of Cheronkin, and hanging over most conversations like a cloud is the specter of a dark series of events that preceded the mass disappearance.

Earlier this month, in an apparent accident on the area's main thoroughfare, Marble Canyon Road, an area resident drove off the side of the road. The car crash, one of many that have taken place on the winding road over the last five years, was discovered days later. In the ensuing investigation, police discovered, close to the site of the crash, bloodstains spread across the two-lane road. According to police, the car's occupant has only recently been accounted for.

Then, earlier this week, state senator William Clayton, long considered a favored political son of the region, committed suicide at a press conference in Santa Barbara. Police are still investigating the motives and reasons for the shooting, and were not willing to comment while the investigation is ongoing.

Local residents see a link: Clayton was the sponsor of an initiative to repair and improve Marble Canyon Road where the bloodstains were found, and to provide compensation to the families of fourteen people who died on Marble Canyon Road. Authorities were unwilling to comment on the ongoing investigation. Many question whether the road improvements were ever begun.

For those few who returned to find their neighborhoods vacant, the idea of remaining in their homes has proved unnerving.

Said one survivor who is in the process of relocating, who asked not to be named in this article, "Whatever it is out there that took everybody away—who's to say it isn't waiting for the chance to get a few more? Who's to say this isn't just the first time, and there isn't more to come? How could I go to sleep every night not knowing what happened to all those people?"

301

www.ingramcontent.com/pod-product-compliance
Lightning Source LLC
Chambersburg PA
CBHW031109030726
47496CB00002BA/455